One Love

By Matt Cain

Shot Through the Heart

Nothing But Trouble

The Madonna of Bolton

The Secret Life of Albert Entwistle

Becoming Ted

One Love

One Love

MATT CAIN

REVIEW

First published in 2024 by
HEADLINE REVIEW
An imprint of HEADLINE PUBLISHING GROUP

1

Cataloguing in Publication Data is available from the British Library

Hardback ISBN 978 1 4722 9191 2

Typeset in Dante MT by CC Book Production
Printed and bound in Great Britain by Clays Ltd, Elcograf S.p.A.

MIX
Paper | Supporting responsible forestry
FSC® C104740

Headline's policy is to use papers that are natural, renewable and recyclable products and made from wood grown in well-managed forests and other controlled sources. The logging and manufacturing processes are expected to conform to the environmental regulations of the country of origin.

HEADLINE PUBLISHING GROUP
An Hachette UK Company
Carmelite House
50 Victoria Embankment
London EC4Y 0DZ

www.headline.co.uk
www.hachette.co.uk

For Laetitia Clapton, Amy Rynehart and Bianca Sainty
14-04 for ever!

Prologue

2002

With Guy at his side, Danny walked along Princess Street until he arrived at the bottom of Canal Street.

They paused in front of a pub called the New Union, outside which a huddle of men in faded jeans and lumberjack shirts were dancing to Geri Halliwell's version of *It's Raining Men*, cigarettes dangling from their mouths and pint glasses sloshing beer onto the cobbles, while a pyrotechnically drunk drag queen in a synthetic blue wig was attempting to pole dance on a lamp-post.

'So this is it,' Danny said to Guy, his eyes fixed on the scene ahead. 'This is the Gay Village.'

As they stepped onto Canal Street, a couple of middle-aged men strolled past, holding each other's hands and giving them a little swing. Danny had never seen two men holding hands before, at least not in real life – and certainly never in public.

He resisted the urge to give a little jig of excitement.

All that time he'd spent in his hometown of Barrow, dreaming of a better life, dreaming of the person he could be if he could just get to Manchester, if he could just find his people. *And now – finally – it's happening!*

Adrenaline fired through his body.

He turned to face Guy. 'Come on, shall we do it?'

Guy felt his body tingle with fear.

'I don't know,' he said. 'Just give me a minute.'

He watched as a drag queen in a blue wig staggered across the street, leaned over the wall and threw up into the canal. One of the men in lumberjack shirts rushed over to rub her back while his friends raised their pint glasses and gave her a cheer. It was much more boisterous than Guy had expected. *Much more in your face.*

He felt a tug in his gut. *Look at these people. They're* my *people.*

He felt conflicted. On one hand, it was as if some kind of invisible force was pulling him forward, drawing him in. At the same time, he wanted to turn on his heel and run right back to his student bedroom, to shut the door behind him and pretend he'd never even attempted to go out on the gay scene.

'Remember, everyone's at that nineties night in the Union,' Danny reassured him, 'so nobody will see us, or at least nobody we know.'

There was a pause.

'It'll be just you and me,' he added.

Guy ran his hand along the inside of his collar. *Just me and Danny.*

Suddenly, it didn't feel too bad.

He yanked in a breath. 'Come on, let's do it.'

FRIDAY

2022

Danny stands on the concourse of Euston Station and draws in slow, steady breaths. As he catches sight of Guy, a mixture of excitement and fear live-wires through his body. He tries to compose himself.

He sees that Guy's wearing a bicep-revealing short-sleeved shirt with khaki shorts and brown loafers. And he's looking every bit as handsome as he did on the day Danny first met him.

As Guy spots Danny, he tugs his hand through his dirty-blond hair and breaks into a smile. Danny can feel a tickle in his heart.

Act normal, he tells himself. *You're just two friends going away for the weekend.*

'Hi, babe,' Danny chirps as Guy wheels his suitcase to a stop. 'You alright?'

'Hello, hello,' Guy says, leaning in to hug him. As he does, Danny feels the solid slab of Guy's chest muscles pressing against him and catches his familiar scent of shower gel and recently applied deodorant. He hopes he hasn't overdone it on the expensive Tom Ford aftershave.

'So,' he says, 'are you all set?'

Guy nods. 'To be fair, I didn't have to do much. You booked the train and the hotel – and you sorted out the tickets for Pride.'

'Yeah, well, I wanted to treat you,' Danny says. 'Besides, how often do we get to celebrate our twentieth anniversary?'

As he says the words, he hopes he doesn't sound desperate. Then again, the events of the last few years have put their friendship under such strain it's perfectly natural for him to sound on edge. Not that he wants to remind Guy of any of that. *Not now we've come through it. Or at least I hope we've come through it . . .*

Just as an awkward silence is opening up, Danny jumps in with, 'Look at the time! We'd better head over to the platform.'

As they weave their way through the crowd, Danny initiates a conversation about work. While Guy is a corporate lawyer currently embroiled in a major case against an oil company that has something to do with tax regulations which Danny doesn't completely understand, Danny is an actors' agent whose clients are enjoying success with a flurry of headline-grabbing jobs in TV and film. He entertains Guy with the latest exploits of a high-maintenance actress he's nicknamed Demandy Mandy and regales him with the story of a self-obsessed actor called Lance Forster who's having an affair with a man who works as his lookalike.

'I might start calling him Lance's doppelbanger,' he jokes.

Guy breaks into a laugh and Danny feels a surge of confidence. It's good to be back on familiar territory. *You've always been able to make him laugh, you know that.*

He checks himself. *You're trying to make him see there's more to you than making him laugh, remember?*

They flash their tickets at the station staff and make their way down the platform towards the carriage on which Danny has booked two seats on opposite sides of a table. He knew he'd find it too stressful to spend the entire journey from London to Manchester sitting next to Guy, their skin touching on the armrest, Guy able to sense his every tremor. Although Danny must have sat next to Guy hundreds of times before, somehow it would feel different today. He only hopes no-one gets on the train and sits next to them.

As Danny lifts his suitcase onto the luggage rack, Guy slides his much smaller duffel bag under his seat. 'Have you packed for a week?' he teases.

Danny dismisses his comment with a wave. 'You know me, I like to have options. Anyway, who said the aim of packing is to bring as little as possible? Who knows *what* might happen this weekend?'

As he says the words, fear catches in his throat. He knows exactly what he's *hoping* will happen this weekend: he's hoping to transform his relationship with Guy into the loving, sexual partnership he's always dreamed of. And he's hoping to prove to Guy that, despite their twenty years of romantic and sexual liaisons with other men – some of them brief, others more significant – all along they should have been with each other. But it's a huge risk and the danger is that Danny will lose his best friend in the process, not to mention having his heart broken. *And cause myself even more pain than I've been caused already.*

He tries to distract himself. 'I've brought us a little picnic,' he announces, lifting a few carrier bags onto the table.

'Oh, you really shouldn't have,' Guy protests. 'Now I feel guilty for doing so little.'

'Stop arguing and start eating,' Danny says. 'Oh and before you ask, yes, I did bring your favourite Kettle Chips.'

Guy's eyes sparkle. 'Really? Sweet Chilli and Sour Cream?'

Danny drops them onto the table. 'How could I forget?'

A grin splits Guy's face. 'Danny, you're a legend!'

Although Danny grins back at him, he feels a pang of hunger as Guy opens the packet. All month he's been starving himself in preparation for this weekend. And it's been tough: his no-carb diet has made him miserable and snappy and he's flown off the handle at his assistant on more than one occasion. He watches Guy attack the bag of crisps and can't help letting out a whimper.

'What's the matter?' says Guy. 'Don't you want any?'

'No, thanks,' Danny replies. 'Honestly, I'm not that hungry.'

Oh, it's alright for Guy; he spends so long in the gym he burns off anything he eats – or somehow it all turns to muscle. But Danny has never been sporty or athletic and has never taken to any of the fitness crazes that have hooked so many of his friends. He's always been susceptible to putting on weight – enough weight for people to describe him as chubby – and during the pandemic a doughy muffin top started to spill out over his jeans. Even worse, when he gave a particularly hearty laugh, he could actually feel it wobble. That's why he decided to take drastic action in preparation for this weekend.

As he gives a little wriggle in his seat, he can feel his jeans sitting much looser around his waist. He glances at his reflection in the window and this confirms that he's looking slimmer than he has for a long time. He may have lost most of his hair but what's left – a thin strip reaching from the back of his head to just above his ears – is still black, as is his stubble. And his skin has relatively few lines for a man of nearly thirty-nine. He assumes this must be down to his half-Mediterranean genes. *Well, at least my dad came in useful for something.*

In any case, Danny tells himself that he's done everything he can to look his best for the weekend and he isn't going to fall at the final hurdle. He opens an artichoke and sundried tomato salad and does his best to look enthusiastic.

A couple of hard-faced teenage girls wearing make-up so heavy it looks like it's been applied by a five-year-old stalk down the aisle. Danny tenses his body in expectation of them sitting next to him and Guy. He tries not to let out a sigh of relief as they check the seat numbers and carry on moving down the carriage.

'Oh, I almost forgot,' he says, pulling down the sides of another carrier bag, 'I've brought us a little something to take us back to our student days.' He pulls out a few bottles of WKD and hands one to Guy.

'My God,' says Guy, as he holds it up to examine the luminous blue liquid, 'do they still make this?'

'Apparently so,' says Danny. He adopts a snooty accent. 'It's just that we've become *much too sophisticated* to drink it.'

'Except for this weekend,' counters Guy. 'I don't plan on doing anything sophisticated this weekend.'

Now that sounds promising . . .

Danny proposes a toast. 'To Manchester!'

'To Manchester!' Guy takes a swig from his bottle and pauses to consider the taste. 'Wow, that really does take me back.'

Danny tastes his. 'Yeah, if we close our eyes we could be in the Union.'

'Or on Canal Street.'

Danny sighs. 'My God, we've got so many memories in that city.'

'I know,' says Guy, 'I'm a bit nervous about going back.'

'Well, maybe we should knock the nerves on the head and

throw ourselves in at the deep end,' suggests Danny. 'Once we've settled into our hotel, why don't we head over to the Village for a drink?'

'OK, let's do it.' Guy dips his hand back into the crisps. 'I'm assuming that's where everything happens at Manchester Pride – on Canal Street?'

Danny opens up his phone and passes it to Guy so he can read the schedule. He explains that Manchester Pride is very different to other Pride events around the country: it's a four-day festival stretching from the Friday to the Monday of the August Bank Holiday weekend and, as well as a huge party in the streets of the Gay Village, there's a parade through the city centre, an open-air arena hosting live music acts, and a programme of LGBTQ+-themed arts and cultural events taking place in various venues. Danny came up with the idea of celebrating their anniversary a month earlier than is strictly accurate as, despite spending three years at Manchester University, neither Danny nor Guy has ever been in the city for Pride: as it didn't fall during term time, it always clashed with summer jobs or family holidays. Perhaps that's why Danny's always thought of it as unfinished business, the missing piece in their shared history.

Just as Guy's handing back his phone, the voice of the train manager comes over the tannoy.

'Welcome to this 17.20 Avanti Trains service to Manchester Piccadilly . . .'

Once again, Danny feels that mixture of excitement and fear pinball around his body. He plugs his anxiety with another swig of his drink and looks up to check there are no last-minute passengers approaching their table. They're in the clear.

'If you're travelling to Manchester for Pride,' the announcer continues, 'we'd like to wish you all a safe and very happy weekend.'

At the other end of the carriage, a man wearing a *Flash Gordon* T-shirt with a glitter beard and the rainbow flag painted on his cheeks gives a cheer. His friends join in, raising their cans of lager in the air.

As the train pulls out of the station, fear suddenly overwhelms Danny's excitement.

What if this all goes horribly wrong?

He exhales slowly. However terrified he is, he knows that he needs to bring things to a head, that at the very least he needs to express his feelings. After everything he and Guy have experienced together, after all the ups and downs of the last two decades, he *owes* it to himself to get them out in the open.

He looks across at Guy, searching for some kind of encouragement, something to cling onto to bolster his confidence.

As if reading his mind, Guy gives him a wink. 'I'm really looking forward to this,' he says. 'How about you, princess?'

'Princess' is his pet name for Danny but one he hasn't used for years. As Danny's ambushed by the memory of the very first time Guy used it, his heart slams into his throat.

He draws in an unsteady breath and rearranges his features into a smile. 'Yes, my prince. I can't wait!'

2002

Did that boy just wink at me? I'm sure he just winked at me!

Danny told himself that he must be imagining it; whoever the boy was, he was way too good-looking to be interested in him. He had dirty-blond hair, a classic jawline, and had to be over six feet tall. When Danny looked closer he saw that he had a cute little gap in between his front teeth and a perfectly formed dimple in the centre of his chin. He felt almost breathless with desire but shook his head and looked away.

It was the second day of term and Danny was at the Freshers' Fair in the Academy concert hall, where later in the year some of the coolest music acts – like Suede, Groove Armada and The Streets – would be playing. Although right now it was difficult to picture the place as a venue for live gigs: it was filled with thousands of wide-eyed first years and over 300 stalls staffed by older students trying to recruit them to whichever group they were representing. The activities on offer catered to every interest – and many Danny hadn't even known existed. So far, he'd spotted societies dedicated to knitting, sack racing, and custard wrestling, as well as being invited to join clubs that celebrated beekeeping,

Bhangra and board games – and even something called the Up Shit Creek Without a Paddle Society, although he had no idea what that was supposed to be. As he walked past the lines of stalls, he tried not to get sidetracked. He needed to stay focused on the reason he was there; he was there to join the Lesbian, Gay and Bisexual Society.

From as early as he could remember, Danny had known he was gay – and so had the other children at school. Although they preferred to use words like 'poof', 'queer' and 'bender', informing him he was a pervert, would end up incontinent, and would die of AIDS. Growing up in 1990s Barrow-in-Furness, Danny hadn't dared to make friends with anyone like him. There were a handful of other boys he'd sensed were also gay, such as Keith Trotter, who was in the year below him, wanted to be a professional dancer, and was obsessed with Janet Jackson. But, like him, Keith was called queer, so the two of them had avoided each other as if magnetically repulsed, as if the combined intensity of their gayness could only attract even more bullying. As if the joint force of their shame would only be suffocating.

When Danny had started at sixth-form college and found refuge in the local drama club, he came into contact with a few boys from other schools who he could tell shared the feelings he was struggling to accept in himself. But, however much he wanted to make friends with them, it was like he was held back by some kind of invisible barrier or force field. In the end, he and the boys just sniffed around each other, preferring to form friendships with the girls in the group. This was around the same time as the only openly gay man Danny had ever known, a man to whom he'd always felt drawn but was only just starting to think he might be able to confide in, had been subjected to an eruption of homophobia so intense it had left Danny terrified of ever coming out – or at least until he moved away from Barrow.

But he wasn't going to let memories like that spoil the start of his new life in Manchester. The important thing was, this was a place where he could feel safe. And now that he was here, he wasn't going to hide his sexuality. *It's perfectly natural that I'll be nervous, but I'm just going to have to get over it.*

In the next aisle, members of the student orchestra took out their instruments and began playing a piece of music Danny soon realised was a classical reworking of *Who Let the Dogs Out*. The grins and giggles coming from the musicians told him the song choice was meant to be some kind of ironic joke. It suddenly struck him how different he was to most of the other students; they were there to work out which activities might give them the most fun, but he was there for something much more serious. *I'm here to become the person I was always meant to be.*

The main reason Danny had applied to university in Manchester was because he'd understood it was somewhere he could live openly as a gay man. He'd read in magazines about the Gay Village around Canal Street and how it attracted men from all over the country. Then *Queer as Folk* had broadcast on Channel 4 and his fantasies had gone into overdrive. The only problem was, he'd be much too nervous to go to the Gay Village on his own – and that was why he needed to make some gay friends. But he still hadn't spotted the stall for the LGB Society and was too frightened to ask one of the officious-looking organisers striding around shouting into their walkie-talkies. He found a quiet spot where he could stand on his tiptoes and look around.

Once again that tall, blond boy strayed into view. He was chatting to a trio of hairy, thick-set boys manning the stall for the university rugby team. As if it hadn't already been obvious that he was out of Danny's league, now he had another reason to look away: *He's hardly going to be gay if he plays rugby.* But just then the boy turned and caught Danny's eye. And from across the room, he gave him another wink.

Danny felt his lungs expel a bit of air.

He wondered if his hangover was making him hallucinate. Last night, he'd gone out with Emma, a confident and sexually forthright English Literature student from Glasgow who had a thick mane of copper hair, wore heavy eyeliner, and lived one floor down from him in the same hall of residence. The two of them had tipped back a plastic bottle of warm supermarket cider on the bus into the city centre and gone to a huge party for freshers organised by the Students' Union at a straight club called Infinity. They'd had a great time dancing under a huge glitter ball to music by Shakira, Sugababes and Blue, but Danny couldn't completely let himself go as he still had no idea how Emma would react if she knew he was gay. After a few drinks, he'd mustered up the courage to come out to her and, when she'd said she'd assumed he was gay and hugged him, he'd felt a rush of such joy he bought them a round of shots of hot cinnamon Aftershock. After downing these, they'd tipped back several more. When they were too drunk to dance, they'd slumped onto a staircase and Emma had slurred her way through an impassioned rant about the moral judgment directed against her as a sexually expressive woman – and Danny had experienced what he'd been convinced was a moment of acute social insight and declared that, as a gay man ostracised for his sexuality, the two of them were natural allies. By the time they'd begun staggering back to Hulme Hall, demolishing a pair of overcooked kebabs along the way, they were vowing to visit each other at home during the holidays, rent a house together in their second year, and even get matching tattoos.

Now it was the next morning, Danny felt embarrassed about having got so carried away and was careful to avoid all mention of tattoos. Thankfully, Emma was preoccupied with nursing her hangover.

'Sorry, pal,' she said as she reappeared from the toilets, 'I had to go and chuck my guts up. Have you got any chewing gum?'

Danny pulled out a packet and gave her a couple. 'If it's any consolation,' he said, popping a few in his mouth, 'I feel just as rough myself. My head's banging and my mouth tastes like I've gargled with sweat.'

Emma held up her hand. 'Don't! You're giving me the boak.'

Danny didn't understand what that meant but could tell from her expression it wasn't good. 'Babe, are you sure you want to be here?'

She nodded slowly. 'Aye. I said I'd be your moral support and I will. But let's get on with it – I don't think I can last much longer.'

Danny spotted an information stand and slid over to pick up a map. He read down the list of stalls. 'According to this, the LGB Society should be in that corner over there.'

He led Emma towards a stall that was tucked away under a staircase, at a discreet distance from the rest of the action. But this was where the discretion ended: the stand had been painted bright pink and was decorated with a pair of rainbow flags and several garlands of silver tinsel. It was staffed by a pale, intense-looking boy with a shaved head and lots of badges emblazoned with political slogans, and a girl in a baseball cap, crop top and combat trousers, with piercings through her eyebrows and a bolt through her nose.

'Fuck me,' said Emma, 'if you were nervous before, I bet you're shitting yourself now.'

Danny elbowed her in the ribs but could feel a coil of anxiety tighten in his stomach. 'Actually, my hangover's worse than I thought,' he said. 'Maybe I'll do this another time.'

'Like hell you will. Get a grip, pal! I've not dragged myself here for you to bottle it at the last minute!'

He drew in a ragged breath and looked over his shoulder to check no-one was watching. Before he could talk himself out of it, he shuffled over to the stall.

'Hello,' he said in a low voice, 'I'm Danny. I'd like to sign up.'

To his left, two well-built boys from the boxing club strode past. He could feel his shoulders stiffen but they strode on without paying any attention.

'That's great news,' said the boy. 'Welcome to the family.'

Danny felt a rush of happiness so strong it left him quite breathless. *Where did that come from?*

'And how about your friend?' asked the girl, nodding towards Emma, who was now putty-faced, leaning over the stall, dry-retching. 'Is she joining?'

Emma didn't look up but waved her hand in the air. 'Sorry, hen, I'm not into minge,' she called out before rushing off in the direction of the toilets.

The girl pulled a face, as if she'd just announced she'd massacred her entire family and eaten the remains.

'Sorry,' said Danny, 'it was a heavy night.'

He quickly changed the subject and asked them about the kind of activities the LGB Society organised. They told him they held regular coffee socials and meetings of their poetry reading collective and book club. They handed him a stack of leaflets with information about the University's LGB policies, initiatives the society organised to raise funds to combat HIV/AIDS, and a march demanding the repeal of Section 28 that members were planning on attending in London. It all sounded very interesting, if slightly earnest.

'Do you ever organise nights out?' Danny ventured.

'What do you mean?' asked the boy.

'You know, like nights out to bars and stuff? In the Gay Village?'

The two of them shot him a frigid look.

'We do organise a monthly trip to the Village,' said the boy, 'but the focus tends to be on LGB culture and history, rather than just getting drunk.'

Danny tried not to see his more riotous *Queer as Folk* fantasies skipping away up Canal Street. *This is just a start,* he reassured himself. *Once you've made some gay friends, you can arrange to go out under your own steam.*

'If you give me your details,' the boy went on, 'I'll let you know when the next one is.'

He handed over a clipboard and a pen and Danny began filling in his contact details, including the number for the brand new Nokia mobile phone that was clipped to his belt. Although he was worried about how he was going to afford his new life as a student now the government had axed all maintenance grants, he'd spent some of the money he'd earned from working in his local Blockbuster video store over the summer on his first mobile. He couldn't bear the idea of the other students thinking he had less money than them and couldn't bear the idea of missing out on anything.

'OK, well, thanks,' he said. 'And I guess I'll see you both soon.'

He gave them a smile and stepped away.

Once he'd rounded the corner, he texted Emma to say he'd wait by the main entrance. He found a quiet spot, closed his eyes and began massaging his temples. But it was no use – his head was pounding so violently he wondered if he might be having an aneurism. He looked at his watch and decided it was just about safe to take another couple of Ibuprofen tablets. He pulled a bottle of water out of his bag, downed the pills and drained the bottle dry. He changed his chewing gum and leaned back against a wall to read one of his leaflets.

'Hello, hello,' came a deep voice.

He looked up. Standing in front of him was the tall, blond boy he'd noticed earlier. The sight of him knocked the breath out of Danny's throat. He was even more handsome close up, with arresting blue eyes set perfectly apart, a light dusting of freckles over his thick, muscular forearms, and that mesmerising dimple on his chin.

'Oh, hi,' Danny said as casually as he could.

When the boy smiled, Danny got a glorious view of the little gap between his front teeth. As he did, his stomach flipped, just like it had when he was little and his mum had taken him to Blackpool to go on the Big One rollercoaster.

'What's that you're reading?' the boy asked.

Danny felt awkward but checked himself with a reminder that now he was in Manchester, he wasn't going to lie about his sexuality. 'Oh, it's just something about the LGB Society,' he answered, handing over the leaflet. He hoped the chewing gum stopped him smelling of rotten alcohol.

'LGB?' asked the boy, turning it over in his hands. 'What's that?'

Danny could feel the heat prickling his face but forced himself not to lower his voice. 'Lesbian, Gay and Bisexual.'

There was a pause.

'Cool,' said the boy, handing back the leaflet.

'Yeah, apparently it used to be called GaySoc but they changed its name.' Danny hoped he wasn't rambling.

The boy nodded and tucked his hands under his armpits. 'Well, maybe I should sign up.'

Danny stepped back in shock. *What? Did he just tell me he's gay?*

'I'm actually here to join the rugby club,' the boy added, before Danny could say anything.

Oh no, don't change the subject!

'I've come with a friend from school,' he went on. 'We went to Radley.'

Danny was pretty sure Radley was a posh school, and the boy did speak with a slightly plummy voice. He suddenly felt conscious of his northern twang. 'Oh yeah, so where are you from?' he asked.

'Buckinghamshire,' the boy replied. 'But I boarded. How about you?'

'Barrow-in-Furness. And there was no boarding at my school; I went to the local comp.'

'Cool,' the boy said again.

Danny chuckled. 'You wouldn't be saying that if you'd seen the state of it. It was a right shithole.'

'Oh, OK, sorry . . .'

'Don't be daft, it's fine.'

They hit another bump of silence. Danny felt almost dizzy with desire. *Oh my God he's gorgeous. But surely he can't be gay?*

'Anyway, I should probably introduce myself,' said the boy. 'I'm Guy, Guy Falconer.'

He held out his hand and Danny took it. His grip was sturdy and Danny tried to shake his hand firmly. 'Danny. Danny Baxter.'

'Good to meet you.'

'Oh and I'm doing Drama. How about you?'

'Law.'

Danny gave an exaggerated frown. 'Very serious.'

'Yeah it is, kind of.' Guy looked around cautiously. 'I doubt there'll be any other gays on my course.'

Fuck, so he IS gay! Danny thought his legs might be about to give way. *What am I supposed to say to that?*

'No, I expect not,' was all he could manage, his voice cracking.

'Not that I'm out yet,' said Guy, scrunching up his nose. 'Except to you now. But I guess I had to tell someone. You know what it's like.'

Danny nodded; he *did* know what it was like. But at the same time, he was struggling to understand this. How had he gone from being the effeminate boy everyone hated to making friends with the most gorgeous boy he'd ever seen – and one who'd just told him he was gay? Not in his most optimistic fantasies about his life in Manchester had he dared imagine anything like this. He tried to remain calm. 'Yeah, well, I feel honoured,' he said with a smile.

A flash of fear passed across Guy's face. 'I hope you don't mind keeping it to yourself though, at least for now.'

'Of course not,' Danny reassured him. 'I totally get it, don't worry.'

They were interrupted by a pair of actors in Elizabethan dress who were reciting a famous speech from a Shakespeare play that they'd adapted to promote the University of Manchester Drama Society. The actors drew out every last syllable as if luxuriating in the lines, projecting their voices as loudly as they could. Danny took a leaflet before the two of them gave a theatrical wave and flounced off.

Danny looked at Guy and pulled a face. 'Just so you know, not all of us who do Drama are like that.'

'What do you mean?' said Guy.

'Just that I am an actor and I do love it but I'm not into any of that hammy, thespy stuff.'

Guy grinned at him, mischievously. 'Oh, I'm sure you can be a real drama queen when you want to.'

Danny clutched his chest and gave a gasp. '*Queen*? I think you'll find I'm a *princess*!'

He felt a flare of self-loathing. *Oh God, why do I have to be so camp?*

Guy gurgled with laughter. 'Listen, how would you feel if I took your number? Maybe we could meet up on our own?'

Fuck, is this really happening?

'Oh, urm, yeah, OK,' Danny struggled.

He fumbled for his phone and just about managed to give Guy his number and save his. *Thank God I bought a mobile!*

As he leaned in to check Guy had entered his details correctly, he noticed that he smelled of fabric conditioner and Wash & Go shampoo. *Oh, he's so* normal. *He's so perfect.*

'OK,' said Guy, 'I'd better go and find Rags.'

'Rags?'

'My friend from school.'

'Oh, OK, great. Speak to you soon.'

Guy gave Danny another wink. 'Speak to you soon, princess.'

Danny felt his heart give a little wobble. As he watched Guy walk away, he shook his head and blinked slowly. Although he was still baffled by their conversation, at the same time it was like the fog of his hangover had suddenly cleared.

He wasn't even sure he had a headache anymore.

2022

As Danny and Guy step off the train and make their way through Piccadilly station, Danny wonders again if he fell in love at first sight. *But, now that I think of it, what does that even mean?*

It strikes him that there are so many different types of love, there should be several words for it. The sparks of new love have to be very different from the love a husband or wife feels for their partner after fifty years. That again has to be so different from the love a parent feels for a child – or, he thinks as a memory of his dad flashes into his mind, is *supposed* to feel for a child. Different again is the love between siblings or close friends. *And then there's the love that all these years I've felt for Guy.*

That love can be joyous and uplifting when Danny and Guy are together, or Guy gives signs that he wants or needs Danny. But for most of the time they've known each other, it's taken the form of a hollow longing, a feeling that something fundamental is missing from Danny's life, and an inkling that the only way he'll ever feel complete is if he finds out his love is reciprocated – in the same form.

As I'm hoping to find out this weekend . . .

He steps out of the station and a barrage of bright sunshine blasts away his nerves. He looks at Guy and feels a grin creeping across his face.

'Babe,' he says, 'we're back!'

'We are, princess. Isn't it great?'

Despite the fact that Manchester was the setting for so many happy memories for the two of them, neither Danny nor Guy has returned much since they left university and moved to London. There's been the occasional trip to visit friends who settled in the north but these have become less and less frequent – and in the meantime, Manchester has undergone some major changes. As they walk through the streets towards their hotel, they can't help commenting on them.

'That bridge didn't used to be there.'

'Where did all those restaurants come from?'

'This city is so much more *glamorous* than it used to be.'

When they come to Piccadilly Gardens, they stumble on a gang of drunks slumped on the grass by the statue of Queen Victoria.

Guy lets out a snort. 'At least Piccadilly Gardens are still as rough as ever.'

Danny chuckles. 'I guess you can't make shit sparkle.'

They move on, engrossed by the city unfolding around them. As they glimpse the top of Market Street, they see that all the shops are decked out in rainbow flags and bunting, and hanging from every lamp-post are banners welcoming visitors to Manchester for Pride. Standing on the corner of the bus station is a man selling rainbow whistles, hats, fans and balloons. And almost everywhere they look, groups of gay men and lesbians are pulling along wheelie suitcases and consulting their phones to find their accommodation. Skipping across the pavement in front of them, two teenagers of indeterminate gender belt out the lyrics to Dua Lipa's *Levitating*. There's such a celebratory atmosphere that Danny can't help but feel uplifted.

They stop on Mosley Street so that a tram can pass.

'Wait a minute, the trams didn't used to be yellow, did they?' asks Guy.

'No, they didn't,' says Danny. 'They were white and turquoise when we lived here.'

Guy nods as if the memories are slowly coming back. 'Hey, do you remember when Emma got so wasted she threw up down the side of that bank?'

Danny smiles. 'How could I forget? She vommed that hard she lost a filling. But she still managed to go off and shag that guy who worked at Old Trafford.'

'Oh yeah,' says Guy, 'she said he looked like Enrique Iglesias but you said it was more like Dean Gaffney.'

They break into laughter.

'Hey,' Danny says as they approach the art gallery, 'do you remember when I made that pretentious short film in there?'

'Which one?' teases Guy. 'I seem to remember there were a few.'

'God knows, I must have blanked it from my memory. All I remember is having to run around the gallery in my underwear wailing like a Spanish widow. Thank God YouTube didn't exist then – or social media.'

'And nobody had camera phones. Can you imagine if people had filmed our nights out? I don't think a single law firm in London would have given me a job.'

Danny waves away his comment. 'That's nothing, babe. I'd have been splashed all over every amateur porn site on the internet!'

Oh, what are you doing, Danny?

Just as he's about to add a line about his reputation for sleeping around being over-exaggerated, they come to the huge round building housing the Central Library. Danny spots an opportunity to revive another memory. 'This place reminds me of our third year, when you were revising for your finals.'

A smile creeps into Guy's eyes. 'Yeah, you used to meet me for lunch and we'd go and sit on our steps next to the Town Hall.'

'You'd wind me up about having no work to do and being on a piece-of-piss course.'

Guy gives him a withering look. 'Yeah, but you've got to admit, Drama *was* a piece of piss.'

Danny roofs his eyes. 'Alright, alright, I admit it. Are you happy now?'

'Finally!' says Guy. 'It only took you twenty years!'

They pass a statue of Emmeline Pankhurst – one of Manchester's most famous daughters – that's currently adorned with a rainbow-coloured garland hanging around the Suffragette's neck and a rainbow flag someone's balanced between her fingers.

'That's new,' says Guy. 'I like it.'

'Yeah and I like the fact she's getting into the spirit of Pride,' quips Danny.

They stride on but when they reach Peter Street they come to a stop.

Danny points down the street towards a grand Victorian stone building. 'There it is, that's our hotel.'

In an instant, his upbeat mood falls away.

The sight of the hotel reminds Danny of something he did when booking their room, something he did that he later regretted but has since tried reassuring himself isn't that bad. In any case, it's something he can't back out of now, even if he wanted to. But he has no idea how Guy will react.

Danny scrunches up his hands into little fists. *Oh, please let this go well. Please, please, please let this go well.*

2002

As Danny walked towards Guy's hall, he tried not to grind his teeth. *Oh, please let this go well.*

It was a week after they'd met at the Freshers' Fair and, after several text exchanges, mainly consisting of small talk about their accommodation and the start of their courses, Guy had suggested that Danny come to his room for a coffee. They both lived on the Victoria Park campus of the University but Guy was in Dalton-Ellis Hall, which was a ten-minute walk away from Hulme Hall.

As Danny entered the grounds, he hardly took in his surroundings; he was feeling far too overwhelmed by a mixture of anxiety and excitement. Since arriving in Manchester, he'd spent a lot of time chatting to his new friends in their rooms and really enjoyed this easy, laidback way of socialising. But most of his friends were girls and he fancied none of the boys he knew – whereas Guy he fancied like mad. *In fact, I fancy him so much, sometimes I think I might be* going *mad.*

He still found it impossible to imagine that Guy might feel anything like the same way about him; not only was he way better-looking than he was but he was also classier than a weekly food shop at M&S, while Danny had grown up with a single mother in a terraced house in a dodgy part of Barrow. Nevertheless, he'd spent the whole day stressing about what to wear, eventually settling on his favourite GAP jeans with a red hoodie his mum told him complemented his olive skin tone. He'd washed his hair with the henna shampoo his mum said made its black colour shine and had smeared Immac onto the dark hair covering his back and shoulders, cursing its ugliness as he contorted himself into shapes he hadn't thought possible – not because he thought there was any chance of Guy wanting to see him naked, but because he didn't want to be standing in front of him feeling repulsed by himself. *I need to give off positive vibes.*

When he reached Guy's room, he knocked on the door. As he waited for Guy to answer, he took deep breaths and scrunched up his hands into little fists.

After a few seconds, Guy's head peered around the door, towelling his hair dry. Danny's heart flinched. Just as he remembered, Guy had blue eyes that sparkled and a gorgeous little dimple in the centre of his chin. When he smiled and revealed the gap between his teeth, Danny felt his insides flip.

'Hello, hello,' Guy said in a voice so deep Danny was sure he could feel the reverberations coming up through the floor. 'How are you?'

'Hiya,' said Danny, worried that his smile might be quivering. 'Yeah, good thanks.'

Just as he was wondering whether to shake Guy's hand, hug him or kiss him, Guy opened the door wide and revealed that he was wearing nothing but a pair of boxer shorts. 'Sorry,' he said, 'I've just had a shower.'

Danny blinked as he took in Guy's body. It was sturdily built and muscular, without any of the ugly hair that plagued him. It reminded him of Brendan Fraser or the men in the Chippendales calendar his mum used to hang in the kitchen. He wanted to come up with some witty, flirtatious line – the kind of thing Samantha Jones would say on *Sex and the City* – but he was stumped. 'It's OK,' was all he could manage, 'I can wait out here if you like.'

'Don't be silly!' Guy insisted. 'Come in!'

Oh my God, oh my God, oh my God.

Danny scrunched up his fists again as he followed Guy into his room. His heart was thumping with such force he could feel his pulse in his fingertips.

Guy gestured for him to sit on his bed while he finished getting dressed. He explained that he'd just got back from his first session with the university rock-climbing society. As he talked Danny through the experience, his words became distant and muffled; all Danny could take in was the sight of his body as he lowered the towel over his shoulder blades and ran it slowly across his back so that every muscle on his chest and abdomen stood out, catching the sunlight that streamed through the window. As he watched a drop of water slowly trickle down Guy's torso, Danny felt an ache in the core of his gut. He imagined his fingers tracing the course of that trickle. *Or then again, tracing it with my tongue . . .*

'Oh and I'm sorry my room's a mess,' Guy said, snapping Danny out of his daydream. 'I've had so much going on I haven't had time to settle in properly.'

Danny looked around and saw that Guy's room was laid out in pretty much the same way as his, with a desk, a wardrobe and a single bed standing against the wall. Except that Guy's had an en suite bathroom, which Danny had stipulated that he didn't want when picking his accommodation as it meant a higher rent.

Plus, most of Guy's stuff was still packed away in boxes and he hadn't put up any posters on the walls, while Danny had unpacked and stored everything away neatly on the day he moved in. And, now that he'd followed up his successful coming out to Emma by broadcasting his sexuality to pretty much everyone he'd met at university, he'd decorated his room with a rainbow flag he'd bought from the Student Union shop and countless posters of half-naked men he'd ripped out of magazines. Brad Pitt, Mark Wahlberg, Vin Diesel – all of his favourites were there. But none of them made Danny feel the way Guy did. *And he's standing right here in front of me!*

He reminded himself that he needed to respond. 'Don't worry about it,' he piped, 'I don't mind at all.'

He leaned back against the wall and watched Guy hang up his towel on the bathroom door and then pull on some jeans and a faded T-shirt, leaving his feet bare. Although he was sorry to lose sight of Guy's body, he was relieved when his heart rate began to settle. He tried not to notice the faint smell of fresh sweat coming from the training kit Guy had taken off and tossed onto the floor. Danny always thought sweat was supposed to smell bad – his own sometimes made him gag – but for some reason Guy's smelled good.

'Do you want a coffee?' Guy asked. 'I have at least managed to unpack the kettle.'

As Guy busied himself making instant coffee, splashing in some milk from a bottle he'd been keeping cool on the windowsill outside, he told Danny that as well as rock-climbing, earlier this week he'd been to his first training session for the university rugby team. Unable to make any meaningful contribution to a conversation about sport, Danny found his memory rewinding to his schooldays and the PE lessons during which a crude, raw masculinity had taken on even more importance in determining the social hierarchy than it had in the playground. It was in PE lessons that the other boys' impressions of his voice and the way he moved became most vicious, when the entire class would gather around and laugh at the way he threw or kicked a ball, when the teacher would become so exasperated with his lack of ability as a footballer that he'd insist Danny didn't just stand in goal but actually *be* the goalpost. In Year 9, the other boys had presented the Head of PE with a petition they'd signed demanding Danny use a different changing room so he wouldn't be able to ogle them naked – and the teacher had instructed Danny to change in the toilets to avoid 'stirring things up any further'. Danny had felt ransacked with humiliation.

The strange thing was, though, he couldn't escape the fact that he *did* find those boys attractive. In fact, of all the boys in the school, it was the sporty, athletic ones he found the *most* attractive, even when they insulted and ostracised him – if anything, this only made him fancy them *more*. It was all so confusing and left him burning with self-hatred. And now here he was, five years later and 100 miles away from Barrow, ogling the half-naked body of another sporty boy, although this one had told him he was gay and invited him into his room. It was a lot for him to get his head around.

He decided to steer Guy away from the subject of sport and towards something he wanted to talk about. 'I'm going to my first meeting of the LGB Society on Friday,' he ventured. 'Fancy coming with me?'

Guy pulled a face. 'I'm not really sure it's my thing.' He handed Danny a chipped mug bearing the coat of arms of Radley College. 'I mean, won't it be all heavy and political?'

Danny remembered chatting to the boy wearing badges emblazoned with activist slogans and the girl with all the piercings on her face. 'You might be right, yeah. But I'm still going to pop along and check it out. I'll let you know if I think you'll like it.'

Guy thanked him and sat next to him. Danny tried not to flinch at the proximity; Guy was so close he could feel his breath moving the hairs on his arms. *And we're on a bed – an actual bed . . .*

He realised how easily he could lean forward and kiss him. *We could just lie back and let one thing lead to another.*

He needed to dismiss the idea before it took hold. 'But if I come back with a bolt through my nose, I might need you to rescue me,' he joked.

Guy laughed. Danny felt good to have made him laugh.

'You know, thanks for being so cool when I came up to you at the fair last week,' Guy said. 'You must have thought I was a total weirdo introducing myself then ten seconds later blurting out that I'm gay.'

'Not at all,' Danny reassured him, 'I hope I didn't give you that impression.'

Guy shook his head. 'The funny thing was, I didn't even intend to do it. But everyone kept talking about university being a fresh start and this amazing opportunity to change your life and everything. And all I could think about was this secret I'd been keeping buried inside me for years – and then suddenly it was bubbling up and coming bursting out.'

Danny blew on his coffee. 'Yeah, well, we've all been there.'

He remembered how keen he'd been to come out to his fellow drama students, gushing away about all the men he fancied when they were supposed to be discussing *The Dance of Death* by Strindberg. He cringed at the memory of his tutor gently steering him aside to suggest he try to focus on the themes explored in the text. The thing was, being able to talk about his sexuality was such a novelty, he'd sometimes get so excited about it that he couldn't restrain himself.

'Anyway, I don't know what possessed me,' Guy went on, 'but I spotted you and just decided I was going to go over and come out with it before I had the chance to change my mind.'

'But how did you even know I was gay?' asked Danny.

Guy gave his feet a little wiggle. 'Don't take this the wrong way or anything but it's kind of obvious.'

Danny's heart sagged. 'Is it?' He wasn't sure why this should bother him when he'd been blabbing the news to anyone who'd listen, but it did. *If only I could be one of those gay men who don't* seem *gay. If only I could be like Guy . . .*

Guy rubbed the back of his neck. 'It is a bit obvious, yeah. Sorry, have I said the wrong thing?'

'No, not at all,' Danny said, breezily. He took a sip of coffee and quickly rewound. 'So am I really the first person you came out to?'

'Yeah. That doesn't freak you out, does it?'

'No, of course not. So you're not out to any of your mates at home?'

'Are you kidding? There's no way I could tell them. Besides, I couldn't risk my mother finding out.'

Guy explained that his mother was a staunch supporter of the Conservative party, attended a service in the local Anglican church every Sunday, and prided herself on having 'traditional family values'. From what Guy had heard her say about gay people, he was convinced that if he ever came out, she'd disown him – and possibly even throw him out of the house.

'It's ironic really,' he added. 'She's a GP so she must have met lots of gay people; you'd expect her to be a bit more understanding. But the truth is she has no understanding at all.'

Danny spotted pain skitter across Guy's face and felt a swell of sympathy for him. This was swiftly followed by a rush of guilt for imagining the two of them kissing then having sex on the bed. Now that Guy was opening his heart, it felt wildly inappropriate. Danny took another sip of his coffee.

'I'm sorry to hear that,' he forced himself to say. 'But how about your dad? Is he any better?'

'Not really, no.' Guy let out a long sigh. 'He's a stockbroker in the City and that's quite a macho world. I doubt it's ever occurred to him that his only son might be anything other than straight.'

Danny wasn't sure what to say but before he had chance to speak, Guy continued. 'Anyway, how about *your* parents? What do they do?'

The question prompted a flicker of embarrassment from Danny but he told himself to shake it off. 'My mum's a hairdresser,' he managed. 'She split up with my dad before I was born. He's never been a part of my life.'

He stopped there. He didn't want to reveal any more. *Not yet.*

'So has your mother ever met anyone else?' Guy asked.

Danny explained that during his childhood his mum had worked her way through a series of boyfriends, each of them less reliable, less respectful and less faithful than the last. Then, when he was about ten, she'd met a scaffolder called Lee who was good-looking and had a rough charm that made him a popular figure about town. Eileen had been smitten and within months Lee had moved in with them and she was starting to talk about the three of them as a family. Danny even dared to think that one day he might call Lee 'Dad', that he might even make up for the absence of his father. But soon Lee was becoming suspicious of Danny's lack of interest in sport and his love of boy bands Take That and East 17. Before long, whenever Eileen was out of the house, he was tormenting Danny, calling him 'pansy' and 'queer'. Suddenly Danny's safe haven was snatched away from him and he had nowhere to hide from the persecution he endured at school. The worst thing was, all he wanted was for Lee to love him – and he blamed himself for not being good enough, for not being enough of a 'proper lad' to deserve his love. Although he stopped short of sharing this last detail with Guy.

'That sounds awful,' Guy said. 'But why didn't you tell your mother?'

'Oh, she'd been unhappy for ages so I didn't want to spoil things for her. And it was all fine in the end because she dumped him anyway.' Danny didn't mention that this had only happened after two long years.

Guy swilled the remains of his coffee around his mug. 'And is she single now?'

'Yeah. So at least I only have to come out to one parent.' It was only now that it occurred to him just how much of a relief this was.

'And what do you think she'll say?'

'Oh, I'm sure she'll be fine about it.'

Actually, Danny *knew* his mum would be fine about it. All through his childhood, Eileen had made him feel loved exactly as he was and would march into school to defend him whenever she had the slightest suspicion that the other kids were picking on him. Not only that but she worked in a salon owned by a gay man called Arthur. Arthur was nearly twenty years older than

Eileen, had a deep sunbed tan and hair dyed a custard blond, and smoked Vogue cigarettes through a silver holder that he'd waft around as he worked. Danny could remember him telling customers with the figures of wheelie bins and faces that had been ravaged by years of hard work that they looked 'stunning' or 'like a Hollywood star'. And he'd often find his mum roaring with laughter at some filthy joke he'd made, gasping in delight as Arthur related his latest sexual encounter, or asking him for advice on her own love life – advice which always seemed to consist of her not putting up with any man who didn't treat her every bit as well as she deserved.

Although Danny liked Arthur and wanted to get close to him, he'd always kept his distance as he was worried Arthur could tell he was gay and he wasn't ready to open up about that side of himself. Then, just as Danny was starting at sixth-form college, Arthur had been beaten up in a horrific homophobic attack. One night when he was shutting up the salon, he'd been accosted by a gang of thugs who'd dragged him down the alley at the back of the building, kicked and punched him till he lost consciousness, then left him lying on the ground until Eileen had found him the next morning. Although he'd eventually recovered from his injuries, Arthur had retreated into himself, selling the salon and the flat above it and moving away to start a new life in Brighton. Eileen had easily found another job but Danny could tell that she missed Arthur and had been shaken up by the attack. That was the reason he still hadn't come out to her.

'I think I'll tell her at Christmas,' he confided in Guy. 'At least that's the plan.'

Guy gave his feet another wiggle. 'You know, you're very brave,' he said. 'I really admire you.'

'What? *Me?*'

'Yeah. I don't think I could do what you've done, at least not yet. It took me ages to even work out I was gay.'

'What do you mean? How could you not *know*?'

'Well, when I was growing up everyone just assumed I was straight and I had no reason to believe otherwise; every time I saw gays on TV they were camp queens like Julian Clary or Graham Norton. I didn't think I could possibly be one of them. Or at least I didn't *want* to be, so I convinced myself I wasn't.'

Danny finished his coffee and put his mug on the side. 'But you must have realised you fancied boys?'

'Yeah, of course.' A smile crept into Guy's eyes. 'I remember every time my mother's Next Directory used to arrive, I'd take it upstairs and pretend to be looking at clothes – but instead I'd be looking at all the bulges in the men's underwear section. I'd wank myself silly.'

Danny almost choked on his laughter. 'That's nothing. I remember once I was off school sick and I had to go to the salon with Mum. Arthur let me watch telly in his flat and I had a nosey around and found his stash of *Playgirl* magazines. I swear to God, all the men had huge muscles and massive dicks and honestly, I didn't stop wanking for days.'

Guy sat forward. 'We found a load of porn at school once. When we were about fifteen we found this old suitcase full of wank mags someone had dumped in the woods next to the rugby ground. I remember being mesmerised by the pictures and hoping nobody would notice I was staring at all the men.'

Danny cackled loudly but his laughter trailed off. He gave a sigh. 'I know all this is funny but don't you think it's a bit sad too?'

'Sad? Why do you say that?'

'Well, just that all the straight boys at school used to talk about who they fancied like it was the most natural thing in the world, but we had to hide it away like a dirty little secret.'

Guy nodded slowly. 'I've never thought of it like that. This is the first time I've talked to anyone about who I used to fancy. But now you mention it, I suppose you're right.'

Danny sat up purposefully. He told Guy that the reason he'd applied to Manchester University was that he'd found out this was a city where he could meet other people like him. He told him about being blown away by *Queer as Folk*, which Guy said he'd been too frightened to watch on TV but Danny promised to buy him on DVD. And he told him how excited he was about visiting Canal Street for the first time.

'Maybe we could go there together,' he said. He spotted a look of fear dart between Guy's eyes. 'Don't worry, we could avoid the student nights. So no-one would see you.'

Guy gave a nervous smile and in that moment Danny felt close to him, much closer to him than he ever had any other friend – which was quite something considering they'd only met a week ago. But already they'd established a bond that was unlike anything he'd experienced with anyone else.

Guy exhaled. 'OK, cool. I'd like that.'

Guy couldn't believe he'd just agreed to go for a night out on Canal Street. But from the moment he'd spotted Danny at the Freshers' Fair he'd felt drawn to him; that was why he hadn't been able to stop himself from marching over and blurting out that he was gay. He'd spent the last half an hour talking to him about things he'd never dared discuss with anyone, revealing feelings he often tried to hide from himself. And now here he was preparing to accompany him on a night out to an area full of gay men. It was something he wouldn't have imagined doing before he moved to Manchester. *But there's something about Danny that makes me feel like I* can *do it.*

He stretched his legs over the edge of the bed and gave Danny another smile. 'I know it might have been weird when I came over and introduced myself,' he said, 'but I'm glad I did.'

A grin lit up Danny's face. 'Yeah, I'm glad you did too.'

As Guy looked into his eyes, he felt strangely close to Danny, much closer than he did to some of the school friends he'd known for years, which was bizarre considering they'd only just met. On the other hand, it wasn't bizarre at all; whenever he was with his schoolfriends he had to be careful what he said about certain subjects. Hearing them make disparaging and sometimes offensive remarks about gay people made him assume they'd reject him if he ever revealed his true self. *But with Danny, for the first time, I feel like I can be me.*

Even though his feet were starting to get cold and he wanted to put on some socks, he decided not to stand up in case it ruined the moment and Danny took it as his cue to leave. *I really don't want him to leave.*

It also hadn't escaped Guy's attention that, all the time he'd been sitting next to Danny, his heart had been beating faster. *But what does that mean?*

Danny was certainly good-looking, although Guy couldn't help thinking he had no awareness of it himself. He wasn't buff or physically fit but he had a cute face, a sweet smile and a mischievous twinkle in his eye – and Guy found his flat-vowelled northern accent charming. A little earlier, he'd imagined what it would be like to lean in and kiss him and it had crossed his mind that, as they were sitting on a bed, things could have very easily developed from there. But since then, the conversation had moved on to some quite intimate subjects and the idea of lunging in to kiss Danny felt wildly inappropriate.

Besides, Danny was the first gay person Guy had ever met – or at least the first one to be open about it. Guy didn't have the slightest clue how you were supposed to work out which gays were meant to be your friends and which were meant to be more than that. Everything he knew about being gay he'd learned from the copies of *Attitude* and *Gay Times* he'd bought on the rare occasions he'd caught the train into London for some sporting event. He'd arrive early, pick them up from the WHSmith's in Paddington station, checking no-one was watching as he approached the till, his heart cannoning in his chest as he handed the magazines over to the assistant. Then he'd sneak off to the canal, where he'd find a quiet spot, hide them in the pages of one of his big college files, and read them from cover to cover, before dropping them into the nearest bin when it was time to move on. But, now that he needed advice, he couldn't remember if the magazines had said anything about identifying your feelings towards another gay man – or his towards you.

In any case, he found it highly unlikely that Danny would fancy him. For most of his teens, Guy had been plagued by spots, spots so angrily red and so prone to erupting in yellow pus that they caused some of the other boys at school to call him 'pizza face'. On one occasion, one of them had said he was so disgusting he should be forced to wear a bag over his head. Whenever the teachers talked to him, they'd talk to his spots rather than looking into his eyes, and sometimes couldn't help giving a little grimace or squirm. He ended up wishing people wouldn't notice him at all, that he could just be invisible. Every evening, he'd lock himself away in the bathroom, staring at himself in the mirror, wishing his spots away. He hated himself for being so disgusting.

It didn't help that his mother was his GP and refused to prescribe him the antibiotics he'd heard could clear up acne, insisting he'd soon grow out of the problem and needed to stop being so sensitive. He'd begged her to reconsider, until the situation came to a head the previous Christmas, when Guy's father wanted to take a photo and Guy broke down in tears in front of the family – one of the most humiliating experiences of his life. After this, his mother had backed down, but by that time Guy was seventeen and had been suffering from acne for years. When the antibiotics worked and his spots eventually cleared up, he still couldn't get used to the idea that he *wasn't* disgusting. When some of the girls from the local sixth-form college started to make it clear they found him attractive, he didn't believe them and felt embarrassed by the attention. He lived in fear of his acne coming back and once again being exposed as the person he really was – the person who made people grimace when they looked at him. Even all these months later, he felt that he was somehow conning Danny and ought to confess what he used to look like, what he still would look like if he weren't taking antibiotics. He certainly couldn't bring himself to consider the idea that Danny might fancy him.

He decided to play it safe and not do anything that ran any risk of losing Danny. *If I've finally gone and made myself a gay friend, the last thing I want to do is scare him off.*

He tried to forget that they were sitting on a bed, leaned back against the wall and listened as Danny talked about the gay-themed sitcoms *Will & Grace* and *Gimme Gimme Gimme*, which Guy had never felt brave enough to watch but Danny said he loved. He listened to him discuss the gay characters in Hollywood films like *My Best Friend's Wedding* and *The Birdcage*, both of which – amazingly – Danny had watched with his mother. And he listened to him rave about an independent British film called *Beautiful Thing*, which was about two teenage boys living on a council estate in London who, quite simply, fall in love.

'Honestly, babe, there's loads of stuff out there now,' Danny said, his eyes glittering. 'Gay's going mainstream. Look at Will Young!'

Guy quirked an eyebrow. 'What about Will Young?'

'Well, he won *Pop Idol*, didn't he?'

Guy ran his hand along his jaw. 'Yeah, but wasn't that before he came out?'

'Alright, but look at all the hits he's had since then. Everyone loves him – and they all know he's gay.'

Guy felt a kick of excitement. 'I suppose you're right, yeah.'

Danny laid a hand on his shoulder. 'Seriously, babe, the world's changing. It's finally ready for us!'

Guy could feel the happiness spreading across his chest. 'In that case, it looks like we've come to Manchester at just the right time.'

'Now let's get out there and show this city what we're made of!'

2022

Danny pretends to be outraged at the news that he and Guy will be sharing a bed. 'What do you mean, it's a double? I specifically requested two singles.'

The hotel receptionist looks at the screen in front of her and bites her lip. 'I'm sorry, Mr Baxter,' she says in a heavy Spanish accent, 'but I cannot find any record of your request.'

That's because I'm lying. That's because I requested a double.

He feels a stab of guilt as he remembers the man on the phone asking what kind of room he wanted, letting slip that there was only one twin left. 'Oh, we'll take a double,' Danny had blurted out, seizing on the idea before he could talk himself out of it – then regretting it as soon as he'd put the phone down.

Well, there's no point regretting it now.

He puffs out his cheeks and throws his hands in the air. 'Yeah, but it's not our fault if someone here messed up the booking.'

'No,' says the receptionist. 'I am very sorry.'

She gives him a weak smile and tucks a strand of hair behind her ear. Danny feels another swell of guilt for putting her through this, but it's an emotion he quickly smothers. *I'm sure she has to deal with this kind of thing all the time.*

'Well, is there anything you can do?' he asks.

As the receptionist taps frantically at her keyboard, Danny can't bring himself to look at Guy. Instead, he directs his eyes around the room and pretends to be appraising the hotel. The entrance hall has been decorated with rainbow bunting and pom-poms, and rainbow flags are flying from each of the reception desks. Underneath the decorations, the lobby is impressive, with an oak-pannelled floor and a crystal chandelier twinkling overhead. Danny knows that inside, the hotel's five-star facilities are even more impressive. When he was researching accommodation, he wanted them to stay somewhere luxurious, somewhere he could relax in the knowledge they wouldn't come up against any problems. *Except for the problem I've created myself . . .*

The receptionist looks up from her keyboard and frowns. 'I'm afraid because of Pride we are completely booked up.'

'It's OK,' Guy says, stepping in, 'we can share a double bed.' He flashes the receptionist a beam. 'Honestly, it's not a problem.'

Danny was hoping Guy would say that – but wanted him to be the one to make the decision. And he may have lied but tells himself that on this occasion it's permissible. *After all, I've waited for twenty years to share a bed with him.*

'Alright,' he says, rubbing his stubble, 'as long as you don't mind. I suppose it's not the end of the world.'

The receptionist gives a sigh of relief and thanks them, promising to send up a complimentary bottle of champagne later.

'That's very kind,' says Danny, desperate to make up for his earlier animosity. 'Thanks very much.'

He makes a mental note of her name and promises himself he'll leave her a glowing review online.

He hands over his ID and credit card and the receptionist inputs the details, then gives them each a key card.

'Here you go,' she says. 'You are in room fifty-three.'

As they make their way across the lobby, Danny has to make a real effort not to break into a smile. In the lift, he and Guy connect their phones to the hotel's Wi-Fi and he makes a joke about how reliant they've become on the internet, something they'd never have been able to predict when they first met, when neither of them had heard the word 'google' used as a verb.

'Hey, do you remember the computer room at uni?' he goes on. 'It always stank of cheese and onion crisps and B.O.'

Guy laughs. 'The computers were the size of tanks and it took ages for every web page to load.'

'Ask Jeeves, do you remember that?' says Danny. 'What a load of crap. And God knows how we survived without Wikipedia.'

By the time the lift arrives at their floor, Danny's satisfied he's diverted Guy's attention from the sleeping arrangements. But, as they walk down the corridor, he knows the double bed is about to slam into view – and the butterflies flap away in his stomach.

When they enter the room, Danny discovers it's spacious and stylish, with a plush carpet, a lounge area with a sofa and two armchairs, and a table on which stand a modern kettle and some kind of vintage coffee-making machine that looks like a steam engine. There's a full-length mirror and several pieces of abstract art hanging on the walls, but dominating the room is the double bed – and it isn't just a double but some kind of Super King. Across the bottom half someone has scattered red rose petals, on top of which have been arranged two white towels sculpted into the shape of swans, their necks intertwined as if they're nuzzling each other. It's an image so blatantly aimed at inspiring romance that Danny feels a rush of awkwardness – not to mention guilt.

He reaches for the remote control to switch on the TV but there are three and they each have so many buttons he can't work out how to do it.

'My God,' he says, 'why do they have to make things so complicated?'

Guy takes the controls off him. 'Leave it to me, princess. Technology's my department, remember?'

While Guy switches on the TV, Danny pokes his head into the bathroom. It's enormous, with a two person shower and a gleaming white bathtub that looks like it doubles as a Jacuzzi.

'Well, I reckon this'll do,' he chirps. 'It's gorgeous, isn't it?'

Guy throws himself onto the bed. 'Yeah, it reminds me of the rooms my PA books for me when I go away with work. Although I'm warning you now – hotel rooms make me horny.'

Fuck!

Danny feels a rush of adrenaline. He can't believe Guy's flirting with him already – and so openly.

But surely it can't be that easy? Not after so long?

He settles for a non-committal 'Is that so?' and busies himself unpacking his shirts and hanging them up in the wardrobe, his heart thumping against his ribcage.

But Guy's keen on running with his theme. 'Honestly, put me in a hotel room and all of a sudden I'm like a bull at a gate.'

'I can imagine,' Danny replies. And he has – on many occasions.

Although hopefully I won't have to for much longer.

He quickly tells himself that he can't go there yet – he needs a drink first. He doesn't want to wait twenty years and blow his big moment by being nervous and awkward. *After all this I can't be shit in bed.*

He tells Guy that he's going to get ready for their trip to Canal Street, grabs a shirt and his washbag, and takes them into the bathroom. Once he's shut the door behind him, he leans over the sink and splashes cold water onto his face.

Fuck! This is happening! It's really happening!

He looks at his reflection in the mirror. He takes a deep breath, then expels all the air from his lungs. He feels confident. This feels right.

And it may have been tortuous to wait so long but maybe this is the way it had to happen. Maybe we were too young to get together when we first met and needed to experience life first.

He picks up a towel and pats his face dry. He changes his shirt, reapplies deodorant and brushes his teeth. Once he's fully composed, he seizes a breath and opens the door.

When he re-enters the room, he sees that Guy's also changed his shirt and is lying on the bed, flicking through the TV channels with his left arm behind his head. Danny looks at the curve of his bicep and feels a pang of longing but tells himself that in just a few hours' time he'll be sharing the bed with him – and this time for the purpose he's dreamed about ever since they first sat on a bed together.

He takes the remote control from him and switches off the TV.

'Come on,' he says, 'let's show this city what we're made of!'

2022

'I don't believe it,' says Guy, 'it's changed its name.'

The two of them stand in front of the bar and look up at a sign that's lit up against the dark sky.

'Shit, yeah,' says Danny, 'it's called ON Bar.'

Guy's forehead creases into a frown. 'I wonder what happened to Manto.'

'I don't know; it must have closed down or something.'

'But how can it have closed down? It was the busiest bar in the Village. And it was our favourite!'

He sounds like a little boy who's just found out his special comfort object has fallen out of his buggy and gone missing. Danny panics that their night is getting off to a bad start. They've already had to stand in a queue at the Box Office for half an hour to collect their Manchester Pride wristbands. *I need to turn this around.*

'Oh, who knows?' he trills with a jollity that sounds borderline hysterical. 'But never mind, I'm sure this new place has got the same spirit. Come on, let's give it a chance.'

Guy reluctantly agrees and they thread their way through the crowd carpeting Canal Street and step inside.

They discover that ON Bar is a bright, stylishly decorated venue with the same ground-floor dancing area as Manto, but the old bar has been ripped out from the back wall and moved to the side, and the first-floor balcony that used to overlook the dance floor has been filled in. Before Guy can express disappointment, Danny suggests they have a look upstairs.

Although it's only 9 o'clock, the venue is already crammed with people, many of whom look like they've been drinking for hours. It takes a while to reach the first floor but once there, they find a newly-created second dance floor and the same terrace that used to jut out over Canal Street, although this has been enlarged to create an outdoor smoking area. A flat-capped lesbian at a DJ desk is playing the latest dance remix by Olivia Rodrigo, and several drag queens wearing architectural wigs, hooker heels and thong bikinis are slut-dropping on podiums. As Danny and Guy squeeze their way into the throng, a man with muscles so hard they look like they've been chiselled from marble spills some of his drink down Danny's right arm, while Guy is accosted by a blonde woman with enormous fake boobs.

'Alright, sweetheart,' she slurs at him, draping her arm around his neck, 'I'm here on a hen night.'

'Oh, OK, right,' Guy says, his shoulders stiffening, 'I hope you're having fun.'

'You're well fit,' the woman goes on, blasting the words directly into Guy's face. 'I don't suppose you're straight?'

Danny can feel the irritation creep up his spine. It was bad enough finding out their favourite bar no longer exists; the last thing he wants is for this woman to ruin their night before it's even started. 'Sorry, babe,' he jumps in, 'you're barking up the wrong tree.'

Danny's alarmed by the note of hostility in his voice but thankfully the woman is too drunk to be offended. She stands back and gives him a glassy-eyed smile. 'So how long have you two been together?' she asks.

This isn't the first time someone has directed this question at them – and Danny usually rejoices at the assumption they're a couple. But on this occasion, the embarrassment screeches down a blackboard in his head.

'Oh, we're not actually together,' he clarifies, 'just old friends.'

'Old friends'? Why the hell did I say that?

The woman shrugs and a hiccup escapes her mouth. 'Well, I think you *should* get together. You'd make a lovely couple.'

Danny can feel himself blushing to the tips of his ears. Like a drag queen whipping off a cape, it's as if the woman has exposed his feelings for Guy – and what he's hoping will happen this weekend.

He can't bear to look at Guy and fixes his features into something approaching a smile. 'Yeah, well, thanks, babe. Have a good night.'

Finally, the woman staggers away.

'Thank God she's gone,' Guy says once she's out of earshot. 'I need a beer – but look at the queue.'

Danny turns to see a mêlée of people elbowing each other to get to the bar. 'Don't worry, my prince,' he chirps somewhat manically, 'I'll go!'

He quickly sets off, leaving Guy to settle into a space by one of the steel girders – another feature to have survived the refurbishment. Although there's an uplifting atmosphere, Danny waits to get served for so long that he worries it'll completely deflate Guy's mood and be the final blow for their night. When a barman eventually takes his order, he decides to double it and asks for two beers for Guy and two vodka and Diet Cokes for himself.

'Doubles or singles?' the man asks.

He feels a surge of self-righteousness. 'Singles,' he replies. Then he remembers that he needs to relax. 'Actually, make that doubles.'

Oh, I can always put the brakes on later.

Danny bunches together the drinks and pushes his way back to Guy. 'Here you go,' he says, 'get these down you. I didn't want to have to queue again so got us two.'

'Good thinking,' says Guy, as he tips back half of his first lager. 'To be fair, I quite like it here. It might be different to Manto but it's still a fun place.'

Danny can feel the tension seeping out of him. 'Babe, that's great.'

He looks around to take in the scene. A trio of middle-aged lesbians are engaging in some kind of three-way kiss while a fourth films it on her phone. A silver-haired drag queen is pouring a bottle of bright pink liquid into the mouths of three shirtless muscle boys, spilling most of it down their chests. And dancing on his own is a stocky man with an almost totally tattooed torso in a strappy, figure-hugging mini-dress.

Danny raises his glass to Guy. 'Happy Pride!'

'Yeah, Happy Pride,' says Guy.

Over his shoulder, Danny spots a drunken trans woman hair-whipping wildly in front of a wind machine then hurling herself at one of the girders and writhing up and down as if in a state of frenzied sexual ecstasy. He reminds himself not to drink too much so that for once he can refrain from that kind of behaviour. *Don't forget, you need to show Guy you've matured and your wild days are over.*

'So have you had any good pulls lately?' Guy asks.

Danny resists the urge to knock back the rest of his drink. 'What do you mean, "had any good pulls"?'

'I don't know,' says Guy, 'it's just that you usually have funny stories about the men you've got off with. What happened to that guy who was obsessed with Jane McDonald?'

Danny remembers going on a date with a handsome Irish guy he later discovered had a flat plastered with posters of Jane McDonald, a shrine to his idol in his bedroom, and a tattoo of her face over his heart. It was an episode he quickly worked up into a comedy anecdote with which to regale his friends – but one that right now he wants to forget.

'Oh, that was years ago,' he warbles. 'And it was just a passing fling, nothing serious.'

Now can we change the subject?

'But didn't you say he had a dick like a rolling pin?'

Danny almost chokes on his drink. 'Did I?'

'Yeah!'

Danny wipes his mouth and waves away the suggestion. 'Oh, I can't remember. Anyway, I'm over hook-ups now. I've given them up completely.'

OK, that's not strictly true but it will be if this weekend goes well.

Guy pretends to stagger back from the shock. 'What do you mean? Where's the Danny I know so well? What have you done with him?'

Danny swats him on the arm. 'Yeah, yeah. I suppose I've got all that of my system. I've done my playing around and I'm ready for something more fulfilling.'

Guy tilts his head as if taking this in. 'Well, joking apart, that's great news.'

'Thanks, babe. Thanks a lot.'

Walking through the doorway, Danny spots a pair of young men who look unsure of themselves; one of them is chewing on the inside of his mouth while the other's dabbing sweat from his forehead. They flash each other a look that says, 'What have we let ourselves in for?'

'Get a load of those two,' he says, nudging Guy. 'Do you reckon it's their first time?'

Guy glances over. 'It wouldn't surprise me.'

Danny gives a loud sigh. 'Can you remember our first time? Our very first night in a gay bar?'

And Guy's smile yanks him right back to 2002.

2002

Danny cast his eyes around the bar. 'So finally, this is Manto,' he said.

Beside him, Guy stayed silent.

'After hearing so much about the place, I can't believe I'm actually here!'

Danny saw that the venue had been fitted out with sleek, industrial décor and spinning balls of flashing neon lights were hanging from the ceiling. The ground floor had a dancing area that was overlooked by a first-floor balcony and a long bar that lined the back wall, which was staffed by unfeasibly good-looking men in fitted T-shirts emblazoned with the venue's logo. In the corner was a DJ desk, behind which a shaven-headed woman wearing cargo pants and a camouflage top was playing *Get the Party Started* by Pink. Even though Danny felt a little uneasy, he found himself smiling.

The only problem was, Guy wasn't smiling.

'Are you alright, babe?' Danny asked.

'Yeah, I'm just a bit nervous,' he replied. 'There's a lot to take in.'

They'd arrived at the venue early to try to avoid the crowds but already it was busy. Most of the people were men but they were accompanied by a sprinkling of female friends and there were a few huddles of women Danny assumed to be lesbians. To their left, a white man with spiky hair and bleach-blond highlights was dancing with a whippet-thin black boy who was wearing a sun visor and matching sweatbands around his head and wrists. To their right, a group of friends in bootcut jeans and Acupuncture trainers were exchanging gossip and giggling loudly. From every direction, eyes flitted towards the new arrivals.

'Why's everyone staring at us?' asked Guy.

'I don't know,' said Danny, 'I suppose they're just checking us out.'

A crease of worry etched across Guy's forehead. 'Well, I don't like it. I don't feel safe.'

Danny was suddenly hit by panic that Guy was going to back out of the night before it had really begun. There was only one thing for it – he needed to get him a drink.

'Come on,' he chirped, hoping his enthusiasm didn't sound too desperate, 'let's get to the bar.'

On their way, Danny noticed that pretty much everyone looked to be under the age of thirty – although he and Guy had to be among the youngest. At least they were wearing clothes that helped them fit in: Danny had opted for distressed jeans and a polo shirt with a popped collar, while Guy was wearing a blue, long-sleeved shirt hanging open over a white T-shirt. The blue brought out the colour of his eyes and made him look more gorgeous than ever – and Danny suspected this was the main reason the two of them were attracting attention. *Not that Guy seems to realise the effect he has on people.*

He told Guy to wait by one of the steel girders while he ordered two bottles of WKD from a barman with a goatee who looked like Beppe di Marco from *EastEnders*. The drinks were nearly twice as expensive as they were in the Student Union bar but Danny tried not to think about money – he didn't want his financial worries to spoil such a momentous night. *This is my first night out on the gay scene; I'm bound to remember it for the rest of my life.*

When he came back, Guy was engrossed in his phone. As he drew nearer, Danny saw he was playing the Snake game.

'What's up, are you bored?' he joked.

Guy shut down his phone and slid it into his pocket. 'No, I just thought if I looked busy there'd be less chance of anyone talking to me.'

Danny felt the love swell inside him.

He instructed himself to get a grip.

'This'll help,' he said, handing Guy his drink. 'Get it down you.'

A grin lifted Guy's face. 'Thanks, princess.'

Danny suggested they go upstairs and find a quiet spot by the balcony. Within minutes, they were leaning over the railings examining the crowd below.

'You haven't spotted anyone from uni, have you?' asked Guy.

They'd come to Manto on a regular Friday night rather than the bar's midweek student night in order to lessen their chances of being seen. The two of them had made separate excuses about feeling ill, waited for their friends to leave for the nineties night in the Union, then snuck out of their rooms to meet up outside St Chrysostom's Church, which was situated in between their halls. Danny felt uncomfortable about lying but he didn't want to force Guy to come out of the closet before he was ready.

'Don't worry,' he reassured him, 'I haven't spotted anyone at all.'

The DJ began playing *Lady Marmalade* from the film *Moulin Rouge!* and there was a roar of approval from the floor below. The boy with the sweatbands began writhing around like a stripper, while his friend with the spiky hair strutted up and down as if he were on a catwalk. At the bottom of the staircase, two pretty boys who looked like they belonged in Westlife leaned against the wall and began kissing passionately. Danny had never seen two boys kissing before, at least not in real life. A bolt of joy shot through him.

'This place is insane,' he gushed. 'I love it!'

But Guy said nothing.

Danny gestured to the floor below. 'I mean, don't you think it's mad that all this was going on while me and you were stuck at home? While I was wanking over Arthur's *Playgirls* and you were drooling over the bulges in the Next Directory?'

Guy nodded. 'It feels like a million miles away from Buckinghamshire.'

'It's like a different planet to Barrow!'

They were distracted by the sound of cheering coming from a table in the corner. They turned and saw a group of young men wearing Triple Five Soul T-shirts and shell chokers who were playing a game of Spin the Bottle.

'Everyone seems so free here,' said Danny, 'it's like they don't have any inhibitions at all – like they don't care what anyone thinks of them.'

But he could tell Guy wasn't paying attention. 'Babe, are you OK?'

Guy blinked. 'Sorry, I'm still a bit nervous.'

A handsome Latino only a few years older than them slid past and ogled at Guy. 'Alright, sexy?' he said.

Danny could feel the terror pierce his chest. *Oh no, don't tell me Guy's going to go off with him?*

Of course he's going to go off with him!

But Guy didn't respond to the man; he just looked down at his shoes.

The Latino continued to hover. 'What's up, lover? Are you shy?'

Guy stayed silent.

Danny willed the man to go away. But it didn't look like he was going to give up.

'Hold on a minute, you're not straight, are you?' he asked. 'Is that why you're not taking the bait?'

Guy looked up. 'Yeah, I'm straight. What's it to you, anyway?'

Without replying, the man scurried off.

Thank God that's over!

'I'm going to the bar,' boomed Guy, slamming his glass down on the ledge. 'Do you want the same again?'

Danny nodded. As Guy walked away, the DJ began playing *Can't Get You Out of My Head* by Kylie Minogue. Danny noticed the couple who looked like they were in Westlife kissing with increased fervour, one of them wrapping his legs around the other's waist. Just as he was wondering if that was what his mum called a knee-trembler, he was distracted by the sound of a high-pitched shriek coming from his left. He turned to see two men who had to be the oldest in there, probably as old as their late thirties. One of them was wearing a diamond stud earring and wafting around a fan, while the other was wearing a black tie over a V-neck T-shirt and waving around a cigarette.

'Honestly, I've never seen a dick like it,' said the one with the cigarette. 'I swear to God, it was like a flask.'

The two of them cackled riotously.

'I once saw a dick that was like a fire extinguisher,' said the one with the fan. 'Seriously, I was worried it would dislocate my jaw.'

His friend let out another shriek and gave him a floppy-wristed slap on the shoulder.

Although Danny couldn't help giggling, it was like his school days had just picked him up and whacked him over the head. Suddenly, he was back in the playground, being assaulted by the other boys' impressions of his effeminate voice and limp wrist. A shrapnel of shame went through him. *God, I hope I'm not as camp as they are.*

No, I can't be.

One thing's for sure – I'll never turn into an old queen hanging around bars joking about big dicks.

''Ere, can you smell fish?' said the man with the fan. He pointed to the entrance, where a group of women in what looked like a hen party had just appeared. 'Honestly, this place is full of tuna these days.'

'I blame *Queer as Folk*,' said his friend, dragging on his cigarette and blowing out extravagantly. 'It's ruined the Village.'

The one with the fan let out an exaggerated sigh. 'Canal Street isn't what it used to be.'

Danny couldn't believe what he was hearing. *What are these two on about? This place is amazing!*

Before he could listen to any more, Guy reappeared with their drinks. Danny smiled his thanks and took a swig. He began commenting on some of the fashions he observed around them but soon was distracted once again by the older men.

'Honestly, his dick was as thick as a pint glass,' crowed the one with the fan. 'It was that big it could block out the sun.'

Once again, the men cackled loudly. Once again, Danny couldn't resist giggling. But Guy pulled a face as if he'd just swallowed a mouthful of milk that had gone off.

'Have you heard those two?' he said. 'They're camper than Julian Clary. Why do they have to be such a cliché?'

'I know what you mean,' said Danny. 'They're not really our kind of people. Come on, let's move away.'

They crisscrossed the crowd and settled in a spot further along the balcony.

'Sorry,' Guy said, 'I know I'm not being much fun. But I still can't relax. I don't know what's wrong with me.'

'There's nothing wrong with you,' insisted Danny. 'It's perfectly natural to feel on edge. It's your first time.'

Guy pinched at the bridge of his nose. 'It's like, I know I need to be here and I know I *want* to be here, but at the same time I *don't* want to be. Do you know what I mean?'

'Yeah, I do.' Danny finished his drink and gazed at the empty bottle. 'For a long time all I really wanted was to go to a straight bar and fit in; all I wanted was to be like everyone else. I don't feel like that anymore but I still don't think I've shaken it off completely.'

They hit a bump of silence.

'There must be *some* way for us to shake it off,' mused Guy.

Danny gave his bottle of WKD a shake. 'I can think of one.'

Guy laughed and drained his bottle. 'Sounds like a good plan.'

Danny pulled himself back from the railings. 'It's my round,' he said. 'You have another go on that Snake game and I'll be back as soon as I can.'

2022

Danny is sitting in the disabled toilet contemplating his memories.

He's surprised by how hard-going he's finding tonight. Not only is he feeling a pressure to be 'on' all the time, to perform, to do whatever's necessary to make sure Guy's enjoying himself, but he's also feeling unsettled by the resurgence of his past. Of course, he's happy to indulge in nostalgia, but he didn't expect to be confronted so abruptly – and so starkly – by the people he and Guy used to be, by the feelings they used to have about other gay people. *By the feelings we used to have about ourselves.*

That's why he excused himself to go to the toilet: it wasn't to relieve his bladder, he just wanted a breather. He remembered that there was a disabled loo tucked away at the back of the ground floor, one hardly anyone knew about. When he saw it was free, he slipped inside, lowered the toilet seat and sank onto it.

He runs a hand across his eyes. *God, I was so clueless back then. So clueless and so messed up.*

He opens his eyes and blinks. *And I thought we'd only be revisiting happy memories!*

He remembers how recently it was that he and Guy were

able to resurrect their friendship and wonders if his plans for the weekend have simply been over-ambitious. *Maybe I've got ahead of myself . . .*

He's interrupted by a banging on the door. 'Hurry up, I'm desperate for a piss!'

'Alright!' Danny shouts. 'I'm coming!'

He stands up and flushes the toilet. Then another memory rushes into his head. It's of an intense discussion he had with his friend Lynsey. *And that was in a disabled loo just like this one . . .*

It was followed by another discussion, years later, when they revisited the same subject and it snowballed into an argument.

He feels a punch to the gut.

In that moment, he realises his estrangement from Lynsey is hanging over him. As she stayed on in Manchester after graduation, this weekend could offer him the perfect opportunity to make amends. And even though Danny said some terrible things to her – things he regretted almost immediately – he's pretty sure she'd be willing to see him.

But I can't do it. I just can't.

He lets out an unsteady sigh. *I've got enough on my plate already.*

There's more banging. 'Bitch, if you don't come out of there soon, I'm seriously going to piss myself!'

'Sorry, nearly done!'

Danny turns the tap on to pretend he's washing his hands, then flings open the door.

As he walks back upstairs, he thinks he feels worse, not better. He wishes he hadn't even attempted to clear his head.

2002

'OK,' said Lynsey, 'let's see that again.'

Danny moved in to give the girl a kiss. Her lips were surprisingly soft and tasted of cherry-flavoured lip balm. Just when he was wondering how long the kiss should go on for, the girl pulled away.

'Sorry,' she said, 'this isn't working for me.'

Danny reached up to touch his collarbone. 'No, it doesn't feel right to me either.'

'OK,' said Lynsey, moving towards them, 'let's step back for a minute.'

It was mid-morning and Danny was in a studio on the City campus of the university. He was rehearsing for a UMDS production of Shelagh Delaney's *A Taste of Honey*, a play that was set just a few miles away in a working-class area of Salford, although several decades earlier, in the late 1950s. It was being directed by Lynsey, a tall, fine-featured law student he'd originally met through Guy. At his audition, Lynsey had told Danny that she was attracted to the theme of race explored in the play, while he'd commented that he was intrigued by its inclusion of an openly gay character – radical for a play first performed nearly fifty years ago. Once he'd heard he'd been cast, the two of them had met for a coffee on University Green. Over the course of the afternoon, the discussion had strayed from the play to their experiences of growing up and feeling different to everyone around them. Lynsey had revealed that her British father had met her Ghanaian mother while he was working for a charity in Africa, but her mother had died shortly after she was born so she'd been brought to the UK and eventually raised by her father and stepmother in a small – entirely white – village in rural Shropshire. Danny had told her about growing up gay in Barrow, then surprised himself by confiding about his own absent parent, a young Greek man Eileen had met while he was spending a year on some work placement in Liverpool. Before they knew it, the two of them had become so engrossed in their conversation that they were late for lectures and had to hurry off in different directions. But, as Danny said goodbye, he knew he'd made a new friend.

'Come on, guys,' Lynsey said, gesturing to some chairs at the side of the room, 'let's sit down and talk this through.'

Acting opposite Danny was another first year called Daisy Sprogge, who had pink hair that was tied in bunches, spoke in a sweet, girlish voice, but then shattered all her cuteness by swearing like a navvy. She was playing the lead role of Jo, a teenager who's abandoned by her mother and sets up home with a shy, sensitive art student called Geof – played by Danny in his first ever gay role. The two actors were rehearsing a scene in which their characters discuss Jo's pregnancy from a brief relationship with a now-disappeared sailor and consider the possibility of getting married and pretending the baby is Geof's, after which Geof moves in to kiss her.

'I just don't get it,' said Daisy, 'why the fuck would he try and get off with her? I mean, I get the whole marriage of convenience thing, but it's not as if Jo doesn't know he's gay. So what the fuck is he playing at?'

Lynsey let out a long breath. 'The play doesn't give us much detail about Geof's backstory but there is a line in which he says that before he met Jo he didn't care if he lived or died. I think that gives us some idea of what he's been through. We can only imagine how hard it must have been to grow up gay in that kind of society.'

Danny shifted forward in his seat. *I don't need to imagine it. I* know *how difficult it would have been.*

An electric pulse ran through him and his words began racing out. 'Maybe what's happening is he doesn't *want* to be gay. Maybe it's got him into so much trouble, he just wants to be normal.'

'I didn't think of it like that,' said Daisy. 'Fuck.' She reached for her lip balm and smeared her already glistening lips with another coat.

'Go on, Danny,' coaxed Lynsey in her usual gentle voice.

'He's desperate,' Danny continued. 'He feels sad and lonely and unloved. He's only ever been told that being gay is bad so in his head it's a problem he wants to fix. And he sees Jo as his chance to fix it.'

'That's great,' said Lynsey.

'*Fucking* great!' agreed Daisy.

Lynsey inched her chair closer and peered at Danny. 'What you've got to do is get that across in your performance. Try to connect with any feelings *you've* experienced of being sad or lonely or unloved. And dig deep. Dig as deep as you can.'

Danny clutched at his script and nodded intently. He'd never played a character that was remotely like him before, so acting had only ever involved using his imagination. That was why he'd fallen in love with it, because it gave him the chance to escape himself, to pretend to be someone else – and be loved for it. But this was completely different; if he was going to make a success of this role, he needed to channel into it his own feelings and experiences.

'OK,' said Lynsey, 'let's give it another go.'

As Danny sprang out of his seat and opened his script, he felt another tingle of electricity run up his spine.

Lynsey looked at him and nodded. 'You can do this, Danny. I know you can do it.'

2022

Danny steps back from the bar and hands Guy another pint of lager.

They've moved onto Via, a bar that was known as Via Fossa when they were students. But other than the slight name change and the decorations that have been put up for Pride, it remains pretty much as they remember: it's fitted out in the style of a traditional English pub, with exposed stone walls and fireplaces, a polished oak bar and matching banisters lining the stairs, and brown leather sofas and armchairs tucked away in cosy alcoves. For Pride, the floor-to-ceiling doors have been opened up onto Canal Street, to allow people to pass in and out freely. And the DJ is playing a nostalgic set of music from the early noughties, currently *Murder on the Dancefloor* by Sophie Ellis-Bextor, which is greeted enthusiastically by a crowd that's mainly male, mainly bearded, and mainly over the age of thirty.

'Do you remember when we were at uni,' says Danny, 'and we always thought this place was full of uncool old people?'

Guy gives a wry smile. 'Well, maybe we just got old and uncool, because I like it now.'

'Me too,' says Danny. 'Me too.'

Just as he's congratulating himself on managing to turn the night around, he spots a man lurking in the corner who he met on Grindr back in London. He was at home late one night, trawling the app – drunk after some party – and ended up lowering his standards below their usual rock-bottom threshold and hooking up with a scraggy old stoner with blond hair and ginger sideburns. He can't remember the man's name but does remember it's something Swedish and sounds vaguely like an Ikea storage unit. *But what's he doing here?*

'Actually,' he says to Guy, fiddling with his wristband, 'do you mind if we go outside? I fancy a smoke.'

He leads him through the doors and they step onto the distinct red-brick paving of this section of Canal Street – not that they can see any of it as the crowd's so dense. All along the waterway, the venues have set up outdoor bars and there are also various DJ desks with speakers blasting out music that battle against each other. They press their way through the crowd and find a spot next to a lamp-post, at the top of which is tied one of the many rows of rainbow-coloured bunting that zigzag the length of the street. Once Danny's satisfied there's no danger of the Swedish man spotting him, he sparks up a Marlboro Light.

'Can you believe it's twenty years since our first night out here?' he asks. 'Since we first came to Canal Street?'

'No,' says Guy, 'it doesn't feel like that at all.'

'It seemed like such a big deal at the time,' reflects Danny, breathing out a curl of smoke. 'I suppose in those days the gay scene was everything. We didn't really have much else.'

'I hardly ever go out on the scene now,' counters Guy. 'I haven't been to Soho for years.'

'Yeah, but you were in a relationship for a long time, babe.' That came out more aggressively than Danny intended. *Well, is it any wonder after everything that's happened?*

He makes a point of smiling.

'Yeah, I suppose so,' concedes Guy. He takes a long pull on his pint. 'Anyway, it's good to be back.'

As if on cue, a voice pipes up behind them. 'You know, Canal Street isn't what it used to be.'

Danny and Guy look at each other and burst out laughing.

'My God,' says Danny, 'people have been saying that since we first came here. Literally, nothing's changed.'

Guy nods thoughtfully. 'But at the same time *everything's* changed. Do you know what I mean? It's just so much easier to be gay than it used to be. Or queer, as everyone says now.'

Danny's gaze settles on a group of effeminate teenage boys wearing make-up and the odd item of girls' clothing – what he calls 'semi-drag' – dancing in the street, flouncing around with no self-consciousness whatsoever, their midriffs exposed, accentuating and celebrating everything that makes them different. *Come to think of it, they may not even identify as boys; they may be non-binary.*

'When we first started going out, I remember thinking the world was changing,' he offers, 'but I had no idea how *much* things were going to change.'

'Absolutely,' adds Guy. 'Or how quickly.'

Danny takes another drag of his cigarette and grinds out the stub under his shoe, tossing a couple of chewing gums into his mouth. He notices a more masculine-presenting young man standing a few metres away eyeing up Guy. *That's one thing that hasn't changed; whenever we go out everyone still fancies Guy.*

Although Guy has just had to retire from playing rugby, although the first wrinkles have appeared on his fair skin and his hair has started to grey at the temples, he still has that same sparkle in his eyes, that same cute gap between his teeth, that same adorable dimple in his chin. *Yeah, he's still got plenty of snap in his celery. And he can still pass for straight, which for some reason continues to carry a premium in places like this*

The young man gazing at Guy certainly seems taken with him. He has a boyish grin, a classically square jaw, and an Instagram-friendly body he's showing off through a tightly fitted T-shirt, the hem of which snakes along the upper ridge of his perfectly rounded bottom. He catches Guy's eye and smiles at him. When Guy smiles back, Danny feels a hook of jealousy rip into him.

Please don't wink at him! Whatever you do, don't wink at him!

Thankfully, Guy announces it's his round and he's going to the bar. While he's away, Danny checks his messages on his phone.

'Excuse me?'

He turns around to see the man who was eyeing up Guy standing in front of him.

'I was just wondering,' the man says, 'are you two together?'

Shit.

Danny doesn't want to lie, not when he's already lied about the mix-up with the beds in the hotel. *But this man's gorgeous and just Guy's type. I don't want to miss my chance now . . .*

In the background, the DJ plays *Can't Get You Out of My Head* by Kylie Minogue. The song snaps Danny back to the first time he and Guy came to Canal Street.

In an instant, he knows just what he has to do.

'Yeah, sorry, babe,' he states, briskly, 'we've been together for years.'

The man smiles meekly and backs away. Danny takes a deep breath and wills his guilt to fade.

Fortunately, Guy soon reappears and hands him another drink. He gives Danny a little kiss on the side of his head and drapes his arm around his shoulders.

Guy often becomes affectionate when he's had a few drinks and this is something Danny sometimes struggles to handle – or always did when Guy had a boyfriend. Tonight, though, he doesn't struggle at all. Tonight it sets the adrenaline firing through his body.

He tells himself that, if everything goes as he's hoping, after tonight he can stop bothering with apps and casual sex. There'll be no more bumping into Swedish men he met on Grindr and would rather avoid. *And I'll be a much better person if it turns out Guy loves me. I'll cut down on the drinking and finally stop smoking. I might even start going to the gym.*

He's distracted by the sight of Guy yawning through his nostrils.

'What's the matter, babe?' Danny asks. 'Are you tired?'

'A bit, yeah. It's been a long day.'

'Well, we don't have to stay out, you know.' Danny tries to sound as casual as possible. 'It's only our first night and we want to be fresh for the parade tomorrow.'

Guy dashes his hand over his eyes. 'Are you sure?'

'Yeah. Come on, let's finish our drinks and head back.'

2002

As Guy looked out over the dance floor, he felt a wave of nausea. He leaned on the railings to try and steady himself. *I don't think I can do this.*

'I might have to head back soon,' he shouted into Danny's ear.

'You what?' shrieked Danny. 'We've only just got here!'

They were in a nightclub called Cruz 101, the one in the basement just off Princess Street, the one you needed a membership key ring to get in, the one that was always packed with shirtless, sweaty men. But that was pretty much all Guy could make out: they'd just finished a long bar crawl and he was feeling stunned by drink and completely disorientated. Neon lights and lasers flashed in his face, dry ice tickled the back of his throat, and loud music he was too wasted to recognise blared out of a speaker next to him. He looked down at his glass and took another swig. He had no idea what it was but it tasted like something from the drip tray.

'Shall we have a dance?' slurred Danny.

'Sorry,' Guy mouthed, 'I'm too pissed.'

'What you need is a shot, babe. That'll sharpen you up.'

Guy couldn't find the words to argue so grinned in agreement.

While Danny careered off towards the bar, he tried to stop his head spinning. He noticed Danny acknowledging a handful people he knew from university. A couple of them spotted Guy and waved in his direction. A few months ago, the idea of being seen in a gay club would have thrust him into a mad panic but now it didn't seem that important. He did have a cover story – that he was here to act as the wingman to his gay friend – but he didn't feel the need to use it. *Could that mean I'm ready to come out?*

Guy remembered the first time he'd stepped foot in Manto, when he'd looked at the crowd of men and felt like they were arranged in some kind of Roman battle formation against him. Now when he looked at the crowd, he didn't feel like they were repelling him at all but inviting him into a group hug.

Although it was less than two months since Guy had arrived in Manchester, already his life had transformed. At university he'd made a whole new set of friends, several of whom were from different backgrounds to him, several of whom were of different ethnicities, a handful of whom were even – for the first time in Guy's life – girls. But there was no doubt that the biggest change in his life came with the exploration of his sexuality. This was something that made Guy feel giddy, sometimes even dizzy, with excitement. But he probably wouldn't have embarked on it at all if it weren't for Danny: it was Danny who'd shown Guy that it was possible to live an openly gay life; it was Danny who regularly took him to the Cornerhouse cinema to watch gay-themed films; it was Danny who made him feel brave enough to go on their increasingly frequent nights out in the Village. He looked at him standing at the bar waiting to be served and felt a rush of an emotion he was too drunk to identify. *Is it fondness? Sexual attraction? Or love?*

He was still trying to work it out when Danny began lurching back towards him, thrusting out two shots.

'Drink one of these and you'll be fine,' he drawled.

Guy didn't bother to ask what it was. 'Thanks, princess.'

As soon as he'd slammed his empty glass down, he knew Danny was right: the drink spiked through him and blasted away the fog that had been clouding his head. Suddenly, he felt a renewed rush of energy – and didn't see why the night had to end soon.

Guy put his arm round Danny and kissed him on the head. But he told himself to be careful. *You don't want to do anything to mess this up. You can't lose Danny as a friend.*

He withdrew his arm and stepped away.

Although he did think Danny was good-looking, he reminded himself that he was surrounded by other good-looking men, men who came without any kind of complications, without any kind of risks. In fact, this club – and the Gay Village as a whole – was full of them. *And so far I haven't pulled a single one. I've been too frightened.*

That didn't mean that Guy had no sexual experience at all. Before coming to Manchester, he'd fooled around with some of the boys at boarding school: there was no shortage of them willing to engage in a late-night session of mutual masturbation, sometimes several at a time. For the duration of these sessions, it didn't matter that Guy's face was erupting in spots as none of the boys were looking at him anyway; the lights were kept low and sometimes the others even closed their eyes, presumably fantasising that the person touching them was a girl. Guy could tell from the expressions on their faces that the activity was, for them, purely functional – and he always understood that he wasn't supposed to enjoy it himself. Once each incident was over, it was never discussed. And once the boys had started sixth form and were allowed to mix with girls, it had all abruptly stopped. Except that for Guy, the desire hadn't gone away.

Next to him, a pair of floppy-limbed drunks were kissing and practically using each other as scaffolding. He was mesmerised by the sight of their hands grabbing at each other, their tongues slipping in and out of each other's mouths, their lips savouring the taste of each other. He tried not to stare but it reminded him of what he'd wanted to do when he'd been masturbating with the boys at school; more than anything he'd wanted to stroke and kiss them, but he'd known that if he did they'd guess he was gay – and he knew how they treated boys they suspected of being gay. So he'd made every effort to keep his desire for tenderness at bay and had adjusted his approach to the sessions of mutual masturbation so that he too saw them as fulfilling a simple bodily function. The whole thing became like scratching an itch – or popping one of his countless spots.

He tried to blink away the memory.

'You know what?' he said to Danny. 'I think I'm getting my second wind. Do you still fancy that dance?'

A smile traced itself across Danny's face. 'Too right I do!'

They picked their way over to the dance floor and pushed themselves into the mass of people. To Guy's ears the music was still an unidentifiable mess of sound but he could just about follow the beat enough to jig around in time – or at least he was pretty sure he was jigging around in time. Danny was a much better dancer, with a repertoire of moves that was much more extensive. As he watched him, Guy could feel his admiration swelling.

But closing in on him from every direction were men who were thrusting, flicking and twisting their bodies along to the same beat. Many of them had taken their tops off, their bare skin exposed and glistening as it caught the light, their muscles tensing and tightening as they allowed themselves to be transported by the music. Many of them were making it clear they found Guy attractive – and this was something he was getting used to whenever he came out on the gay scene. A few weeks ago he'd stopped taking his antibiotics, as it had been a long time since he'd had any spots – and his complexion had remained clear. Although he couldn't entirely shake off the expectation that his appearance would prompt grimaces, when he was given a compliment he no longer felt like a fraud.

The strange thing was, many of the gay men who complimented Guy seemed to comment on the fact that you couldn't tell he was gay, as if this in itself was attractive – his strongest asset, even. But Guy found this confusing. *How can the thing that made it so difficult for me to see myself as gay for so long now be the very thing gay men find attractive?*

A man with a pair of swallows tattooed on his chest gave Guy a grin while another with a pierced nipple blew him a little kiss. As the mass of men closed in tighter around him, he found himself wondering who all of them were and what kind of things excited or inspired them. If he got to know them, might he feel the same way about them as he felt about Danny? *What if one of them stirs up even stronger feelings in me?*

He watched as two of the men caught each other's eye, moved over to each other and began kissing. Although he found what they were doing arousing, Guy wasn't interested in that kind of casual, anonymous encounter. Ever since school, he'd been looking for something more than just physical release. And there were times when he could imagine entering into this with Danny.

But there was so much at stake. And in any case, Danny still hadn't even flirted with him; Guy still had no idea whether he found him remotely attractive. Sometimes he wondered if he was just imagining the energy that fizzed between them. Sometimes he wondered if it existed solely in his head.

The only way to find out if it was real would be for Guy to make a move on Danny. The only way to find out would be for him to initiate a kiss.

But I couldn't do that. It would be way too risky.

He cast the idea out of his head and carried on dancing.

2022

Danny mentally slams his head against a wall.

Oh no, do we have to?

He and Guy are supposed to be on their way back to the hotel but they still haven't stepped out of the Village. A few minutes after leaving Via, Guy spotted the funfair on Sackville Square and declared – as he often did – that he was getting his second wind. He dragged Danny along and, before he could argue, was taking him on the Waltzer, Twister and Dodgems. When Danny finally persuaded Guy to leave, they stumbled into a street lined with stalls selling food of every nationality, from Thai to Tibetan.

Guy declared that he was starving. But he said he didn't want to eat from one of the stalls; he'd rather visit another of their old haunts. And that's how they find themselves on the corner of Canal Street, looking across at the entrance to McTucky's Fried Chicken.

They often used to call into McTucky's on their way home from a night out, especially if this had ended just metres away in Cruz 101. They'd devour their food as they talked through every last detail of the night, what they liked to call their own private debrief. It was something Danny used to love – but going into the cafe now is an idea he hates.

'Look at that,' says Guy, clapping his hands together in excitement. 'The legendary McTucky's!'

'Yeah.' Danny manages to force out a smile. 'Come on, let's do it.'

When they step inside, the venue looks pretty much the same as it did during their student days; it has the same yellow walls and Formica counter, the same harsh strip lighting Danny used to worry would be unflattering, and the same smell of fried chicken that used to make their stomachs roar with hunger. Danny hears his stomach roaring all these years later but knows he has to resist temptation. *I can't spend weeks slimming down, then stuff my face minutes before I finally get into bed with Guy.*

'Actually, I don't want anything,' he says. 'I'm not that hungry. But don't let that stop you.'

They join the queue, standing behind a man wearing a kilt but no shirt, a drag queen in heels so high she might as well be on pointe, and a pair of short-haired lesbians wearing matching rainbow braces. When they reach the counter, they examine the staff but don't recognise any of them. A man with a belly like a boulder takes Guy's order of a chicken burger and chips and Danny smiles in anticipation of what he knows is coming.

'Can I have that with extra mayo please?'

Danny spots a couple of leather queens with padlocks around their necks vacating a bench in one of the wooden booths. He slides into it before anyone else can and waits for Guy to be given his food. He hopes to God it won't take long. *Mind you, I've waited twenty years for this. Another twenty minutes is hardly going to make a difference.*

As the man slaps Guy's burger onto a bun and sprinkles it with salad, Danny remembers watching exactly the same process when he and Guy were in their first year of university. At the time he felt ablaze with love for Guy but was convinced this could never be reciprocated. Then, one night at the start of their second term, they reached a turning point.

2003

Danny couldn't believe what he was hearing.

It was a Thursday evening in February and he'd received a text from Guy asking him to meet him urgently in the Union bar. He'd arrived to find a group of Guy's closest friends trying to work out why they'd been assembled. Then, as soon as Guy had appeared, he'd sat them down and announced he was gay.

Danny had no idea why he'd suddenly decided to come out, but apparently it had something to do with that afternoon's rugby training.

'Go on,' he urged, 'tell us what happened.'

Guy explained that during the training session he'd overheard one of his team-mates making a homophobic joke. When he'd pointed out this was offensive, his team-mate had replied that there were no gay people around to take offence.

'And that's when I told him he was wrong,' Guy said, 'because I'm gay.'

'And what did he say to that?' asked Danny.

'Well, he just went quiet – everything went quiet. Then he

apologised and everyone started congratulating me. I've got to say, it was pretty cool.'

'Pretty cool?' said Emma. 'It sounds cool as fuck.'

You're telling me, thought Danny. But he tried not to show his excitement. He tried not to think about what it might mean for his relationship with Guy.

'I had no idea I was going to say it,' Guy continued. 'It just kind of slipped out. But as soon as it did I thought I'd better tell you guys.'

Sitting at the table with Danny and Emma were Lynsey and Rags, Guy's schoolfriend, who looked like a darker-haired version of Guy and even wore the same gold signet ring on his little finger. Of Guy's closest friends, Rags was the only one who wasn't smiling.

'So let me get this right,' he said. 'You're telling us you're gay, but only because it slipped out while you were playing rugby.'

Danny spotted a wince in Guy's eyes.

'Not exactly, mate,' he replied. 'But yeah, I should have told you guys first. To be fair, that's what I was planning on doing but it just kind of happened this way. And I didn't want you to hear from anyone else.'

Emma nodded. 'News like that spreads around this place like verrucas through a foam party.'

Guy smirked. 'Exactly. Anyway, I'm sorry about the way it happened but I hope you can be happy for me.'

The girls rushed to reassure him that they were thrilled.

Rags gave a slow nod. 'Well, I never had you down for a vagina decliner but fair play, I suppose.'

Guy shot him a grin. 'So can I take that as a yes?'

'Yeah, mate,' Rags said, giving him a pat on his back. 'Congratulations.'

Everyone thrust their drinks – mainly WKD but a pint of lager for Rags and a snakebite and black for Emma – into the centre of the table and gave an enthusiastic toast. Danny couldn't help noticing that Guy didn't seem to care who saw them. And there were plenty of people who *could* see them: the Union bar was one of the busiest areas on campus.

Situated on the ground floor of the Steve Biko building, the Solem Bar – to use its proper name – knew how to attract students, with regular drinks promotions, a snooker table, fruit machines and a jukebox. Its walls were lined with big-screen TVs showing MTV and decorated with posters advertising live music acts playing upstairs in the Main Hall or the Hop and Grape, plus comedy and club nights taking place downstairs in the Cellar. And it had a lino-covered floor that by the end of night would be splashed with sticky drinks and littered with cigarette butts and the remains of old chewing gum.

Tonight, the Solem was as packed as ever and Danny had already spotted several people he knew from his course, plus Daisy Sprogge and some of his friends from UMDS, their loud voices and theatrical laughter carrying around the room. Perched on his usual stool alone at the end of the bar was an older graduate student he'd met through the LGB Society, who had eyes that were set too close together and spoke very quietly, attributes that had earned him the nickname Creepy Phil. Danny tried not to attract his attention but Phil gave him a wave. He returned it with a slightly nervous smile.

Now they'd had time to digest the news, the girls began showering Guy with questions.

'When did you first know you were gay?'

'Have you ever had sex with a girl?'

Guy was happy to answer them all. And he couldn't stop grinning.

'You know, I'm not just saying this but I could tell you were hiding something,' piped Emma.

'All that sneaking off for secret nights out with Danny,' added Lynsey, 'I knew you two were up to something.'

'And we didn't buy all that bullshit about being his wingman,' deadpanned Emma.

Guy explained that Danny had been the first person he'd told. 'And he's been an absolute legend. I don't know what I'd have done without him.'

As he gave Danny's shoulder an affectionate rub, Danny felt a wave of happiness lick his insides.

Unfortunately, Rags didn't look so happy. 'Well, thanks, mate. Thanks for telling someone you've known for a few months rather than someone you've known since school.'

A taut silence set in. Danny wanted to leap to Guy's defence. *Rather than having a go at him, you could try asking yourself* why *he didn't tell you.* But he was wary of inflaming the situation so kept the comment to himself.

'Yeah, sorry, Rags,' said Guy. 'But I didn't plan that either; it kind of just happened.'

'So do you think you'll come out to your family?' Lynsey asked. 'I mean, it went well for Danny.'

That Christmas, Danny had followed through on his plan of coming out to his mum. When he'd arrived home at the end of term, he'd sat her down and explained exactly why he was loving his new life in Manchester: his move to the city had coincided with his decision to live openly as a gay man. As predicted, Eileen had whooped for joy and, after kissing and hugging him repeatedly, had pulled out a bottle of champagne she'd been saving for that very occasion. The following week, she'd whisked him off to visit Arthur in Brighton and the celebrations had continued with a night out in a string of gay bars, where the three of them had hogged the karaoke until the early hours singing increasingly tuneless versions of *I'm Coming Out* and *I Am What I Am*.

Unfortunately, Danny knew there was no chance of that kind of reaction from Guy's family. As did Guy, who greeted Lynsey's question with a frown.

'Not for the time being,' he said. 'I'm afraid my mother isn't anywhere near as enlightened as Danny's.'

Danny intervened, anxious to keep the tone celebratory. 'Well, I think you're doing amazingly, babe.'

Rags echoed his words back at him, deliberately flattening the vowels. 'I think you're doing am*aaa*zingly, b*aaa*be.'

By now, this was something Danny was used to; lots of the students from privileged backgrounds would do impressions of his accent. Although this was usually without malice – and sometimes even with affection – there were times when he felt like he was being put in his place, when he felt like he was being reminded that they were somehow better than him. This was one of those times.

Rags either didn't register his discomfort or just decided to disregard it. 'Go on, Danny, say it again,' he boomed. 'I love the way you say "b*aaa*be".'

At this point, Guy stepped in. 'Oh, give it a rest, mate. I don't see Danny laughing. And I have to say, I don't think you're very funny.'

'Ooooh,' said Rags, 'you've got touchy since you turned gay.'

Danny was about to point out that people didn't *turn* gay when

Emma jumped in. 'Shut the fuck up, pal, or I'll start ripping the piss out of your posho English accent.'

Everyone roared with laughter and Rags had no choice but to join in.

As the banter continued, Lynsey slid over to Danny and whispered in his ear, 'I'm going to the loo. Do you fancy coming?'

'No, thanks,' Danny replied, 'I'm alright.'

She signalled with her eyes that it was important.

'Yeah, urm, OK,' he said. He turned to Guy. 'Back in a minute.'

Danny was intrigued. Lynsey wasn't the type for idle gossip or chatter about some boy she fancied; she was much more sensible and level-headed than that. *What on earth can she want to talk about?*

She pointed to the disabled loo and they slipped inside.

Lynsey looked him in the eye. 'So. How long have you fancied Guy?'

Danny's stomach fell away.

'I've seen the way you look at him,' she went on, 'but I always thought he was straight so just assumed it was some kind of crush. And now I know different.'

Danny closed the toilet lid and sank onto it. He rummaged in his pocket for his packet of cigarettes and pulled out two, lighting them both and handing one to Lynsey. He drew in a long drag and let the smoke out, slowly.

'I've fancied Guy ever since I met him,' he answered. 'Do you think it's obvious? I thought I was doing a good job of covering it up.'

Lynsey blew out a series of smoke rings. 'You know me, as sharp as a stiletto.'

'Either that or I'm not as good an actor as I thought.'

'No, I'm not having that,' Lynsey said, grinning wrily. 'It's just that I can see through your tricks.'

They laughed.

'Now come on, spill.'

Danny told her that, after their first meeting, his attraction to Guy had developed as he'd got to know him. When they'd started sneaking off for secret nights out on the gay scene, his feelings had deepened further.

'Just how deep *are* they?' Lynsey asked.

It struck Danny that it would be too much to tell her he was in love with Guy so he settled for the more retractable, 'I think I might be falling in love with him.'

Lynsey leaned on the wall and blew out another smoke ring. 'Well, that's great, Dan. I think you'd make a lovely couple.'

Danny scoffed. 'Don't be daft. As if Guy would ever fancy me.'

Lynsey gave him a withering look. 'What are you talking about? You're really good-looking, Dan. And in case you haven't noticed, everyone loves you.'

But Danny didn't hear her words; they were drowned out by the echoes of all the insults he'd heard at school, all the insults he'd heard just walking down the street in Barrow. *Even your dad didn't want you.*

'Yeah, thanks, Lyns,' he said, 'but I'm not so sure . . .'

Lynsey tapped her ash into the sink. 'In that case, why don't you find out? Then you *can* be sure?'

'What do you mean?'

'Well, I don't think you should declare your undying love or anything. But maybe you should find a quiet moment later and move in for a kiss. Or at least a little cuddle or something to test the water.'

Danny imagined himself sitting with Guy and moving in to kiss him. But the only outcome he could picture was Guy recoiling in disgust. 'It'd be a disaster, Lyns. I know it would.'

'I don't see why. And even if it was, at least you'd know. At least you wouldn't always be wondering. And then you could move on.'

Danny kneaded his eyelids as he thought it over. Much as it pained him to admit it, Lynsey had a point; he couldn't spend the rest of his life like this.

'You know it's always better to regret doing something than to regret *not* doing something,' Lynsey said.

Danny didn't like to say he could think of plenty of exceptions to that rule.

'No, I can't, I'm sorry,' he said, decisively.

'Alright, alright,' said Lynsey, 'I'll back off. But only for the time being.'

Danny smiled and took one last drag on his cigarette. He wasn't sure how he felt now that Lynsey knew a secret he'd been guarding for months. In a way it was a relief, but it was also unsettling. And, despite what she said, he couldn't bear the idea of her going away and having a quiet laugh at him. *A laugh at my stupid, embarrassing, pitiful delusion.*

By the time they were back at their table, someone had bought another round of drinks and Emma was grilling Guy about the kind of man he fancied.

'I'm not sure I've got a type,' he said. His eyes flitted to Danny as he sat back down. 'Or at least I haven't worked it out yet.'

But Emma wasn't satisfied. 'OK, put these in rank order. Which do you go for first – body, dick or face?'

Guy gasped. 'I can't answer that!'

'You've got very prudish since you turned gay,' grumbled Rags.

'OK,' said Guy, 'face, body and then dick.'

'Same here,' said Lynsey.

'What about you, Danny?' asked Emma.

'Same,' he said. 'Face, body and then dick.'

Emma shook her head. 'Fuck that, I'm all about the dick. It's the only thing you can't change!'

They erupted in laughter and even Rags joined in.

'Sorry to interrupt,' came a voice from behind them, 'but I hear congratulations are in order.'

Danny turned around and saw that it was coming from Drew, a Drama student he knew from his course. Drew had a boyish smile, sparkling white teeth and a solid jawline – and was a trained dancer, with a lithe, muscular physique. But he was one of those good-looking people who constantly moaned to other people about feeling ugly, mainly to be reassured that he wasn't – so Danny usually avoided him. *Although it doesn't look like I can avoid him tonight.*

'I hear you've just come out,' Drew said to Guy. 'That's great news.'

Danny tried not to roll his eyes. *What did Emma say about gossip spreading like verrucas?*

'Yeah,' said Guy, 'yeah I have. Thanks.'

Danny couldn't help noticing that he looked ever so slightly bashful. *Oh for God's sake.*

'Do you mind if I join you?' Drew asked, addressing his question to the group. 'Oh and I'm body, face, dick – just in case you were wondering.'

We weren't. Or at least I *wasn't.*

But everyone else laughed and Drew slid onto the end of the bench.

To Danny's horror, he began flirting with Guy.

For the next hour, Drew mimed fascination at everything Guy said, at one point even complaining about the non-existent heat so he could roll up his already short sleeves and uncover more of his impressively rounded biceps, moaning about putting on weight so that Guy would insist he wasn't fat in the slightest. *Is he for real?*

At first, Guy seemed embarrassed by Drew's attention but, as the evening progressed and he consumed more and more alcohol, his eyes began to sparkle and he inched forward on his seat to anticipate whatever Drew was going to say next. When nobody else was looking, Danny spotted him give Drew a wink – the same wink he'd given Danny on the day they'd met.

It hit him like a blow to the solar plexus.

Fuck.

The pain was quite breathtaking. Danny hadn't felt anything like it since the boys in PE had demanded he use different changing rooms, since his mum's ex-boyfriend Lee had terrorised him for not being a 'proper lad'. And it was the same kind of pain, as if the wounds inflicted by those experiences were being ripped open again.

He could feel his eyes getting hot but, with a great effort and a wobbly intake of breath, forced back a cry. It was something he'd taught himself to do as a child and something he'd done many times since, something he called forcing iron into his soul. Though it was something that when he'd left Barrow he'd hoped never to have to do again.

Don't be stupid! You may have moved cities but you're still the same Danny.

He comforted himself that at least no-one else could tell how he was feeling. But, however hard he tried, there was no hiding it from Lynsey. 'Come on, Dan, it's your round,' she said, gesturing to the bar. 'I'll give you a hand.'

They found themselves a gap in the scrum of people waiting to be served and Danny lit another pair of cigarettes.

'What's going on?' he mewled. 'Is Guy about to get off with Drew or what?'

'Well, it certainly seems like that's Drew's objective,' said Lynsey. 'I'll say one thing for him; he's very forward. And very persistent.'

'Yeah, he's also very good-looking – way more good-looking than me.'

Lynsey opened her mouth to argue but Danny held up his hand.

'Come on, Lyns, I'm not blind. And I'm not thick either. I know Drew's got much more going for him than I have. I know he's got a great body. I know he's middle-class and doesn't talk like someone off *Coronation Street*. I know he doesn't mince around like Julian Clary.'

'Dan, what are you on about? I love all those things about you. Everybody does.'

'Well, Guy clearly doesn't.'

Danny tugged in a desperate drag. Over Lynsey's shoulder, Creepy Phil sneaked into view.

'Evening, Danny,' he said. 'Is everything alright?'

Danny forced out a smile. 'Yeah, sorry, babe, if you don't mind we're just in the middle of something.'

He turned back to Lynsey. 'Listen, Lyns, it's really nice of you to try and make me feel better but it's obvious Guy isn't into me.'

'Dan, I'm not doing this to make you feel better. And I'm sorry but I don't agree with you. Don't forget Guy's pissed. Don't forget he's only just come out. Maybe what he's looking for right now is some no-strings fun. Maybe he doesn't even *know* what he's looking for.'

'Well, whatever it is,' said Danny, 'it isn't me.' He gestured to the table and, as if on cue, Drew said something and Guy bellowed with laughter.

'Not now it isn't, no,' Lynsey conceded. 'And I'm sorry, I shouldn't have got your hopes up.'

'Oh, you've nothing to be sorry for.'

I'm the one who should be sorry. Sorry for even allowing myself a tiny glimmer of hope.

He called out to the barman and ordered a round of drinks, switching his WKD for a more potent Fat Frog – made up of a whole WKD, a Reef *and* a Bacardi Breezer, all tipped into one pint glass. As soon as they arrived, he took them over to the table. On approaching, he saw that Drew had slid along the bench and was now sitting next to Guy.

He ground his cigarette out on the floor. As he slumped onto his seat, Drew nestled into Guy and the two of them laced their hands together under the table.

Danny could feel the bile leap into his throat and forced it down with a glug of his drink. But he couldn't repress a bone-scorching sense of anger that was surging inside him. And this anger wasn't directed at Guy – or even at Drew. It was directed at himself.

As if Guy would ever fancy you.

He probably only hangs around with you because he doesn't want to hurt your feelings!

He lit another cigarette and downed the rest of his drink.

As soon as he spotted a gap in the conversation, he leapt in. 'Actually, I take back what I said. I'm with Emma; I'm all about the dick.'

Emma gave a cheer.

'I mean, who wants to settle down for the rest of their life with someone with a crap dick? I couldn't think of anything worse.'

Before he knew it, he and Emma were praising the qualities of a large penis and pursuing each other down a path of increasingly bawdy humour. Every now and then, Danny glanced over to check Guy was listening but he seemed more and more engrossed in Drew. Soon, the two of them were holding hands in full view of the group.

Without really knowing what he was doing, Danny stood up, walked back to the bar and sidled over to Phil. *He's actually not that bad looking – and there's not really anything creepy about him at all.*

'Alright, babe?' he said. And without any warning he moved in to kiss him.

'Well, that was a little unexpected,' said Phil, blinking.

'Oh, I've fancied you for ages,' Danny insisted. He had no idea where his words were coming from; it was as if they were saying themselves.

Phil winched an eyebrow. 'Really? Well, that's great because I'm attracted to you too.'

'That's insane!' said Danny. And he moved in to kiss him again.

Phil pulled back and whispered in his ear. 'Listen, it's really busy here.' His breath smelled of whisky and was hot on Danny's skin. 'Do you want to come back to mine?'

Danny paused to think. He'd never been home with a man before – on all his trips into the Gay Village, he'd been far too focused on Guy. Which meant he'd never had sex – or anything approaching it. *I can hardly go and lose my virginity with the first man who asks.*

Why can't I? It's not as if I've had any better offers – or am likely to get them.

He looked over at the table and saw Guy kissing Drew. He

watched as Guy's arm moved down to Drew's bum and he pulled him closer.

'Look at you,' Rags roared at Guy, 'you only came out five minutes ago and you're practically balls deep.'

Danny thought he was going to throw up.

'Oh, shut up, mate,' said Guy, 'you're really not funny.'

Rags shook his head. 'And you really have lost your sense of humour since you turned gay.'

But Danny turned his back on them before he could hear Guy's reply. He took hold of Phil's hand. 'Yeah, let's go back to yours,' he said, firmly.

As Phil looked in his eyes and smiled, Danny's head began to swirl.

Oh, what am I doing?

'Come on then,' said Phil, 'let's make a move.'

Danny drew in a sharp breath.

I'm only doing this once. It won't become a habit.

But even as the thought dashed through his head, he wasn't sure it was true.

2022

Is Danny flirting with me?

The thought has been swirling around Guy's head all night. And, now the night's coming to an end, it's swirling faster and faster.

'Come on,' he says, 'let's get back to the hotel.'

He finishes his chicken burger and they leave McTucky's and walk down Canal Street. Although Guy's not sure what they're doing counts as walking, as the street's so crowded they're barely able to put one foot in front of the other – and have to wade through a sea of discarded cans and plastic glasses. Most people have been drinking for hours and have little awareness of everyone around them: Guy has to dodge out of the way of a man who's spotted Grindr on his boyfriend's phone and is shrieking at him hysterically, a woman who throws up into a plastic glass and then puts it on the ground to casually continue her conversation, and a man who's so drunk he can barely stand up – yet is insulting his friend for daring to suggest he might be drunk. To make matters worse, several people have sat or even lain down in the street and a Saint John's ambulance crew is administering first aid to a woman dressed as a pod of peas who's passed out next to the Portaloos. As Guy forces his way through, he's pushed and pulled in so many directions he's worried he might lose Danny.

'Here,' he says, 'hold my hand.'

Once Danny's palm is in his, he leads him to the edge of the street, where there's a little more space to push forwards. As he drives on, his mind begins to race with ideas of what might happen when they get back to the hotel.

Is this it? Are we finally going to sleep together?

When he and Danny first got to know each other, there were times when Guy felt like they were heading towards a sexual relationship. But back then, Danny didn't so much as flirt with him and Guy was too scared to make the first move. Then came the night he told his friends he was gay, the night Drew introduced himself and came on strong. This ended up being a crucial turning point in his relationship with Danny – and one that set the course it's followed ever since.

And now here we are . . . Right back where we started . . .

Still holding his hand, he leads Danny past a group of male friends who look to be in their twenties, all of them laughing at something one of them has said, some of them with their arms around each other, others standing slightly apart from the group. Guy wonders what the dynamics are between them, if any of them are boyfriends or if they're just affectionate friends, if any of them are hiding deeper feelings for one of the others, feelings they're either trying to resist or possibly planning to act on. *I wonder how those feelings have evolved over the years and how they might still be evolving.*

He presses on.

That night he met Drew may have been a long time ago, but

Guy knows he behaved badly – even if he tried to deny it to himself at the time. *Right from the start there was something between Danny and me, even if I wasn't mature enough to understand it. And it can't have been nice for him to see me suddenly getting off with Drew.*

He wishes that he hadn't been so insensitive but tells himself there's no point tormenting himself with regrets. *What is it Lynsey always says? It's better to regret doing something than to regret not doing something.*

In any case, the night he met Drew was the night he had sex for the first time so there's no point regretting it. Now isn't the time to go over what happened next.

He looks back to check on Danny but into his eyeline strays a woman who's topless for no discernible reason, dancing to Bananarama's *Venus*. He looks at Danny and widens his eyes. 'Things are starting to get a bit bonkers around here,' he shouts.

'I know,' Danny calls back. 'Maybe we're doing the right thing bailing out while we can.'

Danny flashes him a smile but Guy still can't work out if he's flirting. And is the idea of something happening between them resurfacing because he wants it to or just because they're back in Manchester and he's feeling nostalgic?

Whatever's going on, the idea isn't going away.

2003

Danny couldn't believe how quiet Canal Street was; it was empty apart from a couple of vans making deliveries and a middle-aged gay couple toddling along pulling a podgy pug on a lead.

It was a Sunday morning and Guy had suggested they meet for brunch. It was a suggestion that had appealed to Danny's aspirations to be more like the characters on *Sex and the City*, albeit one he knew he couldn't really afford. But he hadn't wanted to say no as he'd just returned to Manchester after the Easter holidays and hadn't seen Guy for three weeks – three weeks during which he'd ached to see him.

'Are you ready to order?' asked the waiter.

Guy ordered a full English breakfast with extra bacon and hash browns, and an extra-large fresh orange juice. 'Oh and a Bloody Mary,' he added with a raffish grin.

The casual way in which Guy spent money often made Danny think his family must be very wealthy. He knew Guy received an allowance from his parents that was so generous he didn't need his student loan; but he'd once told Danny he'd taken it out and 'invested it', whatever that meant. Danny, on the other hand, needed every penny of his, although he had to admit he'd frittered away a large part of it on riotous nights out. But his financial problems seemed so insurmountable and his debts so beyond clearing that he couldn't seem to talk himself out of spending money.

'Go on, I'll have a full English too,' he said. 'And make that two Bloody Marys.'

The waiter nodded and backed away.

They were in a bar called Eden, which was one of the less rowdy venues in the Village and a popular place to eat during the day. It was also one of the few venues to be located on the opposite side of the waterway to Canal Street and had to be accessed by a little footbridge. It had a balcony area projecting over the water, on which Danny and Guy were pleased to find it was just about warm enough to sit.

They were eager to discuss what they'd done over the Easter holidays and Danny told Guy that, as well as returning to work in Blockbuster, he'd enjoyed spending time with his mum; since he'd come out to her they'd grown even closer and over the last few weeks had spent several evenings drinking white wine and eating Cadbury's Celebrations while they watched romantic comedies Danny had sneaked out of the shop. But there was no gay scene in Barrow and he'd soon started to feel like the part of him that had only recently been released, the part of him that had been oppressed for so long but was now flying free, had been thrust back into its cage. As soon as he'd arrived back in Manchester, he'd met up with some of the other gay students on his course and they'd gone for a night out in the Village. Danny had practically bounced into the first bar he was so excited, and after just a few drinks had met a man called James who looked vaguely like Matt Damon but unfortunately had little in the way of personality. Danny had decided to overlook this and within half an hour was on his way to James's flat, desperate to make sure that he was firmly out of his cage – and slamming the door shut behind him.

'And how about you?' Danny asked Guy. 'How was it going back into the closet?'

Guy mopped his hand through his hair. 'Awful. It was like I had to become a different person – and it all felt so wrong. I ended up resenting my parents and hating myself.'

'Oh, I'm sorry, babe,' said Danny. He reached out and gave his hand a squeeze.

'You know, all those years I tried to convince myself that being gay wasn't an important part of my life, that it was just a little, incidental part of me I could keep buried and still be true to myself – well, I can see now that I was wrong. I was *so* wrong. Because I only really started living when I came to Manchester. And I couldn't wait for the holidays to be over so I could come back and start living again.'

'Two Bloody Marys.' The waiter handed over their drinks and Danny and Guy toasted their return to the city.

Then, just as Danny was about to tell Guy how much he'd missed him, Guy jumped in and said, 'Oh and I really missed Drew.'

Danny felt his heart dive to his stomach.

'That was probably the hardest part of the holidays,' Guy went on. 'I hated being separated from him. Can you believe we've been going out for two months now?'

Yes, I can. Because every minute of it has been like torture.

'It's funny because I wasn't looking for a relationship at all,'

Guy breezed on, toying with the straw in his Bloody Mary. 'I just kind of fell into it.'

Yeah, yeah, I've heard this a thousand times before. Danny even knew what was coming next.

'You know, the sex we had that first night was amazing. That's what did it for me. From that moment on, I was hooked.'

Danny thought back to what he'd been doing when Guy had been having sex with Drew: he'd been losing his virginity to Creepy Phil – and his experience hadn't been anything like amazing. Phil's room had been surprisingly messy and even dirty, with a smell of rotten food overlaid with unwashed armpit. The sex between them had been cold and emotionless, or at least it had from Danny's point of view. The fact that Phil insisted on making animalistic grunting noises and telling him over and over again how aroused he was only made it worse. All Danny could think about was Guy and what he was doing with Drew.

'And the sex has been just as amazing ever since,' Guy rattled on. 'Seriously, we can't keep our hands off each other.'

Danny fished the celery out of his drink and crunched into it. *How the hell did I end up sitting here listening to Guy telling me how much he loves shagging his boyfriend?*

But even as he asked himself the question, he knew the answer. He'd tried to stop loving Guy, but he couldn't – and if he didn't see him that same ache always appeared. So he'd settled for being his close friend and confidant, which meant that at least he still played an important role in his life. But this also meant that he didn't just ache to see him; he also ached when he *was* seeing him.

He tried consoling himself with a reminder that the pain he felt had lessened over time. It didn't take his breath away like it did when he'd first spotted Guy winking at Drew or he'd first seen them kissing. Now it had softened to a dull pain that sat in him like some kind of malignant growth.

Guy continued talking. 'The thing is, Danny . . .'

Danny noticed that he no longer called him 'princess'.

'. . . I think I'm in love with him.'

Just when Danny thought the pain was lessening, it surged up and spiked through him all over again.

Guy, can't you see what you're doing to me?

He dismissed the thought with a reminder that he hadn't always been sensitive to other people's feelings either. The morning after he'd spent the night with Phil, he'd tried to sneak away without waking him up but Phil had stirred and invited him to stay for a coffee. Danny had invented some important lecture he didn't want to miss so Phil had suggested they go out for a drink some time. Even though it was clear Phil had feelings for him, Danny had barked out 'no' and bolted. The next time they'd bumped into each other in the Solem, he'd given Phil a greeting so cursory it could have left him in no doubt he just wasn't interested.

Maybe now I'm being punished for that.

If this was the case, his punishment wasn't over.

'I think I'm going to tell him when he gets back tonight,' Guy said. 'Yes, I *am* going to tell him. I'm going to sit him down and tell him I love him.'

Danny tugged the corners of his mouth up into a smile. 'That's great news.'

Guy's face suddenly fell. 'Sorry, I'm sure you don't want to sit there and listen to this when you're single.'

'Oh, it's fine,' Danny managed, his voice faltering, 'I'm totally happy being single. You know me, I don't do emotional attachment. I just want to chuck my muck and go.'

But Danny couldn't help thinking it sounded as if someone else was speaking. Either that or he was just acting again, just playing another role. His only consolation was that the role of resolutely single man-eater was one that was giving him a lot of fun. The problem was, the more he played it, the more people believed it was him, the more they expected him to behave as if it was, and the more he played up to it out of a fear of disappointing them.

Or am I just kidding myself? Am I really that person? He thought of his dad, who'd left his mother shortly before he was born and he imagined to be some sort of philanderer. *Am I turning into the gay equivalent? Has the apple not fallen far from the tree?*

'So what about this bloke from last night?' Guy asked. 'Are you going to see him again?'

Danny shifted in his seat. 'Nah. He was nice enough but not really my type.'

Guy's gaze drifted onto a pair of ducks swimming through a cluster of empty beer cans floating on the canal. Danny felt his lack of interest like a barb in his chest. *I need to up the ante.*

'Oh, but you won't believe this . . .' he said. 'He was wearing loads of leather and was really into it.'

That's not strictly true, but he was *wearing a leather waistcoat.*

'He even had a leather jock strap.'

Guy turned back to face him. 'Really?'

'Yeah. But it didn't do it for me – it was like having sex with a couch.'

'Danny, you are hilarious!'

As Guy threw back his head and roared with laughter, Danny caught sight of the gap between his teeth. *My God, he's gorgeous. And I'm such a bad person, lying about my pulls just to get a laugh.*

'Don't you think it's funny?' Guy asked. 'How you and I get on so well but we're both so different?'

'How do you mean?'

'Well, just that you like to shag around and I don't. I guess you're built for sex with lots of different people but I just want to be in love with one man.'

Danny wanted to scream out loud. *Can't you see? We're not different at all! That's what* I *want with* you*!*

He drew in a shaky breath. 'Yeah, I suppose that is funny.'

He stabbed at the ice in his Bloody Mary.

He was thankful when the waiter reappeared with their food.

2003

Guy stood outside the front door of his family home. As it was December, the blood-red leaves of the Virginia creeper that usually covered much of the façade had fallen onto the gravel driveway, exposing the orange bricks. On the navy-blue door hung a large, handmade Christmas wreath, and through the bay window of the sitting room Guy could make out several cards standing on the mantelpiece, their cheeriness contrasting bluntly with his mood.

He noticed that he was gripping his suitcase so tightly his knuckles had turned white. He drew in a long breath and tried to relax.

He was about to come out to his parents. *And this is going to be the most difficult conversation I'll ever have.*

Guy was in his second year at university and, as he reached the end of his first term and the holidays approached, he knew he couldn't face going back to hiding who he was. Now that he was living so openly in Manchester, when he went home he only felt trapped, like he was suffocating, like his spirit was withering. He needed to tell his parents he was gay, even if his worst fears came true and they threw him out of the house or cut off his allowance. He also thought that at the very least he should give them the chance of accepting him. *Don't I owe them that much as a son?*

At any rate, that's what he'd been thinking in Manchester. Now that he'd arrived back in Buckinghamshire, he was no longer sure he was doing the right thing. He'd lost all confidence in his plan.

It was a plan Guy had spent weeks devising. As he wasn't great at expressing himself and in moments of stress would sometimes get what he wanted to say in a jumble and end up coming out with things he didn't even mean, he'd decided to write his parents a letter. There was another reason behind this: when it came down to it, he wasn't sure he could open his mouth and utter the words, 'I'm gay.' So he'd put his announcement in a handwritten letter, promising that he'd discuss it with them when he arrived home. He'd wanted to run over the letter with Drew but he was performing in a play and said he needed to stay focused. Thankfully, Danny had helped him craft what he wanted to say – and then discuss how best to time the delivery.

As neither of Guy's parents worked on a Saturday, that was the day he'd chosen to arrive home. First-class post was supposed to reach any destination in the UK the day after it was posted but this wasn't guaranteed; to give it the best possible chance, Guy had taken his letter to the central Post Office in Manchester first thing on the Friday morning, then timed his train home the next day so he'd walk through the door just after lunchtime. This would allow his parents a few hours to get over their shock and let their emotions settle. It also meant that, once Guy had posted his letter, he wouldn't be able to back out.

Although now that he was home, he'd give anything to back

out. Anxiety rang in his ears like white noise. His shoulders were up around his ears and panic tightened his throat.

All of a sudden, he was an eleven year-old boy again, waiting to meet his parents during one of their visits to school, desperate to earn their love by impressing his mother with news of his academic achievements – particularly in the science subjects she valued so highly – or by presenting his father with his latest rugby trophy, knowing how much he wanted a son who was good at sports, a son he could show off to the other dads. To his immense frustration, nothing Guy did ever seemed to work; nothing he did ever seemed to be good enough for them – or at least if it was they never showed it. Not that he ever stopped trying. If anything, their coldness only made him try harder.

He took out his key and slid it into the lock. His heart was hammering so forcefully he could feel his pulse in the tips of his ears.

He closed the door behind him, slipped off his shoes and coat, and left his suitcase and rucksack at the bottom of the stairs.

The house had been decorated for Christmas. Gold tinsel was wrapped around the mahogany banister and was hanging from the antique grandfather clock and framed paintings of landscapes that lined the walls. The smell of pine needles was coming from the real Christmas tree Guy knew would be standing in the sitting room.

'Hello?' he called out, his voice emerging as something of a whimper.

There was no answer.

From the kitchen he could hear the sound of running water and the clinking of crockery. As he walked through, he wondered if your heart could beat so fast it could kill you.

Across the room – an enormous room filled with pine furniture, duck-egg blue units, an old AGA, and an overhead clothes rack from which hung antique pots and pans – his mother was standing with her back to him, rinsing plates and loading them into the dishwasher.

'Mother?'

Cynthia spun around. 'Guy! You scared me!'

He frowned. 'Sorry.'

'Oh, darling, I'm all wet.' She held out her hands and gave him an air hug. 'How was the journey?'

Guy's heart dropped in his chest. *Has she not read the letter?*

He felt a flicker of hope. *Maybe she's read it and decided it doesn't matter . . .*

'Yeah, fine,' he said, the moisture draining from his mouth.

Cynthia turned off the tap and wiped her hands on a tea towel. 'What's the matter? You look as if you've seen a ghost.'

Shit, she doesn't know. She genuinely doesn't know.

'Did you not get my letter?' Guy couldn't believe he was asking this; his voice seemed to be coming from somewhere outside his body.

'What letter?'

His insides dragged. 'Has the post not come yet?'

'Yes, but it was just a pile of bills.' Cynthia tucked her shoulder-length hair behind her ear. 'Guy, what's going on? Why are you so interested in the post?'

Through his devastation – a devastation that was making him feel sick – Guy was surprised to sense a glimmer of disappointment. *After all that effort, all that terror sitting on the train, it hasn't worked.*

Almost despite himself, he held onto this. 'Mother, there's something I need to tell you. Where's Dad?'

'Watching the cricket on TV.' Cynthia shouted through to the sitting room, 'Stephen! Guy's home! There's something he wants to tell us!'

Guy felt dizzy. He wished he'd been able to eat lunch but he'd been too worked up to swallow the sandwich he'd bought on the train. He fixed himself a glass of water and sat down at the table.

'Good Lord, I don't like the look of this.' Cynthia lowered herself onto the chair opposite him.

Guy's dad bounded in, wearing his usual winter uniform of corduroys and a V-neck jumper over a checked shirt, a smile on his face. 'Hello, son!'

Registering their grim expressions, Stephen's face fell. 'What's the matter? What's happened?'

'Nothing's happened,' Guy said, sliding his hands under the table so he could knead his knuckles. 'Well, nothing that wasn't happening already, nothing that wasn't always happening.'

'What on earth are you talking about?' said Cynthia.

Stephen leaned back on the kitchen units and folded his arms. 'Son, you're going to have to stop speaking in riddles and spit it out.'

Guy felt like he was choking with dread.

'I'm gay.'

There, I got the words out after all.

A stony silence set in.

Cynthia blinked in confusion. 'What . . .? But you can't be gay.'

'What do you mean? Why not?'

A frown appeared between her eyebrows. 'I've met gay men. We have some who come into the surgery. You're nothing like them.'

'Well, maybe it's time you changed your ideas about gay men.

We're not all queenie and effeminate, you know. We don't all like dancing to showtunes.' He attempted a smile.

Stephen's fair skin was turning ruddy. 'There's no need to be so flippant, Guy. This isn't a joke.'

'Sorry, I didn't mean—'

'Why are you doing this?' Suddenly, Cynthia seemed old; her ash-blonde hair looked grey, her face wrinkled and drawn, the sinews on her neck more pronounced. 'Are you angry with us? Is there something we've done wrong?'

He let out a sigh. 'No, I'm not angry with you. And I'm not *doing* anything. I'm just gay.'

And I've always known you'd hate me for it, he wanted to add.

'I need a brandy,' barked Stephen. He went over to the drinks cupboard, grabbed a crystal decanter and sloshed some into a glass.

Guy laid his hands on the table and did his best to adopt a conciliatory tone. 'I wanted you to know as I didn't want to go on pretending. I didn't want to carry on lying to you. I just couldn't do it anymore.'

'Oh, what self-indulgent poppycock!' erupted Stephen. 'Have you any idea what this is like for a parent? Have you any idea how hard this is for us?'

How hard it is for you? Guy wanted to yell. *Have you any idea how hard it is for* me? *How hard it's always been?* But he'd promised himself he wouldn't be confrontational.

'Maybe we shouldn't have sent you to boarding school,' said Cynthia, rubbing her neck. 'Maybe we should have made sure you spent more time around girls.'

Stephen tossed back his drink and slammed the glass down onto the worktop. 'I did say that, Cynthia.'

'Oh, shut up, Stephen! You're not helping.' Cynthia turned back to Guy, her forehead rutted. 'Is it some kind of – I don't know – sexual experimentation? I suppose it's fashionable amongst students, is it?'

Guy went back to kneading his knuckles, this time not bothering to hide them under the table. 'No, Mother, this has nothing to do with fashion.'

'I blame Manchester,' she went on. 'Everyone knows it's riddled with gays. I always said you should have gone to Exeter or Bristol.'

'I promise you, this has nothing to do with fashion *or* Manchester.' He paused. 'Well, I suppose Manchester did help. But only in that it gave me the confidence to explore what was already there.'

'Crikey,' said Stephen, sloshing more brandy into his glass, 'and I thought it was just ferrets and flat caps.'

'Well, I don't accept it,' Cynthia snapped, knives in her eyes. 'You're confused. You'll grow out of it.'

'You'll have to,' added Stephen. 'There's no way your mother and I can accept that kind of lifestyle.'

'What "lifestyle"?' asked Guy. 'I don't know what you're imagining, but I'm in a monogamous relationship, unlike some people in this family.'

Guy was referring to his brother Barney, who'd slept with a multitude of women, including Emma on a visit to Manchester, including several of his colleagues from work who were attached or even married, one of whom had fallen pregnant and had a termination.

'That's not fair!' bellowed Stephen. 'You leave your brother out of this. Barney's just working out who he is, trying to find his way in the world.'

'I suppose you may think you're doing the same,' said Cynthia. 'Although let me tell you, you've veered off in the wrong direction.'

Guy pushed himself back from the table. 'Mother, I don't need to work out who I am. I know who I am.'

'Well, you'll live a sad, lonely life.' The words flew out of her mouth like bullets from a gun.

Guy gripped the seat of his chair. 'That may have been the case in the past but it isn't anymore. Things have moved on.'

Cynthia gave him a look of derision. 'OK, name me one gay couple who are happy. Name me one gay couple in a long-term relationship.'

'Elton John. He's been with his boyfriend for years.'

She rolled her eyes. 'They're the exception that proves the rule.'

'OK, well, how about George Michael and that Texan guy?' Guy couldn't remember his name. *I wish Danny was here.*

Cynthia scoffed. 'I'd hardly hold that up as any kind of model relationship. In case you've forgotten, George Michael was caught trying to pick up a police officer in a public toilet. Lord only knows what his so-called boyfriend thought about that.'

Stephen nodded. 'Which only goes to prove our point – about the gay lifestyle.'

'You know, the incidence of STIs is much higher amongst gay men,' Cynthia cut in, her tone switching from outraged to authoritative. 'And what about HIV? Doesn't that worry you?'

'Mother, I know how to protect myself against HIV,' Guy protested.

She sniffed. 'I wonder if Freddie Mercury said the same thing to his mother.'

Guy stood up. 'Right, I'm not listening to this anymore. I've tried to include you, I've tried to let you know who I am so that we can have a truthful relationship. But it's obviously not worked.'

He stomped out of the room and up the staircase, grabbing his bags on the way.

Once he was in his bedroom, he slammed the door behind him and collapsed on the bed.

What's the matter with them? Why can't they just love me?

All of a sudden, it was as if he'd never set foot in Manchester. It was as if he'd never been out on the gay scene or fallen in love, as if he'd never met Danny. He felt just the same as he had when he used to lie in this room as a teenager, worrying that his parents would disown him if they ever found out he was gay. *All my life I've felt like I haven't measured up to the son they wanted. This is just the final nail in the coffin.*

He could feel the tears bubbling up in his eyes and at the back of his throat.

You're not going to cry, Guy. Whatever you do, don't cry.

He swallowed his tears and sprung off the bed. He reached into his rucksack and pulled out his phone. He scrolled through his contacts until he came to Drew.

Then he paused. Just above his name was Danny's.

He scrolled up and hit Call.

Danny immediately answered and just hearing his voice made Guy feel better.

'Crack open the champagne!' he announced. 'Job done!'

2022

'Look at this,' Danny bursts out, 'they've left us champagne!'

Guy follows him into the lounge area of the hotel room. 'Well, it'd be rude not to drink it,' he says. He busies himself opening the bottle.

Danny makes a mental note to thank the receptionist as he takes off his shoes and stashes them in the wardrobe. Then he stops in the hallway to dim the lights; they're way too bright for what he's hoping is going to happen. But the control panel looks like something out of a spaceship and he can't work out how to operate it. He ends up plunging the room into darkness, then switching on one light after the other. *God, I can't stand technology.*

'What are you doing?' asks Guy.

Danny tries to sound nonchalant. 'Oh, you know I hate harsh lighting. I'm just trying to turn it down.'

Just as Guy's popping the cork, Danny works out the controls and eases the glare off the lights. He moves back through to the main room and picks up his glass of champagne.

'Well,' he says, sitting in the armchair opposite Guy, 'one day down, three to go.'

Guy tastes his champagne and nods approvingly. 'I can't wait for the parade tomorrow. You know I've never done a Pride march?'

Danny inches forward in his seat. 'You're not serious?'

'Yeah. I'm not sure why but it's just never happened.'

This gap in his knowledge reminds Danny of how estranged the two of them became before their recent reconciliation. But he clears this from his mind.

'In that case,' he says, brightly, 'now I'm even more excited about it.'

Danny takes out his phone and shows Guy the parade route through the city centre then tells him about his experiences of marching at Pride in London. This transports him back to the start of their relationship, when the two of them were new to life as gay men but, because he was slightly more advanced on his journey, he often felt as if he was initiating Guy. *Maybe that's how it's meant to be with us – maybe I'm always meant to take the lead . . .*

Once he's finished his drink, Danny excuses himself to go to the bathroom; he wants to freshen up in case anything does happen. He closes the door and quietly turns the lock.

He whips off his clothes and quickly scrubs around his armpits and crotch. He reapplies deodorant but opts not to respray his aftershave, fearing this will make his intentions obvious. He deliberates whether or not to brush his teeth but doesn't want to taste of toothpaste so quickly chews some gum and spits it out in the bin.

As he re-enters the room, he sees that Guy's taken off his shoes and is lying on the bed watching something on his phone. He lets out a rolling laugh.

'What's so funny?'

Guy holds out his phone and Danny slides onto the bed

next to him. He shows him a GIF of a middle-aged man in a business suit and high heels giving a sassy slut-drop, then sashaying off into the distance.

'That's brilliant,' he says. 'Play it again.'

He nestles into Guy and Guy wraps his arm around his shoulders. As they're both wearing short-sleeved shirts, the skin of their arms touches. Danny feels the heat rising from the pit of his stomach.

Guy puts the phone down. 'Do you remember how cruel we used to be about camp queens?'

'Yeah, we were pretty immature,' says Danny. 'I do feel guilty about that now.'

But is this really the right time to discuss it?

'Me too,' says Guy, 'I'm glad we've grown up since then.'

He lets out a long breath and Danny can feel it tickling the back of his neck.

'I'm glad we've grown up together,' he adds.

Now that's more like it.

Danny rests his hand on Guy's forearm and hopes Guy can't tell he's trembling. 'What was it you used to say about us?' he asks.

'We go together like gin and tonic.'

'Benson and Hedges.'

'Slap and tickle.'

They laugh and fall into a loaded silence. Danny can feel his pulse tripping.

Drawing on all his courage, he begins to very softly stroke Guy's arm. He's so nervous he has no idea how he's even able to move his hand. But somehow he manages it – and somehow he keeps going.

Every muscle in his body clenches, waiting for Guy to respond.

But he doesn't say or do anything. The silence grows thick between them. Danny can feel his heartbeat in his ears.

What am I doing? Am I seriously going to go through with this?

But despite his fears, he knows he has to.

He goes on stroking Guy's arm.

2005

Guy felt the skin of his arm touching Danny's.

'Thanks for coming to meet me,' he said.

I really needed it today. I'm so stressed I can't even think straight.

Danny smiled at him. 'Don't be daft, babe. It's always nice to see you.'

They were sitting on the steps at the foot of a statue in front of the Town Hall on Albert Square. It was a statue of William Gladstone, not that either of them knew who he was – it was just the first sitting place they crossed when walking from the library. It was the summer term of their third year and Guy was revising for his final exams. As he was stressed, he preferred to do this away from his fellow law students at the University, in the city's Central Library. Every day at 1 o'clock Danny would come to meet him and they'd walk around the corner to eat their lunch. But on this occasion, Guy felt like he was being followed by his own personal thundercloud – and he didn't want to infect Danny with his mood.

As Guy took a bite of his sandwich, he decided to fall back on his usual joke. 'You know, I've no idea how I'd cope if you were doing a proper course.'

Danny elbowed him playfully. 'I keep telling you, I *am* doing a proper course!'

Guy grinned and took a swig from his bottle of water. He looked around at the large cobbled square. It was dotted with wrought-iron lamp-posts, bronze and marble statues, a smattering of plane trees, a granite and sandstone fountain – with an ornate monument to Prince Albert standing proudly in the centre. But it was the grand, gothic town hall that dominated the square, its clock tower thrusting up into a sky that was almost completely blue and only broken up by the occasional light cloud. As ever, there were few other people around. It always surprised Guy that such an important public space in such a big city could be so quiet. *But that's one of the reasons I like it; it helps me stay calm.*

He let out a sigh. 'Joking apart, I don't know what I'd do without you.'

'Oh, you always say that,' dismissed Danny. 'I'm sure you'd cope.'

'I wouldn't though, would I? How would I have got through the last few years if it weren't for you?'

Guy thought back to the Christmas holidays of his second year. After coming out to his parents, the atmosphere had been unbearably tense and there were times when he felt like he was being buried under the weight of their strange mix of disapproval, disgust, outrage and pity. Although they hadn't thrown him out of the house or cut off his allowance, they had made it clear that this was on the condition that he didn't discuss his sexuality with anyone outside the home. When the family had gone to the golf club for their annual Christmas drinks, Guy had been forced to pretend he was straight; if people asked if he had a girlfriend, he found himself talking about Lynsey. At the end of the holidays, he'd returned to Manchester feeling broken, only to be met by indifference from Drew, who was much more interested in auditioning for some role he wanted in a student play. Although Danny had also been preparing for an audition, he hadn't let him down; he'd been there for heart-to-hearts and to offer the advice and support he needed.

Then, at the start of his third year, Guy had found out Drew had cheated on him with a professional theatre director who was in Manchester doing a job at the Royal Exchange. He'd been devastated and had once again turned to Danny, who once again hadn't let him down. He'd bundled Guy off to the Village for a series of nights out, but had also been there to listen and offer reassurance when Guy had decided he wanted to work through his problems with Drew and give the relationship another go. *Come to think of it, that can't have been much fun for him – but he never complained.*

Now here Danny was yet again, helping him through another difficult time. Guy had already been offered a job, but it was conditional on him getting a 2:1 in his finals and he knew this would be a stretch for him, not least because he'd fallen behind with work in the midst of all the drama with Drew. He was terrified of losing the job as he couldn't bear the idea of moving back home and the pressure he was under was making him feel frazzled. Although Drew was supposedly still his boyfriend, he was hardly around, often disappearing to London for meetings with some agent who'd signed him up for representation. He hadn't done anything to help Guy through this tough period – but Danny had sensed Guy was struggling and that what he needed was simply to know he wasn't alone, that someone believed in him.

As he thought about everything Danny had done for him,

Guy felt tears welling in his eyes. All of a sudden, the heightened emotions of the last few months felt like they were rising up within him, rushing to break through to the surface.

'You know, you're much more of a partner to me than Drew is,' he stammered. 'You're much more like my other half.'

He spotted a flicker of something that looked like hope lift Danny's face. It stirred something inside Guy that he wasn't able to identify.

Back in the first year, Guy had thought the confusion around his feelings for Danny had disappeared when he'd met Drew; what he felt for Drew was so intense it quite simply swept away any sentiment he had for anyone else. More than anything, he couldn't believe someone as good-looking as Drew would be attracted to him, the boy who for so long hadn't been able to bear anyone so much as glancing at him in case his spots made them grimace. Guy found the realisation that Drew did find him attractive quite intoxicating. But now their relationship was faltering, he couldn't help wondering if all along his connection with Drew had been purely physical. And he wondered if Drew's good looks had blinded him to the fact that the connection he shared with Danny was much stronger.

'But I don't understand,' said Danny. 'What do you mean?'

Guy let out a sigh. With all the pressure he was under, this wasn't the time to work out how he felt about something as important as this. 'I don't understand either. Sorry, I think I just need to keep my head down and concentrate on my finals. I need to try and sort out my future.'

Danny swallowed but didn't say anything.

Guy moved on, trying to sound upbeat. 'Speaking of the future, have you heard from any agents?'

Danny frowned. 'No, not yet. And that's not great to be honest. I'm trying not to think about it.'

'You'll do it,' Guy said, nudging his knee. 'You've been brilliant in everything you've done here.'

Danny gave a weak smile. Guy had noticed that his hair had started to thin over the last year and he knew that Danny was worried about losing it. He also knew that one or two agents had already made comments about it and how much these upset Danny. He didn't want to remind him.

'It's only a matter of time till the rest of the world sees how good you are,' he stated, confidently.

Danny gathered together their rubbish and stood up to toss it into a nearby bin. 'Babe,' he said as he sat back down, 'do you ever wonder where we'll be in twenty years?'

Guy's eyebrows shot up to his hairline. 'Twenty years? At the moment I'm trying to get through the next few weeks – and I'm not sure I'll manage that.'

'OK, how about ten? Come on, I'll go first; in ten years I'm going to be a wildly famous and award-winning actor.'

Guy shrugged. 'If I'm lucky I'll have just about scraped through my finals and will be a mildly successful lawyer.'

A pair of starlings landed at their feet and began pecking at crumbs.

'And how would you feel about that?' asked Danny. 'You know, if you were only mildly successful?'

The question caught Guy off-guard and he wasn't sure how to answer. He looked into Danny's eyes and felt the bond between them pulling tight, the bond that had been there since the day they met, the bond that was now stronger than ever.

'I don't think I'd mind,' he said, 'as long as you and I are together.'

Danny wrinkled his brow. 'What do you mean, "together"?'

'Oh, I don't know. But we go together, don't we? Like gin and tonic.'

A grin crept up Danny's face. 'Dolce and Gabbana.'

'Benson and Hedges.'

'Slap and tickle.'

The two of them laughed and the noise frightened away the starlings.

'Come here,' said Guy.

He held out his arms and drew Danny into a hug.

2022

Danny pulls Guy's arm tighter around him and, when he's sure they're both comfortable, continues to stroke it. Before long, he can feel Guy kissing the side of his head.

He turns around and looks him in the eye. But he doesn't say anything. Neither does Guy.

The silence between them hits Danny's ears as anything but silence – he's so nervous it's more like a shrill shriek. He's not sure he can bear this much longer.

Finally, Guy moves down to kiss his mouth.

Oh my God, this is it!

A jolt of excitement shoots through Danny. As Guy continues to kiss him, it races all the way down to his toes.

Guy kisses him with more and more urgency and Danny feels his breath quicken. His head's spinning with adrenaline but at the same time he doesn't feel dizzy. On the contrary, it's as if everything he's seeing is hyper-real, as if the camera through which he's viewing the world has suddenly been upgraded to high-definition. He wonders if this is because he's imagined the scene that's unfolding so many times, if all the scenes from his imagination are somehow coming together to turbo-charge the reality he's finally experiencing.

He moves to undo the top button on Guy's shirt but Guy pulls back. He takes hold of Danny's face between his hands.

'Wait a minute,' he says, 'are you sure you want to do this?'

Yes, I want to do this! I've been wanting to do it for twenty years!

'What about you?' Danny manages to say. 'Do *you* want to do it?'

You have to make the decision, Guy. It has to be you who makes it.

But he looks at Guy's dimple, his arresting blue eyes and that cute little gap between his teeth and knows he can't let this slip away. He moves in and kisses him again.

Within seconds, Guy whispers in his ear, 'Yes.'

'Sorry?' Danny whispers back. 'What was that?'

'Yes,' Guy repeats.

'Yes, what?'

'Yes, I want to do this,' Guy says firmly.

Danny's face splits into a grin. 'In that case, so do I.'

As if he's just moved up a gear, Guy rushes to unbutton his shirt and pull off his clothes. Danny does the same, thankful he's dimmed the lights. As Guy drops his shorts onto the floor, Danny flings off his jeans but they catch on something at the bottom of the bed.

'Those fucking swans,' he jokes. He shuffles down the bed and pushes them onto the floor.

As he moves back up, he's met by the sight of Guy kneeling in nothing but his underpants. Suddenly he feels a twitch of awkwardness. He's aware that his own body isn't anywhere near as impressive as Guy's, however much weight he's lost, however much he may have spent on laser treatment to permanently blast away his back and shoulder hair. He tries to dismiss his worry but is conscious of a stiffness in his shoulders and struggles to relax.

Come on, you've got to deliver the goods now. You can't wait all this time and then disappoint him!

At that moment, Guy lets out a little burp. His hand shoots up to his mouth. 'Sorry! It must be the champagne.'

The two of them erupt in laughter.

'I'm so sorry,' repeats Guy, 'that's really embarrassing.'

But Danny is glad Guy burped because he can feel himself relaxing. Suddenly, he knows everything's going to be alright.

Feeling a surge of confidence, he draws closer to Guy and runs his hand up and down his torso. He rests his chin on his shoulder and breathes him in. *My God, everything about him's perfect – his smell, his touch, his taste . . .*

He begins kissing him again and their lips and tongues glide around each other's. Guy's arms inch downwards and he begins tugging off his underpants. When Danny hears them drop onto the floor, he removes his own underwear. And the two men draw together again, this time both of them naked.

My God, this is really happening.

Guy presses his hardness against him. 'I told you hotel rooms make me horny,' he says.

'So I gather,' chuckles Danny.

Guy breaks away and reaches into a bag on the floor. He lifts out some lubricant and comes back to kneel before Danny. He pumps out the gel and massages it onto himself. Danny draws a long breath and raises his legs.

Guy takes hold of Danny and pulls him towards him. He gently pushes up against him, then pushes a little harder and enters him. 'Fuck,' he says, 'I'm inside you. I'm actually inside you.'

Danny waits for the initial stab of pain to fade then smiles at him to continue.

Guys takes hold of Danny's face and pulls it closer to him so they're looking deep into each other's eyes. Then he pulls it closer still, so their foreheads are touching, their eyelashes tickling each other's, their breath intermingling. He eases himself further inside.

'This is awesome,' he says. 'Why did it take us so long?'

Danny feels overwhelmed. He isn't sure which emotion is rushing through him but he does know he's never felt any emotion so intensely. He wants to answer Guy but can't get the words out. He isn't even able to order his thoughts. All he can say is, 'I don't know.'

And he doesn't know. Because suddenly everything that's happened between them, everything that's happened over the last twenty years, all of it seems inconsequential. Compared to this, none of it matters.

And the best thing is, Guy feels the same.

As Guy begins moving inside him, Danny can feel his emotion building. This is completely different to any of the sex he's had before. It's so much more intimate – and he feels so much more *present*.

I love you, he wants to say. But he confines the words to his head. *I love you, I love you, I love you.*

Guy moves more forcefully and within minutes, Danny finds himself hanging off the side of the bed. He laughs again and is relieved when Guy laughs too.

'Sorry, princess.'

'That's OK, my prince.'

With an easy strength, Guy lifts him up and repositions him on the bed.

Over his shoulder, Danny catches sight of the alarm clock. It's one minute to midnight.

For a fleeting moment he wonders what will happen tomorrow, what will happen when this is over, when they wake up and remember what they did. He's spent so long fussing and fretting over the build-up to this moment it didn't occur to him to consider what might come afterwards – and in many ways that's much more important. *Much more important and much more difficult to predict.*

He puts the thought out of his mind.

What matters is we're having sex. After twenty years we're finally having sex.

No, we're not; we're making love. For the first time in my life, I'm making love.

And he puts his arms around Guy, eager for him to continue.

SATURDAY

2022

Danny is woken up by the sound of the bathroom door closing. He opens his eyes and rubs them. As he hears Guy turning on the shower, he remembers what happened last night.

Oh my God, we did it. We actually did it.

And not just that but it was better than he'd imagined – better than he'd dared to imagine.

He's so excited that his heart is thumping like a piston. He wants to squeal out loud but somehow manages to restrain himself.

He sits up and sees clothes and underwear belonging to both of them scattered on the floor – and this sets the memories firing.

A flash of anxiety passes through his gut. *But what happens now?*

Danny knows exactly what he *wants* to happen now – he wants to begin a sexual, romantic relationship with Guy. He just isn't sure how to get to that point from where he is.

He looks at the alarm clock; it's 10 a.m. Even though he's excited, he's also very tired. After they made love, he lay in Guy's arms and tried his best to stay awake, eager to prolong the moment. He didn't want to fall asleep, he didn't want to do anything at all to separate them. He's no idea what time he eventually drifted off but he knows that even when he did, he only slept lightly.

From the bathroom comes the sound of Guy switching off the shower.

Shit, what do I say when he comes out? Do I mention last night or just avoid the subject till later? And do I kiss him good morning or would that be too full-on?

Just when he's wondering how he can get into the bathroom and gargle away his morning breath, Guy flings open the door and pokes his head around it.

'Come on, get up,' he says, towelling his hair. 'We're going to be late!'

Danny sits up. 'Late? For what?'

Guy pads into the room with a towel wrapped around his waist. 'Brunch with Emma and Richard, remember?'

'Fuck! I totally forgot!'

Danny checks the alarm clock again: it's 10.04 and they're due at the restaurant at 10.30. He's about to jump out of bed when he remembers he's naked.

He feels a flicker of self-consciousness. Now that it's daylight and they're both sober, he doesn't want to appear without his clothes on. But what he was wearing last night is lying on the floor and all his other clothes are hanging in the wardrobe.

There's nothing else for it: he stands up and pulls the duvet around him, dragging it with him into the bathroom.

'Don't panic, babe,' he calls out, 'I'll be as quick as I can!'

2005

Danny felt a spike of excitement but tried his best to suppress it.

He was standing next to Guy in the Old Quad, a courtyard between the cluster of rather grand, gothic Victorian buildings made out of sandstone – some of them covered in ivy – on the Oxford Road site of the university. They'd just emerged from their graduation ceremony and were still wearing their caps and gowns. Guy had asked Danny if he could have a word and steered him aside – then, without any warning, he'd announced that he was going to end his relationship with Drew.

Halle-fucking-lujah!

'I've known it couldn't last for a while really,' Guy explained. 'I guess I just tried to forget about it and focus on work and enjoying the rest of my time here. But all that's over now and I can't pretend anymore.'

Into Danny's head burst some of the things Guy had said recently, some of the things that had made him think he might just have been wrong and Guy might actually see him as a potential boyfriend.

'You're much more of a partner to me than Drew is.'

'You're much more like my other half.'

His insides tingled.

'So what are you going to do?' he asked. 'How are you going to do it?'

Before Guy could answer, he was interrupted by Emma.

'Oi, oi!'

Oh no! But I need to hear this!

'What are you two blethering on about?' Emma said. 'Come on, we need you for a photo.'

She led them into the centre of the quad, in between the two trees, where their extended group of friends were waiting, poised to throw their mortarboards into the air for a mob of parents who were standing by, cameras at the ready. As Danny and Guy added themselves to the group, Danny reminded himself that today wasn't about Guy splitting up with Drew. *It's about our graduation. And it's a big day – I should make the most of it.*

The formal ceremony had taken place in the vast and atmospheric Whitworth Hall, which resembled a church with its stained-glass window, wood-pannelled walls, wrought-iron chandeliers and breathtaking oak hammer-beam roof. The soon-to-be-graduates had sat in the front half of the hall, their guests seated behind them, all of them facing the stage and the huge pipe organ that stretched the height of the wall behind it. They'd listened to a speech by the cheery Vice-Chancellor, who'd been keen to impress on them that they weren't leaving the university but merely starting a new chapter in their relationship with it. Then they'd taken it in turns to go up onto the stage, shake his hand and receive their degree, to the sound of impassioned applause from their families and friends. As Danny had stood on the stage, he'd looked into the audience for his mum and she'd given him a wobbly smile, the tears streaming down her cheeks.

As soon as the ceremony was over, everyone had spilled out into the quad, blinking to adjust to the July sunshine, the boys loosening their ties, all of them erupting in animated chatter, many of them keen to make a photographic record of the occasion.

'OK,' called out Emma's mum, 'on the count of three, throw your hats in the air. One, two, three!'

As soon as the hats had landed, she turned to Emma's dad. 'Did you get that? Don't tell me you missed it!'

'Yes, I got it!' the man snapped. 'I keep telling you, it's a digital camera. I can take loads.'

As they descended into full-scale bickering, Danny gave Emma a smile: he knew from their late-night chats that this happened a lot – and she found it difficult to handle. She rolled her eyes back at him.

'Hey, gang,' she said to Danny, Lynsey and Guy, 'come over here a minute. We need a group chat.'

Over the last few years, Danny, Emma, Lynsey and Guy had formed a tight unit, although when it had come to moving out of halls and into houses, Guy had lived with Rags and a group of straight friends, while Danny had lived with the girls and a few friends from his course; he'd dodged the idea of living with Guy, knowing he'd find it too painful to have such a frontline view of his relationship with Drew.

Drew himself wasn't able to attend today's ceremony as he'd just been cast in his first professional play and couldn't get time away from rehearsals. Of all of them, he was the one who'd moved on from university the fastest – and the easiest, Danny couldn't help thinking, although he was doing his best not to be too jealous. Of the others, Lynsey had decided to stay on in Manchester, where she'd found a job with a local law firm. Danny had tried to persuade her to try her hand as a professional theatre director but she was adamant that, for her, theatre was only ever a hobby. Guy had just scraped the 2:1 he needed so was preparing to start work in London and Emma still had no idea what she was doing – or where she'd be doing it.

When it came to his future, Danny had finally managed to find an agent to represent him as an actor. Heather Hardman wasn't a very good one and he hadn't actually met her sober but still, she was an agent. She'd started by suggesting he 'do something about' his hair loss, insisting that going bald would greatly reduce his chances of work, although what this 'something' was or how he'd be able to afford it, Danny had no idea. Heather had also made it clear that if he wanted his career to succeed, Danny had to move to London, which he hadn't been intending but at least gave him an excuse to be close to Guy. Before he did that he had to find himself some kind of part-time job so he could afford to rent a flat and start auditioning. The prospect was daunting but he was trying to stay positive – and at least in the celebratory atmosphere of graduation day, this wasn't hard.

'This is it, gang,' said Emma, once they were all together, 'it's the end of an era. How's everyone feeling?'

'You know what,' said Danny, 'I'm sad to be leaving but I'm also looking forward to the future.'

'Yeah, but do you promise we'll stay just as close?' said Lynsey. 'Do you promise you'll come back to Manchester all the time?'

'As if I could stay away from this place,' he said. 'It's my spiritual home.'

'Well, just so you know,' said Emma, 'wherever I end up living, I'll be coming to visit you and Guy in London. So one of you had better have a sofa, as I'll be crashing on it – a lot.'

'Just as long as that's all you do on it,' teased Guy.

They all laughed.

'Seriously, though,' said Emma, 'it might be a while till the four of us are together again. So we've got to make a pact not to grow apart.'

Everyone agreed this was a good idea and Lynsey suggested they seal it with a hug. They drew together in a rough, untidy huddle, pulling tighter so their mortar boards came to rest against one another's. The chatter in the background dimmed to a hum.

'I love you guys,' Danny said, his voice catching in his throat. 'We'll never grow apart.'

'We'll never grow apart!' everyone repeated, followed by a messy jumble of 'I love you's.

For a while the four of them remained in the huddle, none of them wanting to break away. Danny could feel a tear leaking from his eye and a loud sniffing sound told him he wasn't the only one crying.

'Come on,' said Emma, eventually, 'there's no need for us to get upset. We've just made a pact, remember?'

They slowly pulled apart. As Danny wiped the tear from his eye, he noticed his mum was watching.

'Look at you lot,' she gushed, beaming, 'the Fab Four!'

'Come on,' said Arthur, moving in next to her, 'let's have a photo.'

He directed them to drape their arms around each other and smile for his battered old analogue camera. When they'd finished, Guy, Emma and Lynsey drifted off to find their parents.

'So what did you think?' Danny asked his mum. 'Did you enjoy it?'

'Yeah, it were brill, love,' Eileen said in her strong northern accent. She'd dressed up for the occasion and was wearing a mint-green pencil skirt and matching jacket with her long curls of caramel hair tucked underneath a wide-brimmed hat – and had treated herself to several sessions under the sunbed. 'I bawled my eyes out when you went up,' she continued. 'I've just had to nip to t' bogs to redo my make-up. But we were dead proud, weren't we, Arthur?'

Arthur was also dressed up, wearing black leather trousers and a black open-neck shirt, with skin that was even darker than Eileen's and a leopard-print velvet jacket that was attracting attention. It had been Danny's idea to offer him his second guest ticket, as the two of them had grown close since he'd come out. Danny and Eileen would often visit Arthur in Brighton, where Danny and Arthur would go for walks on the beach, during which Arthur would give Danny advice and share stories about what it was like to be gay in the 1960s and 70s. Danny felt lucky and privileged to have him in his life. If he ever missed his dad – which only really happened when people asked about him – he'd tell himself that Arthur's presence more than made up for his absence.

'Yeah, I were bursting with pride,' said Arthur. And a wicked twinkle entered his eye. 'I'll tell you summat else, that vice-chancellor were a bit of a dish. I wonder if he's single.'

Eileen cackled loudly. ''Ere, we'll have to look out for him later.'

That evening, the three of them had arranged to go out on Canal Street: Arthur hadn't been to the Gay Village for years and Eileen wanted to see for herself the place that Danny said had made him so happy.

'Well, if we don't see him,' said Arthur, 'there'll be plenty of others. If you're lucky, dearie, I might even leave one for you.'

Eileen gave another cackle and Danny joined in.

'I tell you what, though,' she said, 'I'm going to have to go back to t' hotel and get changed. I'm sweating cobs in this suit.'

'Why don't you take your jacket off?' Danny suggested.

She looked at him in horror. 'I don't want to show you up, love. I don't want anyone to see my bingo wings.'

As Danny reassured his mum that she could never show him up, out of the corner of his eye he spotted Guy chatting awkwardly to his parents. It hadn't escaped Danny's attention that Mr and Mrs Falconer hadn't smiled all day, not even when they'd watched Guy go on stage to receive his degree. As soon as they'd come outside, they'd positioned themselves at the very edge of the quad, next to that boulder of lava that was supposed to be some kind of geological artefact but Danny always thought looked out of place. They'd refused to meet any of Guy's friends, and had only spoken to Rags's parents, who they knew already. Occasionally, Guy's mum had glanced over at the crowd of excitable new graduates and turned her nose up in distaste. She was insisting they drive back to Buckinghamshire that afternoon.

All this made Danny realise how lucky he was to have a mum like Eileen and a surrogate father in Arthur, a realisation he voiced. 'You two have always been so supportive. And I really appreciate you being here.'

'Oh, that's lovely, dearie,' said Arthur, 'but we're going to have to leave you to it for a bit. I need a brew and a sit-down before we hit Canal Street. Don't forget I'm an old bird now.'

Eileen smiled. 'And I'm desperate to take off this new bra – it's been digging into my back-fat all day.'

Danny laughed and said he'd text them later.

He looked around for Lynsey and saw her standing with her dad and stepmum, a rather earnest couple who ran their own artisanal soap and candle company that used only organic and ethically sourced materials. Although Danny had always got on with them, he didn't want to be drawn into conversation today; there was something he needed to tell Lynsey – and it was something he needed to tell her alone.

He caught her eye and beckoned her over to a quiet spot in the far corner.

'You'll never guess what Guy's just said,' he blurted out. 'He's only going to dump Drew.'

Lynsey arched an eyebrow. 'Well, it's about time. I always thought that should have been just a fling – Guy should never have let it go on for so long.'

'Yeah, well, it doesn't sound like it'll be going on for much longer.'

Danny stopped and considered what he wanted to say next. *But can I really say it?*

He took a deep breath. 'You don't think that when they split up, I might stand a chance, do you?' As he heard the words coming out of his mouth, he felt embarrassed, as if he were making a ludicrous suggestion.

'Dan, I've told you before,' said Lynsey, 'Guy would be lucky to have you. I've always thought you two would make a great couple, you know that.'

Although Danny did know this, it felt good to hear her say it again. 'Aw, thanks, Lyns.' The tassel from his hat swung in front of his eyes and he batted it out of the way. 'But what do you think I should do? How should I go about it?'

Lynsey drew in her mouth tightly. 'Well, I can see it's difficult now you've been friends for so long. Maybe you should go out for a few drinks and see if you can make something happen accidentally.'

'*Accidentally*? How do you mean?'

'First you'd have to create the right conditions; you'd have to make sure you're sharing a room, preferably a bed. Then you go out drinking, come home and fall into bed. I'm thinking you start having a perfectly innocent cuddle, one thing leads to another, you both get carried away, and before you know it – woops! – you're having sex. If it all goes wrong you could always blame it on the booze.'

Danny felt a wave of fear lick his belly. *Could I really do that?*

Despite his doubts, he knew he had to at least try. 'And when do you think I should do it?'

'Well, let him dump Drew first – and give him a bit of time to get over it. Then maybe you should go and visit him in London. Come to think of it, if you're staying at his place, that'll be the perfect opportunity.'

Danny drew in a long breath and let it fill his lungs. 'OK,' he declared, 'I'll do it. I'll try to make it happen.'

Just making the decision and voicing it out loud felt like it took a load off his mind. He thanked Lynsey and she went back to her parents.

He looked around for Guy but he hadn't moved from his position by the boulder. As Danny watched him chatting to his parents, he noticed he was hunching his shoulders and bowing his head, as if physically reduced or cowed. Danny felt his heart heave.

Guy's dad reached into his pocket and pulled out his car keys. *Oh no, you can't go yet! Guy can't go without finishing what he was saying!*

To his relief, Guy scanned the quad for him and jogged over.

'I've got to get off,' he said. 'I wish I could come to the Village with you guys but my parents want to make a move.'

'Don't worry, I get it,' Danny said, nodding. 'But what was it you were saying earlier?' He tried to sound casual. 'About ending it with Drew?'

'Oh yeah,' said Guy, 'I've given it a lot of thought and I'm definitely going to do it.'

Danny selected his words carefully. 'Well, these things are always sad but after everything that's happened I think you're doing the right thing.'

Was that sufficiently sympathetic?

From the expression on Guy's face it looked like it had worked. 'Thanks, Danny, I appreciate that.'

'So when are you going to dump him?' Danny didn't intend this last line to come out so glibly. He tried not to squirm.

'Oh, I'm not sure I'd call it dumping him,' Guy countered. 'I don't think Drew's going to have any objection. Let's face it, his heart hasn't been in it for a while.'

'No, I know what you mean,' Danny managed, diplomatically.

'Anyway, I'm not going to do anything just yet. I've got to find myself a flat first – my mother and father aren't getting any better. I need to get away from them.'

Danny wished he were moving to London at the same time as Guy so the two of them could share a flat, although he also acknowledged that it might be easier on him if they continued to live separately. *At least until he's single.*

'How's the flat-hunting going?' he asked.

'Funnily enough, Rags just told me a friend of ours from school has found somewhere with a couple of spare rooms. I'm going for a viewing at the weekend.'

'Great. Well, I hope it suits.'

'Yeah, me too.' Guy let out a sigh. 'And I guess I'll deal with Drew after that.'

2022

Danny and Guy rush into the restaurant. 'I'm so sorry!' says Danny, panting. 'It's my fault – I completely lost track of time.'

Emma stands up to greet them. She still has her thick mane of copper hair, although her skin is more lined than it used to be and she gave up on the heavy eyeliner shortly after university, around the same time as she ditched the snakebite and black.

'I'll let you off,' she says. 'But only because I haven't seen you for so long.'

The force of her Glaswegian accent hits Danny all over again, although it's softened since their time at university. Once he's given her a hug, he moves down the table to shake hands with her husband, Richard.

Richard and Emma have been together for almost fifteen years, after meeting at an advertising and branding agency for which they both worked. Emma had ended up staying on in Manchester, as shortly after graduation she'd been offered an entry-level position selling advertising space in the *Manchester Evening News* – and from there had moved on to the job in which she met Richard. He's a handsome man, with black hair and a neatly trimmed beard. He's also placid, which makes him the perfect partner for Emma. Or at least he's placid in public; Emma's fond of telling Danny that he isn't remotely like that in the bedroom. *But I imagine she won't go into that today – not when we're with the kids.*

Sitting at the table scribbling on a menu is Scarlett, who's four years old and has Emma's distinctive red hair, and asleep in a pram is Jack, who's just turned nine months. Once Danny has peered in on the baby and told Emma how adorable he is, he hands over two presents. Although he bought them both himself, he tells her they're from him and Guy. Then he worries that this sounds like he's positioning himself as Guy's boyfriend. *Which, of course, I am – I just don't want it to be so blatant.*

Scarlett snatches her present from Emma and begins ripping off the wrapping paper. She yanks out a unicorn-themed colouring-in book with a packet of bronze, silver and gold felt-tipped pens, and squeals with delight. Ignoring her mum's instruction to say thank you, she begins colouring in one of the pictures as Emma opens the baby's present – a sailor's outfit.

'Well, we *are* here for Pride,' Danny jokes.

Emma lets out a laugh. 'I love it,' she says, holding up the outfit. She promises to try it on Jack as soon as he wakes up.

As they sit down and look at the menus, Emma tells them Scarlett won't be eating as she has to stick to regular meal times. 'I was up to give her breakfast at seven,' she says. 'And aye, I'm aware of how boring that sounds. God knows what my younger self would make of it – she'd probably want to take me into a field and shoot me.'

They laugh and a waitress pops over to take their order. Danny fancies a full English breakfast but remembers how self-conscious he was getting out of bed this morning so opts instead for smoked salmon and scrambled eggs.

'And what would everyone like to drink?' asks the waitress.

'I'll have a Bellini!' blurts out Emma.

Richard looks at her and raises an eyebrow. 'I guess that means I'm driving, darling?'

'Don't drink-shame me!' Emma says, pretending to be insulted. 'It's important to show the kids I have a life. As a feminist, I don't want them to think the sole point of my existence is to look after them.'

Richard smirks. 'Yes, of course, you're drinking because you're a feminist.'

'You know me,' says Emma, with a mischievous glint in her eye. 'I'm *very* committed to my principles.'

Once Danny and Guy have ordered two more Bellinis, Danny asks how the family are settling into the house they recently bought. He chooses his questions carefully, hoping Emma's answers might offer Guy glimpses into the kind of life the two of them could share. *Not that I particularly want kids or anything but I know he does. And Emma used to be wild and I've been wild; I want him to see that people can change, that we can all evolve.*

As Emma launches into a long moan about Jack's inability to sleep for more than a few hours and his recurrent bouts of thrush, Danny oohs and aahs sympathetically. But it all sounds so undesirable he eventually zones out and allows his imagination to accelerate. He pictures himself sipping a glass of white wine, relaxing on a plush swing seat in the beautiful gardens of a stylish London townhouse, while a shirtless, sun-kissed Guy cooks delicious cuts of marinated meat on a barbecue, and three impossibly cute toddlers run around, giggling.

'Three Bellinis and one orange juice.'

Everyone takes their drinks from the waitress and they clink them together.

'Anyway, never mind about our life,' Emma says. 'Tell me all your news.'

Danny updates her on some of the deals he's done at work recently and jokes about the latest exploits of 'Demandy Mandy'. But he struggles to finish his sentences because Scarlett keeps interrupting. He takes a swig of his Bellini and tries not to show his irritation.

'Scarlett,' Richard says patiently, 'the grown-ups are talking. You be quiet and do your colouring in.'

'And what about Lance Forster?' Emma asks. 'Do you still look after him?'

Danny begins telling her about Lance Forster having an affair with his lookalike but before long Scarlett interrupts again.

Actually, I definitely don't want kids. The fantasy in Danny's head shifts to a scene in which he and Guy are in the garden of the same townhouse but making mad, passionate love on the neatly manicured lawn, then sipping white wine on the swing seat as the sun slowly sets.

'Scarlett, darling,' Richard says, 'why don't you show me what you're colouring in?'

The little girl tips the book towards him.

'Oh, that's nice. And you haven't gone over any lines.'

When she picks up another felt-tip to resume her colouring, Danny continues his story. 'So I met this lookalike the other day and I swear to God the two of them are practically identical. From now on, I'm going to call him—'

'Mummy, I'm bored!' interrupts Scarlett.

Oh, for fuck's sake!

Emma lets out an exasperated groan and clings onto the table as if to stop herself from losing her temper. Danny knows she doesn't like shouting, as she hated growing up in a house dominated by it – until her parents finally divorced shortly after her graduation. But right now she's clearly struggling to hold back. 'I swear to God that girl can't shut up for two minutes. And to think of all the sacrifices I made to have her. I haven't slept properly in years and my tits look like two cricket balls in a pair of tights.'

Danny laughs but he isn't sure if that's the appropriate response. The fantasies in his head come to an abrupt halt.

Emma turns to Scarlett. 'Go on,' she says, 'go and have a run around or something.'

Scarlett shoots up out of her seat and begins charging down the aisles, wailing at the top of her voice.

Emma turns back to Danny. 'Sorry, what was it you were saying?'

'Oh, nothing,' Danny replies. 'Work's going really well, basically. Things have properly picked up since the pandemic.'

Before he can go any further, Scarlett is back at the table. 'Mummy, I want a poo!'

Almost simultaneously, the sound of crying blares out of Jack's pram. Emma cradles her head in her hands. After a few seconds, she looks up and downs half her drink in one gulp. When she hauls herself onto her feet, she looks grey with exhaustion.

Richard jumps up. 'I'll take her, darling. You settle the baby and chat to the boys.'

Emma gives him a weak smile. She checks on Jack and discovers his dummy has fallen out and just needs putting back in. At which point her smile brightens. 'I can't believe it,' she says. 'Peace – finally!'

She sits back at the table. 'Right, where were we?'

Danny corrugates his brow. He's forgotten all about showing Guy a vision of their future together and is concerned about Emma. 'Are you sure you're alright, babe?'

'Aye, don't worry about me. This is normal. This is family life.' She drains her glass dry. 'I wouldn't care but I only wanted one baby.'

'Oh. So was Jack unplanned?' asks Guy.

Emma leans towards them, a twinkle in her eye. 'Richard might look like the sweet, sensitive type but he's an animal in the bedroom; I only got pregnant because he banged me so hard he dislodged my coil.'

The three of them roar with laughter and, just like that, the Emma they both know and love is back.

She shouts over to the waitress, 'Three more Bellinis, please!'

Danny looks at Guy and grins.

'Anyway, never mind my sex life,' she says. 'Tell me about yours.'

Danny trains his eyes on the table. Suddenly, he daren't look at Guy.

'What are you looking so embarrassed about?' Emma says. 'You normally can't wait to tell me about your latest pull. Go on, who was he?'

'Oh . . . You know . . . I've not really . . .' Danny can feel the heat flooding his face.

When the waitress reappears with their drinks, he grabs hold of his like a drowning man reaching for a life raft.

'Come on,' Emma persists, 'when you walked in here you were grinning from ear to ear. I can recognise that post-sex glow when I see it. So who was he?'

'No-one, I was just excited to see you!' Danny attempts. 'And, you know, it's Pride, the sun's shining . . .'

'As if you've ever given a fuck about the sun shining.'

Thankfully, Guy comes to his rescue. 'Hey, what's this I see on Facebook about Lynsey having a new man?'

'Yeah, they've been together for six months now,' Emma says. 'She met him on an app. He's called Ben and he's a teacher. He's nice, I like him.'

Guy strokes the stem of his glass. 'Danny, I still don't understand why you and Lynsey fell out.'

Oh God, not this!

'That doesn't matter now,' Danny trills. 'It was ages ago!'

Guy frowns. 'Yeah, but whatever it was, surely it's not so bad you can't patch it up? For old times' sake?'

'Now that you two are here in Manchester, it does feel like she's missing,' Emma chips in. 'Don't you think?'

Funnily enough, I do.

Funnily enough, I would like to see her.

But Danny remembers what happened the last time he saw Lynsey. It was seven years ago and one of the most distressing days of his life. Then his memory flashes further back, to graduation day and their vow to stay friends for ever. The guilt swells inside him.

'Why don't you pop round and see her while you're in town?' Emma persists.

Danny waves away the suggestion. 'We've already got loads on, babe. I'm not sure we could fit it in.'

Just then, Richard comes back to the table with Scarlett. 'All done,' he announces.

'I just had a poo!' shouts Scarlett.

'Good girl,' says Emma, her earlier impatience erased. 'Now would you like to sit down and have something to eat with Mummy?'

Scarlett nods. 'Yes, please.'

Emma leans in to Danny. 'Forget the routine,' she whispers. 'Those Bellinis have kicked in and I couldn't give a fuck.'

2022

An hour later, Danny flashes his wristband at a steward and stands back as he opens the barrier. They're at the top of Liverpool Road, just in front of the junction with Deansgate; Beetham Tower, which houses the Hilton Hotel, reaches up into the sky behind them. Once he and Guy have slid through the barrier, they pause to take in the scene.

Stretching out before them are thousands of people preparing to take part in the parade. Waiting to head up the procession is a float on which are gathered several members of the cast of *Coronation Street*, many of them doing interviews with TV news crews. Behind them stand floats run by each of the bars and restaurants situated in the Gay Village, gay and lesbian sports clubs, LGBTQ+ charities and youth groups, and queer staff representing Manchester-based shops and businesses and each branch of the Emergency Services and Armed Forces. Danny has no idea what the theme of this year's parade is supposed to be, but he spots people dressed up as characters from *Star Wars*, as well as Freddie Mercury at Live Aid, David Bowie as Ziggy Stardust, and Elton John wearing a 1970s feather-lined cat-suit and diamante-encrusted sunglasses.

'This is insane,' says Danny.

'I know,' says Guy, 'I had no idea there'd be this many people.'

They edge their way into the crowd and down the street. Music is pumping out of each float, the bassline, beats and vocals from one sound system blending into the next, competing with the sound of steel drums, brass bands, a barbershop quartet and a male-voice choir. People are taking selfies or posing for photographs, rehearsing or even devising the choreography for dance routines, and gobbling down last-minute snacks and meals. There's a queue of women waiting for the Portaloos, a line of men urinating down an alleyway, and a steady stream of people emerging from the White Lion and Oxnoble pubs clutching bunches of drinks in plastic glasses.

'Do you know where our group's meeting?' asks Danny.

Guy frowns. 'Sorry, I didn't ask.'

They've signed up to march with AKT, a charity that supports young homeless people whose families have thrown them out for being LGBTQ+. Guy is one of the charity's major donors and often helps them out with free legal advice, which is why they've invited him on the march. They've also provided him with a pair of T-shirts bearing the charity's logo that he and Danny slipped on before leaving the hotel.

'Well, do you have anyone's number?' Danny asks, rubbing his stubble. 'Is there anyone we can call?'

Guy grimaces. 'Sorry, it didn't occur to me. But I do remember we're group ninety-seven.'

They press on, scanning all the placards that are being waved in the air and looking out for number ninety-seven.

'Twenty-eight, thirty-five, forty-three . . .' Danny reads. 'We're getting closer.'

They pass a group of drag queens dressed in sequinned leotards and feathered headdresses and weave their way through a group of fetishists who are wearing dog masks, Speedos and thigh-high PVC boots, some of them pulling others along on leads. As they slowly inch forwards, Danny smiles at everyone, then remembers he was planning to keep his head down, at least until they've found their position in the parade – because there's someone taking part that he doesn't want to see. And that's Guy's ex-boyfriend, Spencer.

He knows Spencer's there because on the train journey he saw a social media post in which he announced that he was going to be dancing on a float promoting the launch of a new hook-up app. *As if the gay community needs another one of those.*

Not that it matters to Danny *what* Spencer's promoting; all that matters is he doesn't want to see him again – and he doesn't want Guy to see him either.

He spots a steward and tramps over to him. 'Excuse me, we're looking for group number ninety-seven.'

The steward explains that all the walking parties are assembling on the lawn by the ruins of the Roman fort. He points them in the right direction.

It's already hot and volunteers are handing out rainbow fans that many people are using to cool themselves down. Danny grabs one and fans himself as they pass a female vicar and a group of nuns he assumes to be in fancy dress, then wonders if they might actually be members of an LGBTQ+ Christian group. On the corner of the street, they come across a fire engine operated by a group of gay firemen who are being mobbed by so many admirers they daren't step out of the vehicle. Banging on the door is an overweight drag queen in badly laddered tights and what looks like a chemotherapy wig.

'I'm on fire!' she yells. 'Somebody put me out!'

Danny erupts in laughter. Then, just as he rounds the corner, he falls silent.

Fuck, there he is.

There's Spencer!

All of a sudden, he can taste acid at the back of his throat. The worst thing is, Spencer's standing so close that – even though he's wearing sunglasses – Danny can't pretend he hasn't seen him.

'Spencer,' he croons, 'fancy bumping into you here!'

But despite his smile, he's already feeling inadequate and unattractive. Despite having spent the night with Guy, he's already feeling like he isn't good enough for him. And despite having allowed himself to think that they might just have a future together, suddenly the idea seems completely implausible.

2005

'Spencer? Who's Spencer?'

Danny was following Guy through the streets of West London, clutching the A–Z he'd picked up at Euston station and pulling along the brand new wheelie suitcase he hoped made him look like a chic, well-seasoned traveller. They'd met outside Fulham Broadway tube station and were walking to Guy's flat, where Danny had arranged to stay for the weekend while he went to a series of interviews for bar jobs.

It had been nearly a month since Guy had split up with Drew and Danny was pretty sure enough time had elapsed for him to no longer be upset or on the rebound. Danny was trying to stay calm but the thought of what he was hoping would happen later made the fear flutter in his stomach. At least for the moment he could enjoy the simple pleasure of seeing Guy again. The only thing was, Guy couldn't stop talking about some man called Spencer.

'He's the cousin of a friend of mine from school,' Guy explained, 'and one of my new flatmates.'

Guy went on to say that Spencer worked in a gym as a personal trainer, and had given him a few training sessions and educated him about the latest protein shakes and muscle-building supplements on the market. Danny zoned out and gazed around him at the rows of beautiful white townhouses, with flash cars parked outside. *I wonder how much each of these costs.*

'Now don't get excited,' Guy cautioned, 'my street isn't anywhere near as nice as this.'

They turned into a crescent that was only marginally less glamorous than the one they'd left, with houses that Danny imagined to be worth more than the entire row of terraces where he was currently living with his mum in Barrow. He tried to look blasé, as if none of it struck him as anything out of the ordinary.

'Oh and Spencer's been taking me out in Soho,' Guy added. 'The gay scene in London's really cool.'

Danny could feel his bones sharpen. 'Oh, so he's gay, is he, this Spencer?'

'Sorry, did I not mention that? Yeah, he's gay.'

Shit. He hasn't stopped talking about this bloke and now he's gay . . .

'Not that you'd be able to tell,' Guy pointed out. 'He's kind of like me – very straight-acting.'

'Straight-acting'. Danny had come across this term on Gaydar, the website on which users set up a profile to meet other gay men in their area, mainly for no-strings-attached sex. While perusing the site, he'd noticed how many users were keen to stipulate that they were only attracted to gay men who acted as if they were straight – something that immediately ruled him out.

But does Guy find it attractive?

He'd certainly never mentioned it before, but now that Danny thought about it, Drew was quite straight-acting and so, apparently, was this Spencer.

A cold slick of dread passed through him.

Oh my God, don't tell me Guy fancies him . . .

What if something's already going on between them?

'Here we are,' announced Guy, gesturing to an enormous four-storey house. 'We've got the top two floors, number 36C.'

As Danny felt the unease shift in his chest, he fell back on a familiar strategy. '36C? That sounds like a bra size.'

Guy laughed. 'Danny, you are hilarious. Spencer's going to love you!'

My God, can you not stop talking about this bloke for just one minute?

Guy opened the door and led them into a communal hallway, up two flights of stairs and through another door that led to their flat. As soon as they stepped inside, they bumped into Rags.

'Danny!' he said. 'Good to see you, mate!'

They came together in an awkward hug.

'You too,' Danny lied, immediately feeling inadequate.

'So you made it down OK?' asked Rags.

'Yeah, why shouldn't I?'

'Well, just that you had to catch the Tube, that's all. I wasn't sure how you'd cope with a train that goes underground. You don't have those up north, do you?'

Oh God, here we go . . .

'No, we don't actually,' Danny said, breezily, 'or at least not anywhere I've been. But don't worry, I coped.'

'I suppose it reminded you of going *down t'pit*, did it?'

Danny unleashed a wintry smile. 'There aren't any pits in Barrow, babe.'

Rags gave a little cheer. 'B*aaa*be! Oh, I've missed that! Danny, you are priceless!'

Guy intervened. 'Give it a rest, Rags. Danny's been travelling for four hours – I'm sure he isn't in the mood.'

Rags backed away down the corridor, shaking his head and chuckling to himself. 'B*aa*be! B*aa*be!'

Guy invited Danny to follow him into his room, where he suggested he leave his suitcase. Like every other room Guy had lived in, it was devoid of personal touches and still had some of his belongings packed away in boxes. There was a pile of sports equipment in the corner, a gym kit hanging on a radiator and several pairs of shiny new dumbbells strewn across the floor. The walls were bare, although Danny's eye was drawn to a single photo that had been stuck on the wardrobe door. It was the photo Arthur had taken of Guy, Danny, Emma and Lynsey on their graduation day, a copy of which Danny had sent to Guy in the post. The sight of it gave him a surge in confidence.

'Well, this is cosy,' he chirped.

'Thanks,' said Guy. 'Dump your stuff wherever you like.'

Danny stashed his suitcase next to the double bed, the bed he was hoping to share with Guy, the bed in which he was hoping the two of them would 'accidentally' get carried away. *Although first I have to find out what's going on with this flatmate . . .*

'So when do I meet the famous Spencer?' he asked.

Guy looked at his watch. 'Oh, he'll be back in five minutes. Why don't we have a coffee while we're waiting?'

He led Danny through to the kitchen, excited to show him his new coffee machine. They entered a well-equipped but messy room and Guy proudly gave a demonstration of how the machine worked. When he handed Danny a finished cup, he smiled in expectation of the verdict.

'Mmm, this is lovely,' Danny said, obligingly.

From the corridor came the sound of a door opening and closing.

Guy's eyes began to sparkle. 'That'll be Spencer.'

Danny turned to the doorway and in walked a handsome young man wearing low-rise jeans, Adidas trainers, a Livestrong wristband, and an achingly fashionable Von Dutch trucker cap. He had the same light brown hair as Drew and just as cute a face, although his chest and arms were much bigger, something he'd chosen to accentuate by wearing a T-shirt that looked like it had been stretched over his muscles.

Danny felt something fall through him.

'Hi, hon,' Spencer said to Guy.

'Hello, hello,' said Guy. And he gestured to Danny. 'Spencer, this is Danny. Danny, meet Spencer.'

Danny wasn't sure whether to hug or kiss him but ended up shaking his hand, then wishing he hadn't been so formal. Already he was feeling reduced in stature and his confidence had deserted him. He went to tug his hand through his hair but this only reminded him that it was thinning. *Whereas Spencer has thick, luscious, shiny hair.*

'Good to meet you,' Spencer said in a voice that revealed he was from a similarly upper middle-class background to Guy. 'Guy's told me so much about you.'

Danny winched his mouth into a smile. 'He's told me a lot about you too.'

Not that I wanted to hear it.

Spencer reached up to slide his gym bag onto a shelf and his T-shirt rode up to reveal the sharp V of his stomach muscles. Danny suddenly became conscious of his own gut straining at his jeans. *Oh, why do I have to be so fat and ugly?*

'Do you want a coffee?' Guy asked Spencer. 'We're just having one.'

'Thanks, hon,' replied Spencer, 'that'd be major.'

Guy busied himself making another drink while Danny asked Spencer about his job and pretended to be interested as he talked him through every last detail of some workout he'd just done with a client. Once the coffee was ready, Guy suggested they move through to the living room.

This had a sofa and armchair that were covered in blue throws and the crumbs left by someone's breakfast. There was a huge stereo with a towering stack of CDs on either side, a DVD player standing on a unit that was bursting with DVDs, and some kind of games console plugged into the bottom of an enormous free-standing TV, the controls spread out on the floor around it. A few plants had been plonked onto the windowsill in uncovered plastic pots, and over an ornamental ceramic fireplace hung that famous black and white photo of construction workers eating their lunch sitting on a girder high above Manhattan, which was slotted into a basic clip frame. Guy dropped himself onto the sofa and Spencer sat next to him, leaving Danny the armchair. He suddenly felt like the odd one out.

'You know, I called at Manchester on my way down,' he said to Guy, hoping he didn't sound desperate. 'I saw Emma and Lynsey and we went out on Canal Street.'

He began telling Guy about their night out but could sense he wasn't really interested. He quickly changed the subject. 'How's the job going? Are you still enjoying it?'

Guy nodded. 'Yeah, it's cool, thanks.'

He told Danny about his office near Victoria, the work he was doing, and some of the new friends he'd made. 'The only thing is, everyone assumes I'm straight. So every time I meet someone I have to come out all over again.'

'Oh yeah,' said Danny, 'I'd never thought of that.'

'You know, in some ways it's easier for people like you,' chipped in Spencer.

Danny tried not to bridle at the comment. 'Oh yeah? Why's that?'

'Well, just that everyone can tell you're gay, so you don't have to keep coming out all the time.'

Danny felt a flash of annoyance. *Try growing up in a rough northern town where everyone can tell you're gay. Try going on public transport or walking past a building site.* Then *do you want to tell me it's easy?*

He took a sip of his coffee. 'Oh, I don't know about easy,' he managed, 'I think the challenges are probably just different.'

A silence curdled between them.

'Anyway, what are we doing tonight?' asked Danny. 'Are we having a big one or what?'

'I thought we'd go into Soho,' said Guy, 'I thought you might like to see how it compares to Canal Street.'

Danny nodded. 'Sounds good to me.'

'Soho's major,' Spencer added. 'You'll love it, hon.'

Oh yeah? And since when do you know me so well?

Danny ignored him and looked at Guy. 'So what's the plan, babe? Which bars are we going to?'

It was Spencer who answered. 'We're going to start in the Edge – I've arranged to meet some friends there.'

What, so you're coming with us?

'Then we thought we'd go on to Escape or Barcode,' Spencer continued. 'That's right, isn't it, hon?'

For God's sake, this 'hon' thing is really starting to annoy me.

'It is, yeah,' answered Guy.

'Then maybe after that we'll go on to Heaven or Wig Out or G-A-Y. Or Popstarz is major.'

According to you, everything's 'major'.

But Guy didn't seem remotely irritated. In fact, whenever Spencer spoke, his eyes glistened at him. *OK, now I really need to know what's going on between you two.*

Very soon Danny got his answer.

As Guy was relating a story about their last trip to Popstarz, Spencer leaned towards him and picked something off his T-shirt. He held it up in the air to examine before dropping it in the bin. 'Sorry, hon, you just had a piece of fluff on you,' he explained.

But Guy didn't even flinch, as if Spencer touching him was the most natural thing in the world. In that moment, Danny understood that the two of them were in an intimate relationship. He understood that they were sleeping together. And all the happiness leaked out of him.

I just can't believe it. I can't believe this is happening to me again!

In an instant, the night before him flashed through his head. He saw himself pretending to have fun with Spencer's friends while Spencer and Guy began pawing each other and kissing. After a few drinks, they'd start to feel horny and announce that they were too tired to go to a club and would rather head home. He'd have no choice but to follow and, once they were back at the flat, Guy and Spencer would slip upstairs to Spencer's room, leaving Danny to sleep in Guy's bed alone, alone with the scent of Guy on his pillow, alone to contemplate his fantasies about drunken accidents unfolding and he and Guy becoming a couple, fantasies that would be completely shattered by the end of the long, miserable, spirit-sapping weekend.

Danny could feel the sadness burning a hole within him. *If only I'd come down to London before Spencer got in there.*

Then he was hit by a wave of self-loathing. *Come on, Danny, Guy would never be attracted to you. You're a balding, hairy, fat bastard who's got no money and is currently living with his mum in a terraced house in Barrow. You're nowhere near as good-looking as Spencer, you're nowhere near as fashionable, and nobody would ever call you straight-acting.*

He imagined Spencer sensing his feelings for Guy and laughing to himself, laughing at him for being such a stupid, deluded, tragic loser.

Oh, Danny, your own dad wasn't interested in you.

Then he remembered some advice Arthur had given him on one of their most recent walks.

'When you come up against any knocks in life, do whatever you have to – cry or scream or bang your head against the wall if you have to – but then straighten out your crown, get back out there and keep going.'

Even though Danny felt like he was almost suffocating with sorrow, he knew this was exactly what he was going to do.

2022

Guy is taken aback by the sight of Spencer.

'Spencer!' he splutters. 'I didn't know you were going to be in Manchester.'

At that moment, stomping through the crowd comes a man dressed as a pirate, complete with a hook in the place of his left hand and a stuffed parrot perched on his shoulder. Guy recovers from his shock enough to lean in and give Spencer a hug.

'Yeah, I'm doing some promotional work,' Spencer says. 'I don't just PT anymore: because of my Instagram following, I get gigs like this on the side.'

Guy leans back to look at his costume: he's dressed as a boxer in a pair of silk shorts and heavy padded gloves, his muscular chest exposed to the sunlight. *That brings back memories . . .*

He also notices Spencer's wearing sliders with thick white sports socks, a fashion Guy thinks doesn't just look daft but has to be seriously impractical. *Is he really going to march through Manchester like that?*

'Well, urm, that's great,' he manages. He feels uneasy and is glad he's able to hide behind his sunglasses.

Thankfully, Danny steps in to steer the conversation. 'So are you an influencer now?' he asks, as he uses a rainbow flag to waft a breeze onto himself.

Spencer shrugs. 'Oh, I don't know. I get sent freebies and do paid posts. But I tend to do more bod pics and thirst traps – I make much more money from my OnlyFans.'

Guy's shocked to hear that Spencer earns a living by charging people to see X-rated videos of himself – so shocked that he can't think of any response.

Fortunately, Danny steps in again. 'How enterprising,' he comments. 'I hear you can make a killing if you've got the bod for it.'

Guy's about to tell Spencer that he certainly has the body for it; he's in even better shape now than he was when they were together. Then he remembers what happened between him and Danny last night.

'Well, I hope you get lots of attention in the parade,' he attempts. 'I hope you pick up lots of new subscribers.'

Guy can't believe he's even having this conversation. He remembers how quickly he fell for Spencer when he first moved to London and how unexpected this was when he was still getting over his break-up with Drew. But he'd been stunned that someone as attractive as Spencer could fancy him and felt powerless to resist a desire that had him completely gripped. All of a sudden, he'd fallen in love again – and the emotion had hit him with just as much force as it had first time around. *But how weird that I could have felt so strongly about someone, then fifteen years later feel nothing.*

He kneads his knuckles as the man dressed as the pirate stomps past again.

'Number eighteen,' the man calls out, 'does anyone know where number eighteen is?'

'What number are you?' Danny asks Spencer.

'Fifty-six,' he replies.

Danny frowns. 'In that case we're miles away from each other. We're ninety-seven.'

'Oh, that's a shame,' says Spencer. He turns back to Guy. 'Funnily enough, I was thinking about you the other day. I heard you were single again. I hope you're alright, hon.'

Guy sighs. 'Yeah, it's been more than a year now. And we've been divorced for a couple of months.'

He's about to say that he's actually enjoying being single, then remembers what happened last night. *I've got to get my head around this. I've got to work out what to do next.*

'But it's cool,' he adds, vaguely. 'I'm fine with it.'

Spencer nods. 'Good to hear it.'

There's an uncomfortable pause.

'Oh and I've got a new man,' pipes Spencer. 'He's a PT I met at a circuit party. He's got an OnlyFans too. Honestly, the bod's unreal.'

Guy smiles. 'Fantastic. I'm really happy for you.'

Spencer turns to Danny. 'I take it you're still single?'

Danny fans himself more vigorously. 'Well, I . . . I don't know . . . I wouldn't say . . .'

'I *knew* it!' says Spencer. 'You're going to be like the gay Hugh Hefner. You'll *never* stop shagging around!'

Now it's Guy's turn to step in and save Danny's embarrassment. 'Oh, I wouldn't be so sure, Spencer. You never know what's going to happen.'

Why did I just say that? What do I even mean?

'Spencer!' shouts a voice from behind him.

Guy turns around to see that it's coming from a shaven-headed black man who's also dressed as a boxer and has an even more muscular physique than Spencer.

'Come on,' the man shouts, 'we're about to start moving!'

Spencer quickly says goodbye and gives them both a kiss on the cheek.

Once he's gone, Danny turns to Guy and opens his mouth to say something. But Guy doesn't want to dissect what just happened. He doesn't want to compare the person he is now with the person he was when he went out with Spencer. He doesn't want Danny to tell him that he could see through Spencer all along – or that everyone thought he was a fool. So he jumps in quickly and tells Danny they should hurry up and find their group.

'Alright,' Danny replies, 'let's go.'

They thread their way through the various walking parties that are assembling on the lawn. They pass a team of chubby gay footballers from Chester and political and community support groups campaigning for an end to the stigma around HIV, equal rights for trans people, and better support for LGBTQ+ asylum seekers. Standing in the centre of the ruins is a man dressed in full drag as Dorothy from *The Wizard of Oz*, complete with gingham dress, ruby slippers and a real-life Toto the dog that several people are stopping to stroke.

Before long, they find AKT and Guy greets the staff and introduces them to Danny. In turn, they're introduced to some young people the charity's helping, teenagers whose families have thrown them out of their homes for being gay, lesbian, bisexual or transgender. As he hears their stories, Guy remembers just how scared he was of the same thing happening to him – which is why he started donating to the charity. But he doesn't have much time to chat before a steward beckons their party forward and they're being funnelled down a side street and into the parade.

'Brace yourself!' says Danny.

All of a sudden, they're crossing the start line.

'And we're off!'

As soon as they hit Deansgate, Guy's struck by the sight of thousands of rainbow flags being waved at them. Everywhere he looks, he sees bright, smiling faces, and there are so many people in the crowd they have to be held back behind crash barriers. People are hanging off lamp-posts, leaning out of windows, and standing on the roofs of bus shelters. And everyone's screaming, cheering or blowing whistles, noises that compete with the music blasting out from the various floats. It's all very disorientating and this is only exacerbated by the stifling heat and the glare of the sunlight. *I feel like I've just hit my head and am suffering from concussion. I'm not even 100% sure this is happening.*

Danny looks at him and widens his eyes. 'It's a bit full-on, isn't it?'

Guy's too stunned to say anything but nods in agreement.

As they press on, waving at the crowds, he gradually adjusts to the situation. A statuesque black man wearing nothing but a pink wig and a matching thong totters past him on stilts and wishes him a Happy Pride. Someone – or possibly two people – bounce alongside him in a huge astronaut costume, giving him a high five. And a woman rumbles past, pulling along a trailer carrying a machine that's firing out bubbles. Guy's face fixes into a grin and rivers of adrenaline course through him.

This is amazing. Why did I never do it before?

The group directly in front of AKT is an LGBTQ+ dance troupe whose members are dressed in silver cat suits, performing an energetic routine on and around a float that's the shape of a giant mirror ball. Behind them are the staff of an airline who are in full uniform and pulling along rainbow-coloured wheelie suitcases, surrounding a float that's been transformed into a huge model aeroplane. Every now and then, the pace of the procession slows and the groups bunch together, giving everyone the chance to chat and exchange messages of solidarity.

Just as they're coming to the point where the procession veers off Deansgate, Guy and his group are brought to a stop and he has a brief opportunity to examine the faces in the crowd. As far as he can tell, the majority of the people crammed behind the barriers are straight, many of them clutching drinks they've bought in pubs. He has to stop himself from staggering back from the impact of being caught between two such thick, roaring walls of approval.

I just can't get over it. I've never experienced anything like this in my life.

After less than a minute, the procession starts moving again. Shortly after turning up Peter Street, the atmosphere takes on a more serious tone when they come to a building with a sign identifying it as the Fourth Church of Christ, Scientist. At the side of it is a group of Christians waving banners and telling those taking part in the parade that they're evil and are going to burn in hell.

'Homosexuality is a Sin!' declares one.

'Adam and Eve, not Adam and Steve!' shouts another.

Standing next to them is a counter-protester with a banner that reads, 'Homophobes are Statistically More Likely to be Gay.'

Guy and Danny look at each other and laugh. But the protesters have reminded Guy that the march isn't just a celebration – and it only feels joyous because it's set against a background of persecution, a persecution that everyone taking part must have experienced in some form. *So I don't just feel happy. I feel moved. I feel humbled. And most of all I feel proud.*

As he marches on, he looks at Danny and the emotion he's feeling swells in intensity. He puts his arm around him and kisses him on the forehead.

'I love you, princess,' he shouts. 'I don't think I've ever told you that but I really fucking love you.'

2006

Guy marched around his childhood bedroom, waiting for Danny to arrive. From the floor below, he could hear the sound of his father watching the cricket on TV and his mother issuing orders to the housekeeper. Beneath his feet, the floorboards of the old house creaked. He told himself to stand still or everyone downstairs would be able to tell he was nervous.

Oh, Danny, where are you?

He'd invited Danny to his family home for lunch with his parents. It was nearly three years since Guy had told them he was gay and their coldness towards him still hadn't thawed. They studiously avoided all mention of anything to do with his sexuality, although trying to disguise their disapproval was like applying cover-up to a huge spot, the bump only remaining visible underneath. Guy had made a point of letting them know he had a boyfriend, someone he said he'd met through friends from school, hoping this might arouse their interest and possibly even the start of something approaching approval – but it hadn't. They'd simply ignored it.

Rather than feeling any anger towards his parents, Guy found himself wanting to fight for their acceptance. He remembered how he'd felt when he was sent away to boarding school, how he'd lain in bed feeling abandoned and rejected, and how, even then, he hadn't felt anger but a desire to prove to his parents that he was worthy of their love – or to *make himself* worthy of it. He wondered how much had changed. He sat on his bed and drew in a ragged breath. *Come on, Danny, don't let me down.*

He'd invited Danny in the hope that, if his parents could see him interacting with another gay man, this might make his sexuality seem more real – and they'd realise there was nothing to fear. But he'd decided that this shouldn't be Spencer: it would be too much for them to see him with a sexual partner. In any case, Guy had been seeing Spencer for a year now and, much as his love for him hadn't dimmed, he wasn't sure Spencer had the intellectual capacity to handle his parents. *To be fair, they'd probably eat him alive.*

Danny, on the other hand, would be much more able to defend himself and was much brighter and more quick-witted. Now that Guy thought about it, he was also more charming and fun. *You never know, if things go well, my mother and father may even surprise themselves by* liking *him.*

It was only as this thought occurred to him that he realised just how much he wanted them to like Danny. He could only assume this was why he was in such an anxious state.

And he did realise he was asking a lot of Danny. But ever since they'd become friends he'd wanted to meet his parents – and to see the house he'd grown up in. When Guy had offered him the opportunity, he'd accepted in an instant.

So why the hell is he late?

He realised he was kneading his knuckles so stood up and

began rearranging his old sports trophies and academic awards. Suddenly, he felt overwhelmed by the futility of what he was attempting – and today's lunch seemed pointless. *What if my mother and father hate Danny? What if this only makes things worse?*

Then another thought occurred to him. *What if Danny hates them?*

He felt a trickle of sweat run down his back. He looked at his watch and saw that Danny was nearly an hour late. *But this is so unlike him.*

Guy had originally arranged to pick Danny up from the station, but Danny had texted to say he'd missed his train and would come straight to the house. He hadn't given away any more details and Guy hadn't wanted to ask. Realising he was kneading his knuckles again, he went over to the book shelves and straightened out his old books.

Oh, I just want him to get here now. I just want to get on with this.

The doorbell rang.

Guy shot out of the bedroom and raced down the stairs.

As Danny heard the sound of someone thundering down the stairs, he took a swig from a bottle of water and hoped his hangover would clear soon.

God, why do I do this to myself?

When the door was flung open, a flustered-looking Guy appeared, wearing chino shorts, a plain white T-shirt and flip-flops. 'Hello, hello,' he said.

'Hi, babe,' said Danny.

Guy threw his arms around him and hugged him much more tightly than usual. *It looks like I'm not the only one feeling nervous.*

'Are you alright?' Danny asked.

'Yeah, I'm cool. It's just good to see you, that's all.'

Danny forced out a smile. His tongue was so dry it was sticking to the roof of his mouth and his head was throbbing so violently he could see stars. *Oh, how could I have let this happen, today of all days?*

'Shall I take my shoes off?' he asked as he stepped into the hall.

'No, don't worry, we'll go straight through to the garden.'

Guy gestured for him to follow, but they'd only gone two steps when he stopped and put a hand on Danny's arm. 'Just a minute, what's that smell?'

Danny said he couldn't smell anything. *Then again, I smoked so many cigs last night I've probably lost all sense of smell.*

Thick lines appeared on Guy's forehead. 'You haven't stood in dog shit, have you?'

Danny looked at the soles of his shoes. 'Fuck, yeah, I have.'

With a rush of panic, he saw there was a trail of dog dirt running from the door to where he was standing. He must have stepped in it on the pavement when he got out of the cab. *God, this is all I need . . .*

This was shaping up to be one of the worst weeks of Danny's life. Over the last seven days, he'd auditioned for several jobs and been rejected from them all. His self-belief was running lower than at any point since graduation, as were his finances. He'd just transferred his rapidly mounting debt onto yet another interest-free credit card, with no idea of how he was ever going to pay it off. He'd been so worried he'd accepted every shift his boss had offered him in the bar where he worked in Soho. Then yesterday his agent Heather had called to tell him she'd heard that a job for which he'd been recalled, a job he'd thought he stood a strong chance of getting, had been offered to a different actor – a better-looking, middle-class, straight actor, with a full head of hair. Danny had been devastated and had ended up going out with some friends after work on a drunken rampage that had only finished at 4 a.m., when he'd remembered what he was supposed to be doing in a few hours and had caught the night bus home. But half a bottle of wine had been waiting for him on his kitchen table so – despite himself – he'd carried on drinking and had made the mistake of firing up his computer and logging onto Gaydar. At 5.30 a.m. he'd hooked up with a man whose profile name was *@mascdude32*. After grabbing a couple of hours sleep, he'd rushed to the station but missed his train, forcing him to catch a taxi he couldn't afford. He'd arrived at Guy's more than an hour late, worrying that he smelled of alcohol and cigarettes. *And to top it all, I've just trailed shit into the house.*

'Babe, I'm so sorry,' he yowled, his eyes bulging. 'I had no idea.'

Thankfully, most of the dirt was smeared on the welcome mat. 'Don't worry,' said Guy, 'that's what mats are for.'

'What are mats for?'

Danny looked up to see Guy's mum entering the hallway. Before he could say anything, the smell registered on her face.

'Actually, don't tell me,' she said, pulling her cardigan around her. 'I can smell for myself.'

'Smell what?' said Guy's dad, stepping in beside her.

'Nothing,' Guy bleated. 'We've just had a little accident.'

Even in the midst of his corrugating shame, Danny couldn't help feeling touched by Guy's use of the word 'we'.

'Crikey!' said Guy's dad. 'That really is rank.'

'It's definitely a job for Maria,' said Guy's mum, shouting the name down the hallway.

Scurrying in almost immediately came a stout Spanish woman

dressed in overalls, who Guy explained was the family's housekeeper. Danny held out his shoe and showed her the dirt. He wasn't sure he'd ever felt so wretched.

I've wanted to meet Guy's parents for so long – I can't believe this is how it's finally happening.

'Maria will take care of this,' brayed Guy's mum. 'Just leave your shoes on the mat and come through to the kitchen.'

Danny did as he was told and joined Guy in washing his hands at the sink.

'Sorry,' Guy said, drying himself on a tea towel, 'in the midst of all that I forgot to introduce you. Danny, this is my mother, Cynthia. And this is my father, Stephen.'

Danny wanted to offer them a hand but they were both wet. 'Pleased to meet you,' he said, meekly.

'Pleased to meet you too,' they both said, neither of them sounding like they meant it.

As he contemplated their expressions of distaste, Danny remembered how thrilled he'd been when Guy had invited him to meet them – how thrilled he'd been when he realised he'd been chosen over Spencer. *I don't understand how I've managed to make such a mess of things.*

'Well, this is a gorgeous place!' he tweeted, drying his hands as he looked around at a vast kitchen that had to be twice the size of his London flat. The cupboards were painted duck-egg blue and there were various dried grasses arranged in vases and an overhead clothes rack from which hung a set of copper-bottomed pans. There was a chunky pine table positioned against one wall and something he was pretty sure was an AGA standing against another.

Cynthia and Stephen launched into a detailed account of the

history of the house and Danny nodded, feigning fascination. But his hangover was raging and he could feel the sweat beading on his forehead and forming patches under his arms.

'Guy, why don't you show Danny around?' suggested Cynthia. 'And give him some flip-flops while you're at it. We'll see you in the garden.'

Thank God for that.

Once Guy had found him some footwear, he led Danny upstairs, past a long wall on which hung various photos of the family skiing and on expensive-looking beach holidays, and childhood pictures of Guy and his brother Barney taken in photographers' studios. Danny dared to imagine what the wall would look like with a picture of him hanging on it, maybe even a formal portrait of him and Guy together.

Come on, Danny, you can still do this; you can turn it around!

On the upper floor, Guy pointed out several bathrooms and guest rooms and led him to the bedroom he'd occupied as a child, which had exposed wooden beams running along the vaulted ceiling and a single bed in the corner. Danny tried not to imagine the teenage Guy lying in it, masturbating over the underwear section of his mum's Next Directory.

They went downstairs and Guy showed him a formal dining room dominated by a table that must have been able to seat twenty people, a living room that had three sofas, an open fireplace and a TV that was the only thing smaller than the one in Danny's family home. *Although I won't mention that in case they think I'm common.*

They went outside and Guy gave Danny a tour of the beautiful gardens, complete with tennis courts and swimming pool. They settled in a spot at the far end, from where Danny had an unbroken view of the rear façade of the house, with its leaded casement windows and a deep red Virginia creeper covering much of the brickwork. It struck him that the differences in financial wealth between him and Guy had become much more pronounced since they'd graduated from university. In some ways, student life had been a leveller: no-one in their peer group had done anything that cost much money, so if one of them had more than the others, it rarely became apparent. It was only now that the lifestyle Danny led was starting to diverge from Guy's; while Guy could afford to dine out in expensive restaurants and jet off for glamorous mini-breaks in Europe, Danny had to stay at home in his grotty flat-share in Mile End, eating endless meals of supermarket value-brand beans on toast and trying to make himself feel better by spotting his street on the map in the opening credits of *EastEnders*. Although he'd steer clear of discussing that today.

He finished his bottle of water and dropped it into the recycling bin. 'Babe, if you don't mind I'm going to have to sit down. I need to put my shades on and try to forget I'm apocalyptically hungover.'

Guy laughed and led him back to the house.

Just as they were approaching, Cynthia called out from the kitchen. 'Would you two like a drink? We're about to have one.'

'Yeah, great!' said Danny, before she'd even finished her sentence.

Guy signalled for him to sit at a wooden table on the paved terrace. As soon as he did, Danny realised he'd positioned himself in the direct glare of the sun. He rummaged around in his pocket but discovered he'd forgotten to bring his sunglasses. A jolt of anxiety shot through him.

'Here we are,' said Cynthia as she emerged from the house, Stephen trotting along behind her. She set down on the table a tray carrying four glasses and a big jug of some kind of gloopy green juice. 'It's apple, elderflower and mint.'

My God, I'd kill for a proper drink.

Danny took a sip. 'Mmm, this is gorgeous,' he said, shielding his eyes from the sun and hoping his anxiety would fade soon.

As Stephen droned on about the new juicer they'd bought, Danny's mind flashed back to the end of last night and his encounter on Gaydar. Since losing most of his hair, he'd tidied up his scalp by buying some clippers and giving himself a close-cropped buzz cut, balancing this out by growing a thin covering of stubble on his face. But when he shared photographs of this on Gaydar, most men expected him to be some kind of hyper-masculine stud – even though he made it quite clear in his profile that he preferred the passive role in the bedroom. Last night, *@mascdude32* hadn't bothered to hide his disappointment on hearing Danny's effeminate voice and realising he didn't match up to his expectations. He'd ended up telling Danny to keep his mouth shut, flipped him around and subjected him to rough, angry sex Danny was surprised to find himself enjoying. But immediately afterwards, *@mascdude32* had bolted from the room as if it had caught fire. Danny had been left feeling empty, used and inadequate, scrabbling around for ways in which he could make the experience work better in anecdote than it had in reality.

Not that he'd be able to share that kind of anecdote now. When Stephen had finished talking about the juicer, Cynthia began detailing the flowers the gardener had planted in the various sections of the grounds.

Danny waited for a gap in the conversation and tossed in, 'Well, it really is beautiful. It must have been a lovely place to grow up.'

'Yeah, it was,' said Guy. 'I was very lucky.'

'Guy tells us you're from Cumbria,' commented Cynthia.

'Yeah, that's right.'

'Stephen and I love the Lake District. Don't we, Stephen?'

'Actually,' Danny interjected, 'Barrow isn't quite the Lake District.'

They ignored his comment and Stephen recounted the various walking holidays they'd enjoyed in the Lakes. 'Which would you say is our favourite, Cynthia? Coniston or Buttermere?'

'I'm actually quite partial to Ullswater.'

'Oh and there's Grasmere, of course,' said Stephen. 'Where you can visit Wordsworth's house.'

'Do you like Wordsworth?' Cynthia asked Danny.

He was about to tell the truth and answer that he couldn't name a single poem by Wordsworth but checked himself. 'Oh, I love Wordsworth,' he gushed. 'He's my favourite poet.'

'Ours too,' said Stephen, enthusiastically.

Danny's eyes flitted over to Guy and he saw how relieved he looked. In that moment, he wanted so desperately to be the one to help his parents get over their disapproval; he wanted so desperately to be the one to bring the family together.

Cynthia looked at her watch. 'Good Lord, is that the time? I'd better tell Maria to serve lunch.'

As she stood up and disappeared into the kitchen, Danny pictured himself joining the family on a walking holiday in the Lake District or on one of those skiing trips he'd seen photographed in the hall. *Maybe if I can really get on with them, Guy will forget all about Spencer and realise it was me he wanted all along . . .*

He told himself not to get carried away and cast the idea out of his head.

As Maria began bringing out the food, Stephen went inside and re-emerged with an ice bucket and a bottle poking out of the top of it.

Oh, please let that be booze . . .

First, Cynthia told them they'd be eating a *salade niçoise* and something called a *frittata* with fresh herbs, neither of which Danny had ever come across in Barrow. *Mind you, that* frittata *looks like an omelette with a bit of veg chucked in – and that* salade niçoise *is basically a tuna salad topped off with boiled eggs and a few spuds.*

'We make our *niçoise* with quails' eggs,' said Cynthia, as if to puncture Danny's positivity. 'Isn't that right, Stephen?'

'Yes,' confirmed Stephen, 'they're a tad richer than hen's eggs.'

Danny smiled but was starting to feel tremendously out of place – and all the squinting wasn't helping his headache. He couldn't think of anything to say about quail's eggs so spooned some of the salad onto his plate.

Stephen stood up and lifted the bottle out of the ice bucket. 'Now, who wants wine?'

'Me, please,' piped Danny.

'I'll do it,' said Guy, taking hold of the bottle. He sloshed a generous measure into Danny's glass and Danny tipped most of it back in one.

'Mmm, this is nice,' he said, as Guy poured much smaller measures for his mum and dad. 'And the quails' eggs are delicious.'

Cynthia and Stephen smiled thinly.

'So Guy tells us you're an actor,' said Cynthia.

'Crikey,' said Stephen, for no apparent reason. 'How's that going?'

Suddenly, Danny felt the return of the gloom that had dogged him all week. 'Not very well, to be honest. I've been going to lots of auditions but haven't had any luck.'

'Not yet, anyway,' interjected Guy.

'Do you find your accent puts people off?' asked Stephen. Danny noticed that he had the same gap between his teeth as Guy, although on him it wasn't remotely cute.

'I've never really thought about that,' he said, 'but I don't think so.'

'But surely it must cut down the roles you can play?' offered Cynthia.

'Well, it shouldn't,' Danny answered. 'Just because I speak with an accent doesn't mean I can't speak *without* one – or do other accents, for that matter.'

Cynthia and Stephen stared at him in disbelief.

'You know, you could always get a role on *Coronation Street*,' suggested Cynthia. 'Or what's that series that's set on a council estate up north?'

'*Shameless*,' said Stephen.

'That's it,' said Cynthia. 'Why don't you get a role on that?'

Danny stabbed into a potato. 'I'd love to but it's not up to me, unfortunately – I'd need their casting director to hire me.'

He drained his glass and Guy topped it up. In his peripheral vision, he was sure he caught Cynthia raising an eyebrow.

Thankfully, Guy steered the conversation in another direction by sharing his own work news. Danny went to great efforts to display an interest, offer supportive comments, and make it clear that – as Guy's trusted confidant – he was already across most of the detail. By the time that topic of conversation was drawing to a close, Maria was returning to clear their plates.

Cynthia announced she was going to serve dessert and popped into the kitchen, coming back with a tray of scones she'd baked herself.

'Oh, I love your scones,' Guy told her.

A smile smoothed Cynthia's face. 'And there's clotted cream and jam from the damson tree in the garden.'

As everyone helped themselves, Danny hoped he didn't have to say the word 'scone'. If he pronounced it in his northern accent, it was one of those words – like 'hair', 'toast' or 'Coke' – that he'd learned from experience could prompt derision. Should he soften his accent to make it rhyme with 'gone' or say it as he usually would, so it rhymed with 'bone'?

Before he could decide, Stephen dived in. 'Don't you call scones something different up north?'

Danny snatched a breath. 'No,' he replied, sweetly, 'we just pronounce the word differently.'

Rather reluctantly, he demonstrated.

'Good Lord,' said Cynthia, letting out a loud guffaw, 'it's like a different language!'

Danny tried not to bristle.

'So have your family always lived in Barrow?' asked Stephen, cramming an entire scone into his mouth.

'My mum's family, yeah.'

'And what about your father?' Stephen asked, spraying crumbs onto the table.

Danny gave a wriggle in his seat. 'I don't have a father. Or at least he's never been part of my life.'

Cynthia looked at him as if he'd just announced he'd strangled a litter of kittens. 'Oh. So your mother's a *single* mother?'

'She is, yeah.'

'Crikey,' said Stephen. 'And do you know anything at all about your father?'

Cynthia shot him a corrosive glare.

'What?' he spluttered. 'What did I say?'

'Nothing,' she hissed. 'You've got cream on your chin!'

As Stephen dabbed at it with a napkin, Danny tried to work out how to respond.

As a young boy, he used to ask his mum about his dad, whose name he'd been told was Yiannis Dimitriou. Eileen had met him when she lived in Liverpool in her late teens and Yiannis was working for a shipping company that had some kind of link to a similar company his family owned in Thessaloniki. They'd become caught up in what Eileen called a 'love affair', before she'd fallen pregnant just as Yiannis's work placement was coming to an end and he had to return home. Danny used to picture his dad being wrenched away from his expectant mother but fantasised that one day he'd come back to tell the two of them he'd always loved them and wanted to make up for lost time.

As he grew older and endured more and more intense homophobic bullying, Danny's fantasy had gradually given way to a worry that if he ever met his dad he'd only be hit by rejection, particularly after his mum's boyfriend Lee had rejected him. So he'd stopped asking about his dad – but he hadn't been able to suppress his curiosity. Recently, when Danny had joined Facebook, he'd run a quick search for Yiannis Dimitriou. But he hadn't found anyone with that name. He'd consoled himself that at least he was now on Facebook – so if Yiannis wanted to find him, he could.

'Apparently my dad's from Greece,' he answered, briskly. 'But I don't know much else.'

Danny noticed that the sun had disappeared behind a tree and he was finally able to stop squinting. He took another sip of wine and could feel the alcohol softening his hangover.

'So how did you survive when you were growing up?' asked Cynthia. 'I suppose your mother was on benefits, was she?'

Outrage spiked through Danny. But he quickly forced it back.

You need Guy's parents to like you – even if they do have all the charm of a case of athlete's foot.

'My mum's actually a successful hairdresser,' he answered, 'so she's never needed to claim benefits. But that doesn't mean things weren't tough.'

'Good Lord,' said Cynthia, 'I can imagine.'

Actually, I don't think you can.

But Danny stayed silent and popped the final piece of scone in his mouth. He was finding it increasingly difficult to restrain himself – and still neither of Guy's parents had broached the subject of being gay.

Stephen tossed his napkin onto the table. 'And how do you think it affected you, growing up without a male authority figure?'

'It can cause terrible social problems,' chipped in Cynthia, 'especially amongst young black men. It's why so many of them join gangs.'

Danny realised he couldn't stay silent any longer. He opened his mouth to protest but before he could reply, Cynthia blurted out, 'Do you think that could be what turned you gay?'

Oh, God, here we go . . .

Danny pushed his plate away. By now he was feeling really uncomfortable, however much the alcohol had smoothed out his hangover. 'The thing is, nothing can '*turn*' someone gay. You either are or you aren't.'

Cynthia gave him a hard look. 'Are you saying you think there's a gay gene? Because I have to tell you, the scientific research in that area is very patchy.'

Danny took another swig of his wine. 'I don't know about genetics,' he managed, his heart thumping in his chest, 'but I do know I've always been gay.'

'And have you ever tried *not* to be?' Cynthia asked.

'Of course,' Danny said, 'pretty much every day of my life till I went to uni.'

Despite his best efforts, he was aware of that old feeling of shame leaking into his heart. He saw himself at the age of eleven, preparing to start at secondary school and desperate to escape the homophobic bullying that had plagued his time at primary school. He pictured himself in his bedroom, trying to teach himself to walk like a 'proper lad', trying to make his voice sound deeper and more masculine – but only getting angry at himself for failing. *Just like I've failed at everything ever since. Just like I'm failing to make Guy's parents like me.*

Guy must have spotted his dismay. 'Me too,' he threw in, with a hint of defiance. 'I tried to be straight for years.'

'Well, maybe you didn't try hard enough,' shot back Cynthia. 'Whatever happened to that Lynsey? For a while I hoped you two might get together.'

Guy's face paled. He tugged his hand through his hair. 'Mother, you can't *make* yourself fancy girls if you don't. This is what we're trying to tell you. That's why I stopped trying and decided to accept myself as I am.'

A sneer twisted across Cynthia's face. 'Well, I'm sorry, but I just don't understand how you can accept it.'

Danny felt a clang of doom; it was obvious this wasn't going to end well.

'Neither do I,' said Stephen. 'Some of the shenanigans gays get up to are disgusting. And it's not just in public toilets anymore: I read in the *Daily Mail* that they've started meeting people on the internet – under some sort of code names.'

Danny's mind flashed back to last night and he felt a lick of self-hatred.

'I've told you before, it's a complete myth that all gays behave like that,' Guy argued. 'I've certainly never met anyone off the internet.'

'Have *you*?' Cynthia asked Danny. 'Have you met anyone off the internet?'

Danny reached for his wine but saw that the glass was empty and the bottle upturned in the ice bucket.

'Mother,' Guy interjected, 'how dare you ask Danny such a personal question!'

Cynthia blinked in shock; she clearly wasn't used to him standing up to her. 'Calm down, darling. I'm only showing an interest.'

Guy's face thickened. 'Well, I'd rather you didn't – at least not on that front.'

'In case it's escaped your attention, I do have some professional experience in the area of gay men's sexual health,' Cynthia added, tartly. 'And now we're on the subject, you do know some of the activities favoured by the gay community are extremely dangerous?'

By this stage the adrenaline was firing through Danny. He couldn't resist giving her a smirk. 'Not the way I do them, they're not. If you're interested, I can give you some tips.'

Stephen gasped. 'Now that is out of order. How dare you come into our house and talk about gay sex!'

Danny was about to protest that they'd started it – but he was stopped by the sound of Guy pushing back his chair. Before he knew it, Guy was on his feet, shouting at his parents.

Danny couldn't take in what he was saying; all he could think was that he'd let him down. *I wanted to bring the family together but I've only driven them further apart.*

So much for going on that ski trip.

So much for Guy seeing me as a potential boyfriend.

Very slowly, Danny pushed back his own chair and stood up. There was nothing else for it; he might as well just leave.

Besides, he didn't want to let Guy's parents get to him anymore. He wasn't going to let them make him feel as low or rotten as he had before he'd gone to university. Before he learned to be proud.

2022

As Danny marches through the streets of Manchester, he doesn't think he's ever felt so proud. Because this isn't the first parade in which he's taken part, but it's the first in which he's taken part with Guy. *And I'm proud of both of us.*

On either side of Peter Street, crowds of onlookers roar their support and the sky shimmers with ticker tape. A lesbian in a golf buggy trundles past, her clubs sticking up out of the back, a flag flying from the aerial advertising an LGBTQ+ golf society. But despite all the distractions, Danny can't stop thinking about what Guy has just said to him.

'I love you, princess,' he said, kissing him on the forehead. 'I don't think I've ever told you that but I really fucking love you.'

'I love you too,' Danny blurted back at him. 'I fucking love you, my prince.'

Since that moment, he's been walking around on a high. It's as if every element of the parade exists solely to express their love for each other. And for Danny, his love for Guy is the ultimate expression of his pride in who he is, his pride in who he is as a gay man. *How could it be any other way? I've loved Guy for so long, he's part of who I am. I couldn't be* me *without him.*

A tram crosses the street and the procession slows to a halt. Once again, their group bunches up against the airline staff behind them and the dance troupe in front. It occurs to Danny that he's seen the dancers' routine so many times he could probably join in with them by now. Then it occurs to him that he actually fancies dancing – and not only that but he fancies skydiving, he fancies flying an aeroplane, he fancies bungee jumping, he fancies doing all kinds of extravagant, adventurous things he's never done before. And he feels like he could succeed at every single one of them.

Is this how it's going to be when me and Guy get together? Is this how I'm going to feel all the time?

He notices that the 'if' of his thoughts has switched to 'when'. That's because, since Guy told him he loved him, all Danny's doubts and insecurities have faded. Spencer now seems like an irrelevance, and bumping into him of no importance whatsoever. Not only that but all the shame Danny has been made to feel over the years has disappeared, the shame he was made to feel about himself as a child and on so many occasions since, such as that awful time he went for lunch with Guy's parents. It's been wiped out by this, the most intense pride he's ever felt.

As the procession begins moving again, they pass the accessible viewing area and the grandstand that has been erected outside the Midland Hotel for the celebrity guests. But Danny doesn't even look to see who these are. On the steps of the hotel, a handful of amazingly honed models wearing skimpy vests are handing out promotional leaflets for some nightclub. But Danny doesn't give them a second glance. All he can think about is how proud he is to be with Guy.

He thinks back over all the experiences they've shared, all the times they've been there for each other, all the times Guy was there for him during those first few years in London, when he was feeling low and struggling to hold his life together. And he tells himself that what's happening now proves that he wasn't deluded on all those occasions he convinced himself they had an intense, unbreakable connection, on all those occasions he suspected there might be something more to their connection than just friendship.

No, I wasn't deluded. And our connection's never been stronger.

2008

I just want to see Guy.

Danny staggered out into the street and drew in a deep, calming breath. He looked at his watch and saw that it was 4 o'clock; Guy would still be at work. *But it's a Friday so he might be able to slip away early . . .*

He sent him a text and slumped against the wall.

He'd just experienced his most brutal rejection yet as a professional actor. He'd been auditioning for the role of a chef in a well-known TV hospital drama, a young man who's following his dream but has an accident in the kitchen that cuts it short. Danny had thought the audition went well but then the casting director Doris Slinger, a middle-aged woman who wore a flowing floral-print maxi-dress that was covered in cat hair, had looked at him and pulled a face as if she were chewing on an old dishcloth.

'But this character isn't gay,' she said.

Danny opened his mouth but nothing came out.

I wasn't playing him gay, he wanted to argue. *Just because* I'm *gay doesn't mean* he *has to be.*

'It's not just that,' Doris went on, 'your look's all wrong.'

'W-w-what do you mean?' Danny stammered.

She released a breath. 'You've less hair than in your photos. And that shaved head, it's giving me thug.'

'"*Thug*"?'

'Yes, thug. I'm getting thug, gay, a northern accent . . . It's mixed messaging. And I can't tell what's going on.'

Danny felt his insides compress. 'Oh, urm, OK.'

Doris drew in her mouth tightly. 'Look, Danny, you need to take this up with your agent. You shouldn't have been put up for this. Quite frankly, it's been a waste of everyone's time.'

She took out her phone and checked her messages.

Danny thanked her and began sloping his way towards the exit.

'Oh, Danny,' Doris called after him, 'what *is* your accent? For future reference?'

Danny turned back. 'I'm from Barrow, in the north-west of England. Near the Lake District – but not actually in it.'

She nodded. 'OK. We'll be in touch if anything suitable comes up.'

She gave him a look of something approaching pity. Danny could taste the self-disgust in his throat.

Now that he was outside – slumped against a wall on a cobbled street in Covent Garden – he could see the experience as the latest in a sustained barrage of rejections that had left him feeling worthless. He wasn't sure how he was supposed to go back to believing in himself; it felt like being a failure had become part of who he was. And, despite the success he'd had as an actor at university, he couldn't help thinking that this was how it was always meant to be.

He rested his head against the wall and tried to regulate his breathing. From every direction people rushed past him: wealthy, successful, gorgeous people wearing expensive clothes, shopping for glamorous presents or on their way to high-powered meetings. *Oh, why can't I be like them? Why can't I just get one little break?*

His eyes leaked hot, frustrated tears. Worried that people would see he was crying, he turned to face the wall.

In his head he replayed what Doris Slinger had said to him – and his sense of frustration rose. *I wouldn't care, but that character* could *be gay; there's nothing in the script to say he isn't. And I'm good at accents; I could have made him from anywhere in the country!*

He remembered what Doris had said about his hair. *It's not my fault I've gone bald! It's not my fault I can't afford to do anything about it!*

He considered calling his agent but, as it was a Friday, knew she'd be at the tail end of a long, boozy lunch. Although this didn't just happen on Fridays: the truth was, Heather Hardman was hardly ever in the office – which was why Danny had given her the nickname Heather Hardly. Not that it made any difference when she was around, as she didn't return his calls anyway. And she'd made it clear she didn't see giving pep talks or any kind of moral support as part of her role. Not that Danny would have minded if she'd ever put in any effort to get him a job or had any traction with casting directors. *But I can't really blame Heather – she's the only agent I can get. What does that say about me?*

When Danny had arrived in London, he'd fantasised about having a successful career, picturing himself on red carpets, accepting awards, and being interviewed on TV chat shows. Within a few months he'd downgraded his dreams and would have been happy just being a working actor, just being given the opportunity to continue doing what he loved. He remembered what it was about acting that had first appealed to him: the idea of escaping a life that made him miserable and stepping inside another. *My God, I could do with some of that now.*

His phone pinged to tell him he had a text. It was from Guy. 'Told my boss I've got an emergency,' it read. 'Hold tight, am on my way.'

Oh my God, yes!

Danny gave a sniff and dried his eyes. He slapped his cheeks a few times so it wouldn't look like he'd been crying. And he turned back to face the street.

'Thanks, my prince,' he texted. 'I really appreciate it xxx'

Guy texted back to suggest they meet in Soho, in a gay bar called Rupert Street.

Danny raced over there, all the time keeping his head down. When he arrived, the bar was already starting to fill up. Many of the men were wearing T-shirts by Ed Hardy or rugby shirts by that hot US brand Abercrombie & Fitch that had recently opened its first store in London. Danny wondered why other men always seemed more attractive the worse he felt about himself. He imagined his self-loathing forming a force field around him, repelling strangers and warning them off from even looking at him. He found an empty table that was hidden away in the alcove at the back and sat down.

A few minutes later, Guy arrived and spotted him. He was wearing his work suit, although he'd taken off his tie. He bought two drinks and carried them over.

'Hello, hello,' he said. 'How are you feeling?'

Danny stood up and hugged him tightly. 'Oh, miserable. And pretty sorry for myself.'

'Well, we'll have to do something about that.'

He sat down and Danny filled him in on what had happened

in the audition. 'Honestly, babe, I think I've got to accept the fact that I'm not good enough. I think I'm just a crap actor.'

'In that case, it's a good job I'm here,' said Guy. 'Because I've seen you in every single thing you've done and I can tell you categorically that you *are* good enough. You're a great actor, Danny.'

Danny smiled weakly. 'That's very sweet of you, Guy, but unfortunately nobody else seems to think so.'

Guy shrugged. 'Well, they're wrong. And I know better.'

Danny sipped on his vodka cranberry – a drink he didn't actually like but drank because it was fashionable – and thought back to all the fringe productions he'd done since moving to London, all the jobs he'd undertaken in the hope of enticing casting directors along to dazzle them with his talent, all the shows in which he'd taken part on a profit-share basis only to find there were no profits because nobody came to see them – nobody except Guy, his mum and Arthur. After three years, all his efforts had amounted to nothing.

'I know it's hard but you've got to find some way to block out the negativity and keep going,' Guy continued. 'If you won't do it for yourself, do it for me. Do it for your number one fan.'

Danny smiled, this time with a little more conviction. 'Alright, babe, I'll try.'

'Promise?'

'I promise. And thanks for coming to see me.'

Guy shook his head. 'You don't need to thank me, that's what I'm here for. You and I are partners, remember?'

By now, Danny was smiling brightly. 'Like Dolce and Gabbana.'

'Benson and Hedges.'

'Abercrombie and Fitch.'

'Vodka and cranberry.'

They broke into a rolling laugh, a laugh that warmed Danny from within.

Since that disastrous lunch with his parents, he and Guy had been closer than ever. When his parents had gone on the attack, Guy had taken Danny's side against them – and had followed this up by taking a step back from the family. He hadn't distanced himself completely, and Danny wouldn't have wanted him to. But he was thrilled that Guy had stepped closer to him.

'Come on,' said Guy, 'let's forget about that stupid audition. Let's go out and have a big night.'

Danny looked at his empty glass and hesitated. Lately, he'd been going out more and more and, much as he enjoyed partying, it was starting to dominate his life. As if to exacerbate the situation, most of his friends expected him to be the one who'd whip up everyone's spirits and get them in the mood. He couldn't bear to let them down – and couldn't help worrying that if he did, they wouldn't want to be friends with him anymore. But he also knew that if he wasn't careful, he'd be drunk every night – and the incessant hangovers would send his own spirits spiralling down to rock bottom.

'Oh, I don't know,' he attempted, 'I'm not working tonight so I am free. But aren't you seeing Spencer?'

'I wasn't going to,' admitted Guy. 'He's working till eight and anyway, I'm not sure I feel like it.'

Danny sat up a little straighter. 'Oh yeah? Is everything alright between you two?'

'Yeah, it's fine. I've just been getting a bit bored lately. To be fair, I'm not sure Spencer's the most riveting company at the best of times. And don't tell anyone, but he's starting to get on my nerves.'

Danny raised an eyebrow. 'What do you mean, "get on your nerves"?'

'Well, it's just little things, like the way he calls me "hon" all the time and says everything's "major". I used to think it was cute but now it just annoys me.' He paused to finish his lager. 'What does that mean, Danny? Do you think it means I'm falling out of love with him?'

'I don't know,' Danny said, 'but I think we should discuss it. I think we need that night out!'

2009

By the following year, Danny and Guy had discussed Guy's relationship with Spencer – several times. And it was clear to Danny that it wasn't going to last.

Guy had raised several concerns, most of which Danny could recite off by heart.

'I'm not sure how intelligent he is.'

'I don't think we have much in common.'

'We never laugh together, not like me and you.'

This last one was his favourite, the one he liked hearing the most.

The problem was, Guy still hadn't communicated his feelings to Spencer – and Danny was becoming impatient.

When pressed, Guy had voiced various objections.

'It's just awkward when we live together.'

'Work's so stressful at the moment, I can't deal with a break-up.'

'He's just so fit and I can't stop myself fancying him.'

This was the one he liked hearing the least.

Then, a few weeks ago, Guy had told Danny that finally he had a plan for ending the relationship: he'd somehow saved up enough money to put down a deposit on his first flat, so as soon as he'd found the right property and the sale had gone through, he was going to bite the bullet. But Danny knew that buying a flat took months – and he was struggling to contain his impatience. To take his mind off things, he'd started doing some work that drew on his acting skills and didn't interfere with his job in the bar: he'd started performing in role-play training run by a company that worked for organisations such as the Police, the Social Services, and the NHS. So far he'd played the role of a father reacting to the news that his child had been killed by a knife gang, an employee telling his boss that he'd overheard racial abuse in the office, and a homophobe objecting to his sick mother being treated by a gay doctor. The work allowed him once again to step away from his life and put his worries to one side – and, best of all, it was well paid so helped ease his financial concerns.

It was because of this that he'd been able to justify joining Emma and Lynsey on a cheap holiday to Thailand, a holiday he told himself would be the perfect distraction from the delay to Guy's strategy. So far, the three of them had been having a wonderful time. They'd spent the first few days on Koh Samui, lying on white, sandy beaches and swimming in the turquoise sea, treating themselves to massages and indulging in long, relaxing meals. They'd had plenty of opportunities to discuss Danny's dissatisfaction with the reality of his life as an actor. They'd also spent time discussing Lynsey's trip to meet her late mother's family in Ghana, a trip she'd said had left her with a greater understanding of her identity as a mixed-race woman. And they'd reflected on Emma's latest career move and the colleague she'd met who was making her think she might just be ready for her first proper relationship after years of promiscuity – something she'd always held up as a badge of honour but several months of psychotherapy had taught her might have been her way of trying to smother the pain of growing up with warring parents.

After four days of reflection and relaxation, someone had told them that the famous Full Moon Party was taking place that night on the neighbouring island of Koh Phangan. They'd hopped onto a boat, bought themselves neon vests, and decorated each other's faces with matching neon paint. They'd avoided drinking the buckets of alcohol so many people were sucking through straws and instead took some ecstasy tablets Emma had bought from a man she swore could be trusted, although how she knew that Danny had no idea. But he put this out of his mind and a couple of hours later the three of them were dancing on the beach to a techno anthem, feeling the bass of the music vibrating up through the sand, surrounded by tens of thousands of people, most of them with their arms in the air, all of them lit by the surprisingly bright full moon.

'This is incredible,' said Lynsey. 'I feel so happy.'

'Aye,' said Emma, her pupils dilated, 'it's like being in a warm hug with every single person on the beach.'

'You know I never used to like this song,' Danny commented, 'but now I *love* it.'

'It's the best fucking song I've ever heard in my entire fucking life,' declared Emma.

The three of them chorused their agreement.

'Alright, mate?'

Someone wrapped their arms around Danny and he turned around to see a shirtless man with his hair in a quiff like David Beckham, chains of shells around his neck and wrists, and tattoos of roses, ships, an eagle and a lion covering his chest and arms. When he hugged the man back, he noticed that his shoulders were covered with a thin layer of sweat and he smelled faintly of rolling tobacco. But it was a pleasant smell and one that reminded him of someone, although he wasn't sure who.

'Yeah, I'm brilliant, thanks,' Danny replied. 'How about you?'

'Yeah, pucker.'

The man introduced himself as Dean and said he'd been watching Danny for a while. 'I really like you,' he said in a pronounced Cockney accent. 'You've got a great energy.'

'I really like you too!' gushed Danny, aware that he'd only known him for a few seconds.

Dean smiled, revealing a gold tooth at the side of his mouth. 'Do you fancy going for a walk?'

'How lovely. Yeah I'd love to. That'd be lovely.' Danny hoped it wasn't obvious he'd taken ecstasy. *Mind you, I'm sure Dean has too.*

Danny told the girls he'd be back soon and followed Dean down the beach, past a man juggling with flaming torches, a flaming skipping rope over which several people were jumping, a flaming hoop through which people were leaping, and some scaffolding on which the words 'Full Moon Party' were spelled out in flames. When he reached the shore, Dean stopped, and began rolling himself a cigarette.

'Do you want one, mate?'

'Yeah,' said Danny, 'I'd love one.'

Dean gestured for Danny to hold the packet while he licked the Rizlas. 'So is this your first Full Moon?'

'Yeah. It's insane, I'm loving it.'

Dean lit two cigarettes and handed one to Danny.

'What a gentleman,' said Danny. 'Thanks, babe.'

He asked Dean what he did for a living and Dean said he worked as a labourer on a building site in the City of London.

Danny told him he also lived in London and was trying to make a career as an actor but it wasn't going very well.

'I could look after you,' said Dean.

Danny's heart swung open.

As if it were the most natural thing in the world, Dean took hold of Danny's hand and kissed him fully on the lips.

Oh my God, I think I'm in love with you!

'I'd like to look after you,' Dean reiterated. And he kissed Danny again.

Suddenly, Danny realised who it was Dean reminded him of – it was his mum's ex-boyfriend, Lee. Like Lee, Dean was stocky but good-looking and had an unpolished charm, an unpolished charm Danny found seriously attractive. He remembered that, even though Lee had tormented and persecuted him, when he'd hit puberty and started masturbating, it was Lee who'd become the subject of his first fantasies.

In a flash, Danny imagined returning to London as Dean's boyfriend and the two of them moving in together. He saw them snuggling up together on the sofa to watch *X Factor* or *I'm A Celebrity . . . Get Me Out Of Here!* He pictured himself falling asleep in Dean's strong arms, his head resting on his powerful chest. And he saw himself getting up early in the morning so he could make Dean's sandwiches, handing him his lunch box as he left the house for the building site.

Oh my God, I am *in love with you! I'm completely, madly, wildly, passionately in love with you!*

Then another thought occurred to him.

But what about Guy?

Danny let go of Dean's hand. 'The thing is, I'm kind of seeing someone.'

He checked himself. 'Well, I'm not seeing someone. But I think I might be soon.'

Dean frowned. 'OK, mate. Well, why don't I give you my number? You know, in case it doesn't work out?'

'Alright,' said Danny. 'I'd like that.'

Once they'd exchanged details, Danny took a last drag on his cigarette and stubbed it out in an empty lager can someone had dropped on the sand.

'Maybe I'll see you around then,' said Dean.

'Yeah, maybe I'll see you around.'

Dean leaned forward and kissed him again. It was a longer, lingering kiss and surprisingly intimate. His breath tasted of tobacco and lemonade, but Danny liked it.

He stood back and watched Dean jog away, his muscular calves tightening as his feet hit the sand. He ran his hand over his stubble. *What the hell just happened? Did I really fall in love or is it just the ecstasy talking?*

For a while Danny stood contemplating the scene. Exploding in front of him was an intensely vivid kaleidoscope of neon, tie-dye and human flesh, set against a backdrop of bars and clubs, and beyond that the rich green mountains of the island. In the air he detected a pungent mix of cannabis, sweat and whichever fuel was being burned by all the flames.

He began walking back to his friends, passing a mixed-race girl wearing a straw cowboy hat, her eyes closed, dancing on her own. Next to her was a shirtless man in a Father Christmas hat who was telling anyone who'd listen that he'd had his wallet stolen but he didn't care and was still happy. And jumping into his path came a topless woman with neon-painted breasts who cheered directly into his face, then sprinted off.

As he neared Lynsey and Emma, the music settled into a well-known trance anthem, another song Danny didn't like but suddenly felt he appreciated. He took off his vest, no longer concerned about what anyone might think of his out-of-shape body.

'Girls, this is the best night of my life,' he announced as he slipped in next to them.

'What happened with that guy?' asked Emma. 'Did you get off with him?'

Danny told them they'd had a chat, shared a kiss and exchanged numbers.

'What the fuck?' Emma yelled, her jaw swinging. 'Why didn't you shag him?'

'Nah, I want to be with you girls,' Danny said. 'I love you girls.'

'I love you too!' warbled Lynsey.

'So do I,' said Emma, 'I love you both so much!'

They came together and put their arms around each other.

'What does this remind you of?' said Danny.

'Graduation,' answered Emma. 'Except we're missing someone.'

'Guy,' said Lynsey. 'We're missing Guy!'

Danny broke out of the hug and shouted up into the sky, 'Guy, wherever you are, we love you!'

Then he remembered. *Of course, it's Guy I'm in love with, not Dean. I'll never love anyone except Guy.*

All of a sudden, he understood exactly what he had to do. He wasn't going to hang around and wait for Guy to break up with Spencer, in case once again he missed his chance. He was going to call Guy and tell him how he felt – and he was going to do it now.

He danced for a little longer then told the girls he needed the toilet. Once he'd slipped away, he made his way back to the shore and pulled out his phone.

Wait a minute, do I really want to do this?

Yes, I do.

And what is it Lynsey says? It's always better to regret doing something than to regret not doing it.

Without bothering to calculate what time it was in London, he found Guy's name in his list of contacts and dialled his number. There was a pause before the ringtone started. As he listened to it over and over again, he could feel every cell in his body tensing. After what felt like an eternity, the ringtone stopped and the greeting on Guy's voicemail clicked in.

'Hello, hello,' came the familiar voice, 'you've got through to Guy Falconer. Leave me a message and I'll call you back.'

Danny screwed his eyes shut then thrust them open.

'Hi babe,' he said, 'it's me, Danny. I'm in Thailand and I'm having an insane time but I just want to tell you I love you. I mean, I'm *in love* with you. Not just as a friend but as, you know, everything . . . Like, I'm properly in love with you. I always have been. Anyway, I think it's time you knew. And when you break up with Spencer I think we should get together. You said it yourself – we're good together, we're a partnership.'

He stopped and looked up at the moon.

'Anyway, that's it. Give me a call back and let me know what you think. OK. Bye.'

He hung up.

Oh my God, I did it. I actually did it.

Out of nowhere he erupted in a peal of laughter. He felt so much freer, as if – without realising it – for years he'd been lugging around a heavy weight that he'd just shrugged off.

A little distance down the shoreline, a man was on his knees in the shallows of the sea, trying to wash neon paint off his chest while sucking on an unlit, wet cigarette. Danny wanted to run up and tell him what he'd done. He wanted to tell every single person on the beach.

But he reined in his excitement. This was a secret he was going to keep to himself, if only for the time being. He wasn't even going to tell Lynsey.

No, I'll wait till Guy's replied.

He's bound to come back to me soon.

2022

As Danny and Guy walk across Manchester, Danny remembers how he felt when he left Guy that voicemail from Thailand. He remembers how strangely calm he was as he waited for an answer.

He puts out of his mind what happened next.

All these years later, he feels a similar sense of calm. He wonders if on this occasion it's some kind of afterglow from the joy he felt during the parade. It occurs to him that the way he felt during the parade was the closest he's come to the way he felt during the Full Moon Party. And now that it's over, once again he understands very clearly what he has to do.

I need to open up to Guy and be honest with him. I need to provoke some kind of discussion about our feelings.

But he can't do that right now, not while he and Guy are walking along the street.

I need to create a little time for us away from the crowds.

They're making their way from the end of the parade at the top of Fairfield Street, back down to the Village and Sackville Gardens, which have been transformed into an open-air arena in which live acts are performing. Danny checks Manchester Pride's social media accounts and relays to Guy the performance schedule.

'And what do you want to do about food?' he asks, hoping Guy can't tell it's a leading question.

'I don't know,' says Guy. 'Can't we get something there?'

Danny tugs at his wristband. 'I'm sure we can, but you know what these things are like: it'll be all junk food and massive queues. If you look at the set times, there's a lull around six o'clock. I was thinking we could nip out of the Village and get a proper meal.'

Guy tilts his head as he thinks this over.

'Just so we don't get hungry later on,' Danny adds. 'You know I hate drinking on an empty stomach.'

Guy nods. 'Alright, as long as there's somewhere decent.'

Danny smiles. 'I'll have a look on TripAdvisor and come up with options.'

He consults his phone and tries not to show his excitement. Sitting down for a meal will be the perfect opportunity for him to bring up a discussion of their feelings. Finally, the two of them will have the conversation they've needed to have for so long; finally, Danny will be able to express his feelings and find out for sure how Guy feels. And if he's in any doubt this is the right course of action, all he has to do is remember how frustrated he felt when his last attempt to do this – by leaving the voicemail from Thailand – failed.

2009

'OK, babe, I'm going to work!'

Danny was standing in the hall of Dean's flat with his coat slung over his arm. He lifted the door off the latch.

'Hang on a minute!' shouted Dean.

Danny let go of the latch and braced himself for what was coming.

He'd only been in the flat for half an hour. As it was December and the sun was setting early, Dean arrived home from the building site by four thirty, which gave them just enough time to have sex before Danny had to leave for his shift in the bar. It was something they'd done several times over the last few weeks and when Danny had told his friends about it, they'd thought it was wonderfully wild and racy. Somebody mentioned that it was called an 'afternoon delight', an expression Danny had instantly adopted as his own.

Except in our case, the word 'delight' is hardly appropriate . . .

Dean stepped into the hallway in his dressing gown. When he looked at Danny, his face fell. 'Are you really going to work in that?'

A flash of anxiety passed through Danny's gut. He glanced down at his plain black shirt and blue jeans. 'What's wrong with it?'

Dean grimaced. 'The shirt's a bit tight, that's all. It gives you a spare tyre.'

Danny immediately felt self-conscious. He immediately felt overweight and unattractive. He pulled on his coat and wrapped it around him.

'I just don't want anyone to laugh at you,' added Dean. 'Not when you're surrounded by so many hot bodies.'

'Oh, it'll have to do,' Danny parried, 'I haven't got anything else here.'

He forced out a smile, vowing that next time he'd slip away without telling Dean he was leaving.

More and more lately, Danny had noticed that Dean revelled in putting him down. He didn't just criticise his weight but often made comments about his baldness, telling him he looked like a boiled egg or a pool ball, or that his scalp was so shiny he could check his reflection in it. When Danny complained, Dean would insist he was 'only messing' and call Danny 'over-sensitive'.

But am I being over-sensitive or is he being under-*sensitive?*

One thing Danny was sure of; Dean's criticism was at its worst directly after they'd had sex.

It's as if he's ashamed of what he's done and wants to take it out on me.

He reached for the latch. 'Right, I'd better get a wriggle on. I'll love you and leave you.'

'Jesus, do you have to be so camp?' said Dean. He did an impression of Danny's voice. '"I'll love you and leave you."'

Danny tried not to let his face crumple. He couldn't help wondering how he'd ended up in a relationship with someone who wanted to make him feel bad about himself. He remembered how affectionate Dean had been when they'd met on the beach in Thailand. When they'd become a couple towards the end of the holiday, he'd shown himself to be caring and demonstrative. But as soon as they'd arrived back in London, everything had changed. Dean hadn't wanted to go out for romantic meals or even to the cinema. He tried to avoid spending time with Danny's friends and refused to introduce him to his, insisting they were just 'very different'. This was when he'd started to snap at Danny and make sly digs.

Danny resolved not to let it get to him. 'Well, if you don't like the way I speak,' he chirped, 'maybe you shouldn't have chatted me up in Thailand. Or was I just impossible to resist?'

Dean scoffed. 'Mate, I'd had an E – I was off my face. And in case you didn't notice, you were the only poof there.'

The insult hit Danny like a body blow. He hated the way Dean spoke to him. He hated the way he disrespected him.

If only the sex weren't so good.

It wasn't that Dean was any less disrespectful to Danny when they were having sex. On the contrary, he handled him roughly and refused to kiss him on the lips or even look him in the eye. Sometimes he even spat at him and called him dirty and cheap and queer.

No, 'afternoon delight' could hardly be less appropriate.

But the strange thing was, in a sexual context Danny didn't mind being treated badly. In fact, it turned him on. It turned him on wildly.

The problem is, when the sex is over I have to put up with this.

He looked at his watch. 'I've got to go, babe, or I'm going to be late.'

Before Dean could reply, Danny slid through the door and out of the flat. As he rushed down the stairs, he remembered his wholesome fantasy of making Dean a packed lunch every morning and kissing him goodbye as he left for work.

God, I'm such a desperado.

He fastened his coat against the cold and walked the short distance to East Ham underground station. Once there, he jumped on a train and began the long journey to the West End. As the old train clattered along the tracks, he looked at the map and counted off the stations.

Plaistow . . . Bow Road . . . Whitechapel . . .

As was often the case when he spent time with Dean, Danny found himself contemplating the state of their relationship. But whenever he asked himself why he put up with it, he always came up with the same answer.

It's not just because of the sex – it's because I can't get any better.

He remembered the voicemail he'd left Guy from the Full Moon Party. Despite the fact he'd asked for a response, he hadn't heard anything – nothing at all. He'd been stunned but had thought this had effectively been his answer; he'd thought he'd been rejected and had to move on. That was why he'd texted Dean and thrown himself into the relationship.

When Danny had arrived back in London, he'd been careful to avoid Guy; he would have found it way too humiliating to see him, to see the sympathetic expression on his face, the pity in his eyes. Guy had texted a few times but had made no mention of the voicemail, so Danny had given him vague, evasive replies and fobbed off his attempts to meet up. This had gone on for three months now and he wasn't sure how much longer he could keep it up – but he still couldn't face seeing him.

. . . Tower Hill, Monument . . . Mansion House . . .

When he reached Embankment, Danny exited the station, kept his head bowed and walked the short distance to Soho.

As he entered the bar, he was relieved to find that it was already busy; he hoped it would stay this way and he wouldn't have time to stop and think. He checked out which staff were on duty: it was a smooth-skinned Brazilian called Junior, who had stars tattooed across his pectoral muscles and liked to boast about his background in porn, a hairy-chested Spaniard called Salvador, who claimed to have slept with a Premiership footballer and had a laugh that sounded like he was choking, and a beefy Bulgarian called Valentin, who was fond of demonstrating that he hadn't always been gorgeous by whipping out his new smartphone to reveal pictures of himself as a fat teenager. Danny couldn't help wondering if Valentin only did this to make him feel better about his appearance.

To make me feel better about being the runt of the litter.

Despite the differences in nationality and background, Danny got on with all of his colleagues – and they had a laugh as they worked. It was a long-standing tradition amongst the bar staff to see which of them could collect the most phone numbers from customers in one night. Junior, Salvador and Valentin were at an advantage as they showed off their incredible bodies by working shirtless and in tight shorts, while Danny preferred to stay fully clothed. When they'd taken a set of staff photographs to be used in advertisements in *Boyz* and *QX* magazines, Danny was directed to stand at the back of the group – and in one of the pictures, you couldn't even see his face. He sometimes wondered if his boss only employed him because he was the sole member of the team who spoke decent English and could help out his colleagues when they didn't understand an order. Not that the customers cared if they had to repeat themselves several times, not when the barman was Bulgarian and looked like Brad Pitt in *Troy*. And if Danny was in any doubt, he only had to witness how many of them handed over their phone numbers. The only customers who gave him theirs were the old or ugly ones, or those who looked like they'd just been released from prison.

Well, at least I'm not on the pull anymore. At least I've got Dean.

As soon as he'd greeted his colleagues, Danny threw himself into work. As a DJ in a vintage Adidas velour tracksuit played music by the likes of Beyoncé and Lady Gaga, Danny spent the next few hours zipping around the bar.

At just after 10 o'clock, Salvador nudged him. 'Baby,' he said in his thick Spanish accent, 'is your hot friend.'

'What?' said Danny. 'Who?'

Salvador pointed to the end of the bar – and there was Guy, leaning against the wall, waving at him.

Suddenly, it was as if all the air had been sucked out of the room.

'After you talk to him,' said Salvador, 'you give me his number, baby.' And he gave a peal of the laugh that sounded like he was choking.

Danny ignored him and waved at Guy. He gestured to his watch and mimed that he had a break in five minutes. As he served a few more customers, he tried to keep his panic at bay.

Shit, I wasn't expecting this. What do I say?

He signalled for Guy to squeeze through the crowd to an area of the bar where the staff didn't serve but stayed on the business side so there was a barrier between them.

'Hi, babe,' he began, weakly.

'Hello, hello,' said Guy.

'What brings you here?'

'I came to see you. Why else would I be here?'

Danny scratched the back of his neck. 'Oh, right, well, that's nice.'

'I haven't seen you in ages,' Guy went on, leaning towards him. 'I wasn't sure if you'd been avoiding me.'

'No, no, not at all,' Danny insisted, 'I've just been mad busy, that's all.'

Guy expelled the air from his lungs. 'Thank God for that. I was starting to think I'd done something to piss you off.'

Danny surprised himself by feeling a flash of irritation. *Didn't you get my voicemail?* he wanted to ask. Then, to his horror, he realised he had.

Guy creased his brow. 'What voicemail?'

Danny felt a stab of fear but knew he had no choice but to white-knuckle his way through the conversation. 'The one I left you from Thailand.'

In the background came the sound of a glass smashing, followed by a loud cheer.

Guy frowned. 'No. But I did have my phone stolen and lost loads of stuff. I had to get your number off Spencer.'

Danny was shocked; it hadn't occurred to him that something like this might have happened.

It was only when his body began to relax that he realised how much tension he'd been holding inside him for the last few months.

But his relief was laced with disappointment. *Because now we're back to where we were. And the whole point of making that call was to get away from that.*

‘So what did it say then, this voicemail?’ asked Guy.

As he considered how to answer, Danny realised they didn’t need to go back to where they were; opening up before him was an opportunity to restate his feelings and provoke the discussion he so badly wanted. He remembered how good it had felt to express his emotions and how unburdened he’d felt as soon as he left the voicemail. But he also remembered how devastating it had been to think Guy had rejected him. If he told him how he felt again, there was a chance that same thing would happen for real.

Shit, what do I do?

It was a tough call, but one he had to make in an instant.

‘Oh, nothing,’ he said, waving away Guy’s question, ‘I can’t even remember now. I was off my head at some Full Moon Party. I was just a bit worried I’d annoyed you or something.’

Guy rolled his eyes. ‘How funny – I thought I’d annoyed you and you thought you’d annoyed me!’

‘Insane!’ quipped Danny. ‘Anyway, what do you want to drink? I’ve still got ten minutes so I can come and join you on the other side if you like.’

A smile illuminated Guy’s face. ‘In that case I’ll have a pint of lager.’

Danny smiled back at him. And with that they slipped back into exactly the way they’d always been.

2010

Danny looked out to sea. He remembered standing at the shoreline when he left Guy the voicemail from Thailand. But that felt like a long time ago now.

So long ago that there's no point regretting what happened.

Danny wasn't even sure he felt inclined to regret it anymore.

Not when me and Guy are having such a lovely time. And more to the point, not when he's finally broken up with Spencer!

Guy had revealed the news on the train down to Brighton. Danny had struggled to conceal his delight and at one point had pretended to need the loo so he could stand in front of the mirror, jump up and down and squeal out loud. Ever since, he'd found it hard to keep a smile off his face – although to cover up the real reason, he'd made a point of mentioning several times how happy he was to see his mum and Arthur.

Before Danny had found out about Guy's break-up, the four of them had arranged to spend the Easter weekend at Arthur's little terraced house just ten minutes' walk from the seafront in Brighton. Danny had been worried that Dean would moan about him going away, even if it was just because he'd miss out on sex – but he hadn't seemed bothered in the slightest. At the time, this had disappointed Danny: he'd almost wanted Dean to be annoyed; he'd almost wanted him to act possessive. At least that would have showed he cared.

But the truth is, now I'm here I've hardly given Dean a second thought.

In fact, while he'd been in Brighton, Danny had hardly given a second thought to any aspect of his life back in London – and certainly none of his problems.

He and Guy had arrived late in the afternoon the day before, which was Good Friday. Arthur had made a meal of Cumberland sausages he said reminded him of home, with mashed potato and onion gravy. The four of them had chatted about the celebrations for Arthur's upcoming sixty-fifth birthday and Guy's plans for the flat he'd just bought, but the evening was dominated by Eileen's account of her initial experiences of online dating. She explained that now Danny was firmly settled in London, she'd decided to try and find love again – for the first time since she'd split up with Lee. She amused everyone with tales of her disastrous dates, including one with someone who turned out not just to be married but married to one of her regular customers, a woman who'd ended up blaming Eileen and sacking her as a hairdresser. Then, over dessert of sticky toffee pudding and ice cream, the discussion had turned to what Eileen called her 'near misses', much more positive experiences that had given her a glimpse of a potential future happiness. At one point, their chatter had become so animated – and so *loud* – that Arthur's next-door neighbour had banged on the wall, something that had sent them into fits of giggles.

'You're so lucky to have this,' Guy said to them, once the giggling had died down.

'What?' asked Danny.

'Just, this *family*,' Guy answered. 'It's lovely, it's brilliant. It's just a shame it reminds me of what I've not got.'

Eileen swatted him on the arm. 'What are you on about, love? You're one of us! You're part o' t' family!'

Guy smiled and Danny felt his heart give a little tug.

Once they'd cleared up, they'd said goodnight and sloped off to their beds, with Eileen sharing Arthur's double, Guy in the single in the spare room, and Danny on the sofa bed – sleeping arrangements that had been decided in advance.

This morning, Danny had been woken by the sound of seagulls squawking – and had drawn the curtains to reveal bright sunshine and a sky he couldn't help thinking was exactly the same colour as Guy's eyes. After breakfast, they'd packed a picnic and brought it down to the beach. Arthur and Eileen were sitting on a pair of fold-out canvas chairs Danny had jokingly called 'nana chairs'. Although it was only April and quite breezy, the two of them were wearing shades and short sleeves, as they'd recently made a joint policy decision to switch from sunbeds to fake tan and wanted to show off their newly bronzed, streak-free arms. Danny and Guy hadn't even thought to bring their sunglasses so were sitting with their backs to the sun, on a blanket spread out on the pebbles. Danny was slightly concerned about his scalp burning but didn't want to draw attention to it.

'This is the life,' said Arthur. 'You can't beat Brighton on a sunny day!'

'Yeah, it's gorgeous, i'n't it?' said Eileen. 'Enough to make me forget all about match.com.'

They laughed.

'Who needs dating, anyway?' added Arthur.

'Maybe you've got a point,' mused Eileen. 'All the blokes I've dated have caused me nowt but grief.'

Danny smiled but felt a stab of guilt. He hadn't told his mum that he'd recently run another search for his dad on Facebook – and this time discovered that he'd set up a profile. Yiannis hadn't posted anything and his profile photo was of a ship, presumably one belonging to his family's company. So Danny hadn't even been able to find out what he looked like. But his curiosity had been piqued.

He'd left Facebook and googled the name Yiannis Dimitriou, but his search had returned no results – or, rather, it had returned a few but they were all written in Greek and he had no idea how to even decipher the alphabet, other than by using one of those new translation apps that were so primitive they offered little more than gibberish. He'd told himself to stop there but he hadn't been able to; he'd returned to Facebook and sent his dad a simple message, just telling him who he was and asking if he'd like to talk. Although the message had been marked as read, Yiannis still hadn't replied.

You don't need him, Danny had reassured himself. *You've survived this long without him. And at least this way you don't run any risk of upsetting your mum.*

He lit a cigarette, using his hand to shield it from the breeze. 'How about you, Arthur?' he asked. 'Do you not fancy online dating?'

Arthur crinkled his nose. 'I might have a look for a bit of fun but I'm not that fussed about relationships, dearie.'

Guy lay back, resting his head on his hand. 'Why do you say that? Have you ever tried one?'

'No, not really,' Arthur answered. 'I've always been perfectly happy on me todd.'

'Maybe you should give it a go,' suggested Danny. 'It's never too late to try something new.'

Arthur let out a sigh. 'One of the things I've always enjoyed about being gay is escaping the expectation. Not feeling like we *should* have any particular kind of relationship – or that we'll be judged if we don't. When I were growing up it didn't cross my mind I'd have any kind of relationship at all. It wouldn't have been possible in them days.'

Danny took a drag on his cigarette. 'Yeah, but all that's changed, Arthur. We can get civil partnerships now.'

'Yes, and it's very important that we have equal rights,' said Arthur. 'But I like to think I'm more suited to making – how shall I put it? – non-conventional connections. I like summat more authentic, not feeling like my relationship has been shaped by what other people say is right. If I did want to be with someone long-term, it'd have to be in the way *I* want it.'

Danny realised that this kind of approach to relationships had never occurred to him. He'd always thought he wanted the traditional romance, the fairytale love story, to be part of a committed, monogamous couple.

But I never really grew up seeing gay relationships, not in real life or in the media. So am I just trying to follow the straight model?

'Anyway, right now there's nowt lacking in my life,' Arthur went on, beaming. 'I mean, look at this, the four of us sitting together on t' beach. I've got a flask full of tea, bacon butties for our dinner, *and* some Kendal mint cake for afters. What more could anyone want?'

'Well, I wouldn't say no to Daniel Craig coming out of t' sea in a pair of Speedos,' quipped Eileen.

They all laughed.

'His bulge glistening in t' sunshine like a sack of spuds,' she added.

Danny gasped in mock outrage. 'Mum, you're as bad as me!'

'Well, I hate to say it, but that's one thing you're not going to see in Brighton,' chirped Arthur. 'The water's much too cold to go swimming. It'd shrivel up anyone's bulge!'

When the laughter had died down, the conversation turned to holidays – and everyone's dream destinations.

Eileen gazed off in the vague direction of France. 'I'd love to go to Saint Tropez. Joan Collins has got a place there – I read about it in *Hello!*'

'I've always fancied t' Maldives,' said Arthur. 'Apparently Paul O'Grady goes every year.'

'I wouldn't mind going to Sitges,' piped Guy.

Danny looked at him as if a bowl of fruit had just appeared on his head.

'What's the matter?' said Guy. 'Did I pronounce it wrong?'

'No, it's just . . .' Danny stubbed out his cigarette and rested the butt on a pebble to throw away later. 'You do mean the gay resort in Spain, don't you? The place where everyone goes to pull?'

'Yeah, what's wrong with that?' Guy picked up a pebble and turned it around in his hands. 'I know a rowdy boys' holiday isn't my usual kind of thing, but now I'm single I thought I might give it a go. What do you reckon, Danny? Would you be up for it?'

Before Danny could answer, Eileen cut in. 'So you're not looking for another relationship then, Guy?'

Danny noticed her eyes flit onto him.

What's she getting at?

'Nah, I thought I'd have some fun first,' Guy replied. And he drew back his arm and threw his pebble into the sea.

'Fun!' burst out Arthur. 'It's what life's all about! And never mind Sitges, it's happening right here in Brighton!'

Eileen bent down and unzipped their picnic bag. 'Now, who fancies a bacon butty?'

2022

Guy tries not to think that in just a few hours he and Danny are going to be having dinner – and, he imagines, a conversation that could change the course of their entire relationship. He's pretty sure that's why Danny's suggested getting away from the crowds and eating somewhere quiet.

And if I'm right, it'll probably be the most important conversation he and I ever have.

With Danny beside him, he steps through the crash barrier, rises up on his tiptoes and looks out over Sackville Gardens. The arena is lined with bars, food stalls and toilet blocks and brimming with people – nearly 5,000 of them. To the left of the main audience area is a sound and lighting rig, directed at the stage, and there are several screens dotted around so that the people towards the back can view the action in close-up. Although some of the crowd are drinking and chatting, most are watching the current performance, which is by a young pop star Guy doesn't recognise.

'Who's that?' he asks Danny.

Danny shrugs. 'God knows, I've never heard of her. Mind you, we're probably both old enough to be her dad.'

Guy feigns outrage. 'Excuse me, what's with the 'we'? You're older than me, remember!'

'Only by a few months! Anyway, I bet you're still twice her age.'

Guy gives out an exaggerated huff. 'I need a drink!'

They tread through a cluster of stalls at the back of the arena, including something called the TikTok Sanctuary, which Guy is eager to avoid as he knows he won't understand it. They come out at the back of the crowd, with the stage directly in front of them, a row of trees to their right, and the canal – plus Canal Street – behind them. On either side of the stage are posters advertising Manchester Pride and advising everyone to stay hydrated. And it doesn't escape Guy's attention that rising up into the sky behind the stage is a group of old redbrick buildings that used to belong to the Science and Technology Institute but now form part of Manchester University.

Once they've bought themselves a drink from a bar in a huge tent set up on the left, Guy and Danny pick their way through the crowd and follow the paved pathway towards the stage. When they enter the cobbled circle at the centre of what's usually a park, they come across the famous statue of Enigma code-breaking computer scientist Alan Turing, who currently has a rainbow bandana tied around his neck and is being mobbed by people wanting to sit next to him and have their photos taken. They continue walking, dodging out of the way of several drunken people who are bashing into benches, bins and pieces of park furniture.

Before long, they're lucky enough to slip into a spot that's just been vacated by the railings at the front of the accessible viewing platform. From all around them comes the sound of whooping and cheering and this continues as act after act performs on stage, each of them introduced by popular queer TV presenters or comedians. Not all of the acts are young and some are clearly aimed at more mature members of the audience – even so, Guy finds it difficult to concentrate. All he can think about is the conversation he's about to have with Danny.

I'm not very good at talking about emotions. I'm better than I used to be, but that's not saying much. What if I get tongue-tied and it all comes out wrong?

After a while, he senses that the artist appearing on stage is losing the interest of the crowd. People start slipping off to the toilets or queuing up at the food stalls. He draws in a deep, bracing breath.

'I reckon this might be that lull you talked about,' he says to Danny. 'Shall we nip off and get something to eat?'

Danny looks as nervous as he is. 'Yeah,' he says, 'let's do it.'

2010

'God, I'm starving. What time are we going for dinner?'

Danny looked at Guy and rolled his eyes affectionately. 'You'll have to wait a bit longer, I'm afraid. I keep telling you – nobody eats here till about ten.'

'Oh, I know,' said Guy, 'but I'm going to struggle to last that long.'

Danny smiled at him. 'Come on, let's get you an ice cream to see you on.'

They began strolling along the seafront, towards an ice cream shop they'd visited regularly during their holiday. As they'd just left the beach, they were wearing flip-flops and swimming shorts and Guy was still shirtless, with a canvas bag containing their earphones and suncream slung over his shoulder, while Danny had pulled on a vest plus a baseball cap to protect his scalp. They both had their towels draped around their necks and were wearing sunglasses with big lenses and chunky plastic frames that they'd bought after Danny had read in *Heat* magazine that they were the height of fashion. Their skin was glowing, Guy's hair had been bleached even blonder by the sun, and Danny was so relaxed he didn't even mind that he had sand stuck in between his toes, rubbing at the thong of his Havaianas.

He imagined what the two of them must look like to the other tourists.

I bet they all think we're a blissfully happy couple on a romantic holiday.

They called into the shop, where Guy bought a huge tub of chocolate ice cream and Danny a smaller cone of toffee, and began walking back up the seafront, along a wide gravel-surfaced promenade that was lined with palm trees. On their right was a row of hotels and restaurants, a series of grand, sandy-coloured buildings with balconies and brick-arched windows. On their left was the Mediterranean Sea, the early evening sunlight shimmering on the surface of its gentle, rolling waves.

Danny took a lick of his ice cream. 'Mmm, this is gorgeous.'

'So's this,' said Guy. He stretched his arms out and gave a little roar. 'This holiday is just what I needed.'

They'd come to Sitges for the boys' holiday Guy had suggested in Brighton. As Danny was still earning money from role-play training, he'd decided he could just about afford it – and he'd just have to block out of his mind the mountain of student debt he still needed to pay off. They'd each brought along a friend: Danny had asked Salvador, his Spanish colleague from the bar, and Guy had asked Marcus, a fellow gay lawyer Danny hardly knew. As it happened, he didn't get to know him any better, as Marcus and Salvador had slept together on the first night and promptly struck up a full-blown holiday romance. Not only did this mean that Danny and Guy were left pretty much on their own, but also that they'd had to switch rooms, so that they were sharing with each other rather than with each of their friends.

Danny knew he'd find it difficult to sleep and shower in such close proximity to Guy, not to mention using the toilet. But he'd been relieved to discover that their room was at least fitted with twin beds rather than a double, so – even after a night out drinking – it would be tricky for them to 'accidentally' have sex, as Lynsey had suggested several years ago.

There were a few reasons he didn't want this to happen now. The main one was that he was still in a relationship with Dean and they were approaching their one-year anniversary. He hadn't wanted to break up with Dean as soon as Guy had ended his relationship with Spencer – that would have made his intention way too obvious. He didn't want to cheat on Dean either; their relationship had some serious problems but, after years of sleeping around, Danny wanted to prove to himself that he could be faithful to one man.

I want to prove to myself that I'm not the gay equivalent of my dad.

The other reason was that Guy was going through a rare bout of promiscuity. On their second night in Sitges, he'd disappeared with a handsome Frenchman, only returning the next morning, by which time Danny felt shot through with sadness. But his ordeal hadn't ended there; on a handful of nights since, Guy had met someone new – leaving Danny thrashing around in his hotel bed, screwing up the sheets and pummelling the pillow, consumed by a jealousy so intense it felt like it was corroding his insides.

So no, any kind of 'accident' between me and Guy couldn't be any less appropriate.

'Are you looking forward to tonight?' he asked Guy, casually.

Guy smiled. 'Yeah, I got a text from Tom earlier.'

'Oh, which one's that?' Danny hoped his voice didn't wobble. 'The dentist from Bristol?'

'No, that was Ed. Tom's the one who's staying at a villa inland.'

Danny licked around the perimeter of his ice cream. 'Oh yeah, the short one with the big balls.'

'That's him.'

Even though Danny hated hearing about Guy's sexual conquests, at the same time he found himself weirdly compelled to interrogate him on every detail. At first, Guy had been reluctant to reveal too much, but Danny had pushed him; it was like lifting up a bandage to look at a cut that was infected, or ripping off a scab even though this would only make the wound worse.

'I didn't realise you were that bothered about him,' he said.

Guy wrinkled his nose. 'I'm not really, but he was sweet. And he was really into kissing. You know I love that.'

Into Danny's head flashed an image of Dean refusing to kiss him when they were having sex and insisting on penetrating him from behind, without any intimacy or affection. He remembered the sharp sting he felt when Dean slapped him, something he'd recently started doing in between shouting out his usual insults. On one occasion he'd even put his hands around Danny's neck as if he were strangling him, at which point Danny had stopped being turned on – but he'd continued to feign enjoyment, scared that if he didn't, he might lose Dean. He blinked the memory out of his head.

'Well, I think it's fair to say you've shagged Spencer out of your system,' he said, cheerily. 'So if that was the aim of the holiday, mission accomplished!'

Guy ate another mouthful of ice cream. 'You know, it's a shame you're not single too.'

Danny hoisted an eyebrow. 'Oh yeah, why do you say that?'

'Well, just that we've never really been single at the same time. At least not since our first year at uni.'

Yeah and don't I know it? Haven't I lived through every painful minute of it?

'Maybe I just thought this holiday would be the chance to recreate that,' Guy went on. 'I mean, you've got to admit, we did have a laugh.'

Danny smiled but said nothing.

They came to a stop outside their hotel, which was located directly opposite the gay beach. As they still hadn't finished their ice creams, they drifted over to the stone balustrade, from where they had a clear view of the long stretch of golden sand. Although it was 6 o'clock and some people were packing up to leave, some were still sunbathing, while others were congregating under the parasols, drinking brightly-coloured daiquiris they'd bought from the mobile beach vendors. A group of men raised their glasses and posed for a photograph one of their friends was taking on his smartphone.

'Sitges rhymes with bitches!' they shouted, and erupted into raucous laughter.

Danny knew that in a few hours he'd be seeing all of these men in the Old Town, in any of the long strip of bars that ran from Parrots to Queenz. They'd greet each other like old friends then spend the night drinking, sharing bawdy stories, and casting their eyes around for the subject of the *next* bawdy story. By the end of the night – which in reality would be the middle of the following morning – people would start forming couples and peeling off to go back to their hotels and apartments, those who were less lucky sloping off into one of the darkrooms at the back of the bars, or down to the beach, where underneath the promenade on which Danny and Guy were currently standing there was a late-night cruising ground – a cruising ground favoured by the unsuccessful or unattractive, or those who simply preferred fleeting, anonymous, intimacy-free sexual encounters.

But I can't do anything like that because I've got a boyfriend.

Guy put down his ice cream and looked out to sea. 'You know, I really don't think you should be with Dean.'

Danny's heart gave a little flutter. 'Oh yeah, where's that come from?'

'I just don't think he's right for you. You know that.'

It was true that Guy had said this on several occasions. From the moment he'd been introduced to Dean, there'd been a barely concealed animosity between the two men and Danny had allowed himself to imagine that Guy might just be jealous. Once the thought had lodged in his mind, he hadn't been able to resist stoking the fire, letting slip to both Guy and Dean that they were disliked by the other, subtly reiterating the point until the two of them could hardly bear to be in the same room as each other. More recently, Danny had gone to Guy for support after he and Dean had had another of their blistering rows. When Danny had confessed the way Dean deliberately chipped away at his confidence, Guy had expressed a surprisingly raw anger. Part of Danny enjoyed witnessing this; for a fleeting moment it made him think it was worth being insulted by Dean, just to see how angry it made Guy.

'I just don't think he makes you happy,' Guy argued. 'He's not good enough for you, Danny.'

Danny felt his heart contract. He licked up some ice cream that had dribbled onto his fingers.

'Anyway, you used to say you were happy being single,' Guy went on. 'Whatever happened to "I don't do emotional attachment"? Whatever happened to "I want to chuck my muck and go"? How did you get from that to being stuck in a relationship with Dean?'

Danny let out a sigh.

Where do I start?

'Oh, let's not talk about this now,' he said, 'we're supposed to be on holiday!'

Guy finished his ice cream and tossed the tub into a nearby bin. 'Alright, point taken.'

'Come on, let's go back to the hotel. Let's have a power nap and then get ready for the night.'

'OK,' said Guy. He reached out and touched Danny's arm. 'I'm serious, though – please think about ending it with Dean. I don't like seeing you unhappy, princess.'

That was the first time Guy had called him 'princess' for years. And Danny was powerless to suppress his feelings, the same feelings he'd experienced the first time Guy had used what had become his pet name. Flickering back to life in some long-forgotten corner of his being came all the innocent hope and excitement of his first year at university.

But now here I am and the only way I can get Guy to call me princess is by going out with some bloke who treats me like shit.

Danny crammed the rest of his cornet into his mouth. 'Right, now we've demolished those ice creams, let's start thinking about where to go for dinner.'

2022

'Spanish omelette, *patatas bravas*, chorizo,' Danny reads. 'It looks good to me.'

They're in Manchester's Northern Quarter, outside a Spanish restaurant Danny found on TripAdvisor, scouring the app to come up with the perfect combination of low-key setting, no-nonsense service and Guy-friendly food.

'And they do paella!' he comments, as if this should come as a surprise for a Spanish restaurant.

He hopes Guy can't tell how nervous he is. Although it's only a few hours since they took part in the parade, all his doubts and insecurities have come thundering back in advance of the discussion he's about to provoke.

Oh God, what's Guy going to say?

Come to think of it, what am I *going to say?*

As he continues perusing the menu, the various options swirl around the page and dissolve into a blizzard of pixels. All he can think about is his opening line.

There's something I want to tell you . . .

It's about last night . . .

He shivers with fear.

Guy, I'm in love with you.

He has no idea how best to express his feelings. He doesn't want to be too blunt, but at the same time, if he's too subtle, his message might not hit home.

One thing he does know is he must be careful not to tell Guy how long he's felt like this; he doesn't want to freak him out. And he must remember to say 'I'm in love with you' rather than 'I love you'. That's what the two of them said to each other during the parade but he can see now that this expression can sometimes be used to describe the love between friends. In the absence of any wider vocabulary to differentiate between the various types of love, he'll have to rely on nuance to make his feelings clear.

This time I'm not going to leave any room for misinterpretation.

'Well, what do you think?' he asks.

'Yeah, it looks great,' says Guy.

For the first time, Danny notices his voice crack.

Oh God, don't tell me he's nervous too.

Danny draws in a long, steadying breath. 'Come on then, let's go in.'

2011

Danny walked into the restaurant and saw Guy sitting on a bench waiting for a table. He took off his coat and hugged him.

'Come on,' said Guy, 'what is it you want to tell me?'

Earlier that day, Danny had texted him to say he had important news – but news he wanted to share in person. It was something he'd been looking forward to for a couple of weeks, something he didn't want to waste.

He sat down and put his hands on his knees. 'I've dumped Dean,' he announced.

'That's brilliant news!' said Guy.

The smile that appeared on his face gave Danny a little glow inside.

'So how did you do it?'

'It was weird but I just woke up on New Year's Day and all of a sudden it was like I couldn't stay with him a minute longer. I just knew it. And the second it entered my head I couldn't get rid of it. I'd slept over at Dean's place so I just got my stuff together, told him and left.'

'And he didn't have a go at you, did he?' Guy asked.

'No, he was too hungover,' said Danny. 'But he's been sending me nasty texts since.'

Creases appeared on Guy's forehead. 'Do you want me to do anything about it? I could always tell him to back off.'

Danny tried not to let his mouth creep into a grin. 'No, it's alright, thanks. He's lashed out now so I think he's probably got it out of his system. And I'm pretty sure it was his pride that was hurt more than anything else.'

To be honest, I'm not sure he was that bothered about me. I'm not sure he even liked *me.*

The indignity of it suddenly hit Danny all over again.

Thank God I've got out now.

'Well, that's a great way to start the New Year!' said Guy, clapping his hands together. 'I'm so happy for you, I really am.'

'Thanks, babe.'

Guy shifted in his seat. 'While we're at it, I've got some news too.'

'Oh yeah, what's that?'

'I've met someone.'

Danny felt like he'd been winded. For a moment, he wasn't sure he'd heard Guy correctly. 'You what?'

'I've met someone,' repeated Guy.

Oh no, please don't tell me that. Not now. I don't think I can take it.

'You've *met* someone?' Danny managed to say, his voice straying into a higher pitch. 'What, like a boyfriend?'

'Yeah, why are you so surprised?'

Come on, Danny, style this out.

'Oh, I don't know, I just thought you were enjoying being single, that's all.'

'Yeah, well, I was at first. And I know I went for it in Sitges but it's different when you're on holiday. I think I probably just needed a blow-out.'

Danny wasn't sure what to say. He tried to swallow but his mouth was dry.

'Once I got home I started to miss having a boyfriend,' Guy continued. 'And I know you and I went on the pull a few times but I wasn't really feeling it. And I couldn't handle Gaydar so I knew I wouldn't stand a chance on Grindr.'

'Mr Falconer,' interrupted the hostess, 'your table's ready.'

Danny and Guy followed her through the entrance hall and into the restaurant. It was a smart brasserie that was located in Mayfair, in a building that used to house a bank, with marble pillars, studded leather banquettes, and a mahogany bar that looked like it must have been the old cashiers' counter. It was the kind of place that would have been much too expensive for Danny, but every January Guy liked to take him out somewhere special, something he called his New Year treat. As they wound their way between tables of expensively suited men and lavishly decorated women, Danny tried to project the image of someone who didn't have the slightest insecurity about fitting in. But inside, all he could think about was Guy's news.

When they reached the table, a waiter appeared and pulled out Danny's chair. Danny thanked him and tried to study the menu. But he couldn't concentrate.

'So who is he then, this new man?' he asked.

Guy smiled and seeing him look so happy ripped at Danny's heart.

'His name's Henry and he's an art dealer. He's two years younger than us and doesn't really go out on the scene so I doubt you'll know him.'

'I don't *only* go out on the scene,' Danny mumbled.

But Guy didn't hear him. 'Oh and guess what? He's from a village a few miles from where I grew up. It turns out we had the same swimming teacher *and* the same driving instructor.'

'That's insane,' Danny mouthed.

'Best of all,' Guy rattled on, 'I was nervous about telling my parents, but it turns out Henry's mother and father go to the same golf club as them. They've even met a few times.'

Of course they have.

Of course you'd go out with someone like that.

Of course you wouldn't go out with someone like me.

Guy put down his menu. 'What's the matter? You don't look very happy.'

Danny cast around for an excuse. 'Oh, I was just looking forward to us both being single at the same time. It's like you said in Sitges, we've never really had that.'

He returned to his menu and scanned down the list of food.

'No, and that is a shame,' said Guy. 'If it's any consolation, I wasn't planning on meeting anyone – I certainly didn't go looking for it. But I met Henry through a colleague at work and he completely knocked me for six. I can't wait to introduce you to him.'

Danny tried not to choke on his bile. 'Steady on, cowboy. You've only known this bloke for five minutes. Are you sure you're ready to start introducing him to your friends?'

'Actually, we met a few months ago,' Guy said, 'but I didn't want to tell you till I was sure it was serious.'

Danny could feel the heat of humiliation staining his face.

'Sorry,' Guy went on, 'I just wanted to keep this one to myself for a while.'

Except you told your parents.

Guy cracked a smile. 'I don't know, maybe it's because it feels different.'

Danny began to fan himself with his menu. ''Different'? How do you mean, 'different'?'

'I think this is it, Danny. I think Henry's The One.'

Danny felt the deep burn of heartache.

Oh, why does this have to hurt so much? Surely loving someone shouldn't be this painful?

And the worst thing is, now I have to sit through the entire meal.

'Well, that's great,' he managed, thinly. 'I'm really chuffed for you.'

He felt hot-eyed and his chin gave a little wobble. He pretended to have something in his throat and coughed it away. 'Now come on, what are we going to eat?'

He looked back at the menu but couldn't care less what he ate. It hardly mattered anymore; the way he was feeling, he wasn't sure he'd even taste it.

Oh, how can Guy go out with all these other men and not me? Just what's wrong *with me?*

Then another voice popped into his head.

Men like Guy don't go out with men like you. He's a nice, lovely, respectable gay, whereas you're a dirty gay who slaps it about and goes on Grindr to hook up with strangers.

Rising up through his humiliation, Danny was surprised to detect a rush of satisfaction. It was as if part of him felt vindicated, as if he'd always known what he was like and had just had his assessment confirmed.

Now come on, get back in your box and stop making a fool of yourself.

The waiter came back to their table and took out his pad and pen. 'Are you ready to order?'

2022

Once they've ordered, Danny starts rambling.

'You know, all this Spanish food is making me think about Salvador.'

'Who?' says Guy.

'Don't you remember, my Spanish friend? The one who came with us to Sitges?'

'Oh yeah, Salvador. The one from the bar.'

Danny tells Guy he's no longer in touch with any of the boys from the bar, but the last time he checked on social media, Salvador had gone back to Madrid and moved in with a chiropodist.

'I wonder if he still has that funny laugh,' he says, desperately trying to lift the tension. 'Do you remember? The one that sounded like he was choking.'

Guy smiles but doesn't say anything.

An uneasy silence sets in between them.

'You know, I'm very impressed with the Northern Quarter,' Danny chirps. He adds that when they were at university and the area was still very deprived – with bohemian cafes, loft apartments and vintage clothes stores only just starting to spring up amongst the derelict mills and warehouses – they could have had no idea that within twenty years it would have developed into Manchester's coolest neighbourhood.

For God's sake, Danny, stop rambling.

The waitress comes back with a bottle of wine.

'Thanks *so* much!' Danny practically shrieks at her.

Once she's left, he takes a sip from his glass.

Come on, you need to pull yourself together.

He takes a moment and looks down at the table. When he looks up again and his eyes meet Guy's, he suddenly stops rambling and says exactly what he wants to say.

'Guy, we need to talk about last night.'

Guy gives a barely perceptible nod. 'And what would you like to say?'

Danny speaks slowly, choosing each of his words carefully. 'I think it would be easy for us to get freaked out by what happened. But I really don't want to. I really enjoyed it.'

His words linger in the air between them.

Guy takes a sip of his wine and slowly sets down his glass. 'Yeah, I enjoyed it too.'

Danny feels encouraged. 'Anyway, it's made me think about my feelings for you.'

He clears his throat.

'What I've realised is I'd like to explore them. I'd like to see if we can be more than just friends.'

Guy sits in silence. He picks up the pepper grinder and begins turning it around in his hands.

'So what do you think?' Danny asks. 'How do *you* feel about it?'

Oh God, this is it. After twenty years, this is it.

Guy takes a loud breath and places the pepper grinder back on the table.

'Like I said, I really enjoyed it,' he says. 'And I'll always be glad we did it. But I don't want to take things any further. At least not in the direction you're talking about.'

Danny blinks, very slowly.

'I guess, what I'm saying is,' Guy goes on, 'I'm happy being friends.'

Fuck.

Danny's body becomes rigid. He just about manages to open his mouth. 'I understand.'

'I'm sorry if that's disappointing,' Guy goes on.

Oh no, here comes the sympathy. Here comes the pity.

But Danny knows he has to see this through. 'It is disappointing,' he says, the banality of the word stinging, 'but it's also a bit confusing. I mean, the sex we had was really intimate. And some of the things you said . . .'

Danny pauses, aware that he's throwing away his dignity.

'I don't know,' he continues, 'I just maybe got the impression that what we did was more than just sex.'

I thought we made love.

Guy screws up his face. 'Yeah, sorry, I do tend to get a bit emotional when I have sex. But you know I've never really been into one-night stands. You know I like to feel a connection with someone.'

Danny notices a little rip in the tablecloth and finds himself staring at it.

I can't believe this is happening.

Is *this really happening?*

For a second he wonders if he's in the middle of a nightmare.

'And I did have a lot to drink,' Guy adds. 'I might have got a bit carried away.'

Oh my God, now he's blaming it on the booze. Just like Lynsey told me to do.

Danny looks up. 'But I don't understand,' he protests, repulsed by how feeble he sounds. 'When we were in the parade you said you loved me.'

Guy takes a sip of his wine. 'Yes, well, I'm sorry if I gave the wrong impression. What I meant is, I love you as a friend.'

His words hit Danny harder than any physical blow.

How could I have got it so wrong?

'Look, I really don't want this to affect what we have between us,' Guy adds. 'We've been through so much together, Danny. You're my best friend.'

Suddenly it strikes Danny that the word 'friend' has to be the ugliest word in the English language. It strikes him as trite and insignificant and dull and facile. It strikes him as an insult to everything that's happened between them, to everything they've done together.

Oh God, this is horrendous. And now I have to sit through the entire meal, just like I did when he told me he'd met Henry!

He glances around and spots the waitress at the service hatch, transferring what looks like their food onto a tray.

Actually, I don't *have to sit through it. There's nothing to stop me from standing up and walking away.*

He tugs in a breath.

'Sorry, babe,' he says, pushing back his chair, 'but I'm not hungry.'

He shakes his head.

'Actually, that's not true; I *am* hungry. I just don't want to do this.'

Guy looks shocked. 'Oh. Are you alright?'

Danny stands up but doesn't answer. 'I just want to go for a walk and clear my head. I just want to be on my own.'

Guy picks up his napkin and starts coiling it around his finger. 'That's cool. I get it.'

Without saying goodbye, Danny nods and walks away.

As he pushes open the door and steps outside, he remembers Arthur's advice about straightening out his crown. It's advice that has helped him through many a tough time.

But this time he isn't going to take it.

2022

Danny leaves behind the Northern Quarter, with its distinctive red-brick buildings, wide boulevards and rejuvenated mills and warehouses. Without any route in mind, he begins walking around the city.

Daylight is fading, but the streets are still busy with people coming to the end of a shopping trip or embarking on a night out. To avoid them, Danny ducks down as many side streets as he can – but all the time he keeps walking. And he walks and walks.

He passes Afflecks and the Arndale Centre, the Corn Exchange and the Cathedral, Castlefield and the Bridgewater Hall. When he hits Deansgate, he retraces the route of that afternoon's parade, amazed that already the crash barriers have been removed, the grandstand dismantled, and the streets cleaned so thoroughly it's almost as if the parade never happened. Although he does spot one solitary rainbow flag, trampled with mud and frayed along the edges, lying discarded at the side of the road.

He walks on.

After a few hours, daylight disappears and night sets in. Danny retreats to Albert Square and, without really thinking about it, finds himself looking for what he and Guy used to call their steps, around the statue of William Gladstone. He lowers himself onto them and stretches out his legs. He's tired and his stomach rumbles with hunger. But he can't face eating.

The square is busier than it used to be, with several new bars around the newly pedestrianised perimeter, most of these with outside seating areas that are teeming with people. But Danny looks away. He notices that the Town Hall is fenced off and undergoing what looks like a major renovation project. He picks up his phone to google the details but can't muster up the interest to read about them.

He feels as if all the love has been wrung out of him.

The love that's kept me alive pretty much all my adult life.

He leans back and closes his eyes. He remembers how he felt when Guy told him he'd met Henry. He wasn't sure he'd cope, but somehow he got over the disappointment. But that disappointment wasn't definitive. There was always a tiny sliver of hope.

And now there's no hope at all.

Or is there?

He opens his eyes. The time on the clock tower reads just after 10 o'clock. A lone starling has landed on the head of the statue of Prince Albert. Apart from the construction site, the square hasn't changed at all since his final year of university. Danny tries to picture what he and Guy must have looked like then. He tries to bring back to life the connection that existed between them.

No, it wasn't just friendship. I wasn't imagining it.

He finds himself wondering if Guy might simply be scared by what they did the night before, if he might just need time to digest it.

After all, it is only a couple of months since his divorce came through.

Maybe he didn't wait long enough before bringing things to a head.

His memory rewinds to the way Guy defended him in front of Spencer before the parade. 'Oh, I wouldn't be so sure,' he said when Spencer joked that Danny would always be single. 'You never know what's going to happen.'

Now, why would he have said that the night after sleeping with me?

Come to think of it, why would he have said hotel rooms make him horny?

And why's he's been calling me 'princess' all weekend?

No, Danny can't just forget that.

He sits up on the steps with a new resolve. He isn't going to worry about acting with dignity – he's going to fight for what he knows is right. He can't discard all the history he has with Guy. He can't discard everything that's happened between them.

And surely, once Guy's thought about it, he'll feel the same . . .

2005

Guy broke out of the hug and leaned back on the steps. He felt better now Danny had come to meet him for lunch. He felt like he could face his finals, like getting that 2:1 wasn't out of reach. He wasn't quite so daunted by the idea of his future once he left university. He even felt like he could cope with the occasional outburst of homophobia from his parents.

And all that's because of Danny.

'Promise me we'll always be together,' he said to him.

'I promise,' said Danny.

'So you'll never leave me?' Guy asked.

Danny shook his head. 'I'll never leave you.'

Guy nodded and smiled.

As the starlings they'd scared off with their laughter returned to peck at the crumbs left by their lunch, he found himself wondering once again if he and Danny could be more than just friends.

The only thing is, I'm not sure I'm attracted to him sexually.

But what would happen if we actually had *sex?*

If he was being honest with himself, Guy knew the answer to this question – rather than making things clearer, it would only make them more confusing. Because he knew he was turned on by feeling connected to someone and he and Danny were so close they were bound to experience certain feelings, the same feelings that had flickered on and off over the first few months they'd known each other. But since then, Guy had realised these feelings didn't reflect what he wanted in the long term. However much he might like them to, he couldn't avoid the fact that they didn't. He didn't doubt that he loved Danny, but he loved him more like a brother or sister – not someone with whom he wanted to share his life romantically.

And OK, sometimes I might think we'd make a good couple. But that's only when I'm feeling tired or stressed or I need him and he's there for me.

Guy knew Danny well enough by now for this to be absolutely clear. And he impressed on himself that he had to keep this in mind or it wouldn't be fair on Danny.

I don't want to lead him on or toy with his emotions just to make me feel good about myself.

He acknowledged that he'd probably been guilty of this during their conversation today and felt a rush of remorse. He resolved to try his hardest not to do it in the future.

He thanked Danny for coming to see him. 'You know, you're the best friend anyone could ask for,' he said, taking care to emphasise the word 'friend'.

The emphasis seemed lost on Danny. 'You're not too bad yourself, my prince.'

Guy smiled. 'And I'm sorry for being so needy. I promise normal service will resume soon.'

'It's fine, babe. Honestly, there's no need to apologise.'

Guy stood up to go back to the library. As he said goodbye, he reminded himself to make sure he had no need to apologise in future.

2022

Danny stands up from the steps and takes out his phone. He's going to text Guy.

'Hi, where are you?' he types.

Guy replies immediately. 'Went back to Sackville Gardens but wasn't feeling it. Just got to Via.'

'OK,' Danny writes. 'See you there?'

Guy texts back the emoji for thumbs up.

Right, I'm going to do this . . . I'm going to take decisive action and fix this situation . . .

Before doubt can set in, Danny sets off for the Village. He doesn't think for the entire time it takes to get there; he just concentrates on regulating his breathing and putting one foot in front of the other.

When he arrives, he queues at the entrance to the street party on Sackville Street. His legs are aching and he's so hungry he's starting to feel faint. But he blocks that out of his mind. When he reaches the front of the queue, he flashes his wristband. Without waiting, he thrusts himself into the crowd.

He passes the Molly House pub, outside which a DJ is

playing Steps to a crowd who are singing along with their arms in the air. He dodges out of the way of the Saint John's ambulance crew who are carrying someone on a stretcher. And he inches around a stall set up by a face painter who's decorating a man holding a cockapoo with a rainbow bandana around its neck.

When he finally reaches Canal Street, he turns left. He forces his way through the mass of people until he sees the sign for Via. Then, just as he's taking out his phone to text Guy, he spots him. He's standing in the same place in which the two of them stood last night, next to the same lamp-post. Danny opens his mouth to shout his name but stops.

No, it can't be . . .

He notices that Guy is talking to a young man. The young man has a boyish grin, a square jaw, and a well-maintained body. Danny realises it's the same man who was checking Guy out last night, the same man who asked Danny if they were together.

And I told him Guy was my boyfriend.

Now this man isn't just talking to Guy but he's also laughing loudly at something he's said. His eyes are sparkling and he's puffing out his chest and popping out his arm muscles. There's no question he's flirting with him.

Danny freezes. As Guy's standing with his back to him, he can't see how he's responding. Then the man moves in for a kiss.

Danny watches to see how Guy will react, the blood singing loudly in his ears.

Oh, please don't kiss him. Please don't do it!

Guy kisses him.

Fuck!

Danny's breath fails. He can't help letting out a little scream.

But it's a scream that isn't heard, a scream that's lost underneath the thumping music and the noise of the crowd.

He can't watch any more and turns away. He feels hollow in the pit of his stomach.

There's no way he can face speaking to Guy. Instead, he writes him a text. 'Just seen you but you're clearly busy. Am going back to the hotel. Have a good night.'

He hits Send.

As he shuts down his phone, he notices from the clock that it isn't yet midnight. He feels around in his pockets and pulls out his cigarettes. As he lights one, he remembers his vow to give up if Guy fell in love with him.

As if.

He breathes in the smoke and breathes it out slowly. Then he begins pushing his way back through the crowd.

He feels like everyone's looking at him and can tell what's just happened. He feels like they're all laughing at him, or – even worse – feeling sorry for him.

It wasn't meant to be like this.

When I pictured this weekend in my head, it wasn't anything like this.

Above the swarm of people ahead, a balloon in the shape of a unicorn breaks free from its owner. Danny stops and watches it slowly drift up into the sky. He stands mesmerised as it becomes smaller and smaller then, finally, disappears from view.

And he understands that he no longer has any hope.

His love has died.

And he has no idea where to go from here.

SUNDAY

2022

Where am I?

As Danny wakes up, all he can see is darkness. His neck is stiff, he's desperate for the loo, and he feels disorientated. Then it hits him.

Oh yeah, I'm in a hotel in Manchester.

Fuck, I told Guy I'm in love with him!

When he remembers Guy's response, that hollow feeling slams into him again.

He rises up onto his elbow and switches on the bedside light. His eyes are dry and he has to blink to see properly. The alarm clock says it's 4.13 a.m. He looks across to the other side of the bed. But Guy isn't there.

Oh no, he must have stayed out with that twink.

My God, I knew I was stupid but I had no idea I was that *stupid.*

Danny hauls himself out of bed and totters through to the bathroom. As he empties his bladder, the conversation he had with Guy replays in his mind. And he may have spent much of last night fighting against it but he can't fight against it anymore;

what Guy said changes everything. It makes him view their whole relationship differently.

He shudders with shame at some of the things he's done over the last twenty years, at some of the things he's said to Guy. As the memories rush back into his head, he lets out a groan.

He flushes the toilet and crashes back into bed.

2011

It was a fine summer's evening and Danny was in Ladbroke Grove, sitting on the roof terrace of the flat Guy had bought just before he split up with Spencer. It occupied the top two floors of a Victorian conversion and the terrace offered an uninterrupted view of London's skyline. When he'd moved in, Guy had hired a gardener to cover it with decking and install chrome pots containing grasses, ferns and bamboo. In the centre he'd positioned a large, durable barbecue, on which he enjoyed cooking for friends – as he was doing this evening.

'Now, who wants a burger?' he said, with a big smile on his face.

Danny, on the other hand, wasn't enjoying the evening; he was feeling agitated and on edge. This had nothing to do with Guy; it was all down to Henry. Danny couldn't help resenting how quickly he'd manoeuvred his way into Guy's life. Danny had still only met him a handful of times, yet here he was, acting like he was Guy's co-host and making sure Danny knew he'd been downgraded to guest. It was only a few weeks since Henry had moved into the flat, but he'd wasted no time in marking his territory by arranging scented candles and diffusers on every surface and plastering the walls with prints, paintings and collages by artists who were much too cool for Danny to have heard of – and if he didn't know who they were, he was sure Guy wouldn't have the faintest idea. Gone was the black and white photograph of New York construction workers and there were no more sports kits hanging on radiators or dumbbells strewn across carpets. Although Danny could begrudgingly admit that Henry's alterations represented a marked improvement, at the same time he didn't think they were in keeping with Guy's personality – and saw this as evidence that Henry was wrong for him.

When everyone had finished their main course, Henry stood up to open another bottle of wine. As he poured it into everyone's glasses, Danny took in his beautifully ironed shirt and the fair hair that was – as always – so neatly trimmed it looked as if it had only just been cut. Much as Danny hated to admit it, Henry was probably the best-looking of all Guy's boyfriends. His skin was blemish-free, his face perfectly proportioned, and his smile almost impossibly symmetrical. A clutch of jealousy caught in Danny's chest.

Although he wasn't proud of this feeling, Danny consoled himself that it wasn't entirely his fault. On the few occasions Danny had met him, Henry had been smug and condescending towards him. Danny had only agreed to come tonight because he'd imagined Henry's smugness would be diluted by the presence of the other guests – although this was an assessment he'd been forced to reconsider when he'd found out who they were. Among those joining them was Guy's colleague Marcus, who seemed to have aged ten years since their holiday to Sitges the previous summer and whose brown hair was already greying at the temples. He'd come straight from work and was still wearing a suit and tie, albeit with his sleeves rolled up, his tie loosened and his belt undone so that his expanding gut could sag freely. Shortly after returning from Sitges, he'd ended his relationship with Salvador, declaring that it was 'just a holiday thing'. Tonight, he was accompanied by his new, blond boyfriend Oliver, although when Danny had used the word 'boyfriend', he'd been corrected and rather snootily informed that he was actually Marcus's 'partner'.

For most of the evening, the conversation revolved around work and the couples exchanged news of pay rises and promotions. Danny didn't mention that his main financial focus was still trying to pay off his student debt. When he asked Oliver what he did for a living, he described himself as a management consultant specialising in 'transformation', something Danny thought sounded delightfully camp but Oliver clearly took very seriously. As Danny had still had no success as an actor, he had nothing to contribute to the conversation and gradually shrank further and further back in his chair. *I feel like a nun who's accidentally wandered into an orgy.*

After a while, he pulled out his cigarettes and lit one. As he blew out a curl of smoke, Henry looked at him as if he'd just defecated in the centre of the table.

'I didn't know you smoked!' he said, his hand flying to his heart.

'Oh, only after a few drinks,' chirped Danny. 'I'm just a social smoker.'

'But don't you think smoking's *anti*-social?' Henry said, not bothering to hide his disdain.

'Not really, not if we're outside.'

Danny made a big show of breathing his smoke away from

the others and over the side of the terrace. He turned back to Henry. 'Have you got an ashtray, babe?'

'Sorry, no, we don't.'

Danny's attention snagged on the 'we'; it was as if Henry was trying to weaponise the word against him.

'That's OK,' he said, smiling, 'I'll use this.' He casually tapped his ash onto a plate, into the remains of a stuffed aubergine.

Oh God, am I starting to be difficult? Am I turning into the guest from hell?

The conversation moved on to the recent riots in London and the current political situation. When Marcus and Oliver mentioned that at the last general election they'd voted Conservative, Danny sat up.

'But how can you be gay and vote Tory?' he asked, stubbing out his cigarette.

Marcus and Oliver looked incredulous. 'What do you mean?

Danny reeled off a long list of anti-gay legislation either introduced or upheld by Conservative governments, a list he remembered well from his time as a member of the university LGB Society.

Marcus batted away his objection like a mildly annoying fly. 'Oh, I'm sure we can forget about that now. It was a long time ago.'

Danny remembered the celebrations around the repeal of Clause 28, the Tory government's anti-gay propaganda law – and that most Conservative MPs had voted to keep the law, a fact he repeated out loud. 'I don't think eight years is *that* long ago,' he said. 'Most of those same MPs stood at the last election.'

Oliver swilled the wine around his glass, his fingers gripping the stem like a row of pink sausages. 'Yeah, but we've got to get over that and move on. Besides, I much prefer the Conservatives' policies on taxation.'

Danny let out a gasp. 'So you're putting financial self-interest above social justice, are you? You're putting it above what's right for your own community?'

He was surprised at the fervour of his political conviction.

Henry arched an eyebrow. 'It sounds like someone's got a chip on his shoulder.'

'It's not a chip,' Danny corrected him. 'It's what's called integrity.'

He looked to Guy for back-up, but he just sat there kneading his knuckles. *Oh God, am I causing a scene?*

He decided to lighten the tone by relating a story about the time he'd had sex with a man who worked in the House of Commons, in a role he couldn't remember but had something to do with office admin. 'Honestly, he was gorgeous,' he trilled, 'but totally OCD. He made me sanitise my hands before he'd let me into his flat and pulled out a wet wipe to clean up my jizz before I'd even finished shooting my load.'

Guy giggled but Henry, Marcus and Oliver looked at Danny as if a particularly crusty cold sore had just erupted on his face. *Oh, what's the problem? Since when is it a crime to have a sex life?*

He could feel himself getting fired up and knew there was no holding himself back. 'So how about you four?' he asked. 'Are you towel, tissue or duvet men?'

His question landed like a dagger between them.

'I *beg* your pardon?' spat Oliver.

'Come on, what do you use to clean up after sex?' replied Danny. 'I think the answer reveals a lot about a man. I'll go first; I grab whatever's at the top of my laundry basket.'

Guy opened his mouth to answer but Henry shot him an icy glare. The air around the table sharpened.

'The trouble with the gay community,' Oliver pronounced, 'is it's obsessed with sex. It's all anyone talks about. Everything's one-night stands, saunas, cruising grounds . . .'

Marcus nodded. 'Every time you open a gay magazine these days all you read about is Grindr.'

'Yes, but Grindr's not just about sex,' Danny pointed out. 'I've seen people on there looking for dates or relationships.'

'Oh, so do you use it a lot?' Henry asked, his mouth flickering into a sneer.

Funnily enough, Danny wanted to say, *I checked it under the table ten minutes ago.* But he noticed Guy shifting in his seat.

'Oh, you know,' he said with a shrug, 'every now and then.'

'Well, I think it sends out the wrong message about the gay community,' brayed Oliver. 'How are we ever going to be fully accepted by society if all we do is have casual sex?'

'I think they should ban Grindr,' declared Marcus. 'And Gaydar too.'

'That's easy for you to say,' Danny couldn't resist hitting back, 'you've got a boyfriend.'

'Actually,' said Marcus, 'Oliver's my *partner*.'

For God's sake, get over yourself!

'I agree with Marcus,' twittered Oliver, 'and while they're at it, they should ban sex clubs and saunas.'

'Hear, hear,' said Henry. 'That kind of thing really damages our reputation. And it has nothing to do with my life; it's not *my* culture.'

Danny was about to lay into him when Guy shot out of his seat.

'I don't know about you boys,' he said, 'but I've got a craving for something sweet. Who fancies dessert?'

'Me!' barked Danny, desperate to move the evening on.

'I'll just clear this away,' said Guy, and he began stacking the plates.

'I'll give you a hand,' volunteered Danny.

Once they'd loaded up two trays, they carried them through to the kitchen, where they began rinsing the crockery and loading it into the dishwasher.

'Well, that was awkward,' said Danny. He thought about what he wanted to say: *I don't think Henry likes me.*

He paused and reconsidered.

'I don't think your friends like me,' he ventured.

Guy screwed up his nose. 'What do you mean?'

'Oh, come on, babe,' Danny said. 'They're making me feel as welcome as a bacon butty at a bar mitzvah.'

'I wouldn't say that,' said Guy. 'You probably just lead different lives, that's all. You're just looking for different things.'

Danny scraped away the remains of the aubergine with his cigarette butt sticking out of it. 'Well, I hope you don't let them get to you; I hope *you're* not going to start looking down on me for smoking and having casual sex.'

Guy frowned and slid a plate into the dishwasher. 'Danny, as if.'

'Please don't lose sight of who you are.'

Guy drew himself up to his full height. 'Don't worry, I've no intention of doing that. But we all evolve, Danny. We all have to grow up some time.'

Somewhere in his words, Danny detected an accusation. He detected a judgment. And suddenly he felt like a failure.

'Come on, we're not kids anymore,' Guy went on. 'We're not even going to be in our twenties much longer.'

A lump swelled in Danny's throat. He was about to turn

twenty-eight and was still nowhere near achieving what he wanted in life. *So far I've amounted to nothing.*

He yanked his mouth up into a smile. 'Don't remind me, babe, I can't believe I'm staring down the barrel of thirty. The next thing I know, it'll be Botox and a boob job!'

Guy laughed. 'Yeah, well, I'm only a few months behind you so I might go the same way.' He let out a sigh. 'Seriously, though, when I do get to thirty, I just want to feel good about myself.'

Danny nodded and carried on scraping food off the dishes. He knew there was little chance of him feeling good about himself any time soon.

Wait a minute, I might have given up hope of getting together with Guy, but that doesn't mean I have to be unhappy in every *area of life.*

And – much to his surprise – in that moment he came to a realisation. But it was so radical he wasn't sure he could accept it.

2012

'I can't believe this is happening,' said Emma. 'I can't believe I'm actually getting married.'

'Well, you'd better believe it,' said Danny, 'because this is only the beginning.'

They were in Glasgow to celebrate Emma's hen weekend, the first stage of which was taking place in a swanky, stone-fronted Georgian hotel that was situated on a grand, tree-lined square. Everyone in the party had spent the last few hours having treatments in the spa and beauty studio before reconvening in the lounge area for afternoon tea. There were twenty of them in total, spread out on the heavily cushioned lime-green suede sofas. Sitting at the table opposite Danny and Emma was Emma's mum, who was chatting to Lynsey.

Emma looked over and massaged the back of her neck. 'I think because my parents were so unhappy for so long,' she reflected, 'I never grew up dreaming about getting married myself.'

Her mum let out a loud laugh. Since she'd split from Emma's dad, Danny couldn't help thinking she seemed much happier.

'But one of the things I learned in therapy was that I had to let go of the past,' Emma continued, 'as I was letting it intrude on the present and this was stopping me from evolving as a person.'

Danny swallowed, slowly. He remembered what Guy had said to him at his barbecue the previous summer: *We all evolve, Danny. We all have to grow up some time.*

'My God, you're speaking like someone who's had a *lot* of therapy,' he joked. 'You sound like a talking textbook!'

She gave him a wry smile. 'Aye, I know. But it really helped me, Danny. I don't think I'd be here now if it weren't for therapy.'

They were interrupted by a female voice that sounded breathy with excitement. 'Now, I've ordered us a selection of cupcakes,' it said. 'I can't wait for everyone to taste them!'

Danny turned around to see that the voice belonged to Emma's childhood friend, Claire. She was a short, blonde woman who was bright-eyed, always smiling, and – possibly because she worked as a primary school teacher – had a tendency to speak to adults as if they were eight-year-old children. Emma had told Danny that she'd felt obliged to appoint Claire chief bridesmaid because of a pact the two of them had made as girls. But Danny could tell that already Emma was doubting she'd made the right decision. Claire's enthusiasm often tipped over into bossiness and in the run-up to the weekend she'd bombarded everyone with emails about the itinerary, the kitty, the matching T-shirts they all had to wear – and the cupcakes.

'Honestly,' she squeaked, 'these cupcakes are better than sex!' Then she clapped her hand over her mouth as if she'd said something naughty.

Danny leaned in to Emma and whispered, 'That depends on the sex you've been having, babe.'

The two of them couldn't help giggling.

Emma waited until Claire was out of earshot, then said, 'You know what, that's the first laugh I've had all day. Isn't a hen weekend supposed to be a laugh a minute? I think we might need to fuck off these cupcakes and bring in some booze.'

'Don't worry,' said Danny, 'Claire's put me in charge of organising tonight. And trust me, there'll be plenty of booze.'

What he omitted to say was that Claire seemed fixated on the idea of going out for cocktails and thought that sipping on a single drink with a mildly suggestive name represented the height of transgression. To placate her, Danny had booked the group into a smart cocktail bar for the first part of the evening. But he knew Emma would be irritated by the idea of having to wait ten minutes for each drink – and when they eventually came, having to battle her way through twigs, flowers or leaves to get a swig. So he'd researched some much less smart nightclubs on to which he could corral everyone once the cocktails had got them in the mood.

The only thing was, he wasn't sure he'd be able to get himself in the mood. Although Danny was totally committed to his role as the life and soul of the party, he knew he wasn't going to enjoy spending the night in a rowdy, straight nightclub. While he appreciated being included as 'one of the girls' – something Claire insisted on calling him – Danny couldn't help feeling uncomfortable being the only man in a group of twenty. Although he acknowledged that in some ways he had lots in common with the women, in other ways he was very different. Already today, a few of the hotel and spa staff had peered at him curiously, as if trying to work out why there was one man in a party of so many women. In each case, their curiosity had been swiftly followed by a visible realisation, as if they were at the zoo and had just come across the nameplate for an animal they didn't recognise. Danny knew this would be much less subtly expressed in a nightclub, as most people would be drunk. His stomach dipped in dread.

When a waitress appeared with several stands of cupcakes, various members of the party widened their eyes and made appreciative noises. Claire emitted a loud whinnying sound, as if she were having an orgasm. Danny was suddenly possessed by the urge to run to the nearest gay bar and have sex with the first man he met.

'Come on, girls,' commanded Claire, 'we need to line our stomachs before those Pornstar Martinis!'

Danny was about to make another snide comment to Emma but told himself to rein it in. *Come on, don't turn into a bitter, twisted old queen.*

'Can I ask you something, babe?' he said, finishing a cupcake and wiping his mouth.

'Aye, course you can.'

'It's just that all the time I've known you, you've been wild and outrageous.'

She finished chewing and arched an eyebrow. 'Yeah . . .?'

'Well, aren't you worried that when you get married, it'll be all cupcakes and afternoon tea? Aren't you worried you'll somehow stop being *you*?'

Emma batted her crumbs onto a plate. 'Not really. First of all, I've only slept with Richard since we got together – and you don't think I've stopped being me, do you?'

'No. Not at all.'

'Well, in that case, wild and outrageous mustn't have been me – or it mustn't have been *all* of me. Now you mention it, I hope you think there's more to me than one-night stands and mad nights out.'

'Yeah, of course!' Danny reassured her.

He clenched his jaw. *But is there more to* me?

'When I get married I'll still have the same spirit,' Emma went on. 'I just won't act on it in the same way. And anyway, I've said to you before, a lot of all that I was doing for the wrong reasons.'

'Yeah, I know . . .'

Emma narrowed her eyes. 'Why are you asking me this, anyway? Are you worried about something yourself?'

'No, no.' Danny realised he'd slipped out of character and re-focused on his role. 'I was just checking you were up for tonight, that's all. You know, having one last blow-out? Celebrating the end of your life as a single girl?'

Emma gave him a wicked grin. 'Up for it? I'm fucking *mad for it!*'

The two of them laughed loudly.

'What are you two laughing about?' asked Lynsey, as she rejoined their table.

'Oh, we're just getting excited about tonight,' said Danny. Then he wagged a finger at her. 'But you're going to have to keep your hands off all those gorgeous Glaswegian men now you've got yourself a man back in Manchester.'

'Oh, it's only early days,' she protested, 'and nothing serious.'

Emma sat up. 'Yeah, yeah, that's what me and Richard said at the start. And look at us now.'

'Come on,' said Danny, 'tell us all about him.'

Lynsey explained that she was seeing a Cheshire-based property developer called Magnus, who she'd met in a bar. 'He's quite posh,' she said, 'and very white. He's not what I'd go for on paper – but I like him. I really like him.'

The three of them continued discussing Magnus as they demolished what was left of the cupcakes. Danny was genuinely happy for Lynsey – as he was for Emma – but behind his cheery exterior he couldn't escape the idea that everyone around him was moving on with their lives.

He returned to the idea that had been flitting around the outer edges of his mind ever since Guy's barbecue. And he couldn't banish it to the outer edges any longer.

The more he thought about it, the more he realised that there was one thing that would improve his life more than any other – and that was giving up acting. This made him feel sad, because acting had been a lifeline for him in his teens and it was something he'd done for so long it felt like it was part of who he was. *But it's time for me to grow up. It's time for me to evolve.*

He had no idea what he was going to do instead of acting. Whichever career he pursued, it occurred to him that he might just fall flat on his face. He could end up working in Starbucks. *But I can't carry on like this. I can't go round and round in circles while everyone else is moving forwards.*

He waited for a pause in the conversation then cleared his throat.

'Ladies, I've got some news,' he announced.

Emma and Lynsey turned to look at him.

'I'm giving up acting.'

2022

Guy places his order and the barista asks his name.

'Guy,' he says. 'G-U-Y.'

He watches as she writes 'Greg' on the side of his mug.

He's in the branch of Starbucks that's almost opposite his hotel, a little higher up Peter Street. He'd been on his way back to the room after spending the night with Josh, the young man he met outside Via. But, as he drew up outside the hotel, fear shot up his spine. At least he thought it was fear but, equally, it could have been guilt.

Whatever it was, he couldn't face Danny, at least not yet. When he spotted the Starbucks, he ducked inside.

As he watches the barista making his coffee, he thinks about Josh and what happened last night. He'd been entranced by his cute smile and classically square jaw, not to mention his amazingly rounded bum. But his attraction was really aroused when he discovered that Josh wasn't just good-looking but intelligent and ambitious too. He's originally from Shropshire but settled in Manchester, where he works in tech design – and is moving to London next year. This last detail sent Guy's interest soaring and made him think Josh might even make a potential boyfriend. At twenty-six, he's twelve years younger than Guy, but that might not be a bad thing; at least he won't have too much baggage or be jaded by too many failed relationships. *You never know, he might even be the one to get me over my divorce.*

At the thought of his divorce, Guy feels a rush of sadness, a specific type of sadness he thinks could be grief. He may have found it easy to take his mind off this over the weekend, but that doesn't mean it hasn't been there all along. *Hiding under the surface, ready to jump out and punch me in the gut.*

The coffee machine shoots out a jet of steam and the barista steps back and wafts it away with a towel.

But what am I going to do about Danny?

He replays in his head the conversation he and Danny had in the Spanish restaurant. He knew the conversation was going to be difficult, but it turned out to be worse than expected. His main worry beforehand had been – as ever – how to express his feelings. But he seemed to cope well on this front and managed to say everything he wanted to say, pretty much how he wanted to say it. He consoles himself that once Danny revealed he was in love with him, he was never going to be happy with Guy's response. But he walked out of the restaurant before the food arrived, leaving Guy to think he must be seriously angry. *And then I went and kissed another man, right in front of him. Or at least I think that's what happened, judging by Danny's text.*

If this is the case, Guy knows Danny will be even angrier with him. *And with good reason.*

His stomach rumbles with hunger. He stands on his tiptoes to peer over the counter just as the barista is lifting up the grill to check on his panini. He tries telling himself that the food and drink will make him feel better, but he's not sure it will.

I messed up; I messed up royally. And now I'm going to have to pick up the pieces.

'Greg!' shouts the barista, holding up a latte and a panini.

Guy blinks himself back to reality. 'Yeah, that's me.'

2013

'What name is it please?' asked the receptionist.

'Danny. Danny Baxter.'

The woman checked her screen and gave him a smile. 'If you'd like to take a seat, Lorraine will be with you shortly.'

Danny lowered himself onto a leather sofa. He was about to have a job interview, one he was hoping would open up a new chapter in his life. If it did, this would coincide – somewhat neatly, he couldn't help thinking – with his thirtieth birthday in a few months' time. *At least I hope to God it does or I'm not sure how I'll cope.*

The interview was the culmination of a long period of deliberation over what would become Danny's second career. *Or second attempt at a career.* The problem was, he had so little experience; he didn't even *know* what was involved in most jobs. One thing he did understand was life as a struggling actor – and he had plenty of knowledge of theatre, TV and film. So it dawned on him that he could be an agent for other actors, not least because he'd learned from Heather how to do the job badly – and if he took the opposite approach then surely it followed he'd be doing the job well?

An actors' agent would also fulfill one of Danny's top criteria for a job: when people asked what he did in a bar or at dinner parties, it would impress them. Telling people he was an actor had worked well in the early days, but invariably this was followed by the question 'What have you been in?' and, as he got older, his response had become less and less impressive. But representing other – more successful – actors could fulfill his criteria perfectly.

After doing some research and chatting to a few contacts, he'd discovered that he would have to start at the bottom of the ladder, beginning as an assistant to an established agent before taking on some of his own clients as what was called an 'associate agent', then eventually flying solo. He'd applied for a few roles that were advertised but hadn't been invited for any interviews. Then Emma's husband Richard had told him his Aunt Lorraine was an agent and had just lost her assistant. As she needed to appoint a replacement quickly, Danny had wasted no time in sending her an email and within five minutes she'd replied with an invitation to 'pop in for a chat'. Now here he was, in a plush reception area in a swanky glass-fronted building on the Haymarket, the walls lined with posters for plays and films starring actors represented by the agency.

While he waited, he gave himself a pep talk. *Just see this as another acting gig. You're auditioning for the role of someone who's always wanted to be an agent. You can manage that!*

When Lorraine appeared, she was in her mid-forties and stylishly dressed, but whey-faced, with shadows under her eyes and hair that had been dyed blonde but had dark roots peeping through. Clearly, she had more important things on her mind than maintaining what Danny had been told was her ordinarily immaculate exterior. Danny hadn't met her at Emma and Richard's wedding as she'd just given birth to twins; Richard had told him that, after several failed relationships and several years as a single woman, Lorraine had conceived the babies via donor sperm – and this had endeared her to him as she was a woman bucking convention and doing things her own way. When she said hello and introduced herself with a Manchester accent, this endeared her even more.

Lorraine led him through an open-plan area full of desks at which people of around his age were tapping on their keyboards or chatting cheerily on the phone. Radio One was broadcasting in the background, two girls were gossiping and giggling, and a camp man was demonstrating his latest yoga pose to a huddle of engrossed colleagues. Danny instantly knew he'd fit in.

I just have to convince Lorraine I can do the job . . .

Inside Lorraine's office, the shelves were crammed with awards, thank-you cards and framed photographs of his potential new boss with her arms around various clients. She plonked herself down behind a desk that was piled high with scripts, contracts, and the remains of that day's lunch – and gestured for Danny to sit opposite.

'So Richard says you're a friend of Emma's from uni,' she said.

'Yeah, we met on our first day and hit it off straight away.'

'I can imagine Manchester's a great place to be a student,' she said. 'Although it must have changed a lot since I lived there.'

He told her a little about the city he knew and, inevitably, came to how much he'd loved the Gay Village – at which point he paused and let out a breath. 'You know, Manchester changed my life. When I got there, for the first time I felt accepted as me. I don't think I've ever been so happy.'

He had no idea where this little speech had come from but it was clear that already he'd stopped acting and was giving Lorraine a glimpse into his true self. Thankfully, she responded with a smile.

'And how are you finding London?' she asked.

He slid his hands under his thighs. 'It'd take me a long time to answer that properly – and not all of it would be work-related. But let's just say if I get this job I'll be a lot happier.'

She leaned towards him and drew in her lips. 'OK, so this is what I'm looking for. I need someone to do all those thankless tasks like picking up my coffee and dry cleaning. I also need someone to call in clothes for clients to wear and deal with all the swag we get sent. Oh and I need help reading scripts and going to showcases to scout out new talent.'

'That sounds brilliant,' said Danny, warming to the job more and more.

'But the main thing I need is someone to do my admin,' Lorraine added, 'taking calls, scheduling appointments, running my diary. I'm crap at all that. Honestly, I couldn't organise a blowie in a brothel.'

Danny laughed. *I can work with her.*

'Well, I'm very organised and very reliable,' he assured her.

'That's music to my ears. And you're obviously friendly and can get on with people. Those are essential qualities in an agent.'

You know what, I might genuinely be good at this.

Lorraine mentioned some of her clients and asked in which direction Danny would steer their careers if he were representing them. As he'd researched her list of actors beforehand, he found this easy to answer.

'Very good,' said Lorraine, 'but a word of warning: some of my clients can be very demanding. You'll need to put up with the odd blast of abuse.'

'No problem,' said Danny, 'my skin's as tough as old boots. It's had to be over the years.'

She picked up his CV and perused it. 'Yes, I see you've been an actor.'

Danny could feel his smile falter. 'That's right.'

She put the CV down and looked him in the eye. 'So how do I know this won't be second best for you? How do I know you don't just want to do it because you didn't make it in your first choice of career?'

Rather than taking offence, Danny appreciated her directness. *And being honest with her has worked for me so far – I might as well forget about acting altogether.*

'Well, it *is* second best,' he admitted. 'Acting *was* my dream. But that doesn't mean my dream can't evolve – as I evolve. And it doesn't mean I wouldn't work really hard and do the job better than anyone else.'

'But you wouldn't be jealous of the clients?'

Danny let out a sigh. 'No, I'm over acting now. It worked for me at a particular stage in life, but it hasn't for a long time. And who knows? Maybe this is what I should have been doing in the first place. Where I come from, I didn't know anyone who did this kind of job. It wouldn't have occurred to me that I could become an agent.'

'If you can't see it, you can't be it,' Lorraine fired back at him. She stood up and moved over to the window. 'I was the same. It's much harder for people like us; there's no obvious path for us to follow. We have to find it for ourselves – and sometimes we have to invent it for ourselves.'

Danny felt a rush of gratitude towards her. He felt like finally he'd met someone who understood his situation – and was explaining it in a way he himself was only just beginning to understand.

Lorraine's phone rang and she said she had to answer. She turned away and began placating an actor who was shooting a film and clashing with his director. Danny wondered who it might be and cast his eyes over the photos looking for some kind of clue. He imagined her clients becoming embroiled in all kinds of dramas. *Just think of the anecdotes . . .*

Before he knew it, he was picturing himself entertaining friends with tales of bust-ups on film sets and torrid affairs in the West End. He was attending awards shows flanked by glamorous movie stars and celebrating box-office successes over champagne at exclusive private members club Soho House. *Yeah, this is a job that'll impress people. And if I can get it right, no-one will ever look down on me again.*

Lorraine ended her call and turned back to Danny. 'OK, so when can you start?'

He blinked several times. 'Seriously? You mean I've got the job?'

'It's yours if you want it.'

Danny couldn't believe it. Finally, somebody had given him a break. All of a sudden his thirtieth birthday didn't seem quite so daunting.

He couldn't wait to tell Guy.

2022

Danny is lying in his hotel room. As he thinks back to his interview with Lorraine, he feels a kick of annoyance. *All I could think about was impressing Guy. Why couldn't I see what was staring me in the face?*

The time on the alarm clock is 11.23. The sidelight is on, illuminating Guy's half of the bed – revealing he still hasn't returned. *Oh, why did no-one tell me I was making a fool of myself?*

He gets out of bed and opens the curtains, unveiling another sunny day. He pads over to the kettle and begins making a cup of tea. All of a sudden, he stops. *Actually, somebody did tell me.*

Lynsey told me.

He remembers what happened the first time she told him, at Guy's thirtieth birthday party. He remembers how carefully she chose her words and how wildly he reacted.

But that was nothing compared to what happened the second time she told him.

Before he can talk himself out of it, Danny picks up his phone and composes a text. 'Hi Lyns, am in Manchester for the weekend. Don't suppose you're around?'

Just as he's about to add a kiss, he stops himself. He hasn't seen her for seven years; he can't just pretend things are normal. He can't just pretend he didn't stop being her friend.

'Sorry it's been so long,' he adds, 'but it would be good to see you. And there's something I want to say. Danny'

He quickly hits Send.

Right, it's done now.

Once the kettle has boiled, he finishes making his tea. Just as he's stirring in one of the little cartons of milk, he receives a reply.

'Hi, good to hear from you. Am going out for a late lunch but you can come round this morning if you like?'

He feels a judder of fear. *Fuck. Am I ready for this?*

But even as he's asking himself the question, Danny knows he has to be. *I owe her an apology.*

He accepts Lynsey's invitation and asks for the address.

2014

Danny was flabbergasted. 'What a bastard. I can't believe he'd do that.'

Lynsey was telling him that Magnus had left her for another woman – after more than two years of dodging her attempts to formalise their casual relationship into something more serious. But that wasn't the worst of it. A few days later, Lynsey had been contacted on Facebook by another woman, who'd said she'd been dating Magnus – and had also been dumped by him. When the two women had joined forces to confront him, he hadn't even flinched. He'd simply laughed in their faces and told them it wasn't his fault if they'd misinterpreted his intentions, insisting he'd always made it clear he didn't want anything serious with either of them.

'He actually accused me of "turning psycho" on him,' Lynsey blustered. 'Can you believe it? He actually called me a "bunny boiler"!'

'Oh my God,' said Danny, 'that's outrageous!'

She let out a sigh. 'I feel so stupid, Dan. All the time I thought we were in love and Magnus was just being commitment-phobic, but the truth was he was only ever using me and having a good laugh at my expense. But I was too needy and desperate to see it.'

Danny shook his head. 'Don't say that, Lyns. It really isn't your fault.'

'Oh and get this,' she went on, 'this other woman he dumped is also mixed-race – actually, she's darker skinned than I am – but the woman he's dumped us for, the woman he actually thinks is good enough to have a *relationship* with, is white.'

'I'm sure she is,' snarled Danny. 'I'm sure she's white and blonde and posh. Her parents probably know his from the golf club.'

Shit, am I starting to sound bitter?

Lynsey drained her glass and set it down on the windowsill. 'Anyway, the whole thing was awful. I just want to forget about it tonight.'

Danny clapped his hands together. 'That's where I come in!'

They were at Guy's thirtieth birthday party, which was taking place in the upstairs function room of a trendy gastro pub on London's Portobello Road. The floorboards were exposed, the Georgian wood panelling painted sage green, and the walls hung with copies of eighteenth-century cartoons by the likes of Hogarth and Gillray. It was a hot summer's evening, the room was at rain-forest humidity, and Danny and Lynsey were hovering around a sash window they'd managed to prise open by a few inches.

Standing with his back to them were Guy's parents, who Danny was studiously avoiding. Not that he was having to try very hard; they were clearly avoiding him too. It was the first time Danny had been anywhere near them since that disastrous lunch eight years ago. He knew Guy had been seeing more of them lately but hadn't expected they'd be here tonight. He felt intrigued – not to mention unsettled – by their reappearance.

Currently, Cynthia and Stephen were in conversation with Rags, who had a sweat patch on his shirt that was roughly the shape of Italy, and his new wife Poppy, a skinny blonde recruitment consultant who looked vaguely like an Afghan hound. Danny listened as the two of them loudly informed Guy's parents they were 'trying for a baby', news that was greeted with excitement and congratulations.

'Steady on,' said Rags, 'I'm hoping it won't happen for a while yet; we're having too much fun trying!'

As Cynthia and Stephen erupted in laughter, Danny remembered how disapproving they'd been of gay sex. *Oh, but it's fine for Rags to have sex, is it? Because he's straight and married and respectable? And he might get Poppy up the duff?*

'My God, it's roasting in here,' said Emma, elbowing her way towards them. 'I'm sweating like a virgin on a date with a porn star.'

Danny stepped to one side to make room for Emma and Richard. He hadn't seen them since their wedding day, when he'd slipped away in between courses for a hook-up he'd arranged on Grindr with some Turkish businessman who'd been staying in the same hotel, only to return thirty minutes later – just in time for dessert – and delight everyone with the tale.

'So have you seen anyone you fancy?' asked Emma, trying to direct the air from the window onto her.

'I have,' he said, 'that barman looks like Michael Fassbender. The only thing is, I don't know if he dances at my end of the ballroom. I'll have to find out later.'

He was distracted by the sound of Henry's laughter. When he turned to look, he saw Henry putting his arm round Guy. Danny felt a rush of irritation at the way he was revelling in his role of consort and lording it around the party. But he was determined not to let it affect him. He told himself that he was looking sharp in slim-fitting designer trousers he'd borrowed from some fashion publicist who wanted one of Lorraine's clients to wear her clothes, together with a geometric print shirt he'd bought from Reiss and was taking on its maiden voyage, and a pork pie hat he'd cocked at a jaunty angle. And three double vodka and Diet Cokes had nicely softened the edges of his anxiety.

'So how's work going?' asked Richard. 'My Aunt Lorraine tells me you're smashing it.'

'Oh, I don't know about that,' Danny said, 'but I am really enjoying it.'

Danny was being modest: although he'd only been at the agency for just over a year, he'd already been told he was the best assistant Lorraine had ever had *and* been rewarded with a pay rise. And not just that but he'd become good friends with several of the other assistants and they'd often go out after work to industry events like film premieres or opening nights at the theatre. On top of that, he'd discovered that people were indeed impressed when he told them what he did for a living. And – as predicted – he'd already amassed an extensive repertoire of anecdotes.

'Hey, you'll never guess what happened the other day . . .'

He began regaling them with a story about two high-profile actresses who were always competing for the same roles and had recently been cast as co-stars in the same film. Just as he was building up to the climax – a vicious but highly camp catfight that only vaguely resembled the argument that had taken place in real life – the music stopped and Guy took hold of a microphone.

'Hello, hello,' he boomed, giving off a blast of feedback.

As he fiddled with the levels, Danny couldn't help thinking that he looked as gorgeous as ever. That dimple in his chin and the gap between his teeth were still insanely attractive. And because of the heat, he'd undone a few buttons on his shirt, revealing a thin layer of sweat glistening between the groove of his chest muscles.

'As you know, I'm not one for speeches,' Guy said, 'but I just wanted to thank you all for coming. Thanks for helping me celebrate reaching my thirty spins around the sun.'

A rowdy cheer broke out from Rags.

'When I was opening my cards, someone sent me one saying "Inside every thirty-year-old, there's an eighteen-year-old asking what the hell happened".'

Danny stabbed at the ice in his glass. *'Someone'? That was actually me.*

'But I just want to say I'm glad I *don't* feel like that. Because I'm very happy with where I am in life. And that's largely down to one man.'

Danny inched forwards, hoping to hear his name.

'Henry.'

Danny felt the jealousy explode in him. He scoured the room for Henry and arrowed him a murderous look. *Oh God, I really am a nasty old queen.*

'Now you all know I'm not a gushy person,' Guy went on, 'but Henry brings out the best in me; he makes me a better man. And that's why I'm delighted to announce that I've asked him to marry me – and he's done me the honour of saying yes.'

A surprised gasp darted around the room.

Fuck, Guy's engaged.

Fuck, he's marrying Henry!

'Ever since gay marriage became legal,' Guy bellowed, 'I've

been wanting to ask him. Anyway, I did and now it's happening. So tonight's a double celebration – we're also celebrating our engagement!'

All around Danny, people began cheering and clapping, but his stomach burned as if he'd just downed a bottle of bleach.

Fuck, marriage means for ever.

So for me that means never.

He blinked as he tried to take in the news. He caught sight of Guy's parents drawing both him and Henry into a hug. *Wait a minute . . .? But how can . . .?*

With a clang of doom, he understood.

Even so, the gall of them!

As the applause faded, he retreated to his conversation with Lynsey, Emma and Richard. But he couldn't concentrate. And he couldn't stop his eyes from following Guy and Henry as they worked their way around the room, lapping up the congratulations. Before long, they approached his group.

'I can't believe you're engaged!' burst out Emma as soon as she saw them. 'That's such brilliant news!'

'Congratulations,' Danny managed, his jaw stiff. 'I'm really happy for you.'

'Thanks,' said Guy, 'that means a lot.'

'You never know,' chirped Henry, 'it could be you next!'

In a flash, Danny wondered if he could spill a drink down Henry's pristine white shirt and make it look like an accident. *God, I'm such a terrible person.*

He fixed his face into something approaching a smile. 'Oh, you know me, I don't do emotional attachment. I just like to chuck my muck and go.'

Henry rolled his eyes. 'Yeah, yeah, we've heard all that before.

But I'm not sure I buy it; if you ask me, it's people like you who always fall the hardest.'

Oh, you've no idea . . .

'Yeah, well, let's see,' was all he could say. He suddenly felt like the room was becoming even hotter.

But Henry wasn't going to let the subject go. He turned to Emma and Lynsey. 'What do you think, girls? Could you see Danny settling down?'

Emma fixed her eyes on Danny. 'All I'll say is, if you do want a relationship, don't go changing yourself to please someone else.'

'Hear, hear,' chimed in Lynsey. 'What you need is someone who accepts you exactly as you are.'

Henry screwed up his nose. 'The thing is, though, a lot of gay men don't go for camp and outrageous.' He tilted his head in a performance of sympathy. 'That must be hard for you, Danny.'

Danny took off his hat and began fanning himself. 'Henry, I keep telling you, I don't want a long-term relationship.'

He looked to Guy for some kind of intervention, but Guy seemed cheerily unaware that Henry's sympathy was disguising a slight.

'Look on the bright side,' Henry continued. 'You used to be an actor; I'm sure you could easily dial things down a bit.'

Yeah but I wouldn't do that, Danny wanted to say. *I've told you – I've got integrity.*

But the comment stayed in his head; he didn't want to be accused of spoiling Guy's party.

'Thanks,' he warbled, 'I'll bear that in mind. Right now, though, I need the bog.' He turned to Lynsey. 'Are you coming, babe?'

Without needing an explanation, she followed him through to the disabled loo.

'What the fuck was that all about?' Danny spat, as soon as they were inside. He untucked his shirt and held it over the hand drier, directing the hot air over the damp patches. 'Can you believe Henry said I should tone myself down?'

Lynsey folded up some toilet roll and used it to dab her top lip. 'I have to say, he was very patronising. I was disappointed Guy didn't pick up on it.'

Danny flapped his shirt over the drier. 'Oh, he's totally under his spell.'

'Well, at least he's happy.'

'"At least he's happy"? What are you on about, Lyns? Guy should be with me, you know that. And if it weren't for Henry, he probably would be.'

Lynsey tossed the tissue into the toilet bowl, closed the lid and sat down. 'I'm not sure, Dan. I'm not sure anymore.'

He stepped back from the drier and waited for it to snap off. 'What do you mean? Where's that come from?'

There was a beat.

'Dan, I think you need to get over Guy. It's quite obvious it's not going to happen.'

Danny felt broadsided by the sting of humiliation. 'But I don't understand,' he said, his voice moving up an octave. 'Why are you suddenly saying this?'

Lynsey steepled her fingers under her chin and let out a breath. 'Do you remember the first time we talked about this? In the Solem?'

Danny raised an eyebrow. 'Yeah. We were in the disabled loo then too.'

'OK, well how many years ago was that?'

'Ten. No, eleven!'

'Exactly.' Lynsey pressed her palms onto her thighs. 'That's why I think you need to draw a line under this; it's gone on far too long. And now Guy's getting married he's effectively drawing the line for you. You've got to move on, Dan.'

Danny felt each of her words tearing into him. He had to make an effort to stop his chin from trembling.

'Look, I'm sorry if I egged you on,' Lynsey continued. 'I think I must have misread the signs. I don't know, maybe I deliberately misread them because I *wanted* you two to get together.'

Danny folded his arms. 'So is that what you think *I* did? Saw things that weren't there because I wanted them to be?'

She frowned. 'Maybe, yeah. And I know that might be difficult to hear. But that's basically what I did with Magnus.'

'Lyns, this is nothing like what happened with you and Magnus. It's a totally different situation.'

Oh, I know it isn't, but I don't need reminding of it.

Lynsey stood up and looked him in the eye. 'Right, I've tried to say things sensitively, but now I'm going to give you some tough love. You've got to listen to me, Dan. Guy is not interested.'

Danny could feel his humiliation morphing into anger. *What's her problem? It's like she's actually* trying *to hurt me.*

'Lynsey,' he snapped, 'I know you've just been dumped and I know you're pissed off about it. But I don't see why you've got to take that out on me.'

'Danny, that's not what's going on here. That's not what's going on at all.'

But Danny wasn't listening. 'Right, I've had enough of this. I'm going back in. I'm going to chat to that barman.'

'But Danny—'

'Danny nothing, Lyns. I can't be arsed with this anymore.'

And with that he stomped out.

He didn't bother closing the door behind him.

2022

The door opens and there's Lynsey, standing before Danny in jeans, flip-flops and a vintage T-shirt. He remembers how tall she is and is struck by how well she's aged; she hardly looks a day older than the last time he saw her. *The time I told her I didn't want to speak to her again.*

He greets her with a hesitant smile and a stiff kiss on each cheek.

'Hi, babe,' he says, 'it's good to see you.'

'You too,' she says, her smile trembling ever so slightly. 'Come in.'

Lynsey lives in a cute little red-brick terraced house in Chorlton, a residential area a few miles south of the city centre. The hallway has a floor tiled with slate and walls painted in one of Farrow & Ball's signature chalky greys, but what makes the most impression on Danny is the series of art works running up the stairs.

Lynsey tells him she's recently started collecting work by British African artists like Sola Olulode and Yinka Shonibare. 'Only prints,' she points out, 'not originals. They're all I can afford at the moment but I really love them.'

Danny compliments her on her taste. 'You always did have an eye.'

He follows her through to the kitchen. This room has an industrial feel, with exposed brick, stainless steel splashbacks, and modern units finished in a gleaming, royal blue. Sunlight streams in through glass doors that open onto a little garden and on the windowsill stands a vase of white calla lilies.

'Well, this is nice,' says Danny, sitting on a stool and pulling it up to the counter.

'Thanks,' says Lynsey. 'Do you want a coffee? I was just going to make a turmeric latte. And yeah, I'm aware that makes me sound like a twat.'

They laugh, but it's not a relaxed laugh. Danny can tell Lynsey is as nervous as he is.

'Great, yeah, I will have one, thanks.'

As she busies herself making the drinks, Danny explains that he's in Manchester for Pride and shares some of his observations about how the city has changed since he last visited. But his chat is formal and stilted. *God, this is more difficult than I thought.*

Lynsey hands him a mug of coffee and sits down opposite him. But Danny still can't bring himself to talk about the subject he's come to talk about.

'So how's it going?' he asks. 'By the looks of things, life's treating you well.'

Lynsey updates him on her career, telling him she moved firms a few years ago and has recently been made a partner. Danny congratulates her and fills her in on his career, at the first available opportunity drawing on his stock of tried and tested anecdotes about his famous clients.

'Oh and I saw Emma and Richard yesterday,' he chirps. By this stage, the subject of Guy doesn't so much feel like the elephant in the room, more a whole herd of elephants that have plonked themselves down between them. 'Emma said something about you having a new man?'

Lynsey nods and tells him about Ben, who she met on Tinder and teaches in a high school. 'I really like him,' she says. 'He's a grown-up. We've only been together for six months but it's going well so far. And I don't want to speak too soon but I think the final piece of my jigsaw might actually be falling into place.'

'Lyns, that's great. Honestly, it's brilliant news.'

She takes a sip of her coffee. 'You know, it's the first time I've ever been out with a black guy. It's not that I didn't want to but they always seemed to get snapped up by white girls – you know, the type who want to parade them around and show them off like some kind of trophy.'

Danny scoffs. 'Yeah, I know the type. At least I know gay men who do that.'

'Anyway,' Lynsey goes on, 'maybe Ben isn't enough of a stereotype for that kind of girl, maybe he's too nerdy and not cool enough. But that's fine by me; I'm not complaining.'

'Well, good on you,' says Danny. 'You deserve to be happy.'

'Oh and get this,' she adds, her voice quickening, 'he teaches English and Drama so directs all the school shows. Right now they're doing a production of *A Midsummer Night's Dream*. Do you remember when we did that?'

'Of course I do. Your staging was insane.'

Lynsey smiles. 'And your Puck was hilarious!'

As Danny remembers the bond he used to share with Lynsey, he feels a twinge of sadness.

'So are you seeing anyone at the moment?' Lynsey asks,

running her finger around the rim of her mug.

'Oh, you know me,' Danny sing-songs, 'I'm too much of a free spirit to be tied down.'

She looks him in the eye. 'Yeah, well, you know I was never convinced by any of that.'

Danny takes a deep breath. 'OK, let me answer the question again . . . No, I'm not seeing anyone – because I'm still in love with Guy.'

Something twists in the atmosphere between them. But he's relieved that he's finally broached the subject.

Lynsey cradles her coffee in her hands. 'OK. And how are you feeling about that?'

'Not great. But that's what I wanted to talk to you about.'

2015

'Guy's making a mistake.'

Lynsey shot Danny a warning look. 'You can't say that – not at his wedding!'

Danny shrugged airily. 'Why not? It's true.'

They were standing in the grounds of Guy's parents' golf club, on a lawn that was so uniformly green it looked like it had been coloured in with a felt-tip pen. Guy and Henry had just pledged their vows in the main function room of the clubhouse, a handsome stone building that dated back to the seventeenth century and apparently used to be the country house of a minor earl. As soon as the ceremony was over, the grooms had been whisked off to pose for the official photographs and their guests directed onto the lawn for drinks. Although Danny had been avoiding Lynsey after the discussion they'd had at Guy's birthday party, he'd seen from the seating plan that they were going to be next to each other at dinner – so had decided to face her beforehand.

'And what did you think of the ceremony?' he asked.

She lowered her voice. 'The vows were a bit slushy; I can't imagine Guy had much input.'

'Yeah, well, what about those matching purple suits? Guy *hates* purple!'

Lynsey looked around to check no-one was listening. 'Let's not be bitchy. At least he's happy.'

Oh God, not that again. 'Alright, Lyns, stop rubbing it in.'

He pretended to need a refill and went over to one of the waiters. Hoping no-one would notice, he picked up a lemonade. He'd decided to try and avoid getting drunk as he didn't want anyone accusing him of bringing down the tone. *The day's bad enough as it is.*

At least he'd been able to pretend he got lost trying to find the venue and slip into the ceremony at the last minute, occupying a seat at the end of the back row. As Guy and Henry paraded down the aisle, their happiness so intense it almost formed a halo around them, a gut-wrenching sadness had cut through him. As the ceremony wore on, it only cut deeper and deeper.

He'd tried to detach from what was happening and concentrate on his breathing, fixing his eyes on the grain of the wood on the chair in front of him until everything else drifted out of focus. But the emotion gripping him was so intense it was impossible – and, by the time the ceremony was over, he felt drained, his entire body a dead weight.

At least he had no active role to play and no speech to make at the dinner. He'd been passed over for the role of best man in favour of Rags, a decision that had initially stung but now came as a relief. He hadn't even been offered the consolation prize of usher, with those duties assigned to Guy's other schoolfriends, plus his colleague Marcus. When he'd found out, he'd felt as if Guy was trying to hide him away, like some shameful misdemeanour he wanted to erase from his past. Either that or his parents had a hand in planning the ceremony and wanted to keep him out of it. But Danny comforted himself with the thought that this way he could feign an upset stomach and leave after dinner. *Or maybe I should say nothing and just quietly slip away – like I quietly slipped in.*

If he was leaving early, he needed to make sure he spoke to all the important people now so they remembered he'd been there. He looked around and saw Guy's parents gliding between the various clusters of people on the lawn, Cynthia's lemon yellow dress and hat complementing the powder blue of Stephen's suit. *But can I really face them?*

He decided he had to.

When he spotted them breaking away from one group, he sidled over before they could start talking to another. 'Mr and Mrs Falconer?' he began.

Cynthia turned and looked at him as if he'd just let out a sweaty, pungent fart.

'I wanted to say congratulations,' he managed.

They each shook his hand, limply.

'I don't know if you remember me but I'm a friend of Guy's from university,' Danny went on, smiling sweetly.

'Yes, of course, you came to our house for lunch.' A look of discomfort flashed across Cynthia's face but she swiftly tried to disguise it. 'It's Darren, isn't it?'

'Danny,' he corrected her, maintaining a rictus smile. 'Danny Baxter.'

As if you don't know . . .

'Good Lord, I almost didn't recognise you,' she said. 'Although maybe that's because you're dressed so much smarter today. And you look so much fresher now you're not hungover.'

Is she throwing me shade?

'Crikey,' said Stephen, 'you're the one who trailed dog dirt into our house. It took us weeks to get rid of the stench!'

Danny suddenly felt like his tie was fastened too tightly and strangling him. 'Yeah, sorry about that. Anyway, wasn't it a gorgeous ceremony?'

Cynthia nodded. 'Yes, it was very moving. I don't mind admitting I shed a little tear.'

Stephen's chest swelled. 'Guy's made us both very proud.'

My God, you two have changed your tune!

Danny winched his smile higher up his face. 'Oh, I'm pleased to hear that. I know these things can be challenging but I'm glad you came round in the end.'

Cynthia looked at him as if he'd just announced he'd spotted her at a swingers' party. 'I'm sorry, I don't understand. We didn't need to "come round"; we've never had any problem with Guy being gay. Have we, Stephen?'

Stephen laughed off the suggestion. 'Good heavens, no. I've no idea why you'd think that. It's just – how can I put this? – certain *lifestyles* we found a bit icky.'

Oh, so it's alright if gays behave like straights, is it? It's OK if gays do the respectable thing and get married? But Danny could see his presence was making them squirm; if they were trying to rewrite history, he was an unwelcome reminder of the truth.

'Of course,' he managed. 'Sorry, my mistake.'

Cynthia cast her eyes around with the furious desperation of a wasp caught in a glass. 'Oh look, there's Joan, the lady captain. If you'll excuse me, I *must* speak to her!'

Danny wished them all the best for the rest of the day but he hadn't reached the end of his sentence before they'd left.

Never mind, at least you've done the right thing.

He decided to lean on a wall next to the entrance and wait until Guy and Henry had finished having their photographs taken. *I might as well get all the awkward conversations out of the way at once.*

Swaggering around the lawn in front of him, he noticed Guy's brother, Barney. He joined a group of straight couples, pretended to be listening to their conversation, and manoeuvred his hand around one of the women to squeeze her bum. Danny wondered what Cynthia and Stephen would make of that. *Oh, they'd probably just roll their eyes and say something like, 'Boys will be boys'.*

When Guy and Henry finally appeared, Danny jumped up and grabbed them. 'Congratulations!' he burst out, his voice veering into a screech. 'It was such a lovely ceremony – the vows were so *romantic*!'

He threw his arms around them in a hug so exaggerated Guy came out of it blinking. 'Thanks,' he said. 'We spent a lot of time writing them.'

'And those suits are *gorgeous*!' he gushed. 'Guy, purple really is your colour!'

Was that too much?

'You see, darling, I told you,' jumped in Henry, nudging Guy.

'Alright, alright,' said Guy. And he flashed Henry a smile that expressed so much love it made Danny feel a twinge in his heart.

Henry turned back to Danny. 'Did you get emotional? Did you cry?'

Danny tried not to grimace. 'I didn't cry as such, but I did find the whole thing moving.'

And I'm not lying – I was just moved in a different way to the one Henry wants to believe.

'I guess the fact gay marriage has just been made legal gives it that extra emotional impact,' he added.

'Absolutely,' said Henry. A smile snaked up his face. 'Although don't forget we owe that to the Conservative Party.'

I think you'll find David Cameron brought in equal marriage but most of his party either abstained or voted against it, Danny wanted to say. But he told himself not to rise to the bait.

'In that case, let's toast the Tories!' he chirped, raising his glass.

'Oh, that reminds me,' said Henry, 'I need a drink. If you'll excuse me. Guy, I'll catch you in a minute.'

And he bounded off.

Guy pointed at Danny's glass and contorted his face. 'Wait a minute! What's that you're on? Don't tell me you're drinking lemonade!'

Danny shrugged. 'Yeah, I just wanted a break from the booze. I've had a run of heavy nights.'

Guy gasped. 'But Danny, it's my *wedding*! It won't be the same if you're not drinking!'

Oh, so I'm just some kind of court jester, am I? Here to get the party going and make sure everyone has a good time? But even as the thought occurred to him, he knew he wouldn't be able to refuse.

'Alright,' he conceded, 'I'll get a glass of fizz.'

'That's more like it!'

There was a pause.

'Anyway, I should probably go and circulate,' said Guy. 'I should probably catch up with my *husband*!'

The word cut into Danny like a knife, causing a whimper to rise from his throat. He quickly covered it up with a cough.

'OK, see you later,' he burst out. 'I'll see you on the dance floor!'

Once Guy had gone, he sloped over to one of the waiters and picked up a glass of champagne. *Oh, I might as well force myself to get into this – it doesn't look like I've much choice.*

He found Emma and the two of them took up position overlooking the lawn. Soon, they were reminiscing about the time she slept with Barney.

'I wouldn't care but he was a lousy shag,' Emma commented. 'He had all the passion of a knackered slug.'

Before long, they were on their second glass of champagne and Emma was telling him about her latest experience of her husband's lovemaking. 'Honestly, Richard's an *animal*!'

By their third glass, Danny was revealing that he'd pulled the barman at Guy's thirtieth and they'd had sex that was so frantic and furious it had brought tears to his eyes. 'Seriously, he wasn't so much an animal as a *monster*!'

They laughed so loudly several of the guests looked over. Danny topped up their glasses.

It took what seemed like for ever for the gong to sound for dinner. By the time Danny reached his table, he was sloppily drunk and his stomach was roaring with hunger. He found several bottles of wine and helped himself to a glass of white. When he spotted Lynsey making her way over to the seat next to him, he quickly introduced himself to the woman sitting on the other side. She had long, blonde hair extensions, a newly applied bronze tan and a strong Essex accent. She told him she was Guy's personal assistant and her name was Sandra. When he told her his name, she gripped his arm excitedly.

'So *you're* the gay best friend! I *love* gays!'

Danny tipped back most of his glass of wine. 'In that case, this is your lucky day!' he trilled.

'I've always said I'm a gay man trapped in a woman's body,' Sandra went on.

'Oh, you're much too beautiful for that,' Danny quipped, 'and you don't have anything like enough chest hair.'

She giggled and rolled her eyes. 'What are you like?'

She asked Danny to tell her about some of his adventures with Guy. As he obliged, she howled with laughter. Over her shoulder, Danny caught sight of Henry straightening Guy's tie and kissing him fully on the lips. Once again, sadness crashed into him.

He decided to tell Sandra about some of his adventures on Grindr – and her laughter became even more raucous. By the time the waiter was bringing out their food, he'd gone past hunger and barely touched his plate. Instead, he opened another bottle of wine.

Well, everyone wants me to get into this; I might as well go the whole hog.

After dessert, Rags announced it was nearly time for the speeches and if people wanted to go to the toilet, this was their chance. Sandra snatched her handbag and staggered onto her feet.

'I need to shake the dew off the lily,' she said.

'Don't fall in!' joked Danny, who by now had gone from sloppily to operatically drunk.

'What are you *like*?' Sandra shrieked, before lurching off into the distance.

Danny looked around the table and saw that everyone else had left –except Lynsey.

'Hello again,' he said.

'Hi,' said Lynsey.

Danny turned his chair to face her but nearly slid off it.

'Are you alright?' she asked.

He ran a hand across his eyes. 'Of course I'm not alright. How am I supposed to be alright when the man I love has just married someone else? Someone who hates me but who does such a good job of hiding it, Guy doesn't even notice.'

Lynsey frowned. 'Dan, you know I feel for you but you really need to stop blaming this on Henry; it isn't his fault.'

Danny shook his head. 'Well, I'm sorry, Lyns, but I think it is.'

She glanced around to check no-one was close enough to hear her. 'Look, Dan, I know you didn't get a chance to make your move on Guy. But it's not all down to you. The truth is, if he'd wanted to, Guy would have made a move.'

Danny drained his glass and set it down on the table. 'Oh yeah? And what makes you so sure?'

Just as he was reaching over for another bottle of wine, Lynsey let out an exasperated sigh. 'Because if Guy wants to sleep with someone he just does. I should know – he did it with me.'

2015

Guy saw he'd received a text from Lynsey. *I wonder what she wants . . .*

He was just about to read it when his mother interrupted. 'Good Lord, will you put that phone away?'

'We're in the Lake District!' echoed his father. 'Why would you want to be glued to your phone?'

'Sorry.' Guy tucked it away. 'I won't look again!'

Henry sent him a smile. 'Come on, darling, let's appreciate that view!'

Guy and Henry were on a walking holiday with Guy's parents, staying in an Airbnb in the town of Keswick. They'd arrived the previous day and had enjoyed browsing the shops and market, as well as eating a hearty meal and sampling local ales in a cosy pub. Today, they were undertaking their first walk, following a route known as the Catbells. They'd crossed the town, completed a moderate climb up Skelgill Bank, and were now looking out over Derwent Water, the Newlands Valley and the Western Fells. The September sunshine made the water look stunningly clear, while the odd cloud cast a shadow that slid slowly over the green hillsides.

'"Come forth into the light of things,"' pronounced Henry. '"Let Nature be your teacher."'

'Ah, Wordsworth!' bellowed Stephen.

'"Nature never did betray the heart that loved her,"' picked up Cynthia.

Henry let out a contented sigh. 'It's so beautiful here. Thanks again for bringing us.'

'Don't be silly,' said Cynthia. 'It's our pleasure.'

Guy felt his stomach give a little somersault.

As the trip was their wedding gift from Guy's parents, the conversation turned back to the big day.

'I can't believe it's been six months already,' said Guy, taking off his fleece and tying it around his waist. 'It feels like yesterday.'

'Well, it was an absolutely magical day,' cooed Henry. 'I wouldn't have done anything differently.'

A pair of middle-aged ramblers approached from the opposite direction and the two groups exchanged greetings.

'Actually, there are one or two things *I* would have tweaked,' said Stephen, stabbing his hiking stick into the path.

'Oh yeah, like what?' asked Guy.

Stephen shot Cynthia a knowing look. 'For a start, your brother Barney sleeping with that woman.'

'Your secretary,' clarified Cynthia, curling her lip as if she'd just spotted a dead fly in her salad. 'Although from what Barney said, she didn't give him much choice.'

'Mother, Sandra's a lovely person,' Guy said, wiping a film of sweat from his brow. 'And I don't know what I'd do without her; she's brilliant at her job.'

Cynthia gave him a pinched expression. 'Well, there was no sign of that when she was on the dance floor. She and your friend Danny were simulating some kind of sex act.'

Guy pulled down on the straps of his rucksack. 'I think maybe they'd had too much to drink.'

'That's an understatement,' scoffed Stephen. 'Danny was as drunk as a skunk.'

Cynthia yelped. 'I just remembered, did you see him dancing around that column as if it were a pole? The one engraved with the names of all the former captains?'

'Yes, it was shockingly inappropriate.' Henry shook his head and sighed. 'You know he ended up spending the night with our photographer?'

Cynthia and Stephen gasped.

Actually, they didn't spend the night together, Guy wanted to point out. *Danny told me they had sex on the golf course, somewhere near the eighteenth hole.*

'Crikey, it's so unsavoury,' said Stephen, using his stick to clear a branch from the path.

'So *tawdry*,' agreed Cynthia.

Guy admonished himself for not defending Danny, but he wasn't sure he had it in him. *I don't want to start an argument, not when we're all getting on so well.*

'And to think you wanted him as your best man!' piped Cynthia.

'Your mother was right,' said Stephen. 'We should never even have invited him.'

Guy couldn't stop himself letting out a huff. 'Mum, Dad, we've been through this. Danny's my best friend. I couldn't *not* have invited him.'

Cynthia paused and took a swig from her water bottle. 'Well, all I can say is, I'm glad your life isn't like his. I'm glad things have worked out for you, darling.'

Stephen nodded. 'You know, we're proud of you, son.'

'We are indeed,' agreed Cynthia.

Guy felt a rush of joy so powerful it left him slightly light-headed. For the next hour or so he walked with an added bounce.

When it came to lunchtime, the four of them sat down on a few rocks at the side of the path, overlooking a view of the lake that was so beautiful it seemed almost unreal. From this distance, the water looked perfectly still, like a mirror reflecting the handful of little fluffy clouds in the cobalt blue sky. It brought a tear to Guy's eye, a tear he quickly wiped away before anyone could see it.

'Right, who's hungry?' asked Henry.

Last night, he and Cynthia had gone shopping to the local supermarket and had risen early to pack a picnic.

As Guy helped himself to a spinach and feta pastry, he knew he had a lot to thank Henry for: it was Henry who'd helped heal the rift between Guy and his parents; it was Henry who'd proved to them that being gay wasn't dirty or disgusting. It seemed unimaginable now that they'd said such horrible things about gay men. *But I forgive them; I forgive them for everything.*

Let's just say we've been on a journey – and the important thing is we got there in the end.

He swallowed the last of his pastry and dusted the crumbs from his hands. *What's that saying? The rearview mirror is smaller than the windscreen. Yes, it's what's ahead of us that's important, not what's behind.*

He reached into his rucksack for his bottle of water. As he did, he sneaked a look at his text from Lynsey. 'It's Danny's birthday,' it read. 'I don't suppose you've heard from him?'

As he filled his mouth with water and swilled it around, he made a mental note to reply to her later.

And the answer was that yes, he had spoken to Danny; Guy had texted him from his bedroom that morning, while Henry was downstairs packing the picnic. After wishing him a happy birthday, he'd added, 'You'll never guess where I am.'

'Where?' came the reply.

'I'll give you a clue – I'm in your neck of the woods.'

'What, Barrow???'

'No, the Lake District!' He was teasing Danny and grinned in expectation of his response.

'I keep telling you, Barrow isn't in the Lake District!' Danny retaliated. 'They're very different. Like tits and todger. Boobs and boner. Rack and rod.'

Just as he was chuckling, Henry came back into the room. Guy quickly wished Danny a good day and signed off.

He reached over to the tubs of food, picked up a padron pepper and bit into it, tossing the stem over the hillside. Then it occurred to him: if Lynsey was asking about Danny, the two of them obviously still weren't speaking. After the wedding, Guy had found out that they'd had a massive argument, not that anyone would tell him what it was about. He'd directly asked both of them but his attempts had been swiftly shut down. Part of Guy couldn't help wondering if it had something to do with that awful night at his parents' house ten years ago.

But no, it couldn't . . . Could it?

It had happened when he'd been living at home after graduation, just before he'd moved into his first flat in London – just before he'd finally put an end to his relationship with Drew. If that hadn't been making him feel like a miserable failure already, his parents had been hitting him with regular digs about his sexuality and insisting he pretend to be straight when any of their friends came round. Then Lynsey had arrived, staying over for a night after a training course in the London office of the law firm that had just given her a job. She'd arrived on a Friday evening, just after Guy's mother and father had left for a golfing weekend. Before they did, they'd gone to ridiculous lengths to make sure she felt welcome, leaving a homemade lasagne Guy could heat up for dinner, a bottle of champagne chilling in the fridge, and another of expensive red wine aerating in the antique glass decanter, not to mention vases of fresh flowers and scented candles dotted around the kitchen and dining room. It was obvious to Guy that they were desperate for him and Lynsey to get together.

He could only assume this had been on his mind as he'd shown Lynsey to her room, after the two of them had polished off the whole bottle of champagne *and* the red wine *and* a bottle of cheap plonk Maria used for cooking. His memories from that part of the evening were hazy but he'd somehow ended up making a pass at her, she'd submitted, and all of a sudden they were having sex. Just thinking about it all these years later, Guy felt the flare of shame.

He pictured himself the next morning, lying in bed, stewing in regret, ravaged with guilt, not just for cheating on Drew but for using Lynsey to somehow try and 'straighten himself out', like that character Danny had played in her production of *A Taste of Honey,* like so many other characters he'd seen in films and on TV, like some kind of gay cliché. Ever averse to confrontation, he'd decided that the best course of action would be to just pretend the whole thing hadn't happened. Thankfully, Lynsey had taken a more mature approach. She'd tapped on his door, perched on the edge of his bed and confronted the issue head-on, suggesting they both agree that what happened was a mistake and make a pact not to let it damage their friendship. Although things had never quite been the same since.

Guy gazed out over the water and felt a swell of sadness.

'Guy, are you alright?'

He snapped himself back to the present just as Henry sat next to him.

'Yeah, yeah,' he insisted, giving his husband a smile. 'I'm having a lovely time.'

He paused to appreciate the dimensions of Henry's face. *God, he's so handsome. He's so perfect.*

'What are you thinking?' Henry asked.

'Just how much I love you,' Guy responded.

Henry's face lit up. 'In that case, do I get a kiss?'

'Of course you do.'

Their lips came together for what developed into a succession of kisses.

'Good Lord, can't you two control yourselves?' quipped Cynthia. But Guy saw that she was smiling.

'Honestly, newlyweds!' said Stephen, giving an exaggerated tut. 'I suppose you and I were like that once, Cynthia.'

'All I can say is, enjoy it while you can,' she quipped. 'I can't remember the last time your father kissed me!'

Stephen plonked himself on the rock next to her and planted a theatrically loud kiss on her cheek.

Cynthia giggled, then gave him a slap. 'You mucky pup, you've got mayonnaise on me!'

The four of them laughed. The four of them laughed loudly.

Guy looked up at the sky and another tear came to his eye. This time he didn't wipe it away.

2022

Lynsey leads Danny through to her garden, which is only small but bursting with flowers that are various shades of purple, lilac and pink. She gestures to two rattan chairs on a patio overlooking the lawn and they sit down.

He's just told her what happened between him and Guy that Friday night, then filled her in on the aftermath – including his declaration of love and Guy's admission that this isn't reciprocated. Every bit of it was as difficult as he expected. *And I still haven't broached the subject of what happened between me and her . . .*

He clears his throat.

Right, here goes . . .

'Anyway, I came here to apologise, Lynsey. When I found out you'd slept with Guy I said some horrible things.'

Some of those things Danny hadn't even meant; they'd just come tumbling out in anger . . .

'Oh, it's obvious you're in love with Guy!'

'You've only been telling me to move on so you can have another crack at him!'

'Maybe your love life's such a disaster you can't bear the idea of me having one!'

He feels leaden with guilt.

'I don't know what came over me, but I was bang out of order. What I said was totally unjustified. I'm so sorry, Lyns.'

Lynsey's shoulders rise and fall. 'I totally get why you were angry. And if it's any consolation I really regret what I did. But I hope you understand I never meant to hurt you.'

Danny watches a bee moving between the purple flowers of a lavender bush. 'I do understand that, yeah. I think I probably always did. I suppose in the heat of the moment I was just blinded by jealousy.'

Lynsey nods slowly.

'Obviously, I'd been struggling with my feelings for Guy for a long time,' Danny goes on, 'but I think his wedding must have tipped me over the edge. It wouldn't surprise me if I went through some kind of depression.'

'Yeah, well, it's always easier to make sense of these things with hindsight,' Lynsey comments. 'I certainly did a lot of thinking about it after the wedding. And I came to the conclusion that when I slept with Guy I was feeling low about leaving university and leaving behind my support structure. I was nervous about giving up theatre and becoming a lawyer full-time. I think university had just been such an amazing experience for me, I felt insecure about the future.'

Danny breathes in. 'Yeah, I get that.'

'I was also lonely,' Lynsey goes on. 'I was desperate for affection, for some kind of human connection. And then, all those years later, when you and I fell out at the wedding, it made me stop and look at why I still kept getting those things wrong. Why

I'd been putting so much of my energy into work and my career and going for the kind of men who were obviously never going to make me happy.'

She pauses and stretches out her arms. 'So in some ways you could say our argument wasn't entirely a bad thing. In a roundabout way, it ended up leading me to Ben.'

Danny watches the bee fly away. 'Well, that makes me feel slightly better. It makes me feel like slightly less of a bastard.'

Lynsey sits forward in her chair. 'You know, *I* felt like such a bastard. I felt awful about what I'd done. And you were right: that was one of the reasons I gave you such tough love. I think I was desperate for you to get over Guy and move on so I could stop feeling so guilty.'

Danny runs his fingers over the rattan on his armrest. 'That may be the case but it doesn't change the fact that everything you said about me and Guy was true, everything you said about my feelings for him. If I'd listened to you then, I wouldn't be in this mess now.'

Lynsey lets out a sigh. 'Yeah, well, I don't want to sound glib but at least now you know how Guy feels. At least the uncertainty's over. Isn't that a relief?'

'Hopefully it will be at some point,' Danny says, 'but I'm not there yet.'

'You'll get there, I'm sure.'

There's something about Lynsey's confidence, something about her belief in him after all this time – after all the terrible things he said to her – that makes Danny's chin give a little wobble. He tugs in a breath. 'Anyway, I hope you'll accept my apology.'

A smile crawls into Lynsey's eyes. 'Of course I accept it. I accepted it the minute you walked through the door.'

Danny feels so overwhelmed with gratitude he thinks he might cry.

He slaps his palms on his thighs and switches on a grin. 'Now all I have to do is get over the fact Guy knocked me back and got off with some twink who's half my age. Honestly, you should have seen the state of him; he looked more like a pet than a boyfriend.'

Lynsey laughs. 'Yeah, well, let's not go back to being shady about Guy's men. Let's try and look on the bright side. Twenty years is a long time to be in love with someone who isn't in love with you. At least now you really can move on.'

Move on to what, though?

But Danny doesn't voice his worry. He hasn't seen Lynsey for seven years; he doesn't want to dump this on her now.

'Right, well, I should probably get going,' he says.

She looks at her watch. 'Shit, yeah, I need to make a move.'

He stands up and draws her into a hug. 'Just let me get through this weekend, then I'll be back in touch.'

'You'd better.' And, just as he's turning to leave, she adds, 'Oh, and Dan?'

'Yeah?'

'You'll work it out. You'll get the happiness you deserve.'

He rocks backwards on his heels. 'What makes you so sure?'

'Because you and I have always been so similar. And if it can happen to me, it can definitely happen to you.'

2016

'I'm not single, I'm in between boyfriends,' Danny read. It was a cute line but one that suggested *@accountantinholloway* went through boyfriends faster than Take That changed line-ups.

No, he's not for me.

Danny was swiping through profiles on a dating app called OkCupid. He'd decided to step back from hook-ups and focus on looking for a relationship. It was a decision he'd made a few months after Guy's wedding, once his spirits were lifting – and once he'd recovered from the humiliation of experiencing erectile dysfunction while trying to have drunken sex with the photographer next to the bins at the back of the kitchen. Part of him was worried that he'd made such a show of being defiantly single people might scoff, but he figured that most people who knew him would understand he'd evolved and would be happy for him. That was, if he did find a boyfriend: he'd been searching without success for six months now. But he was determined to stay hopeful.

He perused a profile belonging to a TV producer called Martin, who went by the name *@martyparty*. He seemed fun but – judging from his pictures – spent a lot of time in the gym. Just as Danny was worrying that @martyparty wouldn't be attracted to him, at the bottom of his profile he read a note saying, 'Sorry, can't meet up for a while, I chipped one of my veneers on a protein bar.'

He swiped left.

It was a Saturday afternoon and Danny was sitting propped up in bed. He was living in the latest of a succession of grotty flat-shares, this one in Stratford. His flatmates were a Northern Irish woman who always seemed to be in the middle of a relationship drama, badgering Danny for advice she never followed, only for the boyfriend to cheat on her – at which point she'd promptly restart the cycle with someone else – and a straight American man who described everything as 'dope', pretended to be bad at housework so the others would do everything, and spent all his free time playing video games with his friends back home in Pennsylvania. From the bedroom next door, Danny could hear him grunting and growling.

'Man, that is dope!'

It was a cold March afternoon so Danny was lying under the duvet with the heating on. But the radiator in his bedroom was blocked and only reached a temperature that could best be described as lukewarm. Above it was a window with a crack running down the pane that was held together with Sellotape and a damp patch on the wall that used to be the size of a football but was well on its way to being as big as a football pitch. From outside, Danny could hear the sound of rainwater dripping from the leaking gutter onto the windowsill.

With any luck, he wouldn't be living here for much longer; now he was earning a decent salary, he was paying off his student debt and – as soon as it was cleared – was going to start saving up for a deposit to buy his own place. Occasionally, he had a browse through property apps, just so he could think about the kind of place he might be able to afford. But he was managing his expectations, as Lorraine had told him that any property you bought would only ever be eighty percent right.

I wonder if the same is true of men . . .

He refocused on his dating app and decided not to be so harsh on the men on offer. After swiping through a few more profiles, he found a landscape gardener called *@greatscott*, whose description included the line, 'I'm looking for someone who gets off at my bus stop and decides not to make the return trip.' Danny thought that sounded sweet, noticed *@greatscott* was currently online, so struck up a conversation.

After the initial preamble, they seemed to be getting on well and were soon making plans to meet up. Then *@greatscott* asked, 'In case it comes to it, what do you like to do in bed?'

Just as he was about to reply, Danny noticed that *@greatscott* was typing again.

Another question appeared: 'Are you the mop or the bucket?'

Danny let out a gasp. *'Bucket'? Did he really just call me a bucket?*

He ended the conversation abruptly.

He decided to take a break and wondered what Guy was up to. He considered checking his Facebook, but he was trying to wean himself off making regular checks. Then he reasoned that one little look wouldn't do any harm.

As usual, Guy hadn't posted in a while.

But what about Henry? He never wastes an opportunity to show off his perfect life.

Danny scrolled through his contacts, clicked on Henry's name and found a picture he'd posted the previous evening – from

Courchevel in France. It was of Henry, Guy and both sets of parents standing outside a chalet dressed in expensive-looking ski gear.

With a jolt, Danny remembered his dream that one day he'd join Guy and his parents on a skiing holiday. Suddenly, that idea struck him as ridiculous. *I don't even know how to ski. I'd look as out of place on a ski slope as a feather boa on a donkey.*

He noticed from the Messenger icon that he had an unread message. He clicked through and saw it was from Yiannis Dimitriou.

Fuck!

He felt like he'd been shot.

Can this really be my dad?

Blinking, he opened the message.

'Hello, Danny,' it read. 'Good to hear from you.'

He had to remind himself to breathe.

'How are you doing?' the message continued. 'If you'd still like to talk, I think now would be a good time for us to get to know one another.'

Fuck, fuck, fuck!

'Would you like to schedule a call?'

Then, as if he was writing a letter, he signed off with his full name.

'Yiannis Dimitriou.'

Danny couldn't believe it; something he'd wanted for so long was finally opening up as a possibility.

He imagined what his dad's life might be like in Greece. *Alright, he's a womaniser but that doesn't mean he can't be close to his family.*

Danny wondered if he had aunts and uncles, maybe even grandparents. He pictured them all sitting around enjoying a family meal, himself at the centre, surrounded by loud, effusive and overbearing relatives, like a scene from *My Big Fat Greek Wedding*.

Come on, Danny, stop fantasising. And stop straying into cliché!

Unease crept up his spine as another thought occurred to him. *If I do reply to my dad – if we do get to know each other – how will I tell Mum?*

He worried Eileen would consider any contact as an act of disloyalty, even betrayal. And he didn't want to throw everything she'd done for him back in her face.

He wished he could talk to Guy about it but didn't want to disturb him, especially if he was out on the ski slopes. He'd almost certainly be with Henry – and Danny didn't want him to hear about any of this.

So he decided to do nothing, at least for the time being. Rather than rushing into anything, he'd take his time and think over this properly. *My dad has waited thirty-two years to get in touch with me – I'm sure he can wait a bit longer.*

Out of nowhere, Danny felt a rush of resentment. *Actually, I sent him that message six years ago. Why's he suddenly getting in touch now?*

His resentment hardened. *He can't just decide he's ready and expect me to jump.*

He shut down Facebook and opened up OkCupid. Right now, he was going to forget about his dad and focus on finding a boyfriend.

2016

London's a big city. It's full of gay men. The right one for you has to be out there somewhere.

It was a mantra Danny repeated to himself every time he went on a date. But no matter how convincing it sounded, it wasn't working.

After nine months of looking for a relationship, he still hadn't been able to progress any further than the first or second date – and he'd had a string of those. Some of them made great anecdotes, but Danny was starting to feel seriously disheartened. The dates he found most upsetting weren't the ones with men he didn't fancy; those he could cope with. The worst were those with men who didn't fancy *him*, the ones who texted afterwards to say they just weren't feeling it, or they saw him more as a friend, or – worst of all – just ignored him, a practice the media was starting to call 'ghosting'.

To mitigate the potential damage, Danny had scaled back the effort he put into a first date. He no longer committed to a meal and no longer gave up a Friday or a Saturday night; instead, he arranged to meet on a weeknight for a coffee or a drink after work, with the pre-arranged excuse of having to leave after an hour or so for dinner with friends. That way, if things weren't going well he wouldn't have to invent an excuse his date could easily see through as a hastily arranged escape plan. If he *did* like them, he could always arrange to see them again – and put more effort into the second date.

But *still* it wasn't working. With every failure, he tried consoling himself that he was eliminating unsuitable men from his enquiries, avoiding wasting time on connections that would only amount to nothing. And he'd repeat his mantra to himself. But before every date, he'd started to expect failure.

As he got off the tube at Tottenham Court Road, crossed Soho Square and walked along Old Compton Street, he tried to suppress all thoughts of failure. *Tonight could be the start of something new and exciting.*

The irony was, Danny was feeling more confident about his physical appearance than ever. The last time he'd been given a pay rise, he'd splashed out on a course of laser treatment to permanently remove his back and shoulder hair. It was excruciatingly painful and the smell of his own body hair burning turned his stomach. But it meant he could give up on smearing himself with Veet and, if it did come to taking his clothes off with a man, he wouldn't feel self-conscious about having stubble on his back and shoulders.

Danny was also in a position to finally tackle his baldness. Unfortunately, though, several sessions with several trichologists had taught him that it was too late to undergo any kind of hair transplant. One of them, a kindly man in his fifties, had run him through the various experimental surgeries and drug therapies that were coming on the market, then stopped and suggested the best possible solution would be for Danny to make peace with it. So that's what he did, against all expectations. Or at least, that's what he was in the process of doing. As part of his efforts, he'd decided to own his baldness in the pictures he put on dating apps and to search for men who weren't put off by it, or who even said they found it attractive.

One of those who claimed to find it attractive was tonight's date. Danny was about to meet a man called Paul, who was a data analyst, was brought up on the Isle of Wight, had a pet golden retriever called Max, and described himself as a keen runner. They'd matched on OkCupid, had chatted on the app for a few days before migrating to WhatsApp, then finally agreed to meet for a drink in one of Danny's favourite gay bars, the Yard.

It was a sunny evening in June and warm enough to drink outside in the ground-floor courtyard. Once Danny had bought a drink, he found a quiet spot leaning against a wall. While he waited for his date, he looked around the decked courtyard, its walls covered in ivy, strings of fairy lights hanging overhead. The bar was full of young-to-middle-aged men, many of them wearing the latest fashions by Urban Outfitters or Superdry, many of them sporting beards, which were fast becoming the muscles of the twenty-tens what Danny liked to call the 'push-up bra of masculinity'. *Maybe I'll use that line on Paul . . .*

When he arrived, Danny's date looked pretty much as he did in his photos, with hair the colour of a two-pence piece and an unremarkable but perfectly pleasant face. The only difference was that he too had grown a beard. Danny decided not to share his observation but to compliment Paul on his new look.

'Cheers, fella,' he replied, in a slightly mannered, laddish voice.

'You know, beards are really in at the moment. You should grow one yourself.'

Danny grimaced. 'Oh, I'm not sure about that – I think I'll probably stick with the stubble.'

Paul's eyes scoured his face. 'I think it'd suit you.'

Is that a compliment? Danny felt a rush of relief and told Paul he'd consider it.

Well, this has got off to a good start . . .

But no sooner had Paul come back from the bar than the evening took a turn for the worse.

Danny asked him about growing up on the Isle of Wight, he asked what it was like to be a member of a gay running club, and he asked about his dog. But it was obvious from all of Paul's answers that in person he was boring – extremely boring. He was so boring, in fact, that at one point, Danny found himself drifting off and compiling his to-do list for the next day.

Oh, come on, boring isn't the worst quality in a man. And you want someone who's steady and dependable, not some quick, dirty shag.

'So tell me about you, fella,' interrupted Paul. 'Where do you live?'

'Near the Olympic Park,' Danny replied. 'I still rent but I'm hoping to buy in a year or so.'

Danny sneaked a look at his watch and saw there was still half an hour until he'd said he had to leave for his imaginary dinner date. But he wasn't even sure he could hack it for that long. *Oh, maybe I'm just not meant to settle down. Maybe I'm not meant to be in one of those respectable gay couples.*

He thought about his dad, who'd sent him another message via Facebook. This time, he'd said he was coming to London in the autumn and was hoping they could meet up. Danny had no idea what was behind this sudden interest and couldn't help feeling peeved that Yiannis thought he could just waltz into his life after an absence of more than three decades. If he did agree to the meeting, would he even like him? What if he was such a womaniser he found him repulsive?

He felt all the heat leave his body. *Maybe I'm built like that too. Maybe I'm a chip off the old block.*

He shook the idea out of his head. *No, I don't want to be some embarrassing old shagger. I don't want to end up a sad, lonely queen.*

'So tell me about being a data analyst,' he said, determined to make this work. 'What exactly does it involve?'

Paul's explanation was long and detailed and, by the time he came to the end, Danny realised he hadn't taken in anything beyond the first few words. He wrenched his mouth up into a smile. 'That's fascinating, babe.'

A look of horror darted across Paul's face. 'Don't call me "babe".'

'Why not?'

'I'm not into camp.'

Danny's smile wilted. 'Oh, right.'

Paul took a draught of his pint. 'Now we're on the subject, you're much camper than I expected. Because of the shaved head and the stubble, I was expecting you to be straight-acting. I only date guys you can't tell are gay.'

Danny felt the humiliation thump into him. 'Urm, OK.'

'But I've enjoyed speaking to you, so maybe we could be friends?'

'Friends'? I'm not looking for any friends . . .

Danny breathed in quickly through his nose. 'To be honest,' he stated, briskly, 'I don't have enough time to see the friends I've got. No offence but I don't want any more.'

Paul's face fell. 'Sorry, fella. I've obviously hit a raw nerve. I didn't realise you were that into me.'

But I'm not *into you!*

Danny felt his humiliation bloating. *My God, this guy has bored me to death for the last hour but I was prepared to overlook that. And now* he's *rejecting* me*!*

In that moment he decided his days swiping through dating apps were over. Even if it meant he'd slide back into casual sex and hook-ups, there was no way he could face any more evenings like this.

'Don't worry, it's OK,' he managed. 'But speaking of friends, mine are waiting; I really should head off.'

He gave Paul a curt nod.

Come on, Danny, straighten out your crown and keep going.

'Toodle loo, *babe,*' he chirruped. And with that, he made a big show of flouncing out of the bar, wiggling his hips, waggling a limp wrist, and trying to be as camp and effeminate as possible.

2022

Guy stands under the shower and lets the warm water run through his hair. He closes his eyes as it blasts away his tiredness. *If only it could blast away my guilt.*

It's shortly after midday and he's just returned to the hotel. He was dreading seeing Danny but found no sign of him; the cleaners have been in and done such a thorough job he can't even be sure he slept in the bed. While it's a relief not to have to face Danny, Guy knows he'll have to at some point. *And I'll have to explain why I got off with someone right after he told me he was in love with me.*

He opens his eyes.

How could I have been so insensitive?

As he squeezes out some shampoo and massages it into his hair, he decides not to be too hard on himself. He didn't go out looking for sex or trying to meet someone; he only went to the Village because he was looking for Danny. And the only reason he allowed himself to be drawn into a conversation with Josh was because of what he'd said to him.

'Aren't you out with your boyfriend?'

When Guy had replied that he didn't have a boyfriend, Josh

had revealed that on Friday night Danny told him the two of them were a couple. This had annoyed Guy so much he decided to put Danny's feelings out of his mind and focus on what he wanted. And, the more he spoke to Josh, the more he realised it was *him* he wanted – and maybe still did.

Alright, the timing isn't great but I can't rule out getting together with someone just so I don't hurt Danny's feelings.

Even so, he'd rather not hurt Danny any more than he has already. He remembers their final year of university and the vow he made not to lead him on or toy with his emotions. *Oh, maybe I shouldn't have started calling him 'princess' again. Maybe I shouldn't have told him I loved him when we were in the parade.*

He rinses his hair and lathers his body with shower gel, scrubbing much harder than is necessary.

The thing is, Guy has always enjoyed it when Danny gives him attention – and he's always enjoyed it when he shows him affection. It makes him feel wanted. It makes him feel special. *And I know it's weak to give in to it but I'm still miserable about splitting up with Henry. I still miss him. I'm still lonely.*

He rinses his body and switches off the water. *But I'd also be lonely without Danny. And I don't want to go back to the way things were after I got married. If I lose his friendship again, this time it could be for good.*

He steps out of the shower and towels himself dry. Next to the sink he spots his phone. He picks it up to text Danny.

'Hi princess,' he writes.

His stupidity makes him gasp.

He deletes what he's written and decides to keep the message simple.

'Hi Danny,' he types, 'how are you doing?'

* * *

How am I doing? How does he think *I'm doing?*

Sitting in the back of an Uber on his return to the city centre, Danny has no idea how to reply to Guy's message.

God, he can be so insensitive sometimes. Suddenly, Danny can't bear to tell him the truth about how he's feeling.

He takes in a sharp breath. 'Fine, thanks,' he types. 'What you up to?'

'At the hotel,' reads Guy's reply. 'Wondering if you want to meet up?'

Danny becomes aware of how stuffy the car is and winds the window down.

To be honest, I'm not sure I do . . .

He remembers how he felt when he saw Guy kissing that young man outside Via. When they see each other, he knows they'll have to discuss it – and he'll only end up feeling the same way.

No, I definitely don't *want to see him.*

He leans forward to speak to the driver, an Indian man who's wearing an anorak even though it's a warm summer's day.

'Sorry, change of plan,' he says, 'I'm not going back to the hotel after all. Please could you drop me at the Village?'

The driver nods and Danny turns back to his phone.

'Sorry,' he types, 'something's come up. Have a good day. Have fun with your pet.'

He stops, remembering a hook-up he'd had just before the pandemic, a hook-up with a much younger man. *I can hardly talk.*

He deletes the last sentence, adds a kiss and hits Send.

Within seconds, Guy replies with the emoji for thumbs up.

The casualnesss of it stings.

Right, that's that. He obviously isn't bothered about seeing me.

Danny runs his palms down his thighs. It looks like he's going to be doing the rest of Pride on his own.

In that case, from now on you're not even going to think about Guy.

2016

One mild autumn afternoon, Danny was sitting at a table outside a coffee shop in Regent's Park. He was waiting to meet his dad. *And I'm so nervous I feel like I'm going to explode.*

After mulling over the issue, he'd come to the decision that he had to agree to the meeting. If he didn't, he'd be wondering what might have happened for the rest of his life, wondering what his dad might have been like. This could be his only chance to find out.

They'd exchanged a couple of messages but Danny didn't want to appear too keen. So he'd simply made arrangements for the meeting and promised himself he'd ask all the questions he wanted when they were face to face. *Although now that's about to happen I'm not sure it was the best idea . . .*

For a start, he realised he hadn't told his dad he was gay and wasn't sure how best to do this. *What if he reacts badly?*

Added to that, he still hadn't solved the problem of how to tell his mum. *But I'll just have to deal with that afterwards . . .*

As he sipped his coffee, his heart hammered in his chest. He was trying not to think about Lynsey anymore but he remembered her saying it was only when she'd met her mother's family that she understood why she'd always felt like part of her was missing. Danny couldn't help wondering if something similar might be about to happen to him; he wondered if he too had a key part of his identity locked away, a part of him that so far had been impossible to access. *If that is the case, is this meeting with my dad going to make me feel complete?*

He looked at the empty chair facing him and felt the fear sluice through him.

As it was October, the leaves on the trees were a beautiful golden brown. Many of them had already fallen onto the grass or the pathway that ran past the coffee shop, forming a thick carpet over which tramped joggers, dog walkers, and young parents pushing prams. Opposite Danny, two squirrels chased each other around the trunk of a tree, their claws clutching onto the bark and giving off a skittering sound.

After a while, Danny spotted a dark-skinned man he judged to be roughly the right age walking towards him. Into his head flashed his childhood fantasy about his dad coming to find him to let him know that he loved him and from now on would look after him.

For God's sake, Danny, pull yourself together!

As the man drew nearer, Danny saw that he was wearing a grey trench coat that was unbuttoned, revealing a navy blue business suit and a Paisley tie. When he came close enough for Danny to see his face, the resemblance hit him like a thunderbolt. There was no question this man was his dad. Except he had a full head of hair, hair that was only just flecked with grey, even though he must have been in his mid-fifties. Danny felt floored by something he thought might be indignation. He forced it back.

The man spotted him and approached his table. 'Hello,' he said, 'I'm Yiannis.'

It struck Danny that he didn't say the word 'Dad'.

'Hello,' he replied, feeling all churned up inside, 'I'm Danny.'

He found himself pumping Yiannis's hand as firmly as he could.

That's my dad. That's actually my dad!

Yiannis asked if he wanted a coffee and Danny said thanks but he already had one. He was struck by Yiannis's proper, very correct English, and his lack of a Greek accent; he spoke in what people in the casting industry called Received Pronunciation. This confirmed what Danny had always assumed: that he was from a well-to-do family. When Yiannis excused himself to buy a cappuccino, Danny concentrated on drawing in deep breaths and letting them out slowly.

He was gone for so long that Danny worried he'd taken one look at him and decided to bail out. *Or maybe he can tell I'm gay and doesn't want anything to do with me?*

Just when Danny was thinking he'd have to go and look for him, Yiannis re-emerged, grumbling about the queue. He sat at the table, directly opposite Danny.

'So you said you're over here with work?' Danny asked, his throat dry.

'Yes, this year our industry's annual convention is being held in London.' Yiannis smiled and sipped his cappuccino.

Danny had to make a real effort not to stare at his features. He found the resemblance between them unsettling, as the knowledge they were so closely related created a sense of intimacy – but he couldn't avoid the fact that they were complete strangers.

'And am I right in thinking you live in Thessaloniki?' he asked.

He noticed that as well as giving Yiannis a firm handshake he was deepening his voice and trying to sound as masculine as possible, something he usually refused to do. *Why am I doing it now? Don't tell me I'm angling for his approval?*

'Yes, it's a port city in northern Greece,' Yiannis said. 'I live in the family home, just outside the centre, with a view of the sea. But it's just my wife and me now. All three of our daughters have left home.'

Fuck, he's married.

Fuck, he's got daughters.

Fuck, I've got sisters!

For some reason, none of this had crossed Danny's mind. *I just assumed he was a womaniser.*

A wave of discomfort passed through him. He wasn't sure why, but the information that Yiannis wasn't made him feel unsettled. *So who is he?*

'How old are they, your daughters?' he managed to ask.

Yiannis ran his finger along the rim of his cup. 'Let me see . . . They'll be thirty-one, twenty-nine and twenty-six now. The oldest is just a couple of years younger than you.'

Danny imagined what his sisters looked like. He pictured himself flying to Greece and being welcomed into the family with extravagant hugs and tears of joy.

'We also have four grandchildren,' Yiannis added, 'with another on the way.'

Fuck, so I've got nephews and nieces too!

Yiannis smiled with a pride that confirmed he was nothing like the swaggering stud of Danny's imagination. 'My grandchildren are without doubt the greatest joy in my life.'

Oh, how lovely!

Then he felt a punch to the gut. *Wait a minute, if he's so attached to them, why has he never bothered with me?*

Before Danny could question him further, Yiannis switched the focus onto him. He asked Danny about his job, his flat, and how he liked living in London. Danny gave him a rough outline of his social life but found himself steering clear of any reference to his sexuality. When Yiannis asked about his childhood, Danny described growing up in Barrow – and inevitably began talking about his mum.

'She did an amazing job bringing me up,' he said. 'There were times when it wasn't easy, but she was always there for me.'

He hoped that didn't sound like a criticism of Yiannis.

Yiannis spread his hands out on the table. 'Well, that leads me on to the reason I wanted to see you today.'

Danny winced in expectation.

'I wanted to apologise, Danny. I'm sorry I wasn't able to play an active role in your upbringing. It's no excuse but I just wasn't ready to be a parent. Or should I say I didn't think it was the right situation for me to be a parent.'

Danny was stumped. It hadn't occurred to him that his dad would apologise. 'That's OK,' he replied, a little embarrassed. 'There's no need for you to apologise.'

Hold on, why am I saying that? Of course he should apologise!

'What happened between your mother and me was entirely out of character,' Yiannis went on. 'It isn't remotely like me to have a fling.'

Danny tried not to flinch at the word 'fling'; it stood in stark contrast to the 'love affair' described by his mum.

'Again, it's no excuse but I was very young and a long way from home,' Yiannis continued. 'I suppose what I did was my way of letting loose a little, of getting that urge out of my system.'

Danny swilled the remains of his latte around the mug. *God, did I only come into the world because my dad was 'getting an urge out of his system'?*

'Anyway, all of that's something I'd rather my wife didn't find out about,' Yiannis said, frowning. 'It would only upset her.'

Danny looked up. 'Oh. So were you together at the time?'

Yiannis pulled at his collar. 'We were, yes. So I'm not exactly proud of what I did.'

Everything inside Danny slumped. *Oh my God, he's actually ashamed of me.*

Of course he is. How could I ever have thought otherwise?

'So did my mum know that?' he asked. 'Did she know you were seeing someone in Greece?'

Yiannis gave a tight smile. 'She didn't, no. I didn't want to tell her. Your mother could be very . . . What's the word? Intense. No, over-sensitive.'

Danny widened his eyes. Yiannis's words reminded him of Dean – and what he used to say about Danny. *So I'm not like my dad at all – I'm like my* mum*!*

'You know what women can be like,' Yiannis added, shooting Danny a look he interpreted as trying to establish some kind of male solidarity. 'I didn't want her to become hysterical.'

'Hysterical'? How dare he say that about Mum!

Danny could feel the anger rising from his stomach. He pushed his mug into the centre of the table. 'Actually, I *don't* know what women can be like. Tell me, how are they supposed to react when a man cheats on them?'

He instantly regretted sounding so aggressive.

'Sorry, I don't have much experience of women,' he added. 'I'm gay.'

Yiannis gave a casual shrug. 'Yes, I realised that. Or should I say I found out from your Facebook profile.'

Danny felt the relief slosh through him; he didn't have to come out to Yiannis after all.

Wait a minute, why should I feel relieved? I shouldn't have had to get worked up about it in the first place!

He drew in his mouth tightly. 'And I suppose you think being gay is wrong, do you? I suppose it's something you won't accept?'

Yiannis raised his cup to his lips. 'Not at all; you misunderstand the culture of my country. In Ancient Greece, gay men were part of society. We Greeks have a proud history of acceptance and understanding.'

Oh and I'm supposed to feel grateful now, am I?

But Danny told himself not to sound petulant. Once again, his heart was thumping in his chest. *I can't believe he called Mum over-sensitive and hysterical!*

'For your information,' he said, 'my mum's always been accepting too. She's actually an amazing woman. And yes, she may sometimes get a bit emotional but I've never seen her "hysterical".'

Yiannis put his cup back in its saucer. Danny found the little clinking sound it made excruciating.

'You seem to be getting a little emotional yourself,' Yiannis commented. 'Maybe it's a good thing we're having this conversation.'

Danny folded his arms. 'What's that supposed to mean?'

Yiannis explained that he was about to become active in local politics, running for mayor in his home city. 'I need to keep my wife happy. I need to keep her by my side. Also, I don't want to upset my daughters; they're very close to their mother.'

Danny gave him a curled look. *Well, it looks like that trip to Greece is off . . .*

'When we started planning the campaign earlier this year,' Yiannis went on, 'my team asked if I . . . What's the expression? Oh, yes; they asked if I had any "skeletons in my closet".'

Oh my God, he's actually calling me a skeleton in his closet!

Suddenly, Danny understood that Yiannis was only here to ask him to stay away. The only reason he'd got in touch after so long was to make sure he wouldn't cause any trouble. That was probably the only reason he'd apologised.

It was like a whip had been cracked in his head.

'Actually, I take back what I said earlier,' he snapped. 'You do owe me an apology; you owe me a massive one. But it's obvious you only gave it so I wouldn't get in the way of your plans. You're not remotely interested in me. You're not remotely interested in how I feel.'

'Danny—'

'Oh, give it a rest, Yiannis. You can stick your apology.'

He stood up and Yiannis rose to his feet and held out his hand.

'Can we at least be friends?'

'Friends'? Why does everyone want to be my friend?

'No, we can't be friends,' Danny spluttered. 'You're supposed to be my *dad*! Although you've done a pretty shit job of it so far.'

He looked at Yiannis's hand. He felt as if shaking it would be disrespectful to his mum – and to himself.

No, I'm not going to.

'Goodbye,' he said, brusquely.

He took one last look at Yiannis and turned away.

As he tramped over the golden leaves, he could feel the anger roiling inside him. But he was also aware of a rekindling of the embers of the sadness he'd felt when Lee had rejected him. The sadness and the shame.

He rammed his hands into his pockets. *I don't need a dad. I've always got on perfectly well without one.*

He quickened his step and straightened out his spine, determined to walk tall. *I'm not going to find myself in a stranger who just happens to share my genes.*

He remembered watching Yiannis arrive and feeling an urge to be loved by him. He cursed himself for being pathetic and vowed never to give in to that kind of weakness again.

At least now it would be easier to tell his mum about the meeting. *And once I have, I'm not going to give Yiannis a second thought.*

2022

As he squeezes his way through the Village, Danny does his best not to think about Guy – but so far this is proving difficult.

He's just eaten a double portion of pad thai he bought from one of the food stalls at the side of Sackville Square. As he tosses the empty tray into a bin, he remembers trying to avoid eating on Friday night and all the work he put into slimming down for the weekend. *Well, at least I don't have to worry about that anymore.*

On a nearby pavement he slides into a gap in the crowd and lights a cigarette. *I don't have to worry about giving up smoking either.*

He fills his lungs and lets out a long breath. *You know what, this is going to be much more fun without Guy!*

Although it's only 2.15 in the afternoon, the Village already looks full to capacity. And, although it's the third day of Pride, no-one looks like they're even close to flagging. Danny passes a group of men in matching gold hot pants who are mixing themselves mimosas from supermarket value-brand cava and cartons of Capri-Sun.

'Happy Pride!' they shout, as they bring together their plastic glasses.

Danny thinks about the day and night stretching ahead of him and can feel his excitement spreading.

He heads up Richmond Street, towards a crowd of people who are dancing outside a marquee that houses a DJ booth and a temporary bar. He passes a drag queen with a glitter beard who's cramming a hot dog into her mouth and spilling ketchup down her French maid outfit. He edges around a huddle of policemen wearing Pride badges, with rainbow epaulettes on their uniforms, all of them trying to maintain serious expressions but being encouraged to lighten up and join the party by the crowd. And he skims the entrance to a multi-storey car park that's been converted into the Gaydio Dance Arena, around which the pavement is thrumming with the heavy bassline. When he reaches the marquee, the people outside it are dancing to Gloria Gaynor's *I Am What I Am*.

This'll do!

He ducks into the marquee and tags himself onto the back of a mob of people waiting to be served.

'I'll have a double vodka and Diet Coke please,' he calls out to the barman.

Next to him, a group of young men dressed as fairies – each with a different coloured tutu and wings – are seeing who can down their drinks the fastest.

'Actually,' he calls out to the barman, 'make that two. And go easy on the Diet Coke!'

2016

Danny gave a little jig as *I Am What I Am* came on the radio. 'Oh, I love this song!'

'Me too,' said his mum, 'I've always loved Gloria Gaynor.'

The two of them had just eaten and Eileen was washing up in the sink while Danny was standing next to her, drying.

'But I'm going to have to switch this off in a minute,' Danny commented.

Eileen's face became a question mark.

'There's something I want to talk to you about,' Danny answered.

Eileen froze. 'By 'eck, this looks serious.'

It was Christmas Eve and Danny was in Barrow, staying with his mum in the house in which he'd grown up. It was pretty much the same as it always had been, except Eileen had installed a new fitted kitchen and the calendars she used to hang up, featuring the Chippendales, then Robbie Williams, had been replaced by wicker hearts and a wooden sign saying, 'Live, Laugh, Love'. She'd also had the front room redecorated and swapped her old floral-patterned three-piece suite for a brand new peach-coloured velvet sofa and armchairs that, with just the pull of a handle, slumped into recline mode and thrust out footrests. The whole house had been tidied up and cleaned in preparation for tomorrow – Christmas Day – when Danny and Eileen were due to be joined not just by Arthur, but by Eileen's partner, Gary.

Eileen had matched with Gary online two years ago and it had soon become apparent that their relationship was serious. When he was younger, Gary had spent a decade in the army, but he had left in his thirties to retrain as an electrician and now ran his own business. He wasn't particularly handsome but had a strong presence, with silver hair that almost shone when it caught the light and a frame so large that when he sat down he could fill a two-seater sofa. But he was something of a gentle giant and loved nothing more than spending a quiet day fishing or playing Eileen songs by Eric Clapton and Tom Petty on his acoustic guitar. Gary was divorced with two daughters who were in their twenties and who Danny hoped would one day have children of their own – so his mum might experience being a grandma. Whether or not that did happen, he was glad Gary was in her life and loved seeing how happy he made her.

But now I need to have a conversation with her I'm worried is going to make her un*happy.*

Once they'd finished the washing up, Danny switched off the radio and they went through to the front room with a couple of wine glasses and a bottle of Aldi's premium prosecco. They settled on the sofa, filled up their glasses and Danny told her he'd met his dad.

An emotion zipped across Eileen's face but it was too fast for Danny to read it. 'Well, I weren't expecting that.'

'Are you alright?' he asked.

'Yeah, it's just a shock, that's all.' She took a swig of her prosecco. 'What did he say?'

Danny told her everything Yiannis had said about his life in Thessaloniki, his three daughters, and his ambition to enter local politics. *I'll miss out the bit about the wife – and what he said about Mum.*

'And come on, you're hiding summat,' Eileen said, without missing a beat.

Danny pretended to be surprised. 'What makes you say that?'

'I'm your mum, I can tell.'

Oh no, how do I do this?

'The thing is, I didn't really like him,' Danny attempted.

'Oh yeah?' Eileen cocked her head. 'Why's that?

Danny coughed into his fist. 'He wasn't very nice about you.'

'Well, that doesn't surprise me,' said Eileen. 'I suppose he told you I were just a fling, did he?'

'Actually, he did, yeah.'

Eileen gave a gasp. 'The cheeky get! He used to tell me he loved me. Or at least he did at first, when he were trying to get into my knickers.'

Danny laughed. But he suspected her humour was masking a real hurt.

Eileen drained her glass, then topped them both up. 'Anyway, *I* were in love with *him*. Or at least I *thought* I were in love with him.'

She reminded Danny that she'd been brought up by strict Catholic parents who'd sent her to a convent school, at which the nuns had been even stricter.

'When I were growing up, pretty much all t' adults I knew were small-minded, judgmental, homophobic and racist,' she went on, tucking a strand of hair behind her ear. 'I couldn't stand any of 'em – that's why I moved to Liverpool. And I sometimes wonder if carrying on with a foreigner – someone they didn't approve of – might have been another way of being rebellious, of sticking two fingers up at 'em.'

'Oh, so you *weren't* in love with him?' Danny asked.

She let out a sigh. 'I'm not sure anymore. What I felt for your dad were nowt like what I feel for Gary. It might have been a different kind of love – it might have been more like lust – or I might have just been wrong and a bit messed up. Arthur thinks I were trying to punish myself.'

'How do you mean?'

She let out her footrest. 'Well, I were only ever going to end up hurt because Yiannis were never really available. I always suspected he had a girlfriend back home – although he always denied it.'

Danny let her know that Yiannis had confessed as much.

Eileen quirked an eyebrow. 'That figures. Poor cow. She probably had no idea – she probably still doesn't.'

Danny knocked back the rest of his drink. 'Funnily enough, that was why he wanted to speak to me. He wanted to make sure I wouldn't tell her. He made it clear I was a mistake he wanted to cover up.'

Eileen flushed at the neck. 'How dare he! You weren't a mistake. At least you weren't as far as I were concerned.'

'Oh, come on, Mum,' Danny said, rolling his eyes. 'You don't have to say that to make me feel better.'

She put down her drink. 'What are you on about, love? I'm not saying owt to make you feel better. I'm telling t' truth.'

'But what do you mean? Surely you didn't *plan* on getting pregnant?'

'Well, no, you're right there: I got caught, as we used to say in them days. But that doesn't mean I had no choice about whether or not to go through with it.'

Danny remained silent and traced his finger around the rim of his glass.

'Look, love, I know the female reproductive system i'n't exactly your area of expertise, but it's quite easy to end a pregnancy you don't want to go through with – and it were even in them days. But something told me you were a baby that needed to be born. Something told me you were going to be special. So I took the decision to keep you. You weren't born by mistake; you were born because I *wanted* you.'

Even though this was the first time they were having this conversation, Danny knew deep inside that he'd always understood this. He looked around the room at all the photos of him at the various stages of his life, each of them displayed in a frame engraved with flowers or in the shape of a star. He looked at the photos of him and his mum together, on holidays, at weddings, and in the professional photography studio on the day of his graduation. And he had no doubt that his mum did want him.

'Right from the start I decided that if you weren't going to have a dad, I'd just have to love you enough for two parents,' Eileen continued.

And she did.

When he was at primary school and the bullying started, Danny remembered his mum marching into the headmaster's office and demanding he punish the kids. When it became more intense, Eileen became a regular presence at school, often raising the issue with teachers and parents. By the time he was moving on to secondary school, the shame Danny felt about the insults the other children hurled at him was overwhelming – so he started engaging in all manner of subterfuge to cover it up. But whenever there was a gay-themed programme on TV or any stories in the media that portrayed gay men in anything like a positive light, Eileen made sure he experienced them. He had vivid memories of her watching episode after episode of *So Graham Norton*, laughing loudly at all Graham's jokes. As soon as George Michael was dragged out of the closet, she raced into town to buy his entire back catalogue, manufacturing a love of his music that until then had been entirely absent. And when *Priscilla, Queen of the Desert* was released, she'd whisked them both off to the cinema, claiming afterwards to have enjoyed the film so much she wanted to return for a second viewing a few days later.

Danny felt a rumble of guilt for repeating his dad's claim that he was a mistake.

'Sorry, Mum,' he said, touching her arm, 'I shouldn't have said that. I never thought you didn't want me. I couldn't have asked for a better mum.'

He hugged her and told her he didn't want to talk about his dad anymore but to draw a line under the experience. Eileen agreed.

But reflecting on everything she'd done for him made Danny question if he'd always appreciated her enough. He wasn't sure he'd been as good a son to her as she'd been a mum to him. He remembered how proud he'd made her on his graduation day and he wanted to make her that proud of him again.

I want her to think all her sacrifices and hard work were worth it.

2022

Just as Danny is pushing his way into the Eagle, his phone vibrates. He lifts it out. It's his mum.

Oh my God, I can't speak to her now.

After everything Eileen has done for him, he couldn't bear her to know that this is where it's all led. *That I'm miserable and on my own and trying to drink myself out of it.*

As he lets his phone ring out, he feels a stab of guilt but reminds himself that, since his mum married Gary last year, she's had her hands full; her two stepdaughters each had a baby within a few weeks of each other and Eileen has thrown herself into the role of grandma, helping out with feeds and changes and regularly looking after both babies so their mums can take some time off. He doesn't want to disrupt her stable family life or burden her with his problems.

He eases his way through the entrance to the bar and is funnelled downstairs, into a dimly lit labyrinth of low-ceilinged rooms that smell vaguely of stale beer and fresh sweat. The crowd is men-only and Danny doesn't think he's ever seen so many vests, so many bare chests, so much muscle. He pushes his way over to the bar and stumbles into a man who's wearing nothing but a pair of white Y-fronts and a yellow fireman's helmet.

'Sorry, babe!' he calls out, but the man doesn't even notice him.

Already his head is foggy with drink but the adrenaline's surging through him, making him feel excitable and wired. He orders another double vodka and Diet Coke from a barman dressed only in a jockstrap and squeezes his way through the throng to a quiet spot at the back of the room.

He's standing next to two men of around his age, one with a crew cut, the other with a buzz, both of them with thick moustaches. From what Danny can make out, they seem to be teasing each other about the effects of enjoying too much anal sex.

'I bet yours is like a windsock,' says the one with the crew cut.

'You can talk,' says the one with the buzz. 'I've heard yours is like a clown's pocket.'

They roar with laughter and Danny can't help giggling.

'Alright, chuck?' the one with the buzzcut shouts to him in a northern accent. 'Are you going to stand there laughing or do you want to come and join us?'

Danny slides over. 'Hi, I'm Danny.'

'Danny?' asks the one with the crew cut. 'Is that short for Danielle?'

They all laugh.

The men introduce themselves as Trent and Robbie and tell him they know each other from work: Trent – the one with the buzz cut – is a paramedic, while Robbie – the one with the crew cut – is a hospital porter.

'Are you here on your own?' asks Robbie.

'Yeah,' says Danny. 'Actually, I came to Manchester with a friend but he was getting on my tits so I left him.' *Oh, I know that's not strictly true but it's not that far off.*

'Well, you're welcome to hang out with us, chuck.'

'We're off to a club after this.'

They gesture to a wall of posters advertising clubs with names like Homoelectric and Bollox.

'Which one?' asks Danny.

'We haven't decided yet,' chirps Robbie, 'but probably DILF; there's more sausage in there than a butcher's window.'

'In that case, count me in,' says Danny. 'Right, who wants a drink?'

As he takes their orders, he becomes aware of his phone ringing again. He looks at the home screen and sees it's his mum making another attempt to get through. He glances at the dimly lit space teeming with half-naked men and knows he still can't answer; he'd be too ashamed.

When he reaches the bar, he receives a notification that she's left him a voicemail.

I'll listen to it later.

2017

Danny looked at his mum, sitting across from him in the hot tub. Next to her was Gary, who had his arm draped around her shoulders.

'Now, i'n't this nice?' said Eileen.

'Yeah, it's bliss,' said Gary.

It was a sunny spring day and Danny had come to Barrow to celebrate his mum and Gary moving in together. The two of them had set up home in Gary's house, as it was slightly larger than Eileen's and located in a nicer part of town. Although before she'd moved in, the walls had been bare, the kitchen table constantly littered with Gary's electrician's tools and cables, and the living room cluttered with clothes horses hanging with laundry that had dried days ago. And the house always seemed to smell of wet dog, despite the fact that – to the best of Danny's knowledge – a dog had never lived in it. Thankfully, now that Eileen had moved in, the smell had vanished. And she'd made the place much more homely, tidying away the laundry and tools and cheering the place up with several pot plants and pictures.

To celebrate her moving in, Gary had hired a hot tub. This just about fitted in his yard, or 'yarden' as Eileen insisted on calling it since she'd hung a few baskets of geraniums on the back wall. They'd wanted to keep the party small so the only other guests were Gary's daughters, Angela and Melissa, two blonde women a few years younger than Danny who both worked in women's clothes shops in the centre of Barrow and whose names he often mixed up, and Arthur, who'd travelled up from Brighton. He declared that he was too old for hot tubs but looked happy enough sitting in a deckchair in a leopard-print kaftan, sipping his usual vodka and orange.

'You might have to turn them bubbles off for a bit, love,' said Eileen, nudging Gary.

'No problem, sweetheart.' Gary reached over to the control pad and pressed a button. 'Your wish is my command.'

As the jets of air stopped shooting around the tub, everyone sank onto their seats.

'There, that's better,' said Eileen. 'All that flab around my tummy's stopped wobbling now.' She laughed loudly.

'Get out of it!' said Gary. 'You've no flab on you at all. I keep telling you, you're a cracking-looking bird!'

Eileen giggled coquettishly.

'There's not a day goes by I don't wake up and wonder what I did to deserve you,' Gary added.

'Come here, love.' Eileen pulled his face towards her and gave him a kiss on the lips.

Although Danny adored seeing his mum so happy, at the same time her happiness sometimes reminded him of what was missing in his life. Like him – and like Emma – Eileen had been an outsider, someone who didn't conform to the model of straight respectability that the majority of people seemed to value so highly. And there were days when he couldn't help feeling like all his allies were deserting him. *But come on, stop being selfish and self-absorbed.*

At least his career was going well: he'd just been promoted from associate to solo agent and no longer had to double up as Lorraine's assistant but could concentrate on his own list of actors. He was earning a much higher salary and, as a result, was finally able to put into action his plan to buy his own place. The problem was, nobody wanted to talk about that; so far, the conversation in the hot tub had revolved almost exclusively around relationships – as Angela and Melissa both had new boyfriends. Danny mimed expressions of interest as they listed all the qualities they loved in their men, then moved on to complaining about their bad habits.

'Mine scratches his balls when we're watching telly,' said one of the girls, Danny wasn't sure which. 'And he leaves the toilet seat up!'

'Mine doesn't clean the sink when he's had a shave,' moaned the other. 'He leaves it full of bristles!'

What I'd give to be able to complain about toilet seats and bristles.

'Anyway, how about you?' asked the one he thought was Angela. 'Have you got a fella?'

'Oh no,' he said breezily, 'not at the moment.' *Not at the moment? When do I ever have one?*

'So who was that fit guy you posted a pic of on Insta the other day?' asked the one who was probably Melissa.

Danny's heart plummeted to his toes. It had been Guy's wedding anniversary and in a lonely moment, he'd posted a photo of him and Guy laughing together at university, captioned with the hashtag #ThrowbackThursday.

'Oh, that'll be Guy,' he said.

'Who's Guy?' said Angela. 'An ex?'

Danny forced out a smile. 'No, just a friend.' The word 'friend' caught in his throat.

'So has anything ever happened between you two?' asked Melissa.

Danny could feel the blood rushing to his cheeks. His mum looked away and began picking at a non-existent chip in her nail varnish.

'No, that'd be weird,' he trilled. 'We've known each other for years. We're too close.'

Danny felt a stab of guilt for lying; these days he and Guy could hardly be described as close. Danny had only seen him on a handful of occasions since his wedding and their text and phone conversations were becoming much less frequent.

'Actually, he got married recently,' he added, 'so I haven't seen him as much.' Just sharing this information, he felt the choke of rejection all over again.

'So does the husband not like you being around?' asked Melissa.

'Is he jealous?' added Angela.

'Something like that,' said Danny. 'Actually, I'm a bit hot. If you don't mind, I might get out and sit with Arthur.

He grabbed a towel and held it in front of his stomach to hide his flab. Once he'd dried himself, he wrapped the towel around him and slid into the deckchair opposite Arthur, who was absorbed in his phone.

'Are you alright, babe?' Danny asked.

Arthur put down his phone. 'Yeah, thanks, dearie. I were just checking my apps.'

He explained that he'd recently set up profiles on Grindr, Scruff and Tinder – looking purely for no-strings-attached fun – but was having the most success on an app called SilverDaddies, which was for mature men and their admirers. 'It's amazing,' he said. 'I had no idea there were so many blokes out there who are into older men.'

'Neither did I,' said Danny. 'I hope they're still there when I get to your age.'

As they laughed, Eileen joined them. 'Gary's turned them bubbles on again,' she said, blowing onto her forehead. 'It's too much for me.'

She picked up a magazine and began fanning herself.

'It's this bloody menopause,' she went on. 'I'm sweating like a whore in confession.'

The three of them laughed.

Eileen put down her magazine. 'Anyway, never mind that. Are you alright, Danny? I hope the girls didn't upset you.'

Danny gave a rictus smile. 'Upset me? Why would they have upset me?'

'You know, when they were asking about Guy.'

'Oh, that's OK,' Danny chirped, 'they didn't bother me at all!'

He detected a frown flicker over Eileen's lips.

Shit, does she know?

There was an awkward pause.

'Anyway, if you ever want to talk about it,' she went on, gently, 'you know where I am.'

For a brief moment Danny found himself wondering if he *did* want to discuss it with his mum – if he did want to discuss it with Arthur.

Then, coming from the hot tub, he heard the sound of Angela and Melissa laughing at something their dad had said. Everyone was so happy; he didn't want to sour the atmosphere by moaning about Guy. He didn't want to be the wasp at the picnic.

'Thanks, Mum,' he said, 'but honestly, I'm fine.'

Arthur clapped his hands together. 'Of course he's fine! He's probably just bored stiff hanging around with an old bag like me and all you dreary heterosexuals.'

He turned to Danny. 'Is that it, dearie, have you got het lag?'

'Oh, I don't—'

'Rubbish!' interrupted Arthur. 'I can tell, it's written all over your face. You're probably sitting there wondering how quickly you can sneak off to a gay bar.'

Although Danny insisted this wasn't true, he couldn't help thinking that the prospect did sound appealing.

2022

Danny takes his drinks and leaves the bar to return to Trent and Robbie. He's only moved a few steps when he feels a tap on his shoulder.

'Danny Baxter? Is that you?'

He turns around to see a man in a leather waistcoat and chaps with pierced nipples and a studded dog collar around his neck.

'Danny!' the man shouts. 'It *is* you!'

'Hi, babe,' Danny replies, but he daren't say any more as he doesn't have the faintest idea who the man is. *Is it someone I've slept with?*

'Do you not recognise me?' the man says, pointing at himself and smiling. 'It's Keith Trotter!'

No, it can't be!

Keith Trotter was in the year below Danny at school, obsessed with Janet Jackson, and one of the few other boys Danny could tell was gay. He was also possibly the only other boy to endure the same level of homophobic bullying as Danny.

'Oh my God, *Keith*!'

Danny rests his drinks on the side and they give each other a sweaty, slightly awkward hug.

'Sorry I didn't recognise you, it's been a long time. Anyway, it's good to see you! What are you up to? Weren't you going to be a professional dancer?'

Keith gives an embarrassed laugh. 'Yeah, well, that never happened. I'm the manager of a gay sauna in Newcastle. The owner's thinking of opening a sex club next door so we've come to Manchester to do some research.'

Danny laughs. 'That sounds like my kind of research trip!' But behind the humour, he can't help wondering how Keith can have gone from being a sweet boy who knew every step of Janet Jackson's dance routines to having pierced nipples, a studded dog collar around his neck and a job running a gay sauna.

'How about you?' Keith asks. 'What are you up to?'

As Danny tells him about his job, he wonders what the boy he was at school would make of the man he's become – if he'd even recognise him now, drunk and slurring in a men-only basement bar, planning to move onto some kind of sex club with two men he's only just met. He asks himself if he's made a mess of his life or if he just used to be naïve – extremely naïve.

He decides not to dwell on it and asks Keith what his plans are for later.

'I don't know yet,' he replies, 'and I'll be so out of my head it won't matter!'

'Me too, babe!' Danny fizzes. 'Me too!'

But even as he's speaking, he's blindsided by a wave of sorrow. For a brief moment, Danny imagines throwing his arms around Keith and telling him how sad it is that both of them lived through the same trauma at school but had to suffer alone – how heartbreaking that they couldn't be of any comfort to each other. *But all that's so long ago, it would probably just be weird.*

'Right, I'd better get to the bar,' says Keith. 'I need a drink before I start sobering up.'

Danny pulls a face of horror. 'Oh no, anything but that!'

They promise to look each other up on social media and say goodbye.

As he picks up his drinks and sets off to find Trent and Robbie, Danny concentrates on banishing from his mind any memory of the boy he used to be. The boy he used to be when he was so terrified of what was inside him, he couldn't bear to be friends with Keith Trotter.

2017

'So that's about it,' Danny said. 'There's the living area, one bedroom and one bathroom. I won't show you my secret sex dungeon.'

Guy smiled. 'Nice try, Danny, but we're on the tenth floor. It'd be a long way down to a dungeon.'

It was a Wednesday evening in October and Danny was showing Guy around his new flat. The best he'd been able to afford was a slightly cramped place in a modern development in Canning Town, but it had a little roof garden, a skylight that illuminated the kitchen area, and curved walls that gave it lots of character – or so the estate agent said. It was nearly two months since Danny had moved in and he'd invited Guy to visit on numerous occasions but on every one of them he'd claimed to be busy. Then Guy had surprised him a few days ago by suggesting he come round one evening this week – and had turned up with a potted bonsai as a housewarming present.

'I'm going to put your gorgeous gift on the windowsill,' Danny said, positioning it in the centre, then stepping back to admire it. 'Thanks, babe.'

Although Danny had unpacked all his belongings, the flat was still nowhere near how he wanted it to be: the decorator couldn't start till next week so he hadn't bothered to assemble his dining table and chairs, and the sofa he'd ordered still hadn't arrived. He had no idea why it took eight weeks to manufacture a sofa; he'd known feature films to be shot in less time. Perhaps worst of all, he currently had no way of listening to his music, as he'd invested in a complex audiovisual system that was operated by a 'virtual assistant' called Alexa – but she didn't understand his voice so he'd given up and put her back in her box. *I'm not coming this far in life to be accent-shamed by an Alexa.*

At least having a half-finished flat released Danny from the expectation that he'd make dinner for Guy. He ordered them a takeaway, opened a bottle of wine and they sat down on boxes. He talked Guy through his plans to refurbish the place, including his idea of using hundreds of squares of mirrored glass to transform a wall in the living room into what he was going to call his 'disco ball wall'. But, once they'd finished talking about the flat, the conversation stuttered.

'How's everything with work?' Danny asked.

As Guy updated him on his latest career news, Danny found himself having to feign interest. *How did things get so stilted between us?*

Then another thought occurred to him. *Wait a minute, does that mean I've fallen out of love with him?*

If he had, he wasn't sure how he felt about it.

'How's Henry?' he asked when another gap opened up in the conversation.

'Yeah, fine, thanks,' replied Guy. 'He's on a work trip to New York.'

Oh, so that's *why you've come to see me!*

Danny noticed that they'd reached the end of the bottle of wine. 'Shall I open another, babe?' he asked, standing up and moving over to the kitchen before Guy could reply.

'Not for me, thanks,' he said. 'Henry and I are trying to cut down. It's his idea to be honest, but I do feel much better for it.'

Danny jumped at the opportunity to tease him. 'I don't know, if your teenage self could hear you now. Cutting down on the booze!'

As he topped up his own glass, the two of them fell back on the fail-safe option of reminiscing about the past. Nostalgia reinvigorated the conversation, but Danny couldn't help suspecting that the connection between them belonged in the past. He felt a rush of grief.

Guy's phone buzzed. 'Sorry,' he said, 'it's Henry. Do you mind if I take it?'

Danny nodded and took the opportunity to check his own phone. Seeing he'd received several notifications from Grindr only confirmed to him just how different his and Guy's lives had become. He decided not to read those and opened the messages he'd received from his friends at work. There were two other gay men who were single and around the same age as Danny who currently worked at the agency: Owen, who was Irish and had only recently come out after a short-lived and disastrous marriage to a woman, and Nathan, who used to be a swimmer and had once represented England at the Commonwealth Games, at which he hadn't won any medals but had apparently succeeded in sleeping with half the men in the athletes' village. The three colleagues had become close and set up a WhatsApp group on which they competed against each other to see who could share the most outrageous, often explicit content. Over the course of the last hour, Nathan had posted the link to an article celebrating the bulges of the Brazilian male gymnastics team, and Owen a pic a man had sent him on Grindr comparing the size of his erection to the cardboard tube from the centre of a toilet roll – dwarfing it by a ratio of about four to one.

'That's insane!' Danny typed, tacking onto the end of his message several aubergine emojis.

'Owen, you are cock crazy!' wrote Nathan.

'Takes one to know one!' Owen replied with a winking face.

The group header indicated that Nathan was typing. 'What you up to, Fanny?' It was the group's nickname for Danny and always made him smile.

'Just having takeaway with an old friend,' he replied. He stopped and considered what he was about to add. He decided to go ahead and add it anyway. 'A bit bored TBH.'

At that moment, Guy strode back into the room and Danny felt so guilty his stomach gave a little heave. He shut off his phone and placed it face down.

'Sorry about that,' said Guy.

'Everything alright?' Danny asked, brightly.

'Yeah, Henry just likes us to speak every night when he's away.'

Danny decided he wouldn't acknowledge that comment. 'Are you sure you don't want some more wine, babe?'

'Yeah thanks,' Guy said, sitting back down, 'I'm trying to limit myself to two glasses on weeknights.'

'So where's all this come from? Is it some kind of health kick?'

Guy kneaded his knuckles. 'Well, the main reason is Henry and I are going to try for a baby.'

Danny felt as if all the air had been punched out of his lungs.

Clearly I haven't fallen out of love with him . . .

He did his best to contort his face into a smile. 'Trying for a baby? Illuminate me – how do two blokes go about that?'

Guy laughed. 'Yeah, sorry, what I mean is we're looking into surrogacy. It's still early days, but we're finding out what's involved.'

'Great,' Danny croaked.

'What's the matter?' said Guy. 'You don't seem very taken with the idea.'

Danny gave his head a little shake. 'Sorry, it's just a surprise, that's all. But only because I've never thought about becoming a dad myself. I know more and more gays are doing it and obviously it's important we have equal rights. But I quite like the fact that no-one *expects* us to have kids. Do you know what I mean?'

Am I starting to sound like Arthur?

Guy nodded. 'Yeah, I do. But I hope you'll get into it when the baby arrives. You know, I'd love you to be involved.'

Danny pictured himself at the baby's first birthday party, catastrophically hungover and making an effort to join in as everyone sang *Happy Birthday* to an ugly, unresponsive lump of blubber – and all he could think about was the unbridled, energetic sex he'd had with some stranger a few hours earlier. He pictured Henry, peacocking around the party and looking down his nose at him, puffing himself up like a princess who's just produced an heir. *Do I really want to put myself through that?*

He considered the alternative: growing even more distant from Guy and the two of them having even less in common than they did now. The grief swelled in his throat.

'Of course, babe,' he managed. 'I'd love to be involved.'

'Cool.'

Danny spotted the opportunity for some mischief. 'But only so long as I can be the wicked uncle who comes round in leather trousers and tells inappropriately dirty jokes. And when the kid's old enough I can take him out for his first drink.'

Guy's eyes twinkled. 'I wouldn't expect anything less.'

Danny's phone vibrated to tell him he had a message. 'Sorry,' he said, 'do you mind if I get this?'

He opened his phone and saw it was another message from Nathan.

'Don't go getting pissed,' it read. 'Remember we've got the Diversity Awards tomorrow.'

'Yas queen!' jumped in Owen.

'Free bar!' added Nathan.

'Can't wait!' wrote Danny. He made his excuses and closed WhatsApp.

He told himself that it was a good thing he and Guy were having a quiet night in; he needed to rest so he could be on top form tomorrow.

If Guy doesn't know how to have fun anymore, I might as well save myself for people who do.

2017

As soon as Danny arrived at the Diversity Awards, he could tell things were going to get messy.

'I swear to God, his dick was so skinny it was like a toothpick,' drawled Nathan. 'Seriously, it wouldn't have even touched the sides.'

Everyone around the table burst into laughter.

'Honestly, babe,' said Danny, 'you're such a dirty bitch.'

'Shut up, Fanny,' shot back Nathan, 'you're the filthiest queen in London!'

'Never mind any of that, ladies,' interrupted Owen. He lowered his voice and leaned in. 'Your Auntie Owen has brought us all some fairy dust – two grams of it.'

Excitement spread around the table and Nathan jumped up and sloshed more wine into their glasses. Straight away, Danny tipped half of his down his throat. At least he didn't have to worry about getting up on stage: he hadn't been nominated for any awards as he'd only been a solo agent for six months. He was, however, already building up a reputation in the industry as someone who cared about diversity.

Danny's passion had been ignited shortly after he became Lorraine's assistant and started gaining an insight into how the industry worked. The more he discovered, the more he realised that his sexuality had been a major factor in the failure of his own career as an actor. It hadn't mattered in student theatre, where everyone was still attached to their ideals and commercial factors weren't a concern, but in the real world there was no question it was viewed as an obstacle. As soon as Danny had found himself in a position to push for change, he'd taken on various LGBTQ+ actors and had started to confidently and unapologetically put them forward for roles – around the same time as the industry had gradually begun to open itself up to the idea of casting them. He was doing the same with actors of colour and had just taken on his first client who was a wheelchair user. *I'm going to give this industry a kick up the arse!*

Tonight's event was being held in one of the exclusive – not to mention ruinously expensive – hotels on Park Lane. Sitting in the ballroom underneath the sparkling crystal chandeliers, Danny spotted several heads of film companies and TV channels as well as various casting directors, including Doris Slinger, who years ago had knocked him back for that job in a TV hospital drama on the grounds that there was nothing in the script to say the character was gay. Like many others, she was now signalling to the world what she claimed was a long-held passion for diversity. Also in attendance were various magazine editors and news correspondents, plus several representatives of the new breed of social media 'influencers', many of whom practised a form of activism that consisted solely of expressing outrage at comments made by other people, many of these well-meaning but ill-informed members of other minority groups – and even, on occasion, the same minority group. As Danny tucked into his starter, at the next table he spotted a recent Minister for Equalities who had notoriously voted against equal marriage, chatting to a famous actor who, despite being white, Eton-educated, straight, able-bodied and cis-gender, was here to present an award. *No doubt under the catch-all title of 'ally'.*

But Danny told himself not to be cynical. He was pleased the diversity movement was gaining traction, whatever people's motivations. And he was here to enjoy the evening. He knew he was looking smooth in his black tie, the wine tasted like a spa in his mouth, and the food was lip-smackingly good.

'Mmm, that was gorgeous,' he said to the others as he finished his starter.

'Speaking of gorgeous,' said Nathan, 'check out those guys selling raffle tickets.'

He pointed towards a pair of men who were working their way around the room, charming guests into parting with their money to benefit a leading diversity charity. Nathan and Owen beckoned them over and flirted wildly to try and ascertain if the men were gay. As Danny opened another bottle of wine, he realised that he recognised one of them.

Fuck!

It was Drew, Guy's first boyfriend.

What's he doing here?

'Danny!' Drew squealed, throwing his arms around him. 'It's *so* good to see you!'

'You too, babe,' Danny managed. 'But what are you doing? Have you stopped acting?'

Drew explained that he was still an actor but, after his initial run of success, things had quietened down – so he did jobs like this to supplement his income. 'Actually, I'm thinking of changing agents,' he said. 'I don't suppose you're looking for any new clients, are you?'

Danny remembered how miserable he'd felt on the night he'd watched Drew move in and kiss Guy – and how that same feeling had gnawed away at his insides every time Guy had talked about how much he loved him. He imagined telling Drew his books were full, or – even harsher – that he was sorry but he just didn't rate him as an actor. *But no, I'm better than that.*

Besides, I always thought Drew was a good actor.

'I can't promise anything but I might be able to help,' he said.

A grin swept over Drew's face. 'Really? Oh, Danny, that'd be amazing!'

'But now's not the time,' he said. 'Here's my card. Drop me an email and come in for a chat.'

'Thank you *so* much!'

Danny felt embarrassed by Drew's gratitude – and his whiff of desperation. 'That's alright, just make sure you put my raffle ticket to the top of the pile,' he joked.

Drew laughed and moved on to the next table. As soon as he was out of earshot, Danny's friends pounced.

'My God, he's so hot!'

'How do you know him?'

'Is he gay or what?'

Danny chuckled at their enthusiasm and outlined the basics. But the incident had left him feeling weirdly unsettled. It was a feeling he often experienced at events like this.

Danny had been a failure in life for so long that he'd started to see this as part of his identity, part of who he was. Although he'd been very happy to break free from it, at the same time he felt strangely unmoored, as if failure had been the anchor that for so long had attached him to the world. He wasn't sure he recognised the new, black-tie-wearing, successful Danny – and he couldn't help seeing this version of himself as an interloper, someone who'd conned his way into the industry and would soon be discovered. It wasn't a pleasant feeling and he wondered what he could do to overcome it.

He turned to Owen. 'Hey, shall we have some of that coke?'

2022

Danny looks around and wonders where he is. He's so off his head he can't remember the name of the club but it's a dungeon-like space with low, red lighting and iron bars over blacked-out windows. Hanging from the walls and ceilings is a selection of chains, handcuffs, harnesses and slings. Loud techno music is playing, there isn't a woman in sight, and the atmosphere is edgy and hypersexual. In the far corner stands the entrance to a darkroom that's masked by thick, black curtains, through which several men are passing. Everyone around him is shirtless, so Danny removes his own T-shirt and tucks it into his back pocket. He's gone past the point of worrying about his body.

'What do you think, chuck?' Trent shouts in his ear. 'Do you like it?'

'It's insane,' is all Danny can say. A man brushes past him who's completely naked but nobody bats an eyelid.

'And it's still early,' Trent says. 'Give it an hour or so and it'll really get going.'

'Honestly, it'll be like a Roman orgy,' Robbie promises, his eyes wide.

They introduce him to a friend of theirs, a pink, hairy man whose face is hidden behind a gas mask. Danny doesn't catch his name and can't make out a word he's saying – if indeed he's saying anything.

What am I even doing here?

He's suddenly gripped by an urgent need to prove to the world that he's having a great time. He needs to show the world that his life is wild and crazy.

He squeezes in next to Trent, Robbie and the man with the gas mask and holds up his phone to take a group selfie, raising his drink and manipulating his mouth into what he hopes is a mischievous smile. He starts to construct a post on Instagram but can't think of a caption and can't be bothered choosing a filter. In the end, he just posts the picture as it is.

'Now then, ladies, where were we?'

2018

'I don't know what to do about Danny. I'm just not sure how happy he is.'

It was half past eleven on a Saturday night and Guy was sitting up in bed talking to Henry. His calendar had sent him a reminder to book a table for his and Danny's traditional New Year dinner but he found himself pausing to ask if, for the first time in more than a decade, he wanted to let the tradition slide. However he viewed his friendship with Danny, it was undeniable that they had a lot less in common these days. Just acknowledging this made Guy feel terribly sad. *Could we ever go back to the way we were or have we grown apart for good?*

Henry turned to face him. 'What makes you say that?' he asked.

Guy let out a long sigh and smoothed down the Egyptian cotton sheets. 'It's just that every time I speak to him, he's either wankered or massively hungover – or he's just slept with another man he claims has got a massive dick.'

Guy wondered where all these men came from. He hadn't had half as many sexual partners as Danny, but he had a pretty good idea of the average size of penis. Yet, according to Danny, every single man he slept with was extraordinarily well endowed. It made Guy think he must be making it up, or at least exaggerating.

He had hoped Danny's behaviour would calm down once he'd abandoned acting, a decision Guy had understood and supported, even if he did find it sad. But Danny's career as an agent was going way better than either of them could have predicted and so far this had failed to make any impact. If anything, he was getting wilder and wilder. *And it's frustrating but I just don't understand him anymore. I don't understand who he is.*

Henry gave his shoulder a rub. 'Well, I don't think you should worry about it. If Danny wants to carry on getting wasted and hooking up on Grindr, it's not your responsibility.'

Guy pounded his goose-feather pillows. 'No, but he's not exactly had it easy – and he's much more sensitive than he lets on. I do feel some responsibility towards him. He's my oldest gay friend; we've been through so much together.'

Guy paused as he remembered how they used to joke about being a partnership.

Like gin and tonic.

Dolce and Gabbana.

Benson and Hedges.

He imagined saying these lines to Danny now, but the idea just seemed ludicrous.

'I know, but what about your responsibility to me?' Henry went on. 'Next year we're hopefully going to have a baby. We can't have Danny hanging around wasted or off his face on drugs, droning on about hook-ups and big dicks. You know, I do feel sorry for him but he needs to sort himself out.'

Guy didn't like the idea of Henry feeling sorry for Danny and he wasn't sure things were as simple as he made out. Once or twice, Danny had told him he didn't think Henry liked him and sometimes Guy suspected this might be true – or at least on a few occasions he'd sensed Henry acting superior to Danny. But there was no way he wanted to bring this up with Henry or do anything that ran the slightest risk of upsetting him.

He took hold of Henry's hand and wove his fingers through his. 'Maybe you're right. Maybe I should stop worrying about him.'

Henry gave his hand a squeeze. 'You've got to take a step back, Guy. You can do that subtly, without having any kind of argument or confrontation. But you've got to do it for your own sake. For *our* sake.'

Guy felt a lump of sadness in his throat. 'OK, and what do I do about the dinner we have every January? My New Year treat?'

Henry frowned. 'I think you should forget about that now. But it's alright, you and I can go out for a meal instead.'

He suggested they go to the restaurant in which Guy had proposed, a venue they often revisited when they had something to celebrate or when either of them needed cheering up.

'Cool,' said Guy, 'I'd like that.' And he kissed Henry on the lips.

As he lay back on his pillows, Guy decided that if he was taking a step back, he would do it subtly, without saying anything to Danny. They were speaking less and less often anyway. With any luck, Danny wouldn't even notice. *Besides, he probably thinks I'm boring now. I can see the way he flicks through his phone when we're together or glazes over when I talk about the baby. He's probably hoping I'll forget all about our New Year meal and then he can get out of it.*

But, however much he told himself this, deep down Guy knew it wasn't true.

2022

Danny staggers out of the club and onto the street. He's standing on the edge of a road that's flanked by tall, red-brick buildings. But he doesn't have the slightest idea where he is. *I could be anywhere in Manchester.*

He pulls out his phone and opens up Google Maps but the streets start spinning before his eyes. He tries to search for his hotel but can't remember its name. He looks to his left and right and spots a junction a few blocks away. He begins walking towards it.

He lights a cigarette, telling himself this will have a settling effect. But it makes him feel so nauseous he has to stop and lean against a wall.

My God, what was that stuff Trent gave me? What have I taken?

Suddenly the junction seems like it's miles away and there's no way he can reach it on foot. He tries to order an Uber but it's impossible without the name of the hotel.

On the other side of the road he sees a shop with the light on. It strikes him that if he buys a can of sugary drink, it'll make him feel better. He tosses away his cigarette, fills his lungs with air, and concentrates all his effort on walking across the road. He lurches into the shop and feels his way along the wall until he comes to a fridge. He yanks out a can of Coke and takes it over to the till.

'Are you alright, mate?' asks the man behind it.

Danny tries to look at his face but can't focus. 'Yeah, I'll just take this, please.' He feels around in his pocket and thrusts out a handful of coins.

Once he's tottered outside, he pours the entire can down his throat.

There, I'll be alright soon.

A few doors away, he spots the entrance to a club and, next to it, a small area cordoned off by a velvet rope, behind which stand a huddle of men, smoking. Almost involuntarily, he's drawn towards it.

As he nears the group, one of the men looks familiar. He's a white man of about average height with blond hair and ginger sideburns. *Now he's someone I definitely* have *slept with.*

Just as Danny reaches the velvet rope, it hits him. *It's that Swede I hooked up with in London.*

When Danny had seen the man on Friday night he dismissed him as a scraggy old stoner but now it strikes him that he's not actually that bad-looking. *In fact, from the right angle he could be quite attractive.*

Already he can feel the sugar from the Coke flooding through him. He suddenly feels the urge to touch and hold someone, to experience the warmth of another body next to his, to feel he isn't alone. *And beggars can't be choosers.*

He tries to remember the man's name but can't. *Oh, it'll be fine if I stick to 'babe'.*

He approaches him and says hello. 'Fancy seeing you here,' he adds, trying his best to sound flirtatious.

The man stares at him, blankly. 'I'm sorry, have we met?'

God, how humiliating.

When Danny explains how they know each other, recognition flashes across the man's face.

'Oh yeah, of course,' he says, in a heavy Swedish accent. 'Sorry, it's been a heavy night.'

'Yeah,' says Danny, 'tell me about it.'

He asks if the club's any good and if the man would like to go back inside for a drink.

'Actually, I was about to head back to my hotel,' he says, flicking the butt of his roll-up into the road. 'But you're welcome to join me if you like?'

Danny opens his mouth to say yes but stops himself.

Do you really want to do this? You're tired and you want to go to bed!

He wonders how many times he's tried to talk himself out of this kind of thing but has gone ahead anyway, had sex out of some kind of compulsion, knowing perfectly well it won't give him what he wants. Suddenly, his head is crowding with memories, from the time he lost his virginity to Creepy Phil to all the indistinguishable hook-ups he's had online – pretty much all the sex he's ever had.

Except the sex I had with Guy.

It's the first time he's thought about Guy for hours.

Yeah, but Guy doesn't want you.

'What do you think?' asks the Swede, with a wolfish grin.

'I'd love to,' says Danny. 'Just give me a minute, I need to text my friend.'

He pulls out his phone and opens up his WhatsApp.

'Bumped into a gorgeous bloke I know from London,' he messages Guy. 'He's got a massive dick. Am going back to his hotel.'

He hits Send and within seconds the header tells him Guy's online. The two ticks colour blue to indicate he's read the message.

Despite himself, Danny feels a flicker of hope. *Go on, Guy, tell me not to.*

On the bottom line of the chat, the emoji for thumbs up appears.

Danny's heart drops like a stone.

He sees from the header that Guy's typing again. When his message appears, it's short: 'Take care.'

Those two little words make Danny want to burst into tears. They make him realise that taking care of himself is something he hardly ever does. *And if I go off with this Swede, I won't be doing it tonight.*

He slips his phone back into his pocket. 'Come on,' he says, 'let's go.'

MONDAY

2022

Danny grips the sides of the toilet as the contents of his stomach burn their way up his throat and come shooting out into the bowl. His heaving action is so violent that for a moment he worries he might have dislocated his shoulder. Just as he's ascertained that it's firmly in place, he hurls again and his vomit hits the water with such force that it sends some of it splashing back onto his face.

My God, why do I put myself through this?

He grabs a few sheets of toilet roll and wipes himself clean. He's not sure he's ever had such a bad hangover. He's exhausted. He feels old. He feels like a wreck.

He pictures Guy asleep in the room next door and hopes he can't hear him. He has no memory of getting back to the hotel last night and hopes he didn't make too much noise when he crashed into bed. *Mind you, if I did wake him up he probably just rolled over in disgust.*

Danny grips the toilet and hurls again.

When his heaving has finally subsided, he pushes himself back from the toilet and rests on his knees. He's still wearing last night's clothes and didn't even take off his watch. He looks at the time and sees it's just gone 11 o'clock.

He can't even remember how he got back to the hotel. The last thing he recalls is being in the Swedish man's hotel room and raiding his mini-bar. He assumes that after this they somehow managed to have sex but he can't even be sure of that. *Well, at least I'm on PrEP so don't have to worry about whether or not we used a condom.*

He remembers to take his daily tablet and hobbles onto his feet to dig it out of his washbag. As he swills it down with a couple of paracetamol and a glug of water, he catches sight of his reflection in the mirror. He's ashen-faced, with bloodshot eyes and dark shadows underneath them. He plugs his shame with another glug of water.

Oh God, it's coming back to me now . . .

I did have sex with that guy – and in the middle of it, I asked him something.

Danny shudders at the memory.

'Tell me you love me.' As the words replay in his head, he hears the desperate, pleading tone in his voice.

From what he can remember, the man told him what he wanted to hear but then laughed as if he were embarrassed, embarrassed by Danny's desperation. He cradles his head in his hands.

He hopes that when he got back to the hotel he didn't say anything to Guy. *Shit, what if I texted him while I was out?*

He grabs his phone and scrolls through it until he comes to their WhatsApp chat. He reads it and lets out a sigh of relief. *Although why did I have to lie about that Swedish bloke having a massive dick?*

While he's in his phone, he logs onto social media to check he didn't make a fool of himself online. He sees a pic he posted on Instagram that shows him in a sex club surrounded by Trent, Robbie and some man who's wearing a gas mask. He's shocked by his appearance: he's sweaty-faced and clearly wasted, shirtless and not even bothering to hold in his gut, and plastered across his face is a grin he has a vague memory of thinking should look mischievous but actually makes him look like he's being electrocuted. Thankfully, the post has only received a handful of likes. He deletes it before anyone else can see it.

God, I hope Guy didn't see it.

His stomach dips. When he goes back into the bedroom, it'll be the first time he's faced Guy since Saturday evening, since Guy told him he didn't share his feelings.

The thought of this makes his stomach heave once more. He rushes to the toilet and makes it just in time.

Guy listens to the sound of Danny throwing up in the bathroom and hopes he's alright. He considers knocking on the door and asking if there's anything he can do but expects he wants to be left alone. *Besides, the only contact we've had since Saturday night has been a handful of texts. He's probably still mad at me.*

As he hears the toilet flush, Guy turns away from the bathroom. Draped over one of the armchairs are the clothes he wore yesterday. When Danny replied to the text he sent in the afternoon, making it clear he didn't want to see him, Guy decided to go for a walk around the city on his own. He revisited many of the places he remembered from his student days and even ventured as far out as the university and Dalton-Ellis Hall, where he lived in his first year. He remembered the young man he'd been when he arrived in Manchester, how liberated he'd felt to escape his parents, and how excited – but terrified – he'd been to explore a part of him that had been suppressed for so long. Thinking of that young man, of how lacking in confidence and self-worth he'd been, he had to make a real effort to stop the tears from springing to his eyes. But it was when he visited Albert Square that he felt the strongest pull on his emotions; he sat on what he and Danny used to call their steps and couldn't contain the tears any longer. He let them flow as he remembered all the lunches they'd shared in that spot and how strong the bond between them used to be. It made him realise what a mess he'd made of their relationship. It made him realise how badly he'd behaved towards Danny.

Then Josh interrupted, texting to see if he wanted to meet up for a meal. Guy didn't feel the slightest inclination to see him but they'd made a vague arrangement and he didn't want to treat someone else badly. When they did meet up, though, he didn't feel any of the excitement of the previous evening. He just felt flat. So, as soon as they'd finished eating, he headed off, making an excuse about needing to catch up on his sleep. But the truth was, he was starting to feel concerned about Danny and wanted to be in the hotel when he got back.

Unfortunately, he was too worried about him to be able to fall asleep – and seeing the picture he posted on Instagram only exacerbated this. Just before midnight, Danny sent Guy a text telling him he was going to have sex with someone – and the fact this was someone he already knew meant Guy could finally relax enough to drift off. But he woke up again when Danny clattered into the room at 4 a.m. As he didn't even switch the light on, it was easy for Guy to pretend to be asleep. *But I can't pretend any longer.*

From the bathroom comes the sound of Danny brushing his teeth, spraying himself with deodorant and unlocking the door. As he pads across the room and plonks himself down on the bed, Guy wonders what on earth he should say. Everything he can think of sounds either banal or insensitive. *Oh, I'm so useless.*

As Danny slides under the sheets next to him, Guy's heart gives a little wobble. He can imagine how bad he must be feeling – and not just physically. Guy wishes there were some way in which he could make him feel better. He wishes he could hug him but after what's happened this weekend, he doesn't think that would be appropriate. *Mind you, our feelings are all out in the open now. Maybe it* would *be OK to give him a hug.*

2020

When Danny woke up, he was hugging someone. His face was pressed against the man's back, with his stubble digging into his smooth skin. The man was lying on Danny's arm and it had gone numb.

Shit, I need to get out of this . . .

Dread lodged in his throat. *But what even* is *this?*

He looked around at the cheap wooden wardrobe and chest of drawers, the cork noticeboard onto which were pinned various timetables, and the desk covered with academic textbooks, surrounded by dirty pint glasses and lager cans. He felt around with his foot and confirmed his suspicion: he was lying in a single bed.

Fuck, I'm in student halls.

In a flash, the details of last night came back to him. He and his workmates had gone out for dinner to celebrate Owen's birthday, but Danny had got so drunk that afterwards he hadn't wanted to go home. He'd logged onto Grindr, where he'd met a man with a cut-throat jawline and sparkling brown eyes. *But what was his profile name?*

Oh yeah, @rosstheboss.

He remembered registering that Ross was much younger than him and thinking it would make a cracking story. But now he wasn't so sure. *What if everyone thinks I'm a dirty old man?*

He resisted the urge to groan out loud. He had a pounding headache, a mouth like an ashtray and a raging thirst. And for some reason his left eye was twitching.

In his arms, he felt Ross stirring.

'Will you get off me!' Ross growled, shaking himself free.

Danny sat up and rubbed his arm back to life. 'Sorry, I haven't slept in a single bed for ages. I'd forgotten how small they are.'

Ross turned towards him. 'Yeah, well, I need to get up. Sorry, man, you'll have to shoot off.'

Danny stood up and scanned the room for his clothes, thankful that he was wearing his underpants – and a decent pair.

As he picked up his jeans, he noticed Ross's gaze creeping down to his gut. He watched as horror swept across his face.

Ross let out a wail. 'Man, I must have been wasted!'

Danny felt the stab of humiliation. He held in his stomach as he pulled on his clothes. 'You and me both,' he chirped, 'I went to a fortieth and it got seriously messy.'

'A fortieth?' Ross mouthed, his forehead rutted. 'Wait a minute, how *old* are you?'

Danny wiggled his hips and struck a cute pose. 'Thirty-six and no bra.'

Ross stared at Danny as if a bird had just shat on his face. 'Thirty-six? *Fuck,* I am dead!'

He covered his face, as if unable to contemplate the scene before him. 'My mum's only forty-two!' he added.

'Oh, really?' Danny sing-songed. 'That's the same age as Reese Witherspoon; I read it the other day.'

'Who the fuck is Reese Witherspoon?'

Danny's left eye gave another twitch. *God, this is awkward!*

He gave up looking for his socks and put his shoes on without them. 'If you don't mind, babe . . . I'll just . . . pop into the bathroom . . .'

Once he'd locked the door behind him, Danny let out a long breath. He rubbed his eyes and examined his face in the mirror. *Alright, I'm not the freshest today but I don't look* that *bad.*

Over his shoulder he caught sight of a shower that looked like it hadn't been cleaned in months and a pile of damp towels that had been dumped on the floor. He glugged several mouthfuls of water, then splashed some onto his face.

He needed to empty his bladder so sat on the toilet to check his phone. When he read back over his messages on Grindr, he discovered that Ross had actually pursued him, and been very persistent – so he didn't have to feel bad about that. He also noticed that Ross was upfront in his profile about being a student. *Oh God, was part of me into that? Was this whole thing some desperate attempt to recapture my youth?*

Into his head flashed an image of Guy the first time he'd visited him in his student room. *Oh, Guy, is this all about you?*

Is it ever going to stop being about you?

He stood up and flushed the chain.

He rubbed some toothpaste along his gums, then swilled it around his mouth with water.

When he re-entered the bedroom, Ross was sitting on the bed in his briefs, watching the news on his iPad. A correspondent was reporting from the north of Italy about that virus everyone was talking about, the one the World Health Organisation had recently declared a global pandemic.

Danny decided to follow his usual policy of ignoring it. 'So what are you up to today?' he asked, jollily.

Ross didn't even look up. 'Oh, this and that.'

Danny picked up his coat and saw it was inside out, as if it had been tugged off in a hurry. As he pulled the arms through, he caught sight of a pair of muddy football boots, a hockey stick and a basketball standing in the corner. Once again, he was back in Guy's student room.

'You know, I went to Manchester uni,' he commented. Then his heart sank. 'But that's a long time ago now.'

Ross gave a grimace. 'Alright, don't rub it in.'

'Well . . .' Danny shifted his weight from one foot to the other. 'I'd better get going.'

Without taking his eyes off the screen, Ross made a gesture somewhere in between a salute and a wave. As he did, his bicep flexed.

Danny found himself adding, 'Maybe I'll see you again sometime?'

Ross looked at him as if he'd just suggested the two of them go for a swim in a cesspit. 'Nah, I don't think so.'

Oh God, why did I have to say that?

An expression of pity scudded across Ross's face. 'To be honest, the way things are looking right now, I don't think anyone's going to be seeing anyone. I think we really are going into a national lockdown. Apparently, Boris is making an announcement tomorrow.'

Danny yanked on his coat. 'Seriously? For how long?'

Ross frowned. 'They reckon it'll be a long time, maybe even as long as twelve weeks. I think my uni is sending all the students home.'

All of a sudden, the threat Danny had avoided confronting seemed real. He'd told himself not to worry about Covid, reassuring himself it would be like SARS, Ebola or swine flu: it wouldn't affect him. But he couldn't force himself to think that any longer. And if it was true that they were being thrust into a lockdown, he had no idea what he was going to do. *How will I cope being on my own for twelve weeks?*

It didn't bear thinking about.

He zipped up his coat.

'Alright, well, bye,' he muttered. He was about to offer Ross a hug but thought better of it.

2022

As Guy puts his arms around Danny's back and begins hugging him, Danny's body goes as stiff as a plank. *I don't believe it, does he really think he can hug me after everything that's happened?*

Guy tries to snuggle into him again but Danny refuses to yield. *What the* hell *is he thinking?*

Then it strikes Danny that he isn't thinking – or at least he isn't thinking about him. *No, he's thinking about himself, as usual. Just like he was thinking about himself when he had sex with Lynsey. Just like he was thinking about himself when he got off with that twink after I told him I loved him.*

As if a switch has been flicked, Danny suddenly understands that Guy's always used him for affirmation, that the only reason he ever put any effort into the friendship is so Danny would make him feel good about himself. This explains why he used to call him princess and joke about them being a partnership but then would sideline him to make way for boyfriend after boyfriend. All the time Danny was in love with him, Guy just saw him as some doggedly dependable friend he could toy with, giving him just enough encouragement to keep him hanging on, hanging on so he'd be there for him.

Well, I won't stand for it anymore.

He turns around to face Guy, his heart pounding. 'Excuse me, what do you think you're doing?'

Guy shrinks back. 'Oh, sorry, I just thought you could do with a cuddle.'

'Yeah, well, maybe I could, but not from you. Do you not remember the conversation we had on Saturday?'

Guy's mouth sags into a frown. 'Yeah, sorry.'

Suddenly, it occurs to Danny that he may not have made his feelings clear enough. He raises himself up onto an elbow. His heart's pounding so violently it feels like it's going to jump out of his throat.

'Guy, I need to tell you something,' he states. 'I haven't just developed feelings for you. I've been in love with you for twenty years.'

There's a beat.

Guy nods, slowly and almost imperceptibly. 'I know.'

Danny lets out a gasp. 'You *know*?'

'Well, I haven't *always* known,' Guy clarifies. 'I suspected, I suppose. I only knew for sure after Thailand.'

'You what?'

A frown crosses Guy's forehead. 'After you left me that voice-mail.'

For a moment, Danny's so shocked he can't speak. He shakes his head in disbelief. 'But I thought you said you didn't get that voicemail? I thought you said your phone had been stolen?'

'Yeah, sorry, I only said that because I didn't know what to do about it. I didn't feel the same way as you and I didn't want to lose you as a friend.'

'Oh my God,' Danny splutters, 'this gets worse. So you lied to me so you could enjoy having me around as a friend, even though you knew how hard that was going to make things for me!'

Guy looks around, as if searching for the right words to say. 'It wasn't like that, Danny. It really wasn't like that.'

'Well, it sounds like it was to me!'

'Anyway, I'm not the only one who lied. You lied to Josh about us being a couple.'

'Josh? Who's Josh?'

'The guy I got off with on Saturday night. Apparently he asked you if we were together and you said yes.'

Danny can feel the heat flooding his cheeks. He snatches a breath. 'Babe, I may have told a little white lie in the heat of the moment, but that's nothing compared to the long-term, premeditated *whopper* you've been telling for most of the time we've known each other.'

Now it's Guy's turn to look flushed. 'Danny, I only lied about that voicemail once; I didn't *go on* lying about it. It never came up again so I just tried not to think about it.'

'What, and that's supposed to make me feel better, is it? That you just "tried not to think about" my feelings? That you just blocked them out of your head so they wouldn't interfere with getting what you wanted?'

'Danny . . .' Guy begins. But he stops.

'Danny what? You used me for affirmation, Guy. You always have. Go on, deny it.'

But Guy doesn't reply. His face has clouded with an emotion Danny can't read. And he looks away, as if he's remembering something.

2021

'I don't love you anymore.'

This was the third time Guy had made Henry repeat the line, as he was struggling to understand it.

'You've become like a brother to me,' Henry explained. 'I just don't feel that romantic, sexual connection to you anymore.'

It was the worst thing Guy could hear, worse even than if Henry was telling him he was leaving him for someone else. *He just doesn't love me. He's got to know me deep down, inside out and back to front – and he doesn't love me.*

Then the voice in his head took on a taunting tone. *Of course he doesn't love you! It's amazing you managed to fool him for so long!*

It wasn't as if Henry's announcement was coming out of the blue. Signs that his love for Guy was fading had started to appear after their plan to have a baby had been hit by a series of obstacles. First of all, tests had revealed that Guy had a low sperm count, a discovery he'd found shameful. Then their first surrogate had met a new boyfriend and pulled out, meaning the months and months they'd devoted to finding and getting to know her had been wasted. When they'd eventually found a new one, three rounds of IVF had failed. After this, Henry had announced that he was finding the process stressful and wanted to take a break. But its failure had already infected their relationship.

Soon, the little sweets and chocolates Henry used to slot into Guy's workbag had stopped appearing. The text messages Henry sent him during the day nosedived in frequency and Guy's messages often went unanswered. And the morning coffee Henry made for the two of them in a pot they'd bought on their honeymoon was quietly discontinued. Although Henry claimed this was because he was cutting down on caffeine, for Guy it only served as another reminder that he'd failed to give him what he wanted.

When the coronavirus pandemic struck and the two of them had been thrust into lockdown, suddenly their flat felt like it had shrunk to a fraction of its size and Henry made Guy feel like he was constantly in his way. Most of the things they enjoyed doing together had been wrenched away from them and replaced by the monotony of working from home, online fitness sessions, meal planning and batch cooking, group video calls with parents whose Wi-Fi connection repeatedly dropped out, and hours and hours of washing, Hoovering and cleaning. On top of all this, everything Guy did seemed to irritate Henry, right down to the way he breathed as they watched TV sitting next to each other on the sofa – in the same positions, night after night after night.

Then Guy had caught Covid, although how that happened he was clueless as he only went out to the supermarket and always wore a mask. But Henry blamed him for bringing contagion into the house and insisted Guy stay in the spare room for two weeks, only leaving to go to the bathroom and when he did texting Henry so he could clear the area. He felt like a leper having to ring a bell and shout 'Unclean, unclean!' And worst of all, he actually became very ill. But Henry showed little sympathy. When Guy recovered, their relationship didn't. For the next six months it limped on.

When they finally emerged from the third national lockdown – and the vaccine rollout was making it clear this would be the last – Henry said they needed to talk and suggested they go for a walk along the river. The weather was striving for sunny but not succeeding: the sky was the colour of a white T-shirt that had been washed too many times and had started to go grey. As they set off from Hammersmith Bridge along the gravel path on the South Bank, there was something in Henry's tone of voice that instilled Guy with a sense of dread. He tried to smother it by commenting on the high tide and how good it was to see the rowers back out on the Thames. But the diversion didn't last long. Before they'd even got to Putney Bridge, Henry had made his announcement.

'I don't love you anymore.'

After hearing it for the third time, Guy felt shaky. He grabbed onto the back of the nearest bench. 'So where does that leave us?' he rasped.

'I think we should split up,' Henry said, calmly. 'And I don't see any point in hanging around; I think we should get a divorce.'

Guy felt as if someone cycling along the path had just veered off and crashed into him. 'Wow, that's pretty drastic.'

As he lowered himself onto the bench, he felt an old fear leak into his heart. *What will my mother and father say?*

He couldn't bear to picture their expressions of disappointment. *Mind you, at least this won't come as a shock to them. I'm sure they've been expecting it all along.*

'Are you sure?' he asked Henry, his voice cracking.

'Yeah, I think it's the right thing to do,' said Henry.

'But it doesn't make any sense,' Guy pleaded, repulsed by the pathetic tone of his own voice. 'How can your feelings for me just completely disappear?'

'I'm sorry,' Henry said, sitting next to him, 'but this hasn't happened all of a sudden – I've been thinking it for a while now. The pandemic and all the lockdowns just gave me more time to mull over it.'

'But you said being married was all you ever wanted,' Guy bleated. 'We used to joke about growing old together. Can't we give it another go? Can't we go back to trying for a baby?'

Henry shook his head, as unconcerned as if he were ending their subscription to the wine club or their weekly delivery of organic vegetables. 'That won't change anything, Guy.'

'OK then, tell me what will.' Guy was aware that he was sacrificing his dignity. 'Tell me what to do and I'll do it. I'll do anything, Henry.'

A wiry, white-haired man strode past wearing plastic gloves, a facemask and a protective visor, a Jack Russell trotting along before him.

Henry let out a sigh. 'I don't know what to say, Guy. I don't want you to do anything. I know how I feel and it's not going to change.'

The voices that had taunted Guy in the past struck up again with renewed force. *Can't you get it into your head that he doesn't want you? Can't you get it into your head that you're just not good enough?* It was as if they'd been there all along, lying in wait for another chance to terrorise him.

He began kicking a weed that was sprouting from between the flagstones. He opened his mouth to continue pleading, but he couldn't think of any more arguments to advance. Henry had extinguished all his hopes – and made it quite clear that the case was closed.

Guy nudged the weed loose and kicked it into the river.

'I know that right now this must hurt,' Henry said, softly.

Hurt? How could he possibly think a word as trite as that could describe the deep pit of despair into which he'd thrust him?

'But when the initial feelings fade,' he went on, 'I'd really like it if we could be friends.'

Friends? Suddenly this struck Guy as the ugliest word in the English language.

'Well, not just friends but special friends,' Henry parried. '*Best* friends.'

Then Guy remembered that he already had a best friend. *Or at least I did until Henry came along.*

Thinking of Danny made Guy realise just how much he missed him.

It was nearly three years since they'd lost touch. After Guy had made the decision to step back from the friendship, Danny hadn't done anything to fight for it, which had made Guy conclude he'd only done the right thing. But then the series of lockdowns had happened and being cut off from all his friends had made Guy consider which of them he really valued – and he'd been worried about Danny and how he'd be, adapting to a life without the social hustle and bustle he loved so much. Reasoning that the pandemic was prompting several people to build bridges, he'd initiated a text conversation and had been relieved when Danny had responded straight away. He'd assured Guy that he was doing fine and enjoying the chance to catch up on work and read a pile of scripts. Then the two of them had slipped into banter and exchanging funny memes about lockdown, as well as swapping recommendations for films and TV shows. Guy had wanted to suggest a video call but had backed out of the idea as Henry would have made it clear that he disapproved – and Henry's disapproval was the last thing he wanted when he could already sense him slipping away. But at least he and Danny had re-established contact.

Now, though, with Henry exiting the scene, Guy realised how much he wanted to rekindle his friendship with Danny.

'I'm sorry,' he said to Henry, 'but I've got a best friend. I'm not looking for another.'

2022

'OK, maybe I did enjoy it when you gave me affirmation,' Guy concedes. 'But you make it sound like it was something I did deliberately to hurt you. And the truth is I only did it because I needed you. I only did it because I was desperate.'

Danny shakes his head. *Why can't he just admit he was selfish? Why can't he admit he was using me?*

'Bollocks, Guy,' he erupts, jumping out of bed. 'You used me without the slightest consideration for my feelings. Just like you used Lynsey.'

Guys mouth falls open but no words come out.

'Yes, babe,' Danny crows, 'I know all about you shagging Lynsey. Why do you think the two of us fell out?'

'I don't know . . .' he splutters. 'But I really regret what happened that night. I didn't mean to hurt her either.'

Danny arches an eyebrow. 'Don't tell me, you were desperate again?'

Guy lowers his eyes and looks away. 'You could say that, yeah.'

'Oh, what a load of crap,' Danny hurls at him. 'What have

you got to be desperate about? You've always had it easy. You've always had everything you wanted.'

Guy gives a sharp sniff. 'Danny, how can you know me so well and think that? Besides, *you* were always the one everyone wanted. You were the popular one at uni. Sometimes I think I only got invited to things because you let me tag along. And now you've got this glamorous career and you're always hanging out with celebrities.'

On the bedside table, Danny's phone buzzes. He ignores it.

'Excuse me, but I've had to work really hard for what I've got,' he snaps, 'and there've been times when it's been a struggle – a massive struggle.'

Guy sits upright and pulls the sheets around him. 'Don't you think I know that? I was there for most of it, Danny. But that doesn't mean that everyone didn't love you. Everyone always did.'

Danny snorts. 'Really? Well, you certainly didn't. Most of the time you were too engrossed in your boyfriends.'

'That's not fair,' Guy hits back. 'You and I only grew apart when I was with Henry and I thought we'd got over that.'

'Yeah, well, maybe we haven't.' Danny's aware that he's almost shrieking. 'Maybe I don't want to go back to being your court jester, making sure every party or night out goes with a bang. Even if I'm not in the mood. Even if I'm feeling rotten and miserable.'

His phone buzzes again. He lifts it up and sees that it's his mum. He remembers he forgot to listen to the voicemail she left him last night. *Well, I can hardly speak to her now.*

'Danny, that's not the way I thought of you at all,' Guy protests. 'And as far as I'm aware you always *liked* the fact people saw you as some kind of party animal. Look at that picture you posted on Instagram last night.'

Shit, so he did see it. 'Yeah, well, just because I'm the life and soul of the party, that doesn't mean I don't also have feelings.'

'I'm not disputing that, Danny – I can't believe you'd even think I would.' Guy pauses and lets out a sigh. 'Anyway, I don't know . . . I just don't want this to end our friendship.'

'Friendship'? There it is again, that ugly, ugly word.

'Yeah and what about me?' Danny shoots back. 'Am I supposed to stay friends with you just to make you feel better? Even though it's hard for me?'

Guy inches towards him. 'No, but equally I can't stay celibate for the rest of my life just so as not to hurt you.'

Danny throws his hands in the air. 'Well, in that case, this is fucked, isn't it? What's the point in holding on to it anymore? Maybe we should have just let it die years ago.'

'But I don't want it to die, Danny. You can't just take a unilateral decision to destroy our friendship and give me no say in the matter.'

Danny's phone buzzes again, this time to notify him he's received a text. As the handset is facing up, he can read it on his home screen. 'Am in Manchester. Have come to see you. Waiting in hotel lobby. Mum x'

'Shit, my mum's here,' Danny says.

'What, in Manchester?'

'Yeah, apparently she's downstairs in the lobby. Look, I've no idea what's going on but I've got to go. I need to get a shower and change out of these clothes.'

Guy nods. 'OK. But can we talk about this later?'

2021

From his seat on a sofa in Soho House, Danny read the text message from Guy. 'Which floor are you on?'

'Second,' he replied. 'Red drawing room. Next to fireplace.'

He put his phone down and drew in a deep, fortifying breath.

Danny was about to see Guy for the first time in three years. And he was nervous. He was so nervous he could hardly sit still.

As he had no idea how the meeting would go, he'd decided to follow his rule for a first date and had only committed to a quick drink. He had thought about inviting Guy round to his flat as he hadn't seen it since Danny had finished decorating. But if Guy came round now, Danny knew he'd have to cook him a meal, which would be too much to take on when he was already so nervous. Besides, he didn't want Guy to find out that he'd managed to kill the bonsai tree he'd bought him as a house-warming gift. So he'd suggested they meet for a drink in his private members' club, Soho House. The venue had a relaxed, laid-back atmosphere and Danny knew it wouldn't be too packed. He was also harbouring a little hope that his choice of venue might impress Guy. *But I'm trying not to think like that.*

When Guy walked in, he'd hardly changed, although Danny noticed that tiny flecks of grey had started to appear in his sideburns. He found himself hoping Guy would give him the same greeting he used to.

'Hello, hello.'

Danny smiled and hugged him. The two of them commented on how good it was that all Covid restrictions had finally been lifted and they were able to meet up again in real life, conveniently glossing over the fact that they hadn't seen each other for eighteen months before the first lockdown. As they shared observations about how London was gradually clawing its way back to normality, all the time Danny couldn't help thinking that Guy was still gorgeous.

Danny's feelings for Guy had properly resurfaced during the first lockdown. This had been every bit as gruelling as he'd feared. Initially, he'd tried to focus on the positives: it had been good to catch up on work and spend some time improving his roof garden, and he'd enjoyed chatting to his mum, Arthur and various friends on video calls. But then, as it became clear that the pandemic was going to last a lot longer than twelve weeks – and that theatres, cinemas and TV and film production would be shut down for longer too – the industry had been thrust into crisis and most of the actors Danny represented had started to panic about their careers. In between giving them counselling and solving their problems, he'd started to drink more. Then loneliness had set in and he'd found himself trawling through his phone and messaging former hook-ups, in the hope that drunken sexual attraction might morph into something more meaningful. When none of the men had even bothered to reply, he'd ended up reflecting on all the people who'd passed through his life and which of the relationships he valued most – and that's when he realised just how much he missed Guy.

When 'bubbling' had been introduced for single-person households during the second lockdown, Danny had joined up with Owen and Nathan, who'd recently moved into a flat share in West Ham. As he could walk there in the morning, the three of them set up a little open-plan office in the living room. Their camaraderie went some way to easing Danny's loneliness – and stopped him from thinking about Guy, during the daytime at least.

Then, out of the blue, Guy had texted him. He'd begun with a casual enquiry about how Danny was doing and how the pandemic had treated him, then had told him he'd suffered what sounded like a nasty bout of Covid. As he sounded like he needed cheering up, Danny had refrained from telling him how miserable he'd been and had kept their text exchanges light-hearted. He'd avoided the subject of video calls as he couldn't face Guy seeing how much weight he'd put on from comfort eating, so much weight that, when he pushed his trolley over the textured pavement outside the supermarket, he could feel his belly and sides jiggling – and, if he had to iron a shirt before a zoom meeting, he could feel his arms flapping. But their text exchanges had increased in regularity and, a few weeks ago, Guy had suggested they meet up. When Danny had hesitated, he'd added – as if the information was only of minor interest – that Henry had left him. Danny had rushed onto his roof garden and roared with joy.

Once he'd calmed down, he'd gently questioned Guy about the split, but it soon became clear that Guy didn't want to talk about it. Danny couldn't think of any other way of finding out what had happened. He couldn't ask any of their mutual friends, as he'd always played down their estrangement. He'd scoured social media, but Guy would never post about relationships or advertise his feelings. When he'd tried to access Henry's profiles, he'd discovered that not only had he unfriended him but he'd also blocked him across all platforms. The only way Danny could find out what had happened was by seeing Guy – so he'd just have to get over his self-consciousness about his weight.

Now that Guy was sitting next to him, Danny was desperate to find out all the details. But he didn't want to dive straight in. He wanted to at least show a modicum of sensitivity.

He called over the waiter and ordered a lager for Guy and a large glass of red wine for himself.

'Is this your first time here?' Danny asked.

'Yeah,' Guy replied. He looked around at the impeccably stylish interior design, the plush suede sofa and antique fireplace. 'It's really cool.'

'I joined when I got promoted about four years ago,' Danny explained. 'I come here quite a bit – or at least I did before Covid. But it's good to see it coming back to life again.'

He gave another wriggle in his seat. He was itching to ask Guy about Henry but judged it was still too soon.

'By the way,' he said as the drinks arrived, 'you know I'm looking after Drew now?'

'No, I didn't know that.'

'Yeah, before lockdown I actually got him a few jobs. I'm hoping things will pick up again now.'

'That's great news,' said Guy. 'Give him my best.'

Danny nodded and took a sip of his wine. He couldn't wait any longer. 'Anyway, what's this about you and Henry? You said you'd split up.'

That was casual enough, wasn't it?

Guy looked down and began picking at the label on his bottle of beer. 'Yeah, it happened a couple of months ago now. He's moved back into his old flat. He was renting it out so gave his tenants notice and I stayed in my place. At least that side of things has been straightforward.'

Danny couldn't help thinking that it was so like Guy to concentrate on the practicalities rather than the emotional fallout.

'Yeah but what went wrong, babe?' he asked. 'Why did you break up?'

Guy took a long draught of his lager. He explained that their attempt to have a baby had been hit by a series of setbacks, then failed. 'And shortly after that, the rot set in and we grew apart. Well, I suppose it would be more accurate to say Henry grew apart from me. He just fell out of love with me, basically.'

He stopped and cleared his throat.

'Anyway, I never thought I'd say this but I'm looking forward to the divorce coming through now. It'll be good to put it all behind me.'

Danny could tell how difficult this was for him to talk about so didn't push him for more details. 'Well, I'm sorry you've had such a shit time,' he said. 'I'm sorry you've had to go through that.' He was careful not to say he was sorry they'd split up.

'Thanks, Danny. But I think it's me who should be saying sorry to you.'

Danny arched an eyebrow. 'What do you mean?'

Guy went back to picking at the label on his beer. 'Well, Henry wasn't always respectful to you. He could be quite condescending. You tried to bring it up with me a few times but I shut you down. I'm sorry about that. I'm sorry I didn't stand up for you.'

Danny was shocked. He hadn't for one second expected this.

Although he was glad Guy was acknowledging Henry's animosity, he couldn't help feeling vaguely embarrassed by his apology. 'Oh, that's fine,' he insisted, 'don't worry about it, babe.'

He ordered them both another drink.

'Anyway,' Guy went on, 'it turns out I was wrong about Henry in all kinds of ways.'

Danny tried not to let his excitement show. 'Oh yeah? What do you mean?'

Guy said he'd discovered that, when Henry used to go away with work before the pandemic, he'd visit gay saunas and sex clubs – and, since they'd split up, he'd been attending chemsex parties. 'Apparently he's always off his face on G or crystal meth, whatever they are.'

Danny decided not to tell him. In any case, he was so shocked he wasn't sure he could get the words out. Into his mind flashed a memory of that awful barbecue on Guy's roof terrace when Henry had shamed him for smoking and using Grindr and said he thought sex clubs and saunas should be banned.

'Oh and get this,' Guy went on, 'he's now in an open relationship with a male escort.'

Danny almost choked on his wine and had to spit it back into the glass. 'The absolute fucking slut!' he burst out.

He slapped his hand over his mouth.

'Sorry, I didn't mean that,' he added quickly. 'Obviously, I'd never slut-shame another gay man. Obviously that kind of thing's fine, if that's what someone wants.'

'Well, apparently it's what Henry wants,' interjected Guy, his mouth stiff with emotion. 'Apparently it always was.'

Danny blew out a breath. 'I just can't stand the hypocrisy of people like that. He was always so judgmental about the stuff I did.'

Guy tilted his head and frowned. 'He was, yeah. Little did we know . . .'

Danny enjoyed the reappearance of that little 'we' and had to make a real effort to stop a smile from creeping up his face. If it weren't so obvious Guy was devastated, he'd be jumping up and down with glee.

'Anyway, I feel stupid now for being taken in by it,' Guy muttered.

Danny's heart lurched. 'Don't say that, babe. You did nothing wrong.'

'No, but can you imagine what everyone's thinking?' protested Guy. 'Henry's constantly splashing pictures of his antics all over Facebook. I feel like a laughing stock.'

Danny felt a rush of anger towards Henry. He hated him for treating Guy so badly.

At the same time, it occurred to him that he'd never liked Henry so much. *Because at least Guy needs me again.*

'Babe, I promise no-one's laughing at you,' he insisted.

Guy waved away his objection. 'The worst thing was, my brother saw one of his posts and blabbed about it to my mother and father.'

Danny's eyes bulged. 'Shit. What did they say?'

'Oh, it was awful, absolutely awful.' Guy kneaded his knuckles. 'But funnily enough, it was kind of a turning point. Until then they'd been asking what *I'd* done wrong, implying that I'd done something to drive Henry away. But after that they turned against him. I guess they were angry he'd lied to them too.'

Yeah and – more to the point – that they fell for it. But Danny told himself not to rejoice in his vindication. He'd made peace long ago with the fact that Guy's parents would never like – or accept – him.

Anyway, this isn't about you. You need to concentrate on looking after Guy.

'Let's try to look on the bright side,' he offered, 'at least you found out now rather than further down the line. What if he'd given you some STI like that monkeypox everyone's talking about? You know, you could say you've had a lucky escape.'

Guy nodded but didn't comment. He finished his bottle of lager.

Right, Danny, you need to move things on.

'OK, shall we order some food?' he asked, picking up a menu.

'Oh, I thought you had to go to some dinner.'

Danny remembered his prearranged escape plan. 'Yeah, don't worry about that,' he sing-songed, 'I can easily get out of it.'

'Oh, right. In that case, cool. I'd love to.' Guy smiled, flashing Danny a glimpse of that adorable little gap between his teeth.

As Danny smiled back at him, he told himself there was no longer any reason to suppress his feelings; he could let them come flooding back.

Except . . . What if he's already started seeing someone? You've been here before, remember?

He pretended to peruse the menu and asked as casually as possible, 'You can tell me about all those men who've been after you. I bet there's a stampede now you're back on the market.'

Guy's forehead puckered. 'Oh God, I'm not interested. The last thing I want at the moment is to meet someone new.'

'Yeah, I suppose it's early days . . .' Danny suggested, arching an eyebrow.

Guy shook his head. 'No, it's not that. Or it's not *just* that.'

Danny looked up. 'Oh yeah?'

'Covid gave us all time to think, Danny.' Guy paused. 'And I thought about you – lots.'

Danny felt the excitement rush through him. 'Really?'

'Yeah. And what I want now – more than anything else – is for it to just go back to being me and you.'

Hope bloomed in Danny's chest. 'Well, let me send a quick text and you can have me all evening.'

'Perfect!'

But, as Danny picked up his phone, a voice in his head warned him to watch out – the last thing he wanted was for the two of them to slip back into the way things used to be, just as they had after the mix-up with the voicemail he left from Thailand.

He'd just have to find some way to move their relationship on. But the last thing Guy needed at the moment was to be put under any pressure. *Whatever I do, it has to be light and fun.*

He wasn't sure what the answer was, but for some reason he was sure of one thing: he'd find it right back where they started – in Manchester.

2022

Danny and his mum step out of the hotel and onto the streets of Manchester. His hangover has started to lift since he had a shower and put on some clean clothes, not to mention knocking back a strong coffee and devouring all the biscuits next to the coffee machine – *and* the jellybeans in the mini-bar. Now he's outside, he gulps in the air and can feel himself reviving further.

But he still has no idea why his mum wants to see him. And she greeted him with such a tight, desperate hug, he's nervous about finding out.

Eileen suggests going for a coffee, but Danny tells her he's just had one and asks if they can go for a walk instead. As she's wearing jeans and casual shoes, she agrees. They begin walking down Peter Street in the direction of Castlefield.

'So how are the babies?' Danny asks.

'Yeah, fine, ta,' she replies. 'We're going to Angela's for a little garden party later. You know, for t' bank holiday.'

'Gorgeous,' he says.

'Anyway, never mind that,' Eileen says. 'I came to see you to check you're alright.'

Danny furrows his brow. 'What do you mean? Why shouldn't I be?'

Eileen looks at him as if he's just told her there's a unicorn flying through the sky. 'You didn't answer my calls, love. And then I saw that picture on Instagram. You'd never have posted owt like that unless you were off your face. I were worried, love – dead worried.'

Shit.

'Oh yeah, it was a heavy night,' Danny says, as he directs her to turn left onto Deansgate. 'But I'm starting to feel human again now.'

Eileen puckers her lips. 'Yeah, well, I weren't just worried about your hangover. I were worried about how you were feeling in general.'

What's she getting at?

'Honestly, I'm fine, Mum,' Danny insists. 'There's nothing to worry about. Anyway, how did you know where I'm staying?'

Eileen shrugs. 'You told me, remember? I asked as soon as you said you were coming with Guy. I suspected this might happen.'

Goosebumps race up Danny's arm. 'Suspected *what* might happen?'

'Well, you said it were twenty years since you'd met him.'

Shit, does she know how I feel about him?

'There's no need to look at me like that, love,' she says. 'I know exactly how you feel about Guy. I've always known.'

Danny feels the humiliation slam into him. It only builds as Eileen explains that she could tell he was in love with Guy the first time she saw them together – and has observed his feelings ebb and flow over the years. 'It's alright, love,' she says, softly. 'There's nowt to be embarrassed about.'

He swallows. 'Yeah, well, if you don't mind, I'd rather not talk about it.'

He leads them off Deansgate and they pass the entrance to Liverpool Road, where he and Guy congregated as they waited to set off in the parade. He remembers how he felt that morning, how elated he was after spending the night with Guy and how excited he was about finally moving their relationship in the direction he'd always wanted. As he remembers how his excitement mushroomed during the parade, he feels a stab of sadness. *I only got to feel like that for a few hours – a few short hours in twenty years.*

'Sorry,' he adds, 'it's all still a bit raw.'

'That's OK,' says Eileen, 'but are you at least going to tell me what happened? I don't like seeing you like this, love.'

When they come to Deansgate train station, they cross the road and take a cobbled street that leads into Castlefield. After passing under a bridge, they trot down some steps to the canal, the same canal that runs through the city and all the way up to the Gay Village. As they walk along the towpath, alongside a red-brick warehouse from which sprout clumps of daisies, Danny explains that he and Guy spent the night together, he confessed his feelings, and Guy revealed that he didn't share them.

'Well, you know I think the world of Guy,' Eileen says, 'but if he doesn't realise what a catch you are by now, then he doesn't deserve you.'

A tram glides along the raised line on the other side of the canal. 'Thanks, Mum, but I think it's the other way round; I'm the one who doesn't deserve him.'

'Rubbish! Listen to me, love. I should know – I spent half my life going out wi' men who didn't deserve me.'

Danny is relieved that his mum has shifted the focus away from him. 'Don't be so hard on yourself,' he insists. 'They weren't *all* bad.'

'They were, love; they were terrible. All that time Arthur used to tell me to know my worth – but I just wouldn't listen.'

They come to the old lock-keeper's cottage and climb up and over the little bridge.

'Yeah, well, sometimes it can be hard to listen,' Danny reflects. 'Sometimes the good things people say get drowned out by the bad things.'

'Maybe you're right,' says Eileen, as they cross the seating area outside Barça. 'At least that'd explain why I spent years going out with someone like Lee. God, he were a dead loss. Getting shut of him were one of t' best things I ever did.'

They walk down a short flight of steps and re-emerge on the towpath. Facing them is a junction of canals, overlooked by wharves and warehouses that have been converted into trendy apartments, lined by pretty barges, and traversed by bridges carrying trains, trams and pedestrians. They sit down on a wooden bench, the sound of water rushing through the lock coming from behind them. On the other side of the water, a Pride flag hangs from the window of a top-floor apartment, catching the light breeze.

'I know what he used to say to you, by the way,' Eileen announces.

Danny feels as if all the breath has been smacked out of him. 'What do you mean?'

'I know Lee used to make fun of you and call you names.'

'But how? He never did it around you.'

She explains that one day she came home from work earlier than expected and overheard Lee taunting him. She somehow managed to control her temper until Danny had gone to bed, then confronted Lee and let him have it. By the time Danny woke up the next morning, he'd gone.

'You know, I always wondered why he disappeared so quickly,' Danny says.

'Well, now you know,' says Eileen.

Danny kicks at some of the beer bottle tops lying on the cobbles. A pair of swans sail along the water as a jogger bounds over the bridge.

'I felt terrible about the whole thing,' Eileen continues, 'but I didn't want to put you through any more upset so I just made things right and didn't mention it again. Just like I didn't mention it when I knew t' bullying were carrying on at school – however difficult that were for me. I didn't want to make you any more embarrassed than you were already.'

Danny can feel the heat prickling his cheeks. He wonders why he should still feel embarrassed all these years later.

'I just concentrated on loving you,' Eileen adds. 'I knew you were someone who'd need a lot to feel loved.'

Danny lets out a shaky sigh. 'Thanks, Mum,' he manages. 'You achieved it.'

But did she?

'Anyway, we don't need to talk about any of that if you don't want to,' Eileen cuts in. She turns to face him and looks him in the eye. 'But I hope you know you had nothing to be ashamed of. You never had anything to be ashamed of.'

'Thanks, Mum. I appreciate that.'

'Yeah, well, listen to your old mum. And let that sink in.'

Danny nods, slowly.

'And stop looking so miserable!' she trills, slapping him on the arm. 'If I can find the right fella after all them scrotes I went out with, you can too.'

Yeah, I'm not so sure about that . . .

'Anyway, until that day comes, I want you to remember that I'm dead proud of you. And I always have been.'

2022

As Danny waves off his mum, her words ring in his ears. *'I'm dead proud of you. And I always have been.'*

He grabs some food and another strong coffee to blast away the remnants of his hangover. But he doesn't feel like going back to the hotel and facing Guy so decides to revisit some places from his past: he decides to revisit his old university.

He walks down Oxford Road, past what used to be called the Palace Hotel but has been renamed the Kimpton Clocktower. He passes under the railway bridge just as a train screeches over it, crosses Charles Street, and walks alongside a cycle lane that has been constructed on the main road. He skirts a new development of luxury flats that have replaced the old BBC building, glancing through to an inner courtyard dotted with young people lounging on deckchairs and bales of hay amongst street food and cocktail stalls. He presses on, past hipster coffee shops, noodle and sushi bars, and a whole development made out of reclaimed storage containers that houses vintage clothes shops and vegan cafes. It's achingly cool and very different to the grotty area he knew as a student. Although he's glad that a few fried chicken shops and kebab and pizza takeaways have clung on – plus the Spar where he used to buy his cigarettes and chewing gum before a night out.

As he approaches the main campus of the university, Danny is beset by trepidation. His plan is to revisit the buildings that welcomed him when he first arrived in Manchester. His plan is to reconnect with the young man he used to be.

What surprises him is just how much the university has changed. He almost doesn't recognise the buildings around its edges as they've been remodelled to include branches of Pret a Manger, Brewdog and Five Guys. He crosses Oxford Road to get a better look, and notices that University Green has also been revamped – with new lighting, paving and concrete benches.

He continues down the main road and enters the campus through the archway of the grand, gothic Whitworth Building. As this is the oldest part of the university, he reasons it's the least likely to have changed. Indeed, the old quad is just as it was on his graduation day and he feels reassured by the sight of its handsome stone walls and pretty, calming trees. He presses further inside the campus and strolls around, recognising buildings, lawns and offices where he used to work, eat, do his admin, chat to friends, and learn his lines for plays. He feels a little lift when he spots the steps leading up to the Steve Biko building and the Student Union – including what used to be the Solem Bar – steps on which he and Emma once entertained passers-by with a spirited performance of the Cheeky Girls' *Touch My Bum*, complete with dance routine, interrupted by fits of drunken giggles. The building itself is closed, so he can't go inside. But it looks like it's also been given a revamp and now houses a carbon neutral coffee shop, a Vietnamese restaurant, and a burrito bar. *I didn't even know what a burrito was when I was at uni – and I'd certainly never eaten Vietnamese.*

As Danny continues his tour, he discovers that for every old building, there's a new one – and for every building that's the same as it was, there's one that's been altered or updated. In fact, there's been so much development since the last time Danny was here that it doesn't feel like it's the same university that welcomed him when he arrived in Manchester. Of course, he can appreciate that most of the change represents an improvement, whether that's in the form of the recycling stations dotted around or the posters advertising mental health support and initiatives to boost environmental sustainability. But, as it's outside term-time and there are hardly any students around, it has a slightly eerie feel, as if it isn't quite real. *I'm not sure it even feels like a university, let alone mine.*

Danny decides to walk to the halls where he lived in his first year, hoping this will stir something within him. He powers down Oxford Road, passing the hospital, the Whitworth Art Gallery – also revamped – and the statue of Edward VII at the entrance to the leafy Whitworth Park. When he arrives in Rusholme and the start of the famous Curry Mile, he turns left and continues walking until he arrives at the entrance to Hulme Hall.

Immediately, something warm blooms in his chest.

He walks inside, passing reception, crossing the car park and pausing to take in the main lawn, bordered by Houldsworth block, the oldest building on the complex.

Already the emotions are churning within him.

He walks through an archway, alongside the tennis courts, and follows the footpath until he comes to an unprepossessing 1960s building called Greenwood.

He stops by the entrance. And that's when it happens: that's when the young man – actually, more like boy – that he used to be comes thumping back to life.

2002

In Greenwood block, Danny sat on his new bed and tried to stop wringing his hands. He was terrified of opening his door and going outside. *Manchester may be a safe place for gay people like me, but the other students will have come from all over the country. What if they've brought their attitudes with them?*

Piled up on the floor around him were his belongings, still packed away in a suitcase, a rucksack, several boxes, and a black bin liner. The cupboards in the room were bare and the desk empty, waiting for him to fill them – and the walls were blank, waiting for him to decorate. Before setting off from Barrow, Danny had scoured his collection of magazines, cutting out pictures of half-naked celebrities he fancied, ready to stick them up on what he was going to call his 'hunks' wall'. Now he'd arrived, the idea struck him as ridiculous, an outrageous exhibition of his sexuality. He wasn't sure who'd be visiting his room, but he didn't want to be accused of *asking* for trouble.

From the floor below, he heard the sound of the latest album by Pink. As he and his mum had lugged his belongings up the stairs, a girl with heavy eyeliner and a thick mane of copper hair had been moving into the room directly below his. As she and her bickering parents had said goodbye, Danny was sure he'd detected Scottish accents. He considered going down and introducing himself, but another rush of fear blasted through him.

You don't seriously think the other students will like *you, do you?*

Even though his mum had only left ten minutes ago, suddenly he missed her. He ran his hands over the bare mattress and remembered how he'd felt when he was little and she'd tucked him up in bed every night, then snuggled in next to him to read a story. Before she kissed him goodnight, she'd stand at the bottom of the bed and waft the duvet over him, creating a wind effect that never failed to make him smile. And when she'd return his smile, Danny would always feel happy – he'd feel safe.

He looked at his battered old duvet, bulging out of the top of the bin liner, and felt a pang of loneliness.

He tried to reason it away. *Come on, people don't always hate you. They like you when you're on stage; they like you when you're playing a role. So all you need to do is find out who they want you to be offstage and play that role.*

Then again, for Danny to pull off that kind of thing he'd need to be much more confident – not to mention brave. *Oh, if only it wasn't all down to me. If only someone could come to my rescue.*

In his head, he repeated the words his mum had said to him before she left: *'I'm dead proud of you.'* It was something she said to him often, especially when she'd been out drinking with Arthur: she'd come home and totter into his room, reeking of white wine and Silk Cut, and wake him up to tell him. But this never annoyed him. He loved hearing it.

'I'm dead proud of you. And I always have been.'

He scrunched up his hands into little fists.

Come on, Danny, you can do this!

He stood up and walked over to the door.

2022

As he leans on the wall of his old hall, Danny struggles to hold back the tears. Once he's glanced around to make sure he's on his own, he stops struggling. The tears come shuddering out of him and his whole body crumples.

Oh God, I was so young. I was so naïve – and so scared.

As the tears flow, he sinks into a crouching position. He's startled by how forcefully the tears are coming – so forcefully they make him feel like he's choking or gasping for breath. Soon, his face is drenched and his chin dripping. A low, primal groan escapes his mouth, a noise he didn't think himself capable of making. And still the tears keep falling.

When they eventually come to a stop, he dries his face and slowly straightens himself up again.

Well, I didn't expect that.

As he leaves Hulme Hall and sets off back along Rusholme Place, then up Oxford Road, his sadness lingers – but now it's accompanied by a sense of calm, a sense of something having righted.

After a while, Danny comes to the building that used to house the Cornerhouse cinema. It's one of his favourite buildings in Manchester and he used to love visiting it to watch gay-themed films – often with Guy. He's no idea what purpose it serves in its current incarnation, but this weekend it's plastered with posters advertising Superbia, the programme of cultural events, activities and discussions organised by Manchester Pride.

Danny read about this when he was planning the weekend, but he didn't pay much attention as he couldn't imagine it playing any part in the long-overdue love story he was hoping to set in motion. Now that dream has failed to materialise, he finds himself studying the programme. A panel discussion has just started around the question 'Why are so many gay men so bad at relationships?'

Instinctively, Danny bristles. He objects to the inference that anyone who isn't in a relationship is somehow failing in life. *What if they're like me and just don't* want *to be in a relationship?*

He stops himself. *Oh, pull the other one, Danny: you've always wanted to be in a relationship – you just wanted to be in one with someone who didn't want it with you.*

He decides to pop inside.

'Hi,' he says, flashing his wristband at a group of stewards standing around the reception area, 'I'm here for the debate.'

A woman with a haircut that's too sharp for her face steps forward. 'You do realise this is an alcohol and drug-free space?'

He's about to joke that he drank so much last night there's probably still alcohol in his system, but he stops himself.

'No, I didn't actually,' he says, 'but that's fine; I haven't had any drink or drugs.'

The steward smiles and leads him down a flight of stairs to a packed lecture theatre. Danny whispers his thanks and slides onto an empty seat at the end of the back row. The discussion is already underway and a historian with sloping shoulders and long, grey hair is speaking.

'When I was growing up in the sixties and seventies,' he says, 'gay men were widely denounced as sexual predators who skulked around in the shadows waiting to fulfill their warped, perverted desires. Time and time again, kids heard the message that queers can't love. And that had a big impact on the way people like me saw ourselves. I grew up thinking I'd never fall in love.'

Danny takes a swig from his bottle of water and shifts in his seat. *This is a bit intense.*

'The thing is, I had no reason to think otherwise,' the man goes on. 'When I started going out on the gay scene, all I found was casual sex. And it was all anyone seemed to talk about. Naturally, I believed this was what gay men did – and this determined my behaviour. Yes, I don't mind admitting I slapped it about in my youth.'

A ripple of laughter spreads through the audience.

'But that was never what I wanted,' he adds, 'not really. And I think the same is true of a lot of gay men.'

Danny sits up, his interest piqued.

Next to speak is an effeminate yet earnest journalist who often appears on TV news bulletins, commenting on stories that affect LGBTQ+ people.

'My experience was very different,' he says, clasping his hands. 'I grew up in the eighties and nineties and, like lots of gay men my age, when I was young I was always falling in love with my straight friends. And I'd always be heartbroken when they didn't love me back. But I gradually realised that by falling in love with men who were unattainable, I was denying myself the love I wanted.'

Another of the panellists, a stocky black man in his thirties who has a regular slot as a relationships counsellor on a daytime TV show, chips in. 'I see this kind of thing happening a lot. But unrequited love is more about the person who's in love than it is the object of their affection. If someone's unhappy with the way they are, they can fall in love with a quality or a set of qualities they want to possess. When the person they fall in love with doesn't love them back, this only reinforces their feeling of being unworthy. And sometimes that's what they're looking for.'

'I think all this stems from the shame so many of us are made to carry around within ourselves,' the journalist interjects.

'Absolutely,' comments the historian. 'As I said before, if you're told something all your life, you'll believe it. And if you're told being gay is bad or wrong or perverted, you'll probably hate your sexuality – and as a result you might not treat yourself with much respect. You might even punish yourself or try to self-destruct. I think this explains why the gay community has much higher rates of drink and drug use and why so many of us become addicted to anonymous sex.'

Danny's insides compress. He tips back what's left of his water.

'It also explains why so many of us are desperate for affirmation,' pipes up the relationships counsellor. 'Why so many of us become addicted to likes on social media or hooked on exercise and showing off our bodies and boyfriends. Or why we become people pleasers socially.'

'One of the things I find saddest about all this,' adds the journalist, 'is that often the people who feel they aren't good enough are those everyone else thinks are amazing. *They're* the only ones who can't see it.'

Danny's head suddenly becomes packed with all the people

who've told him he's amazing. His mum, Arthur, Lynsey, Emma, all the friends he's met since leaving Manchester, his boss Lorraine, his colleagues at the agency . . . *Even Guy – or at least he said that when we were arguing a few hours ago.*

Although this has happened pretty much all his adult life, Danny feels like his awareness of it is coming as something of a revelation. He feels like all this time he's been stumbling around in the darkness and someone has just switched on a torch to light up the way.

'If there's one thing I'd like everyone in the audience to take away from this discussion,' says the relationships counsellor, 'it's that happiness is an inside job. It can only come from ourselves.'

Danny feels something igniting within him.

He takes out his phone and texts Guy.

2022

Guy shuffles along to make room for Danny. Unlike the last time the two of them were together – when they were arguing in their hotel room – Danny seems quite perky. *Although what he's got to be perky about, I've no idea.*

Guy clears his throat. 'I'm sorry about earlier,' he says. 'I didn't want us to have an argument.'

'Yeah, I'm sorry too,' says Danny. 'I think we both got a bit worked up.'

'I guess it's been building up for a while.'

Danny smirks. 'Yeah, like, twenty years.'

They both laugh and Guy's relieved that the tension between them has dimmed.

They're on Albert Square, sitting on what they used to call their steps, at the foot of the statue of William Gladstone. Although the square's been fully pedestrianised and spruced up – and the Town Hall itself is fenced off and undergoing renovation – Guy feels comforted by the familiarity of the cobbles, lamp-posts, statues and plane trees, their leaves fluttering in the light breeze. It's late afternoon and, as it's a bank holiday, even quieter than it would be when Danny used to meet Guy while he was revising for his finals.

'Do you remember sitting here and imagining what we'd be doing in twenty years?' Danny asks.

Guy scoffs. 'I think it's safe to say neither of us could have predicted where we'd end up. Or what would happen this weekend.'

Danny gives a chortle. 'What, that we'd shag and I'd tell you I'm in love with you and you'd say you don't feel the same and we'd have a massive row?'

Guy isn't sure how to respond. He hopes Danny's bravado isn't masking any ill feeling. He hopes it isn't the sign of the tension resurfacing.

'Then again,' says Danny, 'in some ways you could say it was perfectly predictable.'

'How do you mean?'

Danny explains that he's just been to a panel discussion exploring why so many gay men are bad at relationships – and summarises some of the main points. He ends by saying that one of the main lessons it taught him is just how much our feelings about ourselves can influence those we have about others. 'Basically, I've realised that I fell in love with you because I didn't love myself. Because I didn't feel like I was good enough and I wanted to go on feeling like that.'

There's a pause.

'It's weird,' Danny comments, 'but saying that now, I don't feel remotely embarrassed about it.'

Guy raises an eyebrow. 'I guess we've gone past that.'

He tries to apply the lesson Danny learned to himself and it occurs to him that maybe he *didn't* fall in love with Danny because he didn't love himself either. *But how can I express that more sensitively?*

'On my part, I think I might have fallen in love with men I thought were better than me,' he begins, slowly. 'And I did that because I wanted to show them off. I was attracted to men who looked good on the surface or men I thought would impress people.'

He has no idea why a thought he usually keeps to himself – and, more to the point, tries not to confront himself – has just come tripping out of him. But now that it has, he can see that it's always been quite obvious. *I only wish I'd faced up to it sooner.*

Danny inches towards him, his face becoming even more animated. 'They talked about that in the debate; apparently it's about wanting to prove to the world that you're better than they thought you were. And to prove it to yourself too.'

Guy tilts his head and nods. 'That makes sense. I mean, if I think about some of the men I've been out with, I'm not sure I even *liked* them. It's just that they were so good-looking I couldn't believe I'd got them.'

Danny shakes his head. 'You see, that's just ridiculous to me.'

Guy moves towards him until their knees are touching. 'Yeah, but it's ridiculous to me that you'd go out with someone like Dean who treated you like shit. Or that you'd have sex with men who are so obviously beneath you.'

Danny laughs. 'Maybe what's most ridiculous is how long it took us to be having this conversation.'

There's a light gust of wind and a rainbow-coloured ribbon appears next to Guy's feet. 'OK, but now that we are having it, how do we stop ourselves from falling for the wrong men? I mean, it's one thing knowing why we do it, but when does that stop it from happening?'

'I've no idea,' says Danny. 'I suppose once we feel better about ourselves, we'll just start genuinely fancying people who are right for us. People who can actually give us what we want.'

'Really? Do you think it's that simple?'

Danny lets out a sigh. 'I fucking hope so.'

Guy chuckles. 'Me too.'

Danny watches as a gust of wind lifts up a rainbow-coloured ribbon and carries it away across the cobbles. The clock tower chimes as it turns 5 o'clock.

Guy claps his hands together. 'Well, I do want to feel better about myself. So I'm going to start by taking responsibility for my actions.'

'Oh yeah, and what does that mean?'

Guy fixes him with a stare. 'Danny, I'm sorry I abused our relationship.'

Although Guy's apologising for the exact same thing for which just a few hours ago Danny had criticised him, Danny no longer harbours any resentment towards him. He can see now that he didn't act out of malice or even selfishness. *Guy isn't to blame for the way things were between us; neither of us is.*

We were both damaged. We were both desperate.

'That's OK,' he says. 'If you did use me for affirmation then I was quite willing to be used – more than willing. And while we're on the subject, so was Lynsey.'

Guy arches an eyebrow. 'Oh yeah? Why do you say that?'

Danny explains that he went to see Lynsey and they discussed what happened and what motivated her to respond to Guy's advances all those years ago. 'She doesn't blame you either,' he reassures him. 'And she isn't remotely resentful.'

Guy nods, slowly. 'That's good to know. Although I do still feel bad about it.'

'Well, you don't have to. From what she said, she was desperate too. It sounds like we all were. I don't know, maybe we should call Emma and see if we can get a full house.'

Guy laughs.

'Although I think she's already covered that off herself,' Danny adds. 'I think she was the first across the finish line in that race.'

Guy runs his hand along his jaw. 'Oh yeah, I think you're right.'

There's a short silence. Danny tugs at his wristband.

'Anyway, since we're doing apologies,' he goes on, 'I'm sorry I also abused our relationship. I'm sorry I looked to you for feelings you didn't have, then blamed you for not having them. Even if I was doing it out of some kind of twisted desire for self-punishment.'

There's another silence.

'My God,' says Danny, 'this feels like a moment.'

'Yeah,' says Guy, 'it feels like maybe we should hug each other.'

Danny grins. 'Come here, babe.'

As he puts his arms around Guy, he enjoys the simple feeling of connection, of being close to him. Though it strikes him that there's something not quite right about the hug.

Then he realises what it is: it isn't Guy he's hugging but himself. He's hugging the young man he was when he arrived in Manchester. He's trying to communicate to him that he has nothing to be afraid of, that everything will be alright – but for this to happen, he has to believe he's good enough; he has to believe he's good enough as he is.

If only I could have told myself that, I'd have saved myself so much heartache.

Then again, he doesn't think he'd have listened.

2002

Danny and Guy were walking back to their halls after their first night out in the Village, a night that was so momentous that – even as they were living through it – Danny knew he'd remember it for ever.

He was so happy he felt like singing falsetto and skipping all the way down Upper Brook Street. But he held back. *Come on, you don't want to act too camp in front of Guy.*

'So that's it,' he chirped, 'our first night out on the gay scene.'

After spending several hours in Manto, Danny and Guy had strolled the length of Canal Street – several times – marvelling at the colour and energy, at just how buzzing and brazenly gay the whole area was. Nestled in between the bars they'd found a takeaway called McTucky's, where they'd stopped for chicken burgers and chips. Guy had said his was the best chicken burger he'd ever tasted. Danny had gazed at him and thought he was perfect.

As they turned off Upper Brook Street, passed St Chrysostom's Church and took the tree-lined Conyngham Road, Danny was eager to talk through every detail of their night. 'I wonder how many WKDs we drank,' he said.

Guy widened his eyes. 'I've no idea but it was a *lot.*'

'Manto was so amazing. Wasn't the atmosphere insane?'

'Yeah, it was cool.'

'And everyone was so gorgeous and trendy. Did you see that barman who looked like Beppe di Marco?'

Guy laughed. 'I can't say I did, no. But I did really like it. And thanks for bearing with me; I'm sorry it took me a while to loosen up.'

Danny batted away his comment. 'Oh, don't worry about it, babe. I totally understand.'

As they came to Dalton-Ellis Hall – with its handsome Victorian red-brick façade – Danny remembered they'd each told their friends they weren't feeling very well. They didn't want to be spotted and have to explain their lie; Danny would hate for Guy to be dragged out of the closet before he was ready.

When they reached the main gate, they came to a stop.

'So this is me,' said Guy.

'This is you.' Danny lowered his voice. 'So do you think you'll be up for going back to Canal Street? Now we know what it's like?'

Guy gave him a grin. 'I'd love to. That is, assuming you would too?'

A streetlight illuminated the blue of his shirt and brought out the colour of his eyes. *My God, he's so gorgeous.*

Danny grinned back at him. 'Just try and keep me away!'

They stood in silence, grinning at each other.

There it is again, that closeness. That special connection.

For a brief moment, Danny wondered if Guy might invite him in, if they might sit on his bed chatting like they'd done the first time he'd been to his room, but this time would end up kissing – then lying back and letting one thing lead to another.

Don't be stupid!

He rubbed his hands together. 'OK, well, you'd better get inside before anyone spots us.'

'Yeah, I suppose so.' Guy gave a shuffle on the pavement. 'Night, then, princess.'

Danny felt his heart take flight. 'Night, my prince.'

He stepped forward and gave Guy a peck on the cheek. Then he watched him disappear into reception, the door closing slowly behind him.

Oh, I don't care if he doesn't fancy me. I don't care if he isn't interested. Whatever happens, I'll never stop loving him.

Danny waved at Guy's back.

Once he was sure Guy could no longer see him, he began skipping down the pavement. And he skipped the rest of the way home.

2022

Guy moves to the side of the pavement and leans against the shop front. He and Danny have just had dinner – accompanied by some relaxed, easy conversation – and Danny has popped into a convenience store to buy some chewing gum. While he waits for him to reappear, Guy checks his phone.

He's received a text from Josh. 'Hi, do you fancy going to the candlelit vigil?'

He lets the phone fall to his side. The candlelit vigil is the closing event of Manchester Pride and he and Danny originally planned on going together to round off their weekend, although Danny hasn't mentioned it for a while. Now Josh is suggesting the two of them go together – and it'll be Guy's last chance to see him before he goes back to London.

He isn't sure what to do.

Josh seems like a great guy, but am I only attracted to him because he'd make another trophy boyfriend?

He remembers how the conversation flagged over dinner yesterday. Suddenly, the twelve-year age difference feels like it's an obstacle between them.

He peers through the window and spies Danny standing at the back of the queue. He knows what to do.

He lifts up his phone to compose a text.

'Sorry but I'm going to pass. I really enjoyed meeting you but I'm afraid I don't want to take things further. Sorry to mess you around but this isn't what I'm looking for. All the best, Guy x'

Before he presses Send, he stops and gazes up at the sky.

Do I really want to do this?

He looks through the window and sees Danny handing over some coins to the cashier.

He hits Send and tucks away his phone.

When Danny re-emerges, he skips over to Guy cheerfully, seemingly unconcerned about how camp he might look. Guy's never thought of Danny as someone who's particularly self-conscious before, but this glimpse of him without any inhibition makes him think he might well have been. *I wonder what else about him I've still got to discover.*

'Here you go, babe,' Danny chirps. He tips some chewing gum into Guy's palm.

'Thanks,' says Guy, popping it into his mouth. 'Now, what do you reckon? Shall we head over to the vigil?'

2022

Danny steps into Sackville Gardens, his hands wrapped around an unlit candle. He's looking forward to what many people have told him is the most meaningful event of Manchester Pride.

Although the sun's only just setting, already there's a crowd of people waiting for the vigil to start. They're standing facing the same stage on which the live acts performed but which is now framed by a huge rainbow flag on one side and several rainbow-coloured balloons sculpted into the shape of an AIDS ribbon on the other. Although the gardens are busy, as no alcohol is being served, there's a calm, subdued atmosphere.

And I like it. It feels right.

The woman standing next to Danny is puffing away on a cigarette and blows smoke in his direction. He doesn't find it remotely tempting but is reminded of his vow to give up smoking if Guy would fall in love him. He cringes at the memory. And he makes a new vow: to give up for himself.

When more people cram into the gardens, Guy shuffles closer to Danny. As their arms touch each other's, it dawns on Danny that a new easiness has set in between them. Now they no longer have anything to hide from each other, he feels much freer. *From now on, there's no need to pretend to be anything other than I am.*

By 9 o'clock, darkness has fallen, and a wave of applause builds as a group of people takes to the stage. In the lead is trans performer and actress Fancy Bliss, who's hosting the event and is wearing a silver sequinned blouse that shimmers under the stage lights and complements the flash of turquoise in her hair. She takes hold of the microphone and explains that tonight's event is being held to commemorate the queer people from history who suffered prejudice or persecution – and references the National Transgender Memorial and the statue of Alan Turing that stand in the gardens. She says that another aim is to pay tribute to all those who died of HIV/AIDS and points out another memorial, the Beacon of Hope. She then reminds the audience of the importance of recognising the challenges still faced by LGBTQ+ people around the world, particularly in countries where being who they are is still illegal.

There's another round of applause.

Next, Fancy introduces another speaker, a portly man with a bushy moustache who's the chairman of a local charity that looks after elderly LGBTQ+ people.

'Every day I feel privileged to work with our service users,' he says into the microphone, 'because every day they teach me so much. As queer people, we're one of the few minority groups who don't grow up in families with older members from that same minority. So it's vitally important that we value all those older people within our community.'

The speech reminds Danny that Arthur said he'd be coming to Manchester for the vigil as he was in the area visiting friends. They promised to grab each other and say a quick hello. He slips out his phone and texts him.

'It's only by engaging with the older members of our community that we can preserve our unique culture and identity,' the man goes on, raising his voice over the wail of a distant siren. 'It's only by bringing together people from different generations that we can truly call ourselves a community.'

As the audience breaks into another round of applause, Danny's phone buzzes to let him know he's received a reply. But Fancy is directing everyone to light their candles in advance of a minute's silence. Danny lights his and Guy's and they hold them up as the noise dwindles around them. A mood of contemplation descends.

Danny glances at the thousands of people in the gardens, their sombre faces all lit up by flickering flames. He wonders how much prejudice or persecution they've suffered, how ashamed of themselves they've been made to feel, how this shame has affected their feelings towards others. Although several people are standing with their arms around each other, he wonders how many of them may be linked by a complicated tangle of unrequited love, unfulfilled emotional needs, and unresolved sexual tension – as he imagines many people are all over the world, for all kinds of reasons. *But what's important is that the people here are still making their relationships work. They're overcoming their issues to bond as a community.*

The end of the silence is marked by more applause, the loudest wave so far.

'We remember!' shouts Fancy Bliss. 'Manchester will *always* remember!'

When the applause has faded, she introduces the first performance of the evening.

Danny turns to Guy and whispers, 'Come on, let's slip away and find Arthur.'

2022

As he kisses Arthur, Danny is mindful of the performance taking place on stage: the Manchester Lesbian and Gay Chorus is singing an a capella version of Labi Siffre's *Something Inside So Strong*.

He lowers his voice to a whisper. 'It's gorge to see you, Arthur! But what are you doing here at the back?'

Arthur gestures to the crash barrier. 'I need to lean on this, dearie. You know I'm an old bird; I can't stand up for long these days.'

Danny curses his insensitivity. 'Sorry, babe. I still think of you as a young slip of a girl.'

Arthur gives him a playful slap. 'Get out of it, I'm nearly seventy-five! Although Alan here makes me feel sixteen again.'

A man who's a couple of decades younger than Arthur steps forward and gives Danny and Guy a hug. He's slim, with brown hair and a kindly face. Guy asks what he makes of the vigil.

'I think it's marvellous,' he says in a northern accent as strong as Arthur's. 'It's great to show that Pride's about more than just getting leathered and watching pop stars I've never heard of.'

'I couldn't agree more,' says Guy. 'It's a lovely way to round off the weekend.'

Danny turns to Arthur and wags his finger. 'But what's all this about? You always said you didn't do relationships. And now we find out you've been hiding a new boyfriend.'

Arthur gives a wince. 'Oh, I don't know about "boyfriend". I'm not sure I'd use that word.'

'Babe, just because you're an old bird doesn't mean you can't have a boyfriend.'

'Trust me, I'm well aware of that.' Arthur gives him an impish grin. 'What I mean is, I don't feel comfortable with the word "boyfriend". All them words come from straight people – boyfriend, lover, companion, friend, partner, husband . . . What if someone comes along who doesn't fit into any of them boxes?'

Danny frowns. 'I've never thought of it like that.'

'You know what,' Arthur goes on, 'I bet lots of straight people hate having to pick from all the same narrow, old-fashioned labels too. Why can't they go for summat in between? Why not bits of all of 'em all, mixed up and put together?'

'Maybe that's what our community can offer them,' suggests Guy.

Arthur nods enthusiastically. 'Going against t' grain comes much more easily to queer people. It's part of who we are – part of who we've been made to be. But being forced to fit into a box i'n't good for anyone. Why shouldn't we all make up our own rules?'

'My God,' comments Danny, 'you're getting radical in your old age.'

Arthur waves his arm around airily. 'Well, dearie, old age is liberating. The things that used to matter just don't anymore. You don't give a fuck what people think – and you don't give a fuck about labels or trying to fit in. Alan's my Alan and, as far as I'm concerned, that's all that matters.'

A heavy-bosomed lesbian standing in front of them turns around and hisses. 'Will you lot keep it down! Some of us are trying to listen!'

Danny apologises and whispers into Arthur's ear. 'We'd better leave you to it.'

'That's alright,' says Arthur, 'it were good to say hello. We're slipping out before t' end anyway. I don't want to get caught up in t' crush.'

'OK,' says Danny, 'but let's speak again soon.'

'Right you are, dearie. Me and Alan are coming to London next month so maybe the four of us can get together.'

But before Danny can say anything, Guy has accepted for both of them.

2002

As Guy came to the bottom of Canal Street, he felt the first drops of rain.

He looked up and saw the sky was the colour of coal. He pulled up his hood as the rain began pelting down, bouncing up from the cobbles and onto his jeans. It was the end of term and as if the famous Manchester weather had turned up to wave him off.

Rain was the first thing people at home had mentioned when Guy had said he was going to university in Manchester. *Well, that and the saying 'it's grim up north'.*

Now that he thought about it, it *had* rained a lot during his first term. But he could hardly say the weather had defined his time here. As far as he was concerned, the sun might as well have shone every day. *It's been the opposite of grim.*

Straight ahead, at the junction with Sackville Street, he spotted Danny. He was trudging along, carrying a heavy suitcase and a black bin bag, a big rucksack strapped to his back. His coat didn't have a hood and he was stooping under the rain.

'Danny!' Guy shouted. 'Danny, wait!'

But Danny didn't hear him.

Guy tucked his umbrella under his arm and ran towards him. On his left, he passed Manto and felt his heart give a little lift. But he didn't slow down; he was too determined to catch Danny.

'Danny!' he shouted again.

This time, Danny heard him. When he turned round, his face lit up. 'Guy! My prince! What are you doing here?'

'I came to see you off, princess.' Guy stopped and caught his breath. 'I wanted to say goodbye.'

Delight flooded Danny's face. 'You didn't need to; I only saw you last night.'

'I know, but I wanted to,' Guy replied.

I'm not going to see you for months and I'll really miss you.

But he kept this thought to himself; it seemed daft and sentimental.

'That's so lovely!' said Danny, the delight now sparkling in his eyes. 'But look at the state of me; I'm pissed wet through.'

'Here, give me your rucksack.'

Danny handed it over and Guy threw it across his back. Then he opened his umbrella, positioning it over Danny's head. Slowly, the two of them began walking to the coach station, the rain pounding on their umbrella, their arms touching.

'You know, I feel bad about you having to catch the coach,' said Guy.

'Oh, it's only this once,' Danny reassured him. 'It's just because it's a Saturday; it's Mum's busiest day of the week in the salon.'

Guy frowned. 'Even so, it can't be much fun.'

'To be honest, I'm gutted about leaving Manchester and going home; I don't think anything would cheer me up.' Danny buffeted Guy's shoulder. 'Although it's good to see you.'

Guy felt the happiness pulse through him.

As they walked up Bloom Street towards the coach station, the two of them made plans for next term, running through all the things they had to look forward to.

By the time they arrived, Danny's coach was boarding. They flung his bags into the luggage compartment and stepped back under the shelter.

'Well, then.' Danny opened his arms and drew Guy into a hug. 'I'll guess I'll see you next term.'

Guy clung onto him. *I love you,* he wanted to say. *I love you, princess.*

But all that came out was, 'Yeah, you will.'

He cleared a lump from his throat. 'But expect lots of texts and phone calls!'

'I'll hold you to that!'

Danny stepped away. He gave Guy a smile, ducked out from under the shelter and boarded the coach.

Guy tried to follow his silhouette along the aisle but soon lost him.

Oh no . . . I want to wave!

The coach's engine revved to life and it pulled away, towards the station exit.

Guy scoured the windows but still couldn't see Danny. Then he appeared, at the second window from the back.

The two of them waved to each other, smiling brightly.

'I love you!' Guy shouted at the back of the coach, just as it turned and disappeared out of the station. 'I love you, Danny Baxter!'

One or two people standing on the concourse stared at him. But Guy didn't care.

I just love Danny.

He didn't really understand what that meant; the kind of love he felt didn't correspond to the majority of the emotions he'd seen expressed at the cinema or on TV, or to anything people in real life had talked about. But it didn't matter to him how his love measured up to anyone else's. *Besides, how can two people ever know that their feeling is exactly the same as each other's?*

He opened his umbrella and stepped out of the station. *Why on earth would anyone* want *to do that? Isn't it better to have a feeling that's completely unique?*

This thought lingered in his mind as he made his way towards Canal Street, under the heavy Manchester rain.

2022

As Guy hugs Arthur goodbye, he ponders on what the older man just told him. *And the more I think about it, the more I agree with him.*

If he considers his relationship with Danny, it doesn't fit into any pre-existing template. It's not a traditional romantic relationship, but nor is it a friendship in the sense that most people understand the word. *Yes, we're friends, and in many ways we're like brothers, but at the same time we had sex – and it was great. So what does that make us?*

As he weaves his way through the crowd, he's struck by the sight of so many people holding up candles, so many of them lost in contemplation, so many of them no doubt trying to make sense of their own lives and relationships. The choir on stage is singing Queen's *These Are the Days of Our Lives* and the lyrics prompt him to look back over his relationship with Danny, over all the memories they've shared.

For twenty years, Guy was worried about losing their friendship, but in some ways he can see that during the course of this weekend he *has* lost it, or at least he's lost what it was. But that's fine. In fact, it's more than fine: it's a *good* thing. Because now they've razed their relationship to the ground, what emerges is the opportunity to build something new, something better. And Guy knows that whatever this is, it will be founded on a much greater understanding of each other – and a much greater understanding of themselves.

I can't wait for us to start building it. I can't wait for us to start again – and this time get it right.

Just as he and Danny are squeezing themselves back into position, the song comes to an end and the crowd breaks into applause.

Once the applause has faded, Fancy Bliss steps forward and thanks the choir. She introduces the final speaker of the evening, a middle-aged black woman who runs a charity that helps LGBTQ+ asylum seekers, people who are fleeing persecution because of their sexuality or gender identity. The crowd falls silent as she approaches the microphone.

'In this time of war,' the woman says, 'I'd like to send a message of love and hope to all LGBTQ+ people who've been displaced by conflict. Or those who've stayed but are struggling to survive. That's not just in Ukraine but also in Afghanistan and Syria.'

'Yes!' shouts someone behind Danny.

'Preach!' shouts a woman a few rows in front.

'War only erupts,' continues the speaker, 'and hatred only ignites when people fixate on the differences between us. Not just national or cultural differences but also the differences between us as individuals, as individual spirits and personalities. But a friend of mine once told me that we see each other best with our eyes closed.'

She pauses so the audience can consider her words.

'What we all have to realise,' she goes on, 'is that we are all the same. We all breathe the same and bleed the same. We all *love* the same.'

Do we though? Danny can't help remembering what he thought as he arrived in Manchester. He remembers wishing there were more words to describe love in its various – very different – forms. And he isn't sure what to make of the speaker's argument. *Is she right?* Do *we all love the same? Or is what she means that all of our loves are equally valid?*

When the speaker finishes – and the applause has faded – Fancy thanks her and returns to the microphone.

'When you think about it,' she says, 'despite all our differences, there's really only one love. Or there's really only one love that matters. And that's the love for ourselves. If we can get that right, everything else will follow.'

Danny draws in a long, slow breath.

That's more like it.

He feels strong. He feels ready. *Ready for whatever the world's going to throw at me.*

Fancy folds her arms and tilts her head. 'You know, that's something that the queer community, with all the challenges we face, with the struggle so many of us have to go through, often understand very well – the importance of self-love. And that's something I think we can teach the world.'

There's more clapping and cheering.

Fancy then introduces the final performance, by House of Ghetto, a group of artists she describes as queer, trans and intersex people of colour belonging to a vogue ball house in Manchester. 'They know a thing or two about overcoming challenges. They know a thing or two about the struggle for self-love. And they've got so much to teach us all!'

As four extravagantly dressed dancers strut onto the stage, Danny recognises the riff from Candi Staton's *You Got the Love*. When the beat kicks in, he stands mesmerised as the performers use their arms and legs to create flamboyant lines and shapes, accentuating their femininity and exaggerating every element of what makes them so striking. Before long, his own arms and legs are tapping along to the beat and the adrenaline is pumping through him.

By the time the performance is over and the sky is lit up with fireworks, he feels invigorated and inspired.

He turns to Guy and shouts over the noise. 'Talk about going out with a bang.'

Guy chuckles. 'Yeah, quite literally.'

The final firework explodes and it's met with one last cheer from the crowd.

'So that's it,' Danny says. 'The end of Manchester Pride.'

All around them, candles are extinguished and the sea of people begins flowing towards the exit.

Danny and Guy allow themselves to be carried by the throng and, as they leave, drop their candles in a bin. They emerge onto Sackville Street and push their way along to Canal Street. There, they begin threading through the masses in the direction of the hotel.

Danny remembers that, when he made the same journey on Friday night, he was gripped by anxiety as he thought ahead to what he hoped would happen in their hotel room. Tonight will be the first time since then that the two of them have got into bed together. But he doesn't feel remotely anxious.

He turns around to check Guy's still behind him and pushes on. He considers what Arthur said about relationships and compares this to what Lorraine once told him about careers. It strikes him that he can also invent for himself a path towards a new relationship, one that's right for both him and Guy – even if, as he sets off on it, he isn't able to identify where the path is leading.

He and Guy arrive at the bottom of Canal Street. But, before they can step away from the cobbles and leave the Village, they're approached by two women.

''Ere,' one of them says to Danny, 'your boyfriend's a bit of alright, i'n't he?'

'Oh, he's not my boyfriend,' Danny says, calmly. Then he smiles. 'To be honest, I've no idea what he is.'

Guy draws up alongside him. 'I've no idea what he is either.'

The two women shrug, as if what they've just heard isn't anything out of the ordinary.

As they watch them walk away, Danny and Guy break into laughter.

Guy holds out his hand. 'Come on,' he says, 'let's go and find out *what* we are. Let's go and find out where we're heading next.'

'OK,' says Danny, 'let's do that.'

And he takes his hand.

Acknowledgements

This book took me four and a half years to write and I put everything I had into it. I also had to fight some major battles along the way. One of the things that kept me going was listening to music by gay or queer artists – especially Erasure, The Communards, Years and Years, and, most of all, the Pet Shop Boys. When I was writing, I'd listen to their music at the start of each day, and it would help immerse me in Danny and Guy's world. In fact, I listened to so much Pet Shop Boys that I'd even go as far as saying it's their book as much as it is mine.

Thanks must also go to my non-musical inspirations. First is the hairdresser in the local salon where I grew up in Bolton. His name was Arthur Lawrence and he lived a gloriously open life as a gay man. At the time I was too frightened of who I was to speak to him or form any kind of relationship. But I can now see that he was a true queer hero and the character of Arthur is my own little tribute.

Speaking of my childhood, I'd like to thank all the detractors, bullies, attackers and tormentors – you instilled me with a rock-bottom self-esteem that has given me such a fierce drive to prove that I am good enough. You have got me where I am today.

Thanks to all the gay friends who were there for me later in life, through the wild days of my young adulthood. You helped me create so much of the material that went into this book. Special mention goes to Rob Hastie – here's to our glory days!

For helping me with my research, thanks to Joe Stafford and Dr James Peters at Manchester University, as well as David Cross for suggesting the halls in which Danny and Guy live in their first year. David, well done for recognising me as I roamed Oxford Road with my research pad, and for introducing yourself and offering to help.

To Mark Fletcher and all the team at Manchester Pride, thanks for running the best Pride in the world (and yes, I would say that as an ambassador, but I've been to loads and I promise it's true!)

Special mention goes to my agent Sophie Lambert and her assistant Alice Hoskyns, who helped steer this book through tough times and supported me through the scraps and the sparring. But was it worth it!

To my eventual editor Jennifer Doyle – the best editor I've worked with and absolutely the right one for this book. Jen, you were more enthusiastic and passionate about my story than I dared to hope for. So thank you!

Thanks to all the team at Headline, including Joe Thomas, Ana Carter, Ellie Wheeldon, Jessie Goetzinger-Hall, Grace McCrum and Sophie Ellis.

Thanks, as ever, to my friends and family. There are too many of you to mention individually but you know who you are. Special thanks to those who helped with the detail of this book – such as my mum, Lynda, who provided the detail for the Lake District walk. And, of course, to my husband Harry Glasstone. I love you, babe. And yes, I do pronounce 'babe' with a flat 'a'.

I owe a massive debt of gratitude to all the bloggers who've supported this – and all my previous – books. I thanked a handful of them by name in the acknowledgments for Becoming Ted but there are far too many to mention now. Please know that your help in spreading the word and building up my readership has been invaluable.

Likewise, to all the authors and influencers who've given me such lovely comments to help generate excitement and get those retailers on board – thank you, thank you, thank you!

Above all, though, I'd like to thank my readers. Being able to interact with you on social media – and sometimes in real life – means so much to me. It keeps me going through all the challenges of the writing and publishing process. I always say that writing is, for me, an act of communication. But I need someone to receive that communication for it to work. So I genuinely couldn't do this without you. Yes, there are different kinds of love but your love for my work has changed everything. It has helped me fulfil my dream and become the person I always knew I was meant to be – even if, like Danny, at first I didn't know how to become that person. So THANKS – this one's for you.